BurNiNG Bright

CATHERINE BROPHY

Published by Catherine Brophy

Copyright © Catherine Brophy, 2013

A CIP catalogue record for this book is available from the British Library.

ISBN 978-0-9576142-0-8

Design and typesetting: www.slickfish.ie

Tyger Tyger, burning bright,
In the forests of the night;
What immortal hand or eye,
Could frame thy fearful symmetry?
                                    - William Blake

ACKNOWLEDGEMENTS

I could not have written this book without the support and generosity of many people.

My husband, Bernard O Kelly, encouraged, supported and fed me, and, when the computer went weird and I freaked, he calmed me down and sorted it out.

My editor, Helen Falconer, used her gimlet eye and laser mind to winkle out anomalies and make invaluable suggestions.

The following people have been generous with their information, inside knowledge and support: Tom King, Susie Kennedy, Lucy Brophy, Amy Boyle, Caroline Freeman, Fiona Brophy, Clare Brophy, Rose Marie Byrne, Peigin Doyle, Barbara Lee, Thomas McLoughlin, Carmel Callan, Michael Delahunty and Marie O'Rourke.

A special thank you to Imogen, Molly and Seán O'Flaherty Falconer for their perceptive insights.

FOR BERNARD

DISCLAIMER

In the interests of verisimilitude I have given several real celebrities roles in this novel. However, all of their thoughts, words, actions and clothing are figments of my imagination and bear no relation of any kind to the real lives of these people.

The fictional characters, are just that, fictional. They are not based on anyone living or dead. They are just my imaginary friends.

GLOSSARY

Aul – old.

Baw-ways – crooked, off kilter.

Beeb – B.B.C. TV.

Bí ulamh – "be prepared" (Gaelic).

Bowsie – a male youth believed to be a troublemaker.

Chip-shop Beninis – many of the Italian community in Ireland run take-away fish-and-chip shops or ice cream parlours.

Clock her – hit her.

Conker – chestnut.

Craic – fun, especially where there is a lot of verbal banter and wit.

Creathurs – "poor creathurs" ie "poor creatures", as in "the poor things".

Culchie – someone who lives in rural Ireland (derogatory).

Cumann – an organisation, used to refer specifically to the local branch of a political party.

Eejit – idiot.

Fair City – a TV soap opera set in Dublin

Gardaí – the Irish police force.

Gas men – characters, life and soul of the party.

Figary – a fit, a notion, something unexpected.

Fleadh ceol – music festival (Gaelic).

Fleadhed out – exhausted, usually by partying too hard.

High Babies – senior infants, a child's second year at primary school.

Hoor for the quare thing – all they want is sex.

Hot from the sticks – just arrived in the city from rural Ireland.

Hurling – Gaelic sport played with broad-ended sticks made of ash (hurleys) and a small ball of seamed leather. With fifteen players a side, it is considered the fastest field game in the world.

ICA – Irish Countrywomen's Association.

Lamp me – hit me

Leaving Cert – the Leaving Certificate, the final state examination taken before leaving secondary school.

Man U – Manchester United, one of the best teams in the English Premier league, with a huge number of Irish fans.

Mhuire-'s-trua – "Mother of God it is a pity" (Gaelic). A phrase used to refer to complaints about the tragedies of Irish history.

Rarin' to go – impatient to get going.

Rossie – a common, badly behaved girl.

Siege of Ennis – an Irish set dance.

Slagging – humorous insults.

Stamford Bridge – the home ground of Chelsea Football Club, London.

Stephen's Day – December 26th, the feast of St. Stephen, Boxing Day.

Taoiseachs – Irish prime ministers (Gaelic)

Templemore – Tipperary town where the Police Training College is located.

Uisce – water (Gaelic).

Vincent De Paul shop – charity shop.

Wenger, Arsene – manager of Arsenal Football club, London.

Woodie's – a cheap, hardware chain store.

Ye boy ye! – remark of approval.

Yiz – you (plural).

CHAPTER 1

KIRSTY

The Pride of the Kerrigans. That's what Dad calls me. Or sometimes, for a laugh, the Revenge of the Kerrigans. You see we live in Balfathery, which is a blink-and-you'd-miss-it country town full of petty-minded snobs. All they want is for their children to be solicitors, doctors and vets. I've no intention of being a small town solicitor or a doctor or a vet, no way. For me, the sky's the limit.

Of course since the whole Celtic Tiger thing started, the snobs are building big houses for themselves. Big, ugly houses, with lawns and patios and plastic tables and chairs out of Woodie's. But none of them have a house like ours. We don't live in the town, our house is too big for that. And it's not in that string of show-off houses on the Athlone road that Dad calls "snoburbia central". Our house is five miles outside, in its own grounds. Dad was thinking more Beverly Hills when he built it. To quote himself: *"Hollywood in Balfathery's Face!"*

And the best bit? Dad was born in Barrack Street – you know, Barrack Street, where the poor people live. The place all the Balfathery snobs look down on. Now he's one of the wealthiest, most successful developers in Ireland! You see, my dad thinks big! And I take after him! So put that in your pipe and smoke it.

JAKE

I watch Mum from the door of the kitchen. She lifts the red enamel casserole out of the all-singing, all-dancing, eye-level, self-cleaning oven and puts it on the matching, seven-ring, electronically lit, shiny gas hob. Take note: *electronically lit*. So why has Mum a lighter in her hand?

She reaches into the cupboard and takes out something small. The something is wrapped in foil. She opens the foil to reveal an irregularly shaped lump, dark brown, about the size of a conker. She flicks the lighter, holds the flame under the lump and crumbles a generous half of it into the garlic and herb butter that she's making for the garlic bread. It's for the adults. Me and Kirsty don't like garlic. She mixes it well, puts it to one side and starts to slice the French stick.

"Hi Mum," I say, and I smile my angelic smile.

"Oh Jake, hi. Are you ready?"

"I'm wearing a shirt!"

"Good lad."

"What was that herb you were adding?" I ask.

She knows I'm interested in cooking – sort of.

"Just some stock cube. It gives it a bit of pizzazz."

My own mother! Even *she* forgets that I'm fifteen years old. I'm plenty old enough to know that you don't use a stock cube in garlic bread and even if you do, you certainly don't need a lighter to soften it! Just because I'm small for my age...

That's the worst about being a boy. Girls grow sort of evenly. Look at the first years there in St Mary's. They're all a bit straight up and down. Second years – shaping up. Third years – melon city! But boys are different. In my class, average age fifteen and a bit, there are two sizes. Mick Wall and Gerry Stanford shot up and got hairy last summer;

they could pass for eighteen. Most of the rest got tall and were shaving by Christmas. Then there's the titches. I'm one of the titches. I *still* look like I'm only eleven.

Mum says not to worry, that I look like a spiky-haired angel. Thanks Mum – all I need now is a white frock and wings! Mrs Lawless in The Gem gives me a lollipop when I go in to pay for the papers. Joe Martin in the bank asks if I'm still into dinosaurs. *Dinosaurs*, for crying out loud – that was when I was in High Babies! Then I look in the mirror and I cannot believe that my body *still* hasn't caught up. You know what? The way I look *I'd* give me a lollipop.

In my mind, I'm grown up. I'm into ecology and stuff. But my big thing is film. That's what I want to do when I leave school. Make at least one good movie. Something great. Something fearless. Like Mr Geoghan says,

"Great Art is fearless."

Mr Geoghan's our English teacher and he's kinda cool for a teacher. He thinks I'm mature for my age.

Dad says that he was a titch too at my age. Then one morning he woke up with his feet hanging out of the bed. According to him, the same thing will happen to me. I'm still waiting.

Mum casually wraps the rest of the dope in the foil and puts it back in the jar with the stock cubes. Mum and Dad never deny they do drugs. But under strict rules. A recreational snort at a party and a couple of joints at weekends. But never, NEVER in front of us. And they still think we don't know about the cocaine.

They let me and Kirsty have a wine spritzer on Sundays and for celebrations and when we're in Spain.

"That's how the Spaniards teach their children about drink," Mum says. "And you never see them getting drunk."

But they're skittish about us and dope. I think they

3

assume that at some stage we'll smoke it, same as they did at our age. What they're really afraid of is us getting caught by the Gardaí. Getting A Criminal Record. And I'm not crazy about that either. Which is why I only ever smoke dope in Niall Flynn's den, in the shed at the end of their garden. And only at the weekends or during the holidays.

Mum wraps the garlic bread in foil and puts it in the oven. "I think everything's under control," she says.

I smile my spiky-haired angel smile.

KIRSTY

The new dress looks fab. But then, dusty pink is my colour. When I did "Seasonal Colours and You" it said I was summer shades, but spring and autumn look good too. For winter, I need the proper make-up and accessories but I can make that work as well. I'm lucky that way.

I stand in front of the mirror and strike a few poses. Cool or what! I've often thought of going in for modelling when I leave school. Only one more year to go, once this term ends! Mum says it's a dog's life but show me the downside? You fly to Paris, Milan, Hong Kong, New York. You wear top designer gear. You have your photo in Vogue. Duh! What's not to love?

In my walk-in closet, I have a special section for shoes. I keep them in their original boxes with a photo of the shoe on the outside. That was Kate's idea, it saves time when you're trying to decide what to wear. Kate is Mum's friend and she was a model when she was young. I asked her if she thought modelling was a dog's life. She said no, she had a great time. I pick out the silver Manolos. Very glam.

Me and Lala – Lala's my best friend – are the only girls in our school who know how to dress, which is not surprising because we go to the local convent school. I wanted to go to

4

a boarding school but Mum insisted on St Mary's because it gets good results and I can live at home. That means all the girls come from Balfathery or the farms around. They're all either stupos, uggos, lezzers or brainiacs. The brainiacs are too busy doing their homework to know anything about fashion. The stupos think that cheap Chinese knockoffs are cool. Please! As for the uggos and lezzers – who cares? But one thing's for sure, none of them would recognise a Manolo if it jumped up and kicked them in their big, fat arses.

And that's 'cause we live in Balfathery. There's Pink Lady Fashions –Polyester Central!!! Minehan's Outfitters – anyone for wellies? Razz-a-Matazz – a glorified pound shop! Then there's Ardrahan out on the Galway road where Balfathery snobs buy dresses for the annual golf-club dinner. Me and Lala only ever shop in Galway or Dublin or – better still – London or Paris. We've planned what we'll do with our lives once we escape from Balfathery.

"If you had to choose," Lala whispers to me in the middle of art class, "which would you rather be – famous or rich?"

"Alanna!" snaps Mrs Melia. All the teachers call her Alanna. "Would you care to share your thoughts with the class?"

Mrs Melia thinks she's dead cool. She's *always* trying to get us to discuss "Important Issues". And the minute we give our opinion she begs to differ and then bores us with all the reasons why we're wrong and she's right. Whatever!

Lala tells Mrs Melia her thoughts.

"Interesting question, Alanna. So, Kirsty, what's your answer?"

"Famous."

"Because…?"

"Because if you're famous you'll get rich anyway."

"I see. So where does that leave James Joyce? He was famous but he didn't get rich."

"Yeah, Miss, but that was the old days. They didn't have telly then, they didn't even have "Hello" magazine." Mrs Melia smiles her teachery smile.

"And what do you want be famous for, Kirsty?"

"I don't care Miss. I just want to be an international celebrity, the Paris Hilton of Ireland."

"Like *that's* going to happen!" snorts Martina Curran.

Martina Curran's a brainiac. In fact, she's the chief brainiac in the school. She has frizzy beige hair scraped back from her spotty red forehead and she hates me. She's jealous of course. Her dad is one of the snobbiest snobs in this town. He wouldn't even talk to my dad when they were in school together but now he's just the local vet and he's all palsy-walsy. But we're not fooled. He's the same snob he always was and Martina's the same.

"Why not?" I ask.

"You think a jumped-up-nobody from Balfathery could be an international celebrity?"

"What about Philip Tracey? " I snap back. "He was a nobody from a hole-in-the wall in Galway and he's a Mega Celeb."

"The difference being," says Martina, "that Philip Tracey's a genius."

"So he sticks a few feathers together and calls it a hat! Anyone could do that!"

"Have you *seen* his hats?"

"I've seen pictures."

"Well I went to the exhibition in Dublin. He's definitely a genius."

"And if you say it then it *must* be true!"

"And you're supposed to be the fashionista!"

6

"Girls please," interrupts Mrs Melia, "let's stick to the point. So Kirsty, what are the advantages of being famous?"

"Philip Tracey begs you to wear his hats," I say. Martina snorts but I ignore her. "*And* it gives you power and position and then you can do anything you want."

"Such as..." prompts Mrs Melia.

"I don't know exactly but I have lots of ideas."

"Well, if being famous is all that important, perhaps you should focus on how to achieve it. You could start by paying more attention in class. Because, Kirsty, you do have a flair and if you take your art seriously and do well in your Leaving Cert next year, it might help you find gainful employment."

Gainful employment! No way! Boring! I want to live the dream. I want my life to be fabulous, thrilling, exciting, and I can't wait to leave school and get started. Mrs Melia is so old-fashioned. Things have changed completely since her day. For a start, we no longer live in the Ice Age! Dinosaurs do *not* roam the earth. Nowadays, anybody can be anything they like — as long as they believe that they're worth it. And I *know* that I'm worth it. I've always known. When I was only eleven I made up my own coat of arms with "Because I'm Worth It" on a scroll underneath. Dad got it laminated for me and I still keep it on the door of my wardrobe. I *know* that I'm going to be famous, because it's my dream. It's always been my dream. And, as long as you believe in your dream, somehow, some day, your dream *will* come true. Everybody knows that.

Besides, I have a plan. Because that's the other thing, you have to have a plan to make your dream a reality. The instant I'm eighteen, I'm going to audition for every reality programme and every pop star competition on television. I'd do it now only Mum won't let me. Actually I'd quite like to be a pop star. Or in a girl band. That'd be cool. Dad says most of them can't sing, they just mime to a backing track. But I can sing.

"*Kirstyyyyy!*"

It's Mum. Gran and Granda must have arrived.

MARIAN

Eamon's parents Minnie and Jim! Jesus wept! Don't get me wrong, I get on grand with them. Minnie thinks I'm the bee's knees and Jimmy, well… Jimmy has a bit of a thing for me. One at a time they're grand. But put them together – Holy God – they're like cats in a bag. How they've stayed married all these years, I don't know. It's one of the mysteries of religion!

Even with other people around they go at it. *"I'm right." "No, I'm right." "No, I'm right."* It'd drive a saint to distraction. Sometimes I wish they'd have a proper row, shout, throw things, get it all out of their system. But no, it's snipe, snipe, snipe, snipe, snipe, snipe, *snipe*. And I'll tell you something for nothing, it sucks all the good out of Sunday dinner.

Lord knows I've tried to distract them. I've tried changing the subject – which works fine for all of two seconds. I've tried plying them with drink but that has its problems. Jimmy believes that he's just a big child and, a drink or two later, he is. A big, mischievous child. He starts making "jokes" at Minnie's expense. Meanwhile, the drink makes Minnie all feisty and sparky. She'll rise to his bait and they're off. *"I'm right." "No, I'm right." "No, I'm right." "No, I'm right." "No, I'm right."*

Last Sunday, after they'd finally gone home, me and Eamon had collapsed on the sofa. The kids were in bed. I got up to pour some wine while he rolled a joint. I put on some Celine Dion and we sat, completely fleadhed out, letting the wine and the smoke do their job.

"You know what they need?" Eamon said after a while.

"A divorce?"

"No."

"What?"

"A dirty, big spliff."

I laughed. I couldn't see Minnie smoking a joint. She thinks marijuana's the slippery slope. One puff and next thing you're robbing the Mace mini-mart with a dirty syringe! Eamon teased three more Rizlas out of the packet and started a new skin. Suddenly he stopped.

"But," he said, and a grin spread over his face like he'd witnessed the Dawn of Aquarius, "they do eat!"

The only thing I'm afraid of is feeding dope to Kirsty and Jake, and that's why the garlic bread is so handy. They both hate garlic whereas Minnie and Jimmie love it. Of course, I wouldn't be shocked to discover that the kids had the odd toke behind the bicycle sheds. As Eamon has pointed out several times, we smoked rakes of dope at their age and we're not living in squats, searching for a vein we can spike. I just don't want them to get into trouble with the police. Or worse, with the dealers. We never get gear from a dealer. We get it from Fergus. Fergus was in the band with Eamon when we were in London. And he's kept up all his old hippie connections.

Come to think of it, it's a shame my mother doesn't like garlic either, because she could do with something to relax her and take off the edge. She doesn't even drink.

JAKE

I take Gran's coat. She takes my face in her hands and kisses it, mwah, mwah, mwah, all over. She also forgets that I'm not still a baby. But I don't mind too much. She smells nice. Granda takes off his new leather jacket and punches me on the shoulder.

"How's she cuttin' son?"

"Grand."

I like Granda and Gran. They're old but they're not old-fashioned if you know what I mean. They don't keep going on about the old days like most old people do. And Gran's not scared of teenage boys. Because that's another thing about being a boy. Once you hit your teens, you're a suspect. Old ladies clutch on to their handbags. Shopkeepers assume that you're up to no good. Young mums cross the street. Even here in Balfathery, where everyone knows us. It's like we send out a dangerous scent, like werewolves.

We actually like that idea! That's me, Brian, Fionnbar and Niall. My Bros. My Posse. We think it's funny. Hilarious really, when we know they've nothing to fear. We're just teenagers having a laugh. We're about as dangerous as a litter of Labrador pups! But we do like to pretend. Say, it's Saturday afternoon. Town's packed. We emerge from Niall's den after a couple of herbals. We're up for adventure. We pull up our hoodies.

"Werewolves," I suggest.

"Yeah! Werewolves."

We bump fists and walk to the top of Main Street. We saunter along, emitting our strange werewolf scent. Everyone yields right of way. It's amazing. Like using The Force. We're always werewolves in town. Except when we go for chips to The Dozy Donkey. Mrs Dozy knows who we are. She knows we're not werewolves.

Dad shoos Gran and Granda into the lounge and he goes behind the bar. God, but he loves that bar. It's a proper bar, made out of sanded glass, with draught beer, an icemaker and all the works. He faces the array of bottles. He takes a deep breath and rubs his hands together. He lets the breath out: *Whooooo*... And now he's ready to wrangle the cocktail.

Back in the eighties, Mum and Dad worked in London. Dad was the best barman in Kilburn – according to himself. An ex-New York cop showed him how to make cocktails and he considers them the height of a barman's skill. But any aul eejit can shake up a cocktail! Has he never seen the guys that juggle the bottles and glasses at the same time as they're mixing and pouring?

He puts the John Rocha glasses on the bar and flicks the rims with his nail. Tiiiiiing, ring the glasses – shows they're quality crystal. He takes out the silver ice bucket and fills it with ice. He puts it beside the glasses. Next comes the silver cocktail shaker that Mum bought for his birthday. He lines that up too.

"Time to work my magic," he says, "but, before I begin..."

He takes up the remote and presses a button. *The Girl from Ipanema* comes slip-slidin' into the room. Gran loves that tune. Dad sashays over to Gran, takes her by hand and gets her up to dance. Mum has warned him to keep Gran and Granda from fighting while she's in the kitchen.

"Tall and tanned and young and lovely...." he sings as he twirls her round the floor. Gran goes pink at the gills and laughs.

"You were always a charmer Eamon, even when you were little."

He gives her another twirl and sways her back. Gran squeals with delight. He dances her back to the sofa.

"Make mine a double," says Granda. "It'll sharpen my appetite."

"Jimmy!" snaps Gran, "can you think of nothing but

drink and your gut? Why can't you dance with me like Eamon?"

"'Cause you'll stand on my toes."

"I will not!"

Ding. Ding. Ding. Seconds out of the ring.

"Harvey Wallbanger, Pop?" Dad interrupts.

"Have you got a sore leg I can have it off?" says Granda laughing. He always laughs at his own jokes.

"Tequila Sunrise, Ma?"

"Yes please, with plenty of fruity bits on the side."

"Wish I could get a bit on the side!" says Granda.

"Too much information," says Dad, but they both do their lads'-night-out laugh.

"Jimmy! Not in front of the child."

"He's not a child."

"Yes he is."

At least Granda knows I'm not a child.

Kirsty comes in. That stops them for the moment. That's Kirsty, my sister, the blister. She flicks her hair like she's Penelope Cruz or something. Jesus, but she's stupid. Not thick, just stupid. Do you know what her motto is? "Because I'm worth it." Seriously! She even drew up a fake coat of arms for herself that she keeps on her wardrobe door. I swear to God. With "because I'm worth it" written underneath – in pink glitter! Vomitorious!

That's Kirsty for you. She uses a shampoo ad as her guide in life! A *shampoo ad!* She acts like she's Queen of the World and you know the worst part? *She gets away with it!*

And she's not even all that good-looking. I mean she's not a hobbit, she's not an uggo, she's just, well, dead ordinary. I know – I've seen her first thing in the morning. But then she does the lip gloss thing, and the mascara thing and all the shiny stuff that girls do and people tell her she's gorgeous.

"Oh Kirsty, you look fabulous," says Gran. "Is that a new dress?"

They huddle together. Gran feels the material. Kirsty smirks. Gran coos. They go on about the dress like it's the answer to peace in the Middle East.

"Have you decided what you want for your birthday?" asks Gran.

"Sweet sixteen and never been kissed!" says Granda.

"Eighteen, Granda, eighteen."

"Eighteen already? Time flies when you're having fun."

"I want a nose job and a boob job but Dad's too mean, he won't let me."

Please no. I do *not* want to hear this discussion. It's been going on for three months and no way do I want to hear any more details about my sister's boobs.

"It's not the money, Princess." Dad hands Kirsty a Buck's Fizz, a little fizz, a lot of OJ.

"Kirsty, come over here," says Gran.

Dad and Granda start to dissect Man U's performance at Stamford Bridge yesterday. Kirsty sits beside Gran. Gran takes her hand and talks confidentially but I can still hear her.

"The Kerrigan women are all big on top. Think of your Aunty Phyllis."

I think about Aunty Phyllis. She reminds me of cushions. And not scatter cushions – the big ones you put on the floor.

"Maybe I take after Mum," worries Kirsty.

"You could do a lot worse," says Gran.

There is a lull in the Man U discussion.

"But I have to use chicken fillets," squeals Kirsty into the silence as she stares down the neck of her dress.

Granda starts to laugh. The Harvey Wallbanger is

beginning to take.

"Take care you don't catch bird flu," he cackles.

"Jimmy!" Gran protests.

"What?" He throws her a look of fake innocence.

"What did you think of Ryan Giggs?" Dad asks very loudly. He's as embarrassed as me.

"Don't worry, pet," Gran murmurs to Kirsty. "I didn't know what I had till I was nineteen."

Now I'm thinking about my grandmother's boobs. Isn't that incest or something?

Mum comes in to save the day. I know by the look on her face that she's heard them gearing up. She hugs Gran and Granda. Dad hands her a champagne cocktail and she takes a good slug.

"Come on, Minnie," she says. "You have to see the new kitchen."

Mum and Gran leave. We hear Gran oooing and ahhing at the new black granite worktops, the central island, the double fridge, the seven-ring hob, the whole cutting edge, up to the nanosecond, fabulous everything.

"'Tis far from granite tops we were reared, Marian," she laughs, "but we sure can get used to it."

Dad and Granda get down to really serious man talk, ie whether Alex Ferguson is the best football manager on the planet and what a boring French fart Arsene Wenger is.

"I rather like Wenger," I say, because I do, I think he's intelligent and thoughtful but mostly I say it just to rile them.

They give me a pitying look and ignore me. Kirsty glugs back her Bucks Fizz in a gulp. When Dad isn't looking she pours another one, light on the OJ, heavy on the fizz. Mum calls her. She heads out to the kitchen.

I'm drinking pure OJ. I'm not great on alcohol, not since

the time Niall Flynn's folks were away and we raided the drinks cabinet. I had a lot of red wine, topped off with vodka and cointreau. I was so drunk I couldn't cycle home and they had to phone Dad. I was humongously sick in the car. Dad made me clean the car the next day but otherwise he was okay. Mum too. It put me off drink though. And that makes me look good.

I take up my book. It's called "Norwegian Wood". It's by this Japanese writer called Murakami. It's on the list of "cool books to read" that Mr Geoghan suggested in case we run into literary types and don't want to look like eejits! Yeah, 'cause as everyone knows, Balfathery is coming down with literary types! In the book, there's a lot of walking around Tokyo with girls and being depressed. And suicide. So it's definitely cool. I think about how I might film it.

Dad doesn't get why I want to make movies when I could easily work with him. But I'm not a builder, I'm not like him, I'm no good with my hands. Besides, business isn't really my thing.

"Why do you want to do that when I have a thriving property empire all ready and waiting? I'll retire when I'm fifty, then it's all yours."

"But I want to make movies."

"Well it's up to yourself but there's a lot of queers in that business."

"So?"

"I'm just saying."

"Working with gay people doesn't make you gay."

"Don't be so sure about that."

Yet he knows perfectly well that Seán, his best friend, is as gay as Honolulu. Dad thinks Seán's cool. Seán's single and fancy free, unless you count Pedro, his "business partner". I saw them kissing one time. No big deal. I like

15

Seán but I don't like Pedro. Pedro's a little scut but Seán thinks the sun shines out of his arse. (Ho-ho! Unintentional joke.)

Dad has no time for anything that isn't straight down the line, especially anything he considers "fancy pants intellectual" ie anything that isn't about developing property, making money, Manchester United or getting one over on what he calls the Balfathery Snobafia.

"All them professors," he says, "they just make the stuff up. I left school with no exams whatsoever, and look at me, I'm doing all right. Check out my bank account... On second thoughts – *heh, heh, heh* – don't!"

Even so, he's chuffed that I do well in school. He thinks of it as some weirdo talent, like sword swallowing or being double-jointed. And he *loves* Parents' Day. Every year, he insists I give him a tour of the school and roams all over, inspecting the classrooms, the library, the science labs, and commenting critically on their construction. He beams his head off at students and greets other parents like he owns the school. Then he heads for the gym hall where the teachers are waiting behind their little tables with their lists of names and reports. He goes to the first table and sits.

"How's she cuttin'?" he grins. "I'm Eamon Kerrigan, Jake's dad, how's he doin'?"

The teacher says I'm doing well.

"Takes after his Da," he says, and moves on to the next teacher.

On Parents Day, Father Cronin, the Principal, always parades around in his cap and gown. He looks like the head teacher out of the *Beano*. All the teachers used to wear that stuff back when St Fintan's was the poshest school in the county. Fr Cronin likes to act like it still is. He wears the gear for special occasions. Dad gives him a friendly punch on the arm.

"How's she cuttin'?"

Fr Cronin is not the arm-punching type. He smiles his ice-cutter smile. The temperature drops about fifty degrees. Dad doesn't notice.

"And you are…?" asks Fr Cronin, even though he knows damn well.

"The one that got away!" says Dad and he laughs and I know he's not going to give in.

"Mr Kerrigan, isn't it?"

"Call me Eamon. So tell us, Joe…" he pauses for effect, "I mean *Father* Joe, – how's the young fella doing?"

This is not the way to talk to Fr Cronin and I hope he won't hold it against me.

"I believe his behaviour is satisfactory."

"Good, grand, that's what I like to hear," says Dad and claps Fr Cronin on the back.

Fr Cronin winces slightly, smiles one of his wintery smiles and moves away. Dad laughs.

"Two can play at that game," he says, loud enough for Fr Cronin to hear.

Dad thinks Fr Cronin's a snob and he has a thing about snobs. He divides them into categories: jumped-up snob, poker-up-backside snob, tuppence-looking-down-on-a-penny-halfpenny snob, village idiot snob, holy-water-hen snob, hypocritical snob… and there's probably more that I can't remember. He thinks Fr Cronin's a hypocritical snob probably just because he's a priest and all priests are hypocrites in Dad's book.

He meets a few more teachers and punches them on the arm as well. I bet when I win the Oscar, Dad'll be there, beaming his head off, punching Martin Scorsese on the arm and going, "How's she cuttin'?". But I won't care 'cause

17

I'll have three Oscars. One for best screenplay, one for best director and one for best movie.

Mum calls us all to the table. She sets the casserole on a mat. Gran comes in with the plates and the garlic bread. Kirsty brings the salad and couscous. We all sit down. Gran knocks her fork to the floor by mistake.

"That's seven years bad luck," crows Granda.

"No, Jimmy, it's not seven years bad luck. It means a visitor's coming."

"It's seven years bad luck."

"No it isn't."

"Yes it is."

"Garlic bread, Minnie?" says Mum, passing the plate.

"Oh yes please."

"I think you'll enjoy the casserole I did today, Minnie." Says Mum as she serves out the food.

"I love your mother's cooking," Gran says to me then she turns back to Granda. "breaking a mirror is seven years bad luck, dropping a fork is a visitor."

"No, dropping a *knife* is a visitor. Dropping a fork is seven years bad luck."

"It's lamb and apricot." Mum sounds a bit desperate. "I think it's one of my best."

"I don't know how you do it, Marian," says Gran. "I follow your recipes exactly but my cooking never tastes as good as yours."

"Maybe you're missing the magic ingredient," I say.

I look at Mum for a reaction. Not a flicker.

"And what's that, Jake?" asks Gran.

"A special herb, a stock cube... who really knows?"

I smile my spiky-haired angel smile and watch Mum like a hawk. She's filling the plates as fast as she can.

"Admit it, Minnie," chuckles Granda, "you were never

18

what you'd call a cook."

"Now, now Jimmy," says Mum. "Minnie makes a mean apple tart."

"Mean is right!" says Granda. Him and Dad do their lads'-night-out laugh. Dad pours the wine. As soon as everyone's served, Mum raises her glass.

"Minnie and Jimmy," she says. "You're both very welcome. Enjoy your dinner."

We all drink to that.

"To the cook," says Granda.

"To the cook."

We drink to that too and then we tuck in.

"I think I'll try the garlic bread," says Kirsty.

"I don't think you'll like it," says Mum, trying to look as if she doesn't mind either way.

"Let her try it, Marian," says Gran, passing over the plate.

Kirsty takes a slice and eats half of it.

"This is quite nice," she says.

I don't much like garlic but I'm tempted to try some too, just to see what Mum will do, but I decide that it's better to watch instead.

Half-way through the meal, Gran and Granda stop sniping. They start grinning instead. Kirsty takes a slice of red pepper out of the salad bowl. She turns the shiny side up and starts to stroke it.

"Look at that colour Gran," she says. "Look at that shade of scarlet. It's like it's lit from inside."

"So it is," says Gran.

She hooks a slice for herself. She starts stroking it too. The two of them lean in together and stare at the slices of pepper and giggle. Mum winks at Dad. Dad gets up and puts on *Dark Side of the Moon*. Everyone nods their heads to

19

the music. It gets to the bit that goes, "the lunatics are on the grass" and we all sing along. Mum and Dad start giggling and nothing can stop them. We all catch the giggles, even me. Gran is doubled-up laughing. Granda throws back his head.

"Aowoooooooooooooo!!" he howls like a wolf.

He gets up and goes to the kitchen and brings back the desert. Tiramisu and ice-cream. We all wire into it.

"Fabulous, Marian," sighs Gran. She wipes her finger round her bowl and licks it. "You know how to sprinkle stardust. I wish I knew your secret."

I smile my spiky-haired angel smile.

CHAPTER 2

KIRSTY

Martina Curran's top of the invitation list… NOT!!!! And she's going to be SICK!!!! She'll pretend she isn't but she will. She'll be biting her toenails. Because my eighteenth is going to be the BEST PARTY EVER!!!!

We're holding it in the swimming pool! I love saying that. You should see the looks on people's faces. But then, our swimming pool is not your run-of-the-mill indoor pool. It's State of the Art. When it comes to gadgety things, my dad is all about State of the Art. Everything is remote control, curtains, lights, the lot.

The pool is in a glass building connected to the house by the atrium. Inside, the floor is goldy marble and there's two statues of Roman ladies with urns, pouring water into the pool. Dad had them made in Italy. And he brought an Italian artist over to do a mosaic of the Kerrigan Crest at the bottom of the pool. Then there's a lift, it takes you down to the basement where there's a gym, Jacuzzi, sauna and stuff.

But that's not the best. When the weather is good you can slide the roof open. The walls as well, so the pool is outdoors. And when you want to have a party, you just press a button and a marble floor slides over the pool and, *voilà*, a dance floor! And the Roman ladies are still there pouring the water. And no, it's not spilling on to the floor because two marble basins come up as well and the water pours there and back down into the pool. It's amazing. No wonder everyone in Balfathery loves coming to our house. Some of what Dad calls the über-snobs like Corky Curran, Martina's dad, pretend they're not impressed but they are. Dad loves showing people round, especially the über-snobs!

"Not bad for a lad from Barrack Street," he'll say.

And they smile their tight smiles and you can see they're mad jealous.

In the run up to my birthday, I get Dad on his own in the den and tell him how every time I look at my nose I get depressed. I know the plastic surgery is not going to happen but I have a plan. Unfortunately, Mum arrives in and – typical Mum – she freaks.

"For the umpteenth time Kirsty," she yells, "there's nothing wrong with your nose! And if you pay for a nose job, Eamon Kerrigan, I'll divorce you, I swear to God."

She sweeps back out and up the stairs.

"You heard your mother," he says.

I sigh and look sad and let the silence develop.

"What?"

"Nothing." I use my little girl voice.

"What's wrong, Princess?"

"I suppose I'll just have to get pills."

"Pills, what pills?"

"For the depression."

He goes out to the hall and stands at the bottom of the stairs.

"Marian!" he yells. No answer. "Marian!"

He strokes the onion domes on top of the Murano glass

pillars at the foot of the stairs. He had them specially made. They have swirls of silver and gold. The stairs themselves float up to a landing before they divide, and look like they're hovering on air. He calls it his Stairway to Heaven. It is his pride and joy.

"Mariaaaaaaaaan. Can you come here and talk to your daughter!"

Mum appears on the landing and stands with her hand on the Versace table – it's Louis Quinze style, done in mirror-mosaic. She's wearing a headband and has cream on her face. She shifts the flower arrangement in the middle of the table a fraction.

"What?"

"Talk to her, Marian. Please. She says she's getting depressed."

"Wakey, wakey, Eamon!"

"What?"

"You still don't know when you're getting played."

"I know, Marian, but you're much better at this sort of thing."

"It's real simple, Eamon. Just say No."

She goes back into her room, leaving Dad staring up at the portrait at the top of the stairs. It's a portrait of Mum, Dad, me and Jake, by an artist Mum found in Spain. There's even a bit of Barrack Street in the background, and the two children playing in the street are Mum and Dad when they were kids. "To remind us where we started and how far we've come," says Mum. She's always on about remembering our roots and not showing off. But I'm with Dad on this – if you've got it, flaunt it.

I go back to the den and flop into a chair. Dad follows me in and sits down to read his paper again.

"You heard your mother."

Now that I have him well softened up, I sit there and say nothing for a good while. Then I ask him for a cherry red Jag for my birthday.

"Mmmmm," he says.

That means he wants to run it past Mum. She'll say no but still, it's worth a shot.

And now I have to get serious because I need to decide on a theme for my party. I'd better call Lala.

MARIAN

We started with nothing you know. When we left school, the very best we could hope for was a reasonable living. We never dreamt of all this. But, along came the Celtic Tiger, God bless it, and now we're living the dream. Still, it took a deal of hard work as well. Here's how we got to where we are now:

Eamon, Seán, Colm and Fergus had been over in London for a year and a bit when Phyllis and I finally decide to take the boat. Phyllis is Eamon's younger sister, we were pals in school. We moved into the lads' decrepit two-up, two-down in Kilburn. The Balfathery Paddys. It was the start of the eighties, and things in Ireland were desperate. At least there was bar work in London.

I'd never known freedom like it. Parties, fights, friends sleeping over, tousle-head girls in the kitchen. Easy access to condoms, the Pill and to dope. It's hard to rebel in Balfathery and I had a lot of lost time to make up for. If you'd told me then that I'd end up back here, I'd have laughed in your face.

The lads were hell-bent on forming a band but they couldn't agree on a name. They weren't aiming for the big time, it was more like a hobby. I came in one day and found them hunched over joints. Fergus had a wrench in his hand and was wagging it at the others while making a long rambling point about Echo and the Bunnymen. Eamon was scratching his armpit. They looked like a circle of chimps.

"I think our name should reflect our image," said Colm.

"You should call yourselves 'Monkey and the Wrenches'," said I.

It just popped out of my mouth like that. And they loved it! They thought I meant monkey as in *Monkey*, the television programme about the Chinese monkey god. I've never disabused them.

Seán was the fixer. He got the gigs. He started with a couple in The Claddagh Ring, an Irish pub in Kilburn. The owner, a Galway man and retired New York cop, had a soft spot for Seán. He helped him get more gigs. Me and Phyllis were the roadies, the groupies and the general support. One night in the back of the van, coming home from a gig, Eamon told me he fancied me something rotten. That's how we started.

Then Seán met this Dutch guy called Jakob. Séan was always meeting unlikely people. (I know now that he met them in gay clubs, but back then he was still in the closet.) Jakob liked Monkey and the Wrenches, or maybe he just liked Seán, I don't know, but he asked the lads to do a tour of his pubs in Holland the following summer. We all jumped at the chance. We saved like crazy, gave up our jobs and took off. Jakob also arranged for "Monkey" to play at a couple of festivals.

It was the trip of a lifetime. We met drop-outs, hippies, punks, alternative lifestyle types, eternal travellers, vegans, Buddhists, anarchists, whatever-you're-having-yourself. We had soulful discussions under the moon, and argued the Meaning of Life until four in the morning. We dropped acid, smoked weed, read tarot cards, swam naked, watched the dawn rise from a beach on Terschelling. We were young, we were free, we were changing the world!

It's true what they say about travel. It does you a power of good. People don't know if you're from Barrack Street or the Athlone Road, whether you're rich or you're poor, they don't know whose daughter you are or what religion. And when you realise that they like you anyway, it's a wonderful thing. You start to breathe deeper, you start to see good in yourself, you start to feel like you can do things, go places, dream dreams.

Eamon and me had often talked about starting a business. Before Holland it was just pillow talk but after that summer there we opened a building society account. We got more bar jobs, grabbed all the overtime going, saved like the dickens. We also took every nixer that Jakob offered – which meant going to Holland and bringing back hash for some woman he knew called Tracey O'Hagan to sell in London. We saw nothing wrong in it because we believed absolutely that if only prime ministers, taoiseachs, presidents, IRA men and loyalists smoked dope, the problems in Northern Ireland would be solved and the rest of the world would be a much safer place. Jakob assured us that it was hippy hash, brought back from India and Afghanistan by people with the same world view as us. We didn't know then who Tracey O'Hagan was, although we knew that she was pure wild out.

We were still going back to Ireland for Christmas and weddings and, every time we went home, we could see that the place was changing. You could nearly smell the shift in the air. There was more money about. Big names were coming to Dublin for gigs. There was a buzz in the streets, people were going out to eat, people were laughing.

26

And one time, mostly out of curiosity, we went to view two cottages up near Christ Church, numbers 27 and 29 William Square. Eamon and me had always agreed that we'd finish with the hash – the smuggling that is, not the smoking – as soon as we'd earned enough to set ourselves up. The cottages were wrecks and they were going for a song. We checked and double-checked our accounts and decided it was time to take the plunge. We bought the cottages outright, got married, moved into 27 and started work on 29.

One morning I answered a knock on the door.

"My name is Miroslav," said the man standing outside.

He had startling blue eyes and was very soft-spoken. He was a builder looking for work and someone had told him that we were gutting the cottages. As it happened we needed the help, and as it turned out Miroslav was a treasure. He could turn his hand to anything and wasn't afraid of hard work. House prices were rising. Banks were throwing loans around like confetti. Christ Church began to get trendy. Young professionals started snooping around. We sold number 29 for a very nice profit indeed. And that's how it all started.

We sold number 27 for an even bigger profit and rented a house while we looked for a site to build our own home. Eamon did more buying, more refurbishing and more selling. He had a nose for what was ripe for development. Then Kirsty came along followed by Jake and we wanted to bring them up in the country because country kids have more freedom. And we wanted them to be near their grandparents. Eamon got a tip that the old Felton estate was coming up for sale. We made an offer and here we are. The house was a wreck so we tore it down and built "Burning Bright".

Now suddenly, Kirsty's eighteen!

EAMON

I do hear people giving out about the Poles and the Latvians coming here looking for work but I've no complaints. I like them. Work their arses off, don't expect to earn millions and do exactly what you tell 'em. It's all them years of Communist rule.

Which reminds me – Miroslav, he has to go on The List. Marian's after me for names, she wants to send out the invitations for Kirsty's party. I'm waiting to hear if Joe Horan can come. He's our local TD, recently made Minister of State for Who-The-Fuck-Cares, but he *is* a government minister. I was two years behind him in school and I'd like him to know that I'm a good party supporter. So I'm inviting him to the party. I'll just give Andy Minehan a call. Andy's chairman of the local Cumann...

Success! The Minister will be at the party. That'll set the town talking. Put a few noses out of joint. Oh I'm looking forward to this. *"Tiger, tiger, burning bright..."* Ye boy ye!

JAKE

It's not that my family is stupid. They're actually quite intelligent. It's just that they *act* stupid. Dad makes money. That's his thing. But after that? Nothing, no interests at all, no hobbies... unless you count listening to the dinosaurs of rock and flying over to watch Man U play at Old Trafford. And we're not talking Ryanair here, oh no, Dad travels by private jet, he shares the lease with some of his pals. He's obsessed with Man U, worships them, the way Nana Jo worships the Infant of Prague.

Mum's different. She's hot on us getting a good education. She thought about going to college herself but instead she set up the Book Club. Otherwise known as Wine Guzzlers Anonymous. There's ten of them. They arrive with salads and desserts and bottles of wine, settle down in the dining room and proceed to get totally tiddly. They talk about men and sex and screech like mad bats with the laughing. Sometimes they even mention the book.

And there's her yoga, which demands the latest in leisurewear and provides an excuse to show off a slice of tanned belly. Mum loves her tan – which needs more help than the Irish climate can provide. Which is why, as well as "Burning Bright", we have "La Casita". That's Spanish for little house. Our "little" house in Marbella has:

Five bedrooms – air-conditioned, ensuite.

Three reception rooms – large, tiled, air-conditioned.

One kitchen – state of the art.

One patio and barbeque area – vine-dappled.

One swimming pool – infinity, of course.

Garden – olive trees, orange trees, lemon trees, cactus, swathes of bougainvillea, picturesque rocks.

Housekeeper – Señora Assunta.

Gardener – Señor Pepe.

Rough life, eh?

Then there's Kirsty. Take for example this party. It's made her go all girly and squealy. Mind you, it doesn't take much, but the party has ramped up the girly squealing and by now it's way off the hook. Especially when Lala comes round. Lala's Kirsty's yes-girl. She's okay, but I wish she'd stand up to Kirsty more. They spend *hours* going over *The List*, deciding who's "in" and who's "out". And the list changes every day, depending on who disses who and who's wearing what! Every girl in St Mary's is, according to Kirsty, agog. And all the horsey girls she meets in The Paddocks for riding lessons are doing fandangos. Even the ponies know something is up. She predicts despair and mass suicides when people find out that they haven't been invited!

The theme of the party is a matter of intense discussion. Kirsty, Lala and Mum go into huddles. Meanwhile, Dad's planning his own party within a party. The local nobs, the local politicos, a government minister! Yippee! A fine combination of showing off and licking arse.

MARIAN

Kirsty's gone all "Beverley Hills 90210".

"Beverley Hills 90210 is television," I remind her. "It's drama. They have to *have* fights otherwise they've no story. They have to *have* poisonous bitches, sex kittens and great hair and shiny teeth. But it's not real life!"

I think she listens too much to her dad. He remembers every slight from the past and there's still people in Balfathery that he's trying to get back at. That's why Kirsty's so keen to be Princess-in-Chief. Me? I don't care. I know there's people in this town who think we're just jumped-up-jacks but so what? They can say what they like. I can afford to be pleasant. Success speaks louder than words.

Kirsty throws a conniption when I insist that she invite every girl in her class. And all the girls in her riding class at The Paddocks.

"But it's *my* party," she squeals.

"Yes, and you live in a very small town."

"Which is why I'm moving out," says she, "the instant I finish school."

"Fine. Meanwhile you live in Balfathery. You can't cut someone off just because you don't like them. You don't have to be their best friend but you do have to be polite. It's called having decent social skills. And that's something everyone needs."

She makes the mumbling noise that she thinks, that I

think, is her agreeing. She imagines it leaves her room for manoeuvre. But I know my Kirsty.

"And if you don't invite them, I will."

"Mumble, mumble."

Thank God for Seán. He's a god-send for parties. He can take an ordinary party and create the event of your dreams. I think he's attuned to the national psyche, that's why he's so successful.

His business started in Holland as well. While the rest of us were discussing the meaning of life, Seán was making a name for himself arranging theme-parties in Jakob's chain of pubs. His bubble parties were legendary and people travelled from Amsterdam, The Hague, even from Germany, for his Angels and Devils.

Success must have given him courage, because one night on the beach in Ameland, he stepped out of the closet. Once he'd told us it made perfect sense to me; things fell into place. Eamon, however, refused to believe him.

"You can't be queer," he squeaked, "I've seen you with women."

"I know… I guess they were a kind of camouflage. Anyway, turns out they're not my thing."

"Jesus, Seán, you're my best friend! For fuck's sake… *Christ!*"

"Relax, Eamon," says Seán. "You can still be my best friend. It's not catching."

Eamon has never mentioned it since.

Somewhere along the line in London, Seán got to meet Elton John. Elton was "straight" or maybe bi at the time. Although Seán isn't telling what happened, he has Elton's number, and they still talk. Work the rest out for yourself! Whatever happened, he organised a party for Elton, and the next thing all of London wanted Seán to organise their parties and that's when his business – Fiesta! Fiesta! – was born, catering to everyone from pop royalty to real royalty.

After several years of the high life, Seán got bored of London and is now based in Dublin.

"Anyway," he explains, "the Irish are spending like Nancy boys. Someone recently ordered two elephants for a wedding. Can you imagine? In Ballydehob!"

"And what did you say?" I ask.

"I said, 'certainly Sir'!"

So who better to organise Kirsty's idea of "the Best Party Ever"?

Seán gathers us all into the den – me, Eamon and Kirsty. Seán sits at the desk with a notebook and pen, all business, all focus. He flashes an encouraging smile round the table.

"I think this is going to be great," he says.

We shift in our seats and grin and relax.

"Whatever it takes Seán," says Eamon. "Nothing's too good for the Pride of the Kerrigans."

"Thanks Eamon. So, Kirsty. As you're the Birthday Girl, you're the one that I have to make happy. What would your dream party be?"

Kirsty wriggles and preens. Oh he's good. She rambles on about lovely, and cool, and dreamy, and fab. And don't forget wicked. Séan doesn't interrupt. He nods and takes the odd note as though she's said something really important.

"Thanks Kirsty," he says, when she's finished. "That's sparked off ideas already."

Kirsty smirks.

"Marian?"

"I'll go along with whatever you and Kirsty concoct."

He grins and wrinkles his nose at me. He knows I am handing it over and I know that he is in charge.

"Eamon?"

Eamon harrumphs, clears his throat, crosses and uncrosses his legs, wriggles and frowns. He likes having his say.

"How about having a circus?" he says. "And the guests could dress as tight rope walkers and clowns."

"Daaaaaaaad!!!!"

"I'm not wearing a leotard!" I say quickly.

"Okay, but I think we should have something spectacular."

Seán looks pensive. He hushes the bubble of talk.

"I think Eamon's got something there," he says.

Eamon sits up straight in his chair. I told you Seán was good! After all, Eamon is paying for this.

"Think Cirque du Soleil," Seán continues. "Very chic, very slick. Exquisite people in beautiful costumes sailing like angels and gods through the air."

"Wow," says Kirsty, "We could match the costumes to the theme."

Seán high-fives her.

"Now all we need is a theme."

"How about Pretty in Pink?" suggests Eamon.

"Daaaaaaaad!!!!"

"I thought you liked pink?"

"Yeah, when I was seven!"

"Why don't we go for something like 'Summer Berries'," proposes Seán. "It is after all a summer party and that covers all the warm summer shades: Madonna in Material Girl, magenta, fuchsia, carnation, strawberry, raspberry, poppy. Picture this. Drinks on the patio first. They come into the swimming pool which has the party floor in place. The walls are hung with pale drapes, back-lit with fairy lights, the tables are set out with tablecloths in deep raspberry, explosions of flowers, punctuations of green, glints of silver and gold, candles, crystal. You on a throne in a killer dress. What d'you think?"

"My God, Seán, that's brilliant!" exclaims a starry-eyed Kirsty.

Eamon grins too, sure it is all his idea. That's what makes Seán so good at his job – he makes everyone happy.

Kirsty is so predictable. At her age I was working full time. I dyed my hair black and put in a blue streak. Mammy had a fit. She was sure I'd end up in a brothel. She bombarded the Infant of Prague with novenas.

"I can't believe Kirsty's so bloody conservative!" I say to Seán afterwards.

"Teenagers," he replies. "They're riddled with hormones. They think rebellion means being stroppy and dressing the same as their mates but it's only their little gonads causing a bluster. You have to know who you are before you can really challenge convention."

He's right. I blustered away when I was a teen but I never really stood up to Mammy until I was thirty! Nowadays I think she's half-scared of me. But back then it was, what if the neighbours heard? The shame of it!

"Temper, temper," she'd exclaim whenever we squabbled.

I don't know if she actually ever said the word "common" out loud but she made it quite clear that losing your temper was something that only tinkers and labouring men succumbed to in drink. I think she's afraid of anger. Nowadays instead of voicing her disapproval she makes snide comments. Mostly I let them slide because I know there's no point in taking her on. She's stuck in her ways so I choose my battles.

LALA

As usual, Kirsty had no notion how lucky she was. Her dad – yes, *her dad* – suggested that her mother take her to Paris to find the perfect dress for her party. Paris! I always agreed with Kirsty that "Yes, Paris was the only place to buy clothes" but really I was only pretending to agree 'cause there was no way my dad would let me go to Paris to shop. He'd consider it "a shocking extravagance in a world where babies are dying from hunger." And I'd have to agree with him, really, but still...

Then Marian, Kirsty's mum, suggested I came with them, to help Kirsty shop. I was afraid my folks would still think it "a shocking extravagance et cetera et cetera" but Marian sweet-talked my mum, who said maybe I could use the experience to further my education.

That is why I'm writing it all down. I want to be a writer. Mrs Brady, our English teacher, told me that I had the makings of a good writer. She advised me to practise describing things. So I've decided to write about Kirsty because I want to write a novel about two girls who are friends, one rich and one poor. (It's not that we're poor but we're not rich like the Kerrigans.)

So here goes:

Paris was so exciting. We went to all the designer boutiques. You couldn't just walk in the door – you had to ring a bell before they would let you in. I suppose if you didn't look wealthy enough they wouldn't open the door. But Marian and her friend Kate, the ex-model, were wearing designer suits and definitely looked wealthy enough. Kirsty and I were in jeans and t-shirts but even Paris Hilton wears jeans, so they let us in too.

Inside, each boutique was scented with expensive

perfume and had an assistant who looked like a Spanish Marquesa who would ask how she could help? Well, not all the assistants looked like a Spanish Marquesa, but they were all equally daunting. They put you sitting on a sofa and brought you champagne and showed you some dresses. Kirsty found what she called The Perfect Dress in Dolce and Gabbana and tried it on. She clearly thought she looked totally fierce, like a Red Carpet Celeb. I wasn't so sure. It was slit down the front to the navel.

"Oh my god Kirsty," said Marian. "You look like a hooker." Then her eyes widened in horror. *"And what's that in your belly button?"*

Oh dear. Kirsty had a gold star in her navel. Her mum was dead against piercing. When they turned thirteen, Marian made Kirsty and Jake swear to God, cross their hearts and hope to die that they wouldn't get any piercings or tattoos until they'd left school. Except for earrings, of course; she didn't mind earrings.

"Give me a proper look at that thing," snarled Marian.

And right there, in the middle of Dolce and Gabbana, in Paris, she demanded to know what Mrs Brady always called the key questions every writer must answer: Who? What? Where? When? Why? How?

Kirsty admitted that she'd got it last year in Marbella. She didn't say that we'd had it done in "Vicious Victim", the tattoo and piercing stall on the beach. That would have freaked her mum out, big time. And she didn't tell her that the only reason we got it done there was because we fancied Stingray, the tattoo guy. (Probably that wasn't his real name but it was what everyone called him.) He was one of those surfer-type dudes, streaky blonde hair, cheekbones, tan, six-pack. We spent the week daring one another to do it. I thought it was just a joke but next thing

Kirsty marched in and I couldn't just leave her there so we both had it done. (My mum was also dead against piercings, but she wasn't going to find out about mine.) It wasn't that bad. Unfortunately, Stingray had a girlfriend.

"It's the twenty-first century, Mum!" Kirsty protested.

The Spanish Marquesa was pretending to do something to a dress but she was obviously listening. Marian didn't care.

"That doesn't mean you're immune from infection. Do you have any idea of the kind of diseases you could have got?"

"But I didn't, did I? And anyway, my body's my own."

"Oh no, it isn't. Not while I'm paying for your clothes and you're eating my food. And I'm definitely not paying for a dress that makes my daughter look like a whore. So get it off now."

Kirsty stood defiantly admiring herself in the mirror, not taking off the dress. Marian was getting the revs up to explode, but Kate put a hand on her arm.

"Let's see what it's like when she walks." She dropped Marian a wink. "Give us a runway view, Kirsty, would you mind?"

Kirsty smirked triumphantly and walked to the end of the shop and back.

"The colour is great," said Kate," and it's fabulous from the front. You might need some tit tape but that's easy enough. Turn round again."

Kirsty turned round.

"Mmm," said Kate, "It's okay, but…"

"*What?*"

"It's all right, I suppose…"

"How do you mean?"

"It's a bit… I'm not saying it isn't nice but… Well…

It's a bit *blah* from the back. I think you'd be better with something that shows off your figure. Because you do have a fabulous figure."

Kirsty examined the back of the dress in the triple mirrors.

"You're right. It is a bit *blah*."

"Why don't we take a break and have lunch?" suggested Kate. "I know this great little place."

Kate seemed to know loads of "great little places" from her days in Paris as a model. Marian and Kate scoffed foie gras and champagne in La Petite. Paris had made them go all "Ooh La La". The champagne went straight to their heads and they started giggling and flirting with the waiters. I thought they were funny, but Kirsty was mortified. She tried to pretend that we weren't with them.

After they sobered up a bit we did "the golden triangle". Marian wanted Kirsty to get a dress we found in Chanel. I thought it looked great: coral silk, criss-cross straps and a diamante belt. Kirsty slouched in front of the mirror.

"Not exactly cutting edge," she said, and for once I could see she was right.

We did Dior, Yves Saint Laurent, Louis Féraud, Cardin, Versace. Oh my God, you should have seen the dresses. I'd have given my right arm for any of them. Kirsty kept on at me to get a dress for myself but I hadn't got that kind of money. It got a bit embarrassing before Marian realised and shut her up. Marian and Kate got themselves dresses along the way but nothing was good enough for our Kirsty. As the afternoon wore on she got grumpy and when Kirsty gets grumpy, she sulks and whinges. She's tired, she's fed up, she wants to go back to the hotel and have a hot bath... But Kate insisted she try a shop called Colette before she gave up. And there it was, on display. Alexander Mc

Queen: luminous pink satin bustier with orange strapping, magenta taffeta skirt with net flowers in orange and pink. Sort of glamorous punk and totally fierce! Kirsty gasped and touched the flowers.

"This is it," she said.

Marian didn't like it but Kate said to try it on. It looked amazing.

"This is what brainiacs like the Martina Currans of this world don't get," said Kirsty as she paraded around. "Designer dresses are flattering."

And she was right; the corset top gave her an amazing figure. Marian still didn't like it.

"Well, I love it," said Kate. "Cool, edgy, young, very twenty-first century."

I agreed with Kate and eventually Marian gave in.

Once we'd found The Perfect Dress things turned fun. Paris was just beautiful. Even just sitting outside a café drinking cappuccinos made me feel sophisticated. I got to try out my French and Kate brought us to this little jazz club she knew where there was an Argentine band and these amazing tango dancers. Even Kirsty thought it was cool.

EAMON

Monkey and the Wrenches are making a comeback. For one night only. It'll be a laugh. We're the warm up act for the Wage Slaves, the band Kirsty wants. We'll bash out a few classics. Give the grown-ups something to dance to before they go home. But I'm not telling Kirsty. It's going to be a surprise.

All the lads are signed up, we reckon it's twenty years since we last played a gig. Doesn't time fly when you're making a dollar! Colm's our drummer. Like me, he's in the property business. Made a fortune in Eastern Europe. When I was talking to him he made a suggestion. He's been looking at a deal in Romania. Castle in the Carpathian Mountains, lakes, scenery, weather, whatever you're having yourself. Luxury development. Wants to know if I'm interested. So I had a word with Marian.

Marian has a good head on her shoulders. Asks all the right questions. And she thinks it's worth looking into. I've done plenty of luxury developments. Colm hasn't. But he knows Eastern Europe. He says there's all kinds of property over there going a begging. I'll fly to Bucharest next week for a look-see.

KIRSTY

Mum has the official invitation list. But I have the *real* list – and a brilliant idea for delivering the invites! White Angels and Red Devils! Here's the plan:

Lala and me will get a limo and go round to everyone's house. The angels deliver the invites and we watch from the car. Won't that be gas? Then, I have these black envelopes with black cards inside saying "You are NOT invited to Kirsty's Eighteenth Birthday". I got them off the internet. We'll drive to Martina Curran's house and the devils will deliver one to her. I can't wait to see her face! Then the same for the uggos and Jennifer Horseface from the riding classes in The Paddocks, the one who thinks she's so great 'cause she has her own horse.

I have decided to ask Johnny Lynch. He owns The Paddocks. He's quite old but he looks like Colin Farrell and he's single. At least I think he is. I've never seen him with a girlfriend.

"That doesn't mean he's single," says Lala.

We are grooming Whispa. She's my favourite horse. I've

asked Dad to buy her but the owner won't sell.

"Here he comes now," hisses Lala. "I double-dare you to ask him."

Johnny comes over and gives Whispa an apple. She's his favourite as well.

"Hey Johnny," I say. "Have you got a girlfriend?"

"That's for me to know and you to find out." And he gives me a twinkly wink and walks off.

"That means he has," says Lala.

"Don't be stupid. He can't say out straight he's got no girlfriend. It's too lame. He's just avoiding the question!"

Lala wants me to ask Paddy White. He's one of the nerdiest nerds in the whole of St Fintan's. That's the boys' school. Both the convent and St Fintan's are single sex. They say it's better for academic achievement – but what about social development? That's what I want to know. Anyway, Paddy White has glasses and looks like a dork. Lala thinks he's way cool 'cause he draws cartoons like Japanese Manga. She has *begged* me to invite him, so I will. But honestly, I don't get it.

MARIAN

Kirsty is all Little Miss Sunshine. Hmm. When Kirsty turns sunny side up, you'd better watch out. She forgets I am her mother and I know her better than she knows herself. So, let's review the situation. She's having two angels for postmen. I assume she got them from Party Favours in Galway. I phone to check.

Ah… She has ordered two devils as well. I have a snoop through her room. I find pink and white party invites in the top drawer of her desk. In the next drawer, I find black cards and envelopes. These cards read, "You are NOT invited…"

LALA

The end of term was here at last and we were free for the summer. I still didn't know if I wanted to concentrate on writing poetry or go back to my rich girl/poor girl story. I asked Mrs Brady her opinion, and she said just to write whatever I felt like at the time. The last day at school felt like a poem, so this is what I wrote:

> **Last Day at School**
> *Sister Agnes speaks from the stage:*
> *Behave, help, credit to the school.*
> *The words are drowned in our excitement.*
> *The Angelus tolls,*
> *Cacophony of chairs,*
> *The Angel of the Lord declares:*
> *We are free! We are free!*
>
> *We race down the avenue*
> *Giddy with freedom,*
> *Sloughing off study and class.*
> *The debris of learning*
> *Abandoned,*
> *We embrace the glory of summer.*

KIRSTY

Summer holidays at last! I thought they'd never come. And only one more year to go before I am totally free. Lala and I do our hair and make-up and try out my new pearly-pink eye-shadow. It is killer. I have the pink and white invitations ready in a box where Mum can see them. I carry my bag, where I have the un-invitations zipped away out of sight.

"My! Don't you two look stylish," says Mum when we arrive down the stairs. "All set?"

"Yeah."

"It's going to be fab!" says Mum.

The doorbell rings. It's the limo. Me and Lala rush out. One of the angels jumps out and opens the door for us. I get in. Straight away, I notice there are no devils but I don't say anything 'cause Mum has followed us out.

"Where are the devils?" blurts Lala.

I kick her hard on the ankle.

"Okay Mum," I say, "we're ready to roll."

When we've left the front gate, I'll ask. Lala is dithering about which seat she wants to take. Mum gets into the limo after her and sits down. What the...?

"I'm coming with you. It's going to be great!"

So that's why there are no devils. Somehow, some way Mum has found out. How? Jake? But I didn't tell Jake. I purposely didn't tell him because I know he's a snitch. So how did she find out? Sometimes I think that she's psychic or that she really does have eyes in the back of her head. She used to say that when we were little, and I used to lift up her hair to see if I could find those extra eyes. I still haven't found them but she must have them somewhere. I give the driver the first address and sit back in my seat. I have to re-think my plan.

Everyone adores the angels. Mammies and daddies come out to take photos and everyone has a good time except me. When we are finished, Mum pulls out a list from her pocket.

"There's still six names left to do."

"Lala and me will do them tomorrow," I say. "We've no invitations left."

"You're in luck," she says. "I've brought some extra ones with me. And a pen."

She makes me write them there and then on the spot

and go round to the houses and get the angels to deliver them.

LALA

As soon as Marian climbed in the limo, I knew that she had Kirsty sussed. It was funny though, watching Kirsty try to deal with it and her mum always being one step ahead.

Martina Curran's house was out the Bog Road and the path to her door was lined with lavender. As the angels brushed past, it released a gorgeous scent. They rang the bell. The housekeeper opened the door and looked surprised. Then she called Martina. Martina appeared in the doorway wearing a tracksuit.

"We're here to ask if it will please you," sang the angels, wiggling their tutus in unison, "to come to Kirsty's eighteenth do."

Martina just stood there and stared. I could see she was flummoxed. The angels handed over the envelope. Martina looked out at the limo, then she snatched the invite and closed the door.

Next day, Kirsty texted me to come over.

"I've been awake half the night," she complained, flinging herself on her bed, "thinking. The uggos and nerds don't matter but I'm not having Martina Curran."

She showed me a black envelope with a stamp. It had Martina's name and address. We cycled in to Balfathery to post it.

After that we wandered down to The Dozy Donkey for coffee and just before we left who should come in, only Martina.

"Gee, Kirsty," she sneered. "Summer Berries! Is it a party or a stall on the side of the road?"

Kirsty just smiled 'cause she'd already posted the letter.

JAKE

It's the first Monday of the summer holidays. We all sleep in except Dad. He's up and off to work ages ago. The kitchen is empty. I prop my book up against the fruit bowl. It's *Adventures in the Screen Trade*.

I make scrambled eggs in a pan, like they do in American movies. I stir the eggs, add salt and pepper and I'm in Hollywood. I put on some toast. Movie executives beg me to direct their scripts. I only take on the best. The toast pops and I remember that Hollywood's crazy. Godzilla-on-Acid crazy, according to *"Adventures"*. Maybe I should be thinking Fellini, Kurosawa, Almodovar, Loach. Independent classics. Work with people you trust, turn unknown actors into stars. Kirsty punctures my daydream by arriving in her bathrobe.

"Make some for me."

"Make your own."

She takes out the Rice Krispies and flicks one at me. I duck. She misses. "You'll need a new suit for my party," she says.

"I have suits."

"None the right colour."

"I'm not wearing a raspberry suit."

"Yes you are!"

"No, I'm not."

"I'll tell Mum."

"Go ahead."

I go back to my book. Kirsty clatters around. Mum arrives down. Kirsty bends her ear about me and the suit. Mum says I can wear a pink shirt. I bargain her down to a red tie. With a black shirt, a red tie will be fine and the tie will be coming off anyway.

I don't want to go to the party. I mean who'll dance with

me? My Gran, my Mum, my aunties, my cousins. None of the cool girls. Because I'm a titch and they're all two years older. If I was taller I might have a chance. But I'm not. On the plus side, there'll be loads of girls in skimpy dresses. But *Summer Berries!* Vomitorious.

MARIAN

When did girls get so horribly bitchy? It wasn't like that in my day. And that's not rosy specs, it really wasn't. Of course there were girls you didn't like. There might be the odd row, a few catty remarks but mostly girls were fun. When did that change? How is it suddenly "typical teen" to hurl vicious abuse at your parents? And who said it was right, commendable even, to go out of your way to score bitch points?

I blame those reality shows. They always pick crazies. Well duh! For the ratings! If a Martian came down and only watched the reality shows he'd think bitchy was normal for human females. Not the ones I know! My friends don't get sarky about your shoes! Or call you two–faced! Normal people don't do that.

God knows I've told Kirsty often enough. But who ever listens to their mother? I certainly didn't, so I can't expect her to. I suppose it's a lesson that she has to learn for herself.

EAMON

Note to self:
1. Amps and mikes.
2. Remind lads to bring gear.
3. Arrange rehearsal – not at home.
4. Play list.
5. Check with Fergus re Wage Slaves.
6. Delivery of Present.
7. Flight to Bucharest.

I think that's all… Seán will look after the rest. He does amazingly well for himself does our Seán. You wouldn't believe his turnover. Jesus but the Irish are spending! And why wouldn't we? We got it, we flaunt it. That's why they love us in Spain, because we spend, spend, spend. Not like the English, who wouldn't spend Christmas – tight as ticks. At last we've got our chance at the high life. And who could begrudge us? We've had our fill of history and famine and all that aul mhuire-'s-trua. It's time to par-tay!

CHAPTER 3

LALA

The day of the party Kirsty, Marian and Kate booked into Balm, a country house spa that they loved. I'd never been there but Marian insisted that I come. She booked us all in for the Total Treatment. Marian and Kirsty often talked about needing to be pampered. Why? I didn't understand, it wasn't like they were slaving in coal mines every day. My mum always said she'd *love* to get pampered but she had to make *choices* and she *chose* to spend her money making sure her children got a good education. It made me feel a tiny bit guilty about going to the spa.

First, they served Macedonian fruit teas, which were supposed to relax us. They were nice, not like that horrible herbal stuff my mum always drank when she felt she needed a detox. Then we hit the Jacuzzi. Once we were inside, they dimmed the lights. I lay back and looked up and there were stars on the ceiling and the sound of waves on a beach. After a while even Kirsty went quiet. The Jacuzzi was to relax the muscles and open the pores.

When we'd been well simmered, they wrapped us in big fluffy towels and took us off for a massage and a facial. It was dim in there too. The lady who did me looked small and I was afraid it might tickle because this was my first proper massage. But it wasn't. While she kneaded the knots out of my body she had this trance music playing and after a while I felt like the music was seeping into my bones and that I had melted into the table. Wow. I decided to persuade my mum to go sometime. She worked very hard at her job as a radiographer, and she could do with a massage.

Lunch was extra healthy, chicken with several salads. Dessert was fresh fruit. Then Kirsty started acting up.

"What if I've put on weight? What if the dress doesn't fit? I definitely feel fatter."

"Don't be ridiculous Kirsty," I said.

Marian ignored her but Kate took her by the hand and brought her out to the dressing room where there was a scales. Of course she hadn't put on weight. She just enjoyed the drama.

EAMON

While the girls are off tittifying themselves, the lads arrive for lunch and a proper rehearsal. It starts off a bit scratchy at first but soon enough we settle into the groove. It's just like the old days. Me singing, Colm doing his Phil Collins thing on the drums, Fergus thinking he's Jimi Hendrix and Seán holding us all together with his bass guitar. Groovy baby.

Fergus had offered to get us a loan of a couple of roadies but we'd said no. We like setting up. It's part of the ritual. I'm not really nervous about going on stage. I just want to get on. I know once I'm out there I can turn it on. But I have to admit to the odd butterfly, this being Kirsty's birthday and all…

Fergus had brought some nose candy for afterwards when the kids were doing their thing with the dancing and us adults can retire and kick back in the living room. I put it out of the way in a drawer in the den with the mirror, the bowl and the spoon. I lock the drawer and put the key in its hiding place. We have a very strict rule, business first and always before pleasure.

Fergus also brought Tracey. Marian is not going to like this. We thought we'd seen the back of Tracey when we came home from London. That's the mad, bad and dangerous-to-know Tracey O'Hagan – Old Man O' Hagan's youngest. Reared her himself when her mother, his third wife, did a runner. You often see him these days in the papers, handing out cardboard cheques to cripples and orphans. Mansion in Wicklow, herd of wild deer, string of thoroughbreds. And none of them got by doing good works. Officially, he's Topaz Security – or was, until he retired. But he was also Ireland's premier drug baron, though that's never been proved. Now Tracey's in charge of both sides of the business. She's gets her kicks from taking risks. Personally, I wouldn't put Tracey in charge of a cardboard box.

Marian thinks Fergus is coming to the party with Laura, his wife. Last time she was talking to Laura, things were going well. She and Fergus were seeing a shrink to sort out their marriage. But Laura hadn't reckoned on Tracey turning up to provide Fergus with wild, freaky sex or, as he himself calls it, "falling in love". Not that I'm dissing wild, freaky sex – it's just, well, it takes too much out of you.

My phone rings and it's Andy Minehan.

"The eagle has landed," he growls.

That means the minister's car has arrived in Athlone. Excellent.

KIRSTY

Gregor is ready and waiting to do our hair when we get

home from the spa. I can't wait to try on the dress, but Gregor won't let me.

"You must wait for hair and makeup!"

"I just want to check it still fits."

"*Dahlink*, of course it still fit."

"And besides," says Lala, in that deadpan voice she uses when she's being sarcastic, "you weighed yourself only an hour ago."

There was no need for her to say that.

Gregor is so into fashion. He's my hairstylist, Mum's too, but it was Kate who discovered him. He trained in Paris, styled hair for all the famous designers, and his hero is Alexander Mc Queen. He's also Russian, so he's very emotional. When we went to his salon in Galway for the trial run, I showed him a photo of the dress.

"Oh my God! Oh my God," he squealed. "Can I show this to the girls?" The girls squealed as well. "For that dress you must wear your hair up. And you must have it tousled and edgy."

Mum wanted it down and sleek but when Kate agreed with Gregor, Mum had to give in.

Most people think hairdressing is only for losers but, hair-styling is different. Hair-*styling* is Art. Gregor says it's like sculpture. Kate says a good stylist is worth their weight in diamonds and Kate believes that Gregor's a genius.

We go up to my dressing-room. When Gregor sees the actual dress hanging up on the door he nearly faints.

"Oh my God! Oh my God!" He fingers the silk of the bodice and fluffs out the skirt. "Oh my God! Oh my God!"

Finally he gets me to sit down in front of the mirror and starts prowling around, lifting my hair, twisting bits, glancing back at the dress. He's being creative. And when Gregor is being creative, you'd better not interrupt. God no, he'd get into a snit. Once he told the Lord Mayor's wife to shut up or fuck off!

Finally he's ready. He spritzes my hair and turns me away from the mirror.

"Better you wait until everything finish, then… *Surprise!*"

I agree not to look till the end. It is agony not knowing. But when Mum and Kate join us they smile and go, *Oh wow!* So far so good. Then Kate and Gregor have a long consultation about make-up and Kate gets out her kit. Kate's a genius with make-up. When she is done she steps back, cocks her head, and looks pleased. At this stage my stomach is churning with the excitement, like I have swallowed an alien life form. Mum and Kate help me into the dress, tighten the bodice, fluff out the skirt and stand back. As I slip on the Louboutin shoes, Mum's eyes fill up.

"Take a look in the mirror," says Kate, turning the pier glass around.

What I see is this gorgeous stranger, looking totally cool. Oh my God, that's *me*. Oh! *My!!* GOD!!!

I look fierce. I could rock any red carpet anywhere in the world. My hair is funky and wild but totally matching the vibe of the dress. Crystal-chandelier earrings, killer dress, shoes to die for. I strike a few poses. Mum is snuffling away in the background.

"Alexander McQueen does Victorian tomboy!" says Kate.

Gregor gasps. "That's it exactly!"

Mum calls Dad in for a preview. He stares for several seconds.

"Jesus, Mary and the holy Saint Joseph," he says eventually. "I told you not to stick your fingers in the electric socket!"

JAKE

I hate to say this. But the party room looks kind of fabulous. High quality schmaltz, not my cup of tea, of course, but it would make a great set. Swathes of gauze, swags of roses, sconces with rose sprays like fountains, sconces with flames made of roses. Lights, silver, candles, everything twinkly, twinkly. Kirsty will adore it.

The riggers are doing their last-minute checks on the ropes and trapezes. The rig for the acrobats is painted gold. The stage at the back is hidden by drapes. A horseshoe table is set between the marble ladies pouring their water into basins and there's a space for performers in front. The rest of the tables are down either side. This party will be some hoop-de-la. I'm bringing my camera.

Next thing we hear a familiar sound: *"Di-doodle, di-doodle, di-doodle, di-do, di-do, di-dooooo..."* Granda's trademark. He tootles the horn as he comes up the drive. Gran hates that horn. That's why Granda does it.

More cars arrive. I come back into the house and out to the patio. My job is to encourage people into the garden to keep the patio from getting too crowded. But the people are happy to go. It's twinkly out there as well and there's a table set up in the summer house with more drinks and snacks and a couple of waiters.

Girls start arriving in bunches. They move around like a shoal of shimmery fish. Except, fish don't squeal. The girls squeal a lot and flick their hair. The shoal splits and one lot swims off to the bathroom. New arrivals merge with the rest. All the girls glitter and gleam. I can't help staring. There's a lot of bootylicious babes. I take a few pictures.

Then the fellas arrive. They stand round in clots and look awkward. They're sheepish about the Summer Berry shirts they have to wear and they josh one another. There's lots of arm-punching and baa-ing laughs. Some of the fellas were too embarrassed to wear the shirts or even a tie that someone might think is pink but Mum has lots of coloured scarves ready for them because all the guests have to wear the Summer Berries colour somewhere. They're flicking the scarves at one another. Every so often the fellas glance at the girls while pretending they're not. They're dying to go over but nobody wants to be first. Jim Buckley swaggers in with Gerry What's-His-Face. They both wear red suits. They get a fierce razz from the rest of the lads. But they don't care. They're sixth years, they play junior county hurling and they're known as gas men. They get themselves drinks and head straight for the girls.

Granda comes over to me.

"How's she cuttin' Jake?"

He wears the magenta jacket he bought in Spain and a dickey bow with flashing pink lights.

"Pink to make the boys wink, eh Jake?" He gives me a dig in the ribs. "I see you're using that camera to pick up the girls." He cackles and digs me once more in the ribs. Then he spots Nana Jo. "Oh-oh," he says. "Here comes The Mother of Sorrows."

Nana Jo joins us. She is Mum's mum. Her name is Josie but we call her Nana Jo. She's very old-fashioned but I get along with her fine. She wears a pink woolly cardigan over a sensible dress and white nurse's shoes. Granda shows her his flashing bow tie. Nana Jo doesn't say it but I know by the look on her face that she thinks it's common. I excuse myself, there's a new knot of arrivals.

One of the arrivals is Gran. She rushes over to kiss me. She's wearing a magenta and gold brocade suit and she has a magenta and purple feather explosion stuck to the side of her head.

"Jake!" she exclaims. "You look very grown up!"

She kisses me, all over my face, like I'm three years of age. She smells of roses. The feathers tickle my nose.

Seán glides in and out through the guests. He checks glasses, nods instructions to waiters, greets people he knows with a hug and a laugh. He wears a discreet silver-grey suit and a perfect scarlet rosebud.

LALA

We waited up in Kirsty's room with Kate, because Kirsty was not going to appear till everyone was sitting down – she was going to make "an entrance". I fixed the blinds so we could see out over the patio. The garden looked magical. There were thousands of lights twinkling in the trees and lanterns lining the paths.

"It's like something a film star would have," I said.

Kirsty was pleased with that.

Most of the girls from school turned up around the same time, and stood in a group on the patio gasping. I would have liked to be down there among them but Kirsty wanted me to stay.

Marian came in. She was wearing the rose-gold silk dress she had bought in Paris; it looked great with her tan.

"You're missing all the fun, Lala," she said and insisted on bringing me down to the patio. Kirsty called me back.

"Let me know if Martina turns up," she whispered.

"She won't."

"Still, I'd like to know. Just in case."

KIRSTY

I'm stuck here watching out through the blinds while

Kate sits on my bed drinking champagne and talking on her mobile. Everyone in the garden below is drinking and yacking away. I'm getting fed up being stuck up here.

"Why can't Seán announce dinner?"

"He has to wait till all the guests have arrived," says Kate.

"I wish they'd hurry up."

"Are you nervous?"

"A bit."

"What could possibly go wrong?"

"It's just I want it to be the best party EVER."

Kate digs in her handbag and takes out a gold pillbox. There are several green tablets inside. She breaks one in two.

"Take that," she says, "and don't tell your mother."

I swig it down with champagne. After a while I feel totally chilled and kinda floaty. Next thing, Seán rings a gong and announces that dinner is about to be served. Pedro is here as well, helping Seán. Pedro rounds up guests from the garden. The wrinklies are the hardest to move. They flock together, nattering to each other. I want to open the window and scream, "get a move on". Lala comes dashing upstairs.

"No sign of Martina!"

"Pity."

"But I thought…"

"I was thinking of accidentally-on-purpose spilling a glass of red wine all over her dress!"

"Oh, don't do that Kirsty," she says. "It'd spoil the party."

Kate checks my hair, my dress and my make-up. Pedro knocks on the door. Kate lets him in.

"*Ay que guapa!*" says Pedro, clearly impressed.

GRANDMA MINNIE

The waiters line up in a guard of honour. Then Kirsty arrives with a fanfare of trumpets. She is sitting in a Cinderella carriage, pulled by four little fluffy white Shetland ponies. I cry. I can't help it. She looks like a princess out of a fairy story. I feel so proud. Everyone is cheering, cameras are flashing and Kirsty is waving to us all like a pro. The ponies flick their tails and toss their manes. They must have come in through the door in the atrium because even Eamon would never have let them come through the house.

Eamon opens the carriage door and helps Kirsty down. I've seen the dress before but this is the first time I've seen the whole look. It's fabulous! When she sits at the head of the table she looks like a picture. That's my granddaughter, I think. Who'd ever have thought that a Kerrigan could end up like this? It's like a beautiful dream – except it's real!

My Eamon did this by himself! And he started with nothing! Not much education, no connections and not a red cent to his name. But he always had brains. Not book-learning brains but practical brains. And of course he had Marian. Without her, things might be different. She's been the making of him. Because, like his father, Eamon's inclined to be wild.

MARIAN

Tracey is wearing Versace, a black and white zebra-print, no hint of Summer Berries. Typical. She's holding court at the table, being terribly gracious, so it has to be one of her good days. When she's on form, she can charm the birds off the bushes. But she's bi-polar – that's not an official diagnosis, but she's definitely bi something or other. She'll turn on you in an instant, for no reason at all. I remember it well back in London. One minute you'd be talking calmly about business, the next she'd be bashing you over the head with her handbag screaming that you're ripping her off. I had to get stitches one time and she gave Eamon a black eye. Which is just one of the reasons we wanted to leave London and finish with her for good. I never expected her to turn up in my house, and I'm praying she doesn't take a figary and ruin the party.

I've warned the staff to keep their eyes peeled for the least sign of trouble. Séan of course knows her well. He carries a pepper-spray and is not afraid to use it. Apparently parties and weddings are great places for fights, but even the mention of pepper-spray calms people down.

Fergus is gazing at Tracey with the soppy expression of the school nerd who, against all the odds, has just scored a date with the prom queen. I wouldn't mind, but he knows right well she's unstable. As my mother would say, when it comes to men and sex there's no rhyme or reason. Eejit. I have to admit that Tracey is very good looking – a figure to die for and she dresses to kill, but she's as mad as a box of babies. Horse's-head-at-the-end-of-your-bed kind of mad. But he's "in love", so there's no talking to him.

He's always been like that. Only ever went out with mad bats. It's a kind of addiction. Freaky women with "exotic" lifestyles. We'd find them in the kitchen in London searching for coffee, panda eyes and hair like a haw bush, wearing only his shirt or, in one remarkable case, only his jocks. It always follows the same pattern. She's gorgeous, he falls "in love", she messes with his head, she leaves him, he's in bits. After one of these loonies had left, he met Laura. She was sensible and safe, his port in a storm. They got married. And it worked for a while.

Some men are adrenelin junkies, they risk life and limb climbing Mount Everest or trekking to the South Pole or swimming with sharks, Fergus gets his kicks from unstable women. Unfortunately, Tracey fits that bill better than most. Look at her gene pool. Father, a vicious criminal. Mother, in jail in Australia for "grievous bodily".

Interesting point: Fergus's PR business keeps him in regular contact with mad people. Rock stars, soap idols and Media Whores. That, incidentally, is what I'm trying to get through Kirsty's head. She thinks celebrities are all glamour, but they're not. They're just egos on legs. Egos that keep leaking and ruining the carpets.

JAKE

I sit beside Helen, my cousin. She's thirteen and a bit podgy but easy to chat to. We watch the acrobats flying through the air overhead. Helen's jaw is down to her knees. I'm trying to look cool, but they are amazing. I take lots of photos. Helen's very impressed with my camera. I take a few more shots and show them to her. She's looks at me like I'm god on a stick. I go round the tables between courses taking shots. Especially of girls that I fancy. I'm looking for unguarded moments.

Suddenly I'm Mr Popular. Everyone wants me to take their photo. And everyone wants copies. I promise to put them up on my website. They can download them themselves. Granda was right, the camera's a great way to chat up the girls. But I'm still Kirsty's cute little brother. Let's hope Dad was right and that I'll wake up some day with my feet dangling out of the bed.

NANA JO

All those children starving in Africa.

That's what kept going through my head, on and on and on, starving children and then look at this! They must have spent thousands. Thousands. It's not right. Of course there's no point in talking to Marian. I know what she'll say:

"Relax Ma, enjoy yourself, life's too short."

But the next life is not short. The next life will last for Eternity.

In my day a girl of eighteen was earning her keep, not making a display of herself in designer frocks. And the state of her hair! Why can't she comb it? It looks so untidy.

The Kerrigans were always the ones for display. Look at Minnie there, in her shiny brocade and earrings like cheap chandeliers. At her age! She was always the same, parading around in her slacks, turquoise blue eyelids and roaring red lips. She was the first woman in Balfathery to be seen wearing trousers. She caused a few tongues to wag I can tell you!

My mother was a lady. On her poorest day she wore gloves in the street and always a hat, not a headscarf. Wonderful woman. She even arranged my marriage. And a very good marriage it was. Benny Murray, quiet, respectable, with his own tidy farm and quite a bit older than me. Some might think his age was a drawback, but it meant he didn't make many demands of the marital type. I was forty-three when he died. Old enough to know there's not much to be got from this life but we'll reap our rewards in the next.

Why Marian had to marry Eamon Kerrigan I'll never understand. She could have taken her pick. The vet's eldest was interested and that Garda in Clonfad. Yet no one would do her but Eamon. I'm afraid he's a very rough diamond. Very Flash Harry.

And who ever thought that having acrobats dangling over your head was clever idea? As good as naked they are, flinging their legs every which way. No one wants that when they're eating their dinner. What if one of them slips? And as for the dinner! It looks like something that wants to be hung on the wall in a frame. Give me a nice leg of chicken, roast potatoes and peas any day.

GRANDMA MINNE

The Mother of Sorrows is at the next table, poking her lovely food like some poor unfortunate searching a bin. It's the fanciest night out of her entire life, and she's complaining. Sweet Jesus, I'd hate to be living inside of that head! Nothing lives up to her standards. It's a mystery to me that Marian turned out the grand girl she is.

Just because her family once had a shop, Josie thinks she's a cut above buttermilk. But her father gambled every farthing they had and when he died all they were left with was debts. Had to sell up and move to Barrack Street until she married. They lived three doors down from us when we were young ones, but they never mixed.

Josie was fit to be tied when Marian announced she was marrying Eamon. Tried to stop it, thought she could do better. And look at him now, a Minister at the top table and the room bursting with the cream of the county.

Money is the root of all evil she says. She says it to get at Eamon. But who built that bungalow for her? Who pays for her flights to Marbella? We've been poor long enough. A few bob won't hurt us. Nor a bit of indulgence. As I always say, 'Tis far from Jacuzzis we were reared, but we can take to them easy enough!

EAMON

Bloody Minister. He can't pass up a mike. He just had to rear up on his hind legs and say something political. At a birthday party! Wanker. Not that it matters, everyone knows what he's like.

After the speeches, me and the lads sneak off to get ready. We're no longer the scrawny youngsters we were, so we've had new outfits made. They look good. We slick back what's left of our hair and put on our fedoras; it was just like the old days. The wait to go on. The nervous jokes. Me pacing the floor.

The MC goes out on stage. I peep through the screen at the crowd. Kirsty is up at the front. The mike squeals a bit.

"Ladies and Gentlemen. For one night only. As a special treat for Kirsty…"

I take a deep breath.

"Please give a big welcome tooooooo…."

I cross myself and mutter a prayer.

"'Monkey and the Wrenches!'"

Everyone starts clapping and laughing. Kirsty goes bright red and covers her face with her hands. Colm runs out and starts up a drum beat. Fergus goes next and then Seán. They lash out a few chords. I take another deep breath and I'm on. We dive head first into *Satisfaction*.

The crowd are all clapping and jigging in time to the beat. Marian drags my dad out, more people follow and next thing the floor is packed, with the youngsters leppin' about like jack-in-the-boxes. We bow to rapturous applause and take it down a couple of notches. I sing the first verse of *The Most Beautiful Girl in the World*. Kirsty looks mortified but I don't care because she is the most beautiful girl in the world. I stop singing, the band vamp behind me. I walk to the edge of the stage and ask Kirsty to dance. Everyone cheers. Kirsty blushes. I come down and lead her on to the floor. Séan takes over the singing.

"Oh my God, Dad!" she says. "I'll never live this down."

But I bet she likes it really because she knows I mean every word of that song, she's my Princess.

All those awkward teenage boys were dancing around us, with only one thing on their squirrely minds. They're being nice to the girls but I know what they're thinking. Every last man of 'em is a hoor for the quare thing. I look down at Kirsty, she smiles up at me and my heart nearly breaks. I wish I could hide her away from all that. Protect her. And I will, any way that I can.

When the dance is over I have go back on the stage. We blaze into *Rock around the Clock*. Jake is dancing around with my mother. Tracey, looking shit-hot, has a schoolboy in her clutches; he looks like he's going to come in his pants. Da, in his flashing bow tie, is pulling some cool moves with Kirsty. He's been teaching her how to rock'n'roll since she was three. There's kids throwing shapes on the floor, parents reliving their youth and everyone's lovin' it, lovin' it, lovin' it. We finish the set with *I Will Survive*. Monkey and the Wrenches can still rock the Kasbah.

JAKE

Johnny Lynch, the manager from the horse-riding school, is dancing with Kirsty. He keeps a decorous distance. She's batting her eyelids and touching her hair. She's had a crush on him since she was twelve. He knows. His girlfriend watches.

Monkey and the Wrenches finish the set and leave the stage – thank God, because they are majorly embarrassing. Dad knows it but he doesn't seem to care. He says it's a parent's job to embarrass their kids.

Johnny says something that makes Kirsty smile. He still keeps his distance. He leaves. Kirsty returns to her posse.

The MC comes out and announces the Wage Slaves.

Kirsty and Co go into hyper-drive. They scream and wave their hands and make a tottery rush to the stage. The guys follow behind. They want to look cool. They're all "let's-go-and-look-for-a-laugh". But they want to, really.

The Wage Slaves strut out. Spike takes the mike. The girls jump up and down with their arms in the air, like a flock of flamingos. They're all of them squealing. Some of them are crying. The noise is enough to alarm every bat in the county. I cover my ears.

The Wage Slaves are so lame. With a name like that, you'd think they'd be cool, but they're not. They're basically a boy band with pretensions. Girls love them. Guys mock them. They start the set with their current hit *Heart Fever*. The girls go deranged. When it ends Spike says something into the mike. I can't hear with the squealing. I catch "something, something, Birthday Girl". He holds his hand out to Kirsty. She takes it. He jumps down beside her; the screaming goes into warp-drive. He leads Kirsty up to the stage. He sits her on a high stool and sings *Coconut Candy* to her. He changes 'Candy' to 'Kirsty'. Kirsty looks at him like he's a god.

It's embarrassing.

EAMON

The Minister's off. Busy man. Rumour has it that when he's on form, he can hit twenty events in one night. Wins a lot of votes that way. Throws local journos a headline, gives them interviews. That's good for votes too.

"Always willing to help," I say, shaking his hand at the door.

"I'll remember that, Eamon!"

We both guffaw.

When I get back to the party, I summon Marian and

Kirsty up on stage. It is time for the present.

"Kirsty, Princess," I say. "Your mum and me are so proud of you. Happy birthday, sweetheart. I hope you like your present."

Kirsty is clutching her hands. I point to the door. Everyone strains to see. The Wage Slaves do a bit of a fanfare like I'd asked them to do and in marches Johnny Lynch, the manager of that horse-riding place, leading a horse. And not any old horse. Whispa. Kirsty's favourite. And a fine-looking beast she is too, gingery brown and all dickied out in red ribbons. Kirsty shrieks and flings her arms around my neck.

"Oh Daddy, I love you." she says.

JAKE
The horse looks embarrassed. And so would you, if you had an enormous red ribbon tied to your tail! Everyone's yammering. The pals crowd round Whispa to stroke her. The Wage Slaves are horsing around on the stage. Someone trips and falls into the drum-kit.

"All together now,' says Spike into the mike and with a crash of cymbals, the Wage Slaves start up *Happy Birthday.*

Whispa takes fright and rears up. I turn my camera to video mode. Everyone screams as the horse starts to plunge. She knocks over a table. People dash for the door. Johnny Lynch keeps his head. He catches the reins and leads Whispa out of the party. The Wage Slaves begin *Happy Birthday* again. Everyone sings.

That's one for YouTube.

MARIAN
The adults are starting to leave so I am on Hostess Patrol, smiling, hugging, being generally gracious. I can see

Mother trying to catch my attention. I wave to let her know I'll be over as soon as I can. My sister Jacinta is leaving with her girls. The girls want to stay, but they're only ten and eleven. I wave them goodbye and turn back to my mother. Miroslav greets me fondly and I have to talk to him and his wife, see them to the door. A car pulls up on the forecourt and out steps one of Kirsty's classmates – attractive girl, honey blonde with subtle high-lights in a midnight blue dress, no hint of Summer Berries.

"Martina Curran," she says.

So this is the arch enemy, the "evil bitch" Kirsty didn't want to invite to the party. Sometimes I despair of my daughter. I know Eamon has a thing about Martina's father but that's no excuse. She seems like a perfectly nice, polite, young one to me.

"Delighted you could make it, Martina," I say, turning the warmth to max.

"Thank you, Mrs Kerrigan."

"Can I give you a scarf to go with the theme of the party?"

"Thank you."

She drapes it over her shoulder and I bring her into the party. I had wondered if she'd show because, in spite of me insisting that Kirsty give her an invitation, I wouldn't be stunned to learn that Kirsty had done all she could to put the girl off. So I'm glad she's turned up, it serves Kirsty right and maybe it'll teach her a lesson. I mean that business with the black envelopes and the devils, that wasn't good. I'm just glad I was able to nip it in the bud.

The Wage Slaves are giving it some welly and the kids are up dancing and whooping and jumping about. Kirsty is right up against the stage with some of her friends. They are having a ball, acting delirious and trying to flirt with the band. I don't get what they see in them. Spike is scrawny and plain, the drummer is pudgy and plain, the other two are just blah and the lot of them look like they've dressed themselves out of a bag that was left for the Vincent De Paul shop.

Someone plucks at my arm. My mother. I walked her into the house.

"How can they stand it?" she says. "I couldn't hear myself think in there."

"Séan and Fergus and the others are in the sitting-room, Mam. Why don't you join them?"

"I'm anxious to get home, Marian, I need a bit of quiet. Is it all right if I use the phone to call a taxi?"

"You don't have to ask, but give me twenty minutes or so and I'll get someone to drive you."

Carol Carson, our local doctor, is adjusting her pashmina and her husband is hovering beside her; they are obviously waiting to bid their farewells. Joe Morrissey, the county engineer, and his wife are also heading my way.

"Wait down in the den," I say to my mother. "Get someone to make you a cup of tea. Put up your feet up for a bit." I smile at the Carsons and the Morrisseys. "Thank you so much for coming," I say.

JAKE

I've decided that Seán is an artist. Not a writing-painting kind of artist, but still an artist. He says he doesn't think of his work as organising events, he thinks more about how can he transport people to a magical world where the décor is fabulous, the entertainment sensational, the music out of this world and they feel like they have got their three wishes. And isn't that what an artist does?

I think he has succeeded tonight. It might be a bit girly

for me but even so, I can't help enjoying it. Of course if you want to keep the world looking magical you need to keep a sharp eye out because when there's drink, guys can square up to each other, or girls can start a cat fight, and pfftt… the magic is gone. Apparently it happens more often than you'd imagine, even at the swankiest affairs.

The instant Blue Dress arrives I clock it. I notice Séan clocking it too. It's the only blue in a sea of Summer Berries. At first I don't recognise her because she looks so pretty, then I realise who it is. Martina Curran. I know her brother from school. I often see her in The Dozy Donkey with her pals but usually she has her hair scrooged back. Obviously she's got it done and it looks, wow! I'm surprised she's here because I know Kirsty hates her.

The Wage Slaves finish with *Feel A Tequila*. Everyone's dancing like crazy. I'm Jake Kerrigan, paparazzo extraordinario, snapping away. Girls looking sexy and cool. Guys throwing shapes. And oh-oh… red alert! Martina is making her way down the room towards Kirsty. She stops to talk and high-five people and laugh, but she's definitely heading for Kirsty. I check that the camera's on video mode.

The set ends. Everyone cheers. Spike thanks us for being a wonderful audience and the band starts to pack up. I notice Seán going over to talk to Spike.

The crowd starts to mill round the stage. I get up on a chair where I have a good shot of Kirsty. If anything's going to happen that's where it'll be. Martina manoeuvres herself into Kirsty's direct line of vision. Kirsty spots her. Martina smiles.

"Hi Kirsty."

Kirsty's face goes all gawpy and sullen. Everyone's watching. The noise level drops.

"What are *you* doing here?"

"You invited me."

"Well you're late!"

"I had better things to do."

"You're wearing blue!"

"It's not a criminal offence."

"The invitation specifically said," says Kirsty, "'you are requested to wear something in Summer Berry shades'. But you're not."

"Oh but I am," says Martina.

"Well I can't see it."

Ho-hum. Irish girls don't really know how to give good cat fight!

But then Martina brings up her fist, and sticks up her middle finger in the universal gesture.

"Happy Birthday, Kirsty," she says. Her nail is long and pointed and painted bright scarlet.

There's a sharp intake of communal breath. Martina looks smug. Kirsty turns red and her jaw hits her chest. I keep the video going. Kirsty can't think what to say. Breaths are now bated in every direction. Spike comes up behind Kirsty and whispers into her ear. Kirsty listens and beams and she turns to him. He takes her by the hand and leads her away. She gives one triumphant glance back at Martina.

Martina ignores her.

KIRSTY

I can't believe it when Spike asks me out to the garden! That's one in the eye for Martina. I was going to clock her but this is sooooooo much better! One of the great moments of my life. You should've seen the look on her face!

We walk hand in hand to the summer house. It's so glowy and romantic with all the lights. There are still some bottles of bubbly and nibbles left in the summer house but no glasses, and the waiter is gone. Spike opens a bottle and necks it, then passes it to me. I neck it too. We bring it to the swing seat and sit swigging and swinging till the bottle is empty.

Then he kisses me!

Oh! My!! God!!!

It is amazing. He is SUCH a good kisser. Not grabby and bumpy like the Balfathery boys. Soft and sort of juicy. It feels like my insides are melting. Then our tongues are slip-sliding around and he is trying to get his hand down my dress. It was a bit awkward, with the boning in the basque. Then one of the roadies comes into the garden.

"We're ready!" he shouts.

"I have to go now," says Spike. "But I had a great time. Would you give me your number?"

HE HAS ASKED FOR MY NUMBER!!!!!!!!!! He keys it into his cell phone but my mobile is up in my room so I can't get his.

"Don't worry," he says. "You'll have it when I call."

I kiss him again. He gives me a wink as he leaves. So *up yours*, Martina Curran.

NANA JO

People are taking forever to go. Laughing like braying donkeys and horsing around. Lord but the drink is a terror. I don't understand the attraction. It makes fools out of people, noisy and boisterous fools. I'd rather die than make a show of myself like that. But then, as my mother would say, some people have no self-respect. I took the Pledge at fourteen and no drink has passed my lips since. I don't even like the smell of it.

I have a bit of headache and would love a cup of tea but

they seem busy in the kitchen so I don't like to interfere. I go on into the den. There's a nice velvet armchair in there that I like, with a footrest. The most comfortable chair in the house. I don't like those big squashy sofas they have. Leather's too slippy and cream is a very impractical colour. I switch off the main light and just leave the one on the desk. I slip off my shoes, put up my feet and start a decade of the rosary.

KIRSTY

It's time to change into my Vera Wang. On my way through the house this woman stops me, Zebra print, red patent belt with silver edging, red patent Manolos with dangerous heels. She stops in front of me and points at my dress.

"Is that Alexander Mc Queen?" she asks.

"Yes, it is."

"Cool. I'm Tracey"

"And you're wearing Versace."

"You know your designers."

"Thank you."

"Sorry I'm not wearing the party-theme colours but I do have some red. Is that close enough?"

"Of course," I say.

As I go on up the stairs, Fergus comes over to her and says something into her ear. She must be Tracey O'Hagan, the girlfriend. Mum says that she knew her in London and that she's a dangerous bitch but that's because Mum is friends with Laura, Fergus's ex-wife. I think Tracey is nice.

NANA JO

I must have fallen asleep. For a couple of seconds I don't quite know where I am. Then I remember. I am waiting for Marian. My mouth is dry. What are the chances, I wonder, of getting a nice cup of tea? I'm about to get up when I realise that I'm not alone in the den. I can't bear to face people just now so I close my eyes again and wait. There is lots of whispering and giggling, like children doing something they oughtn't. I hear a tapping noise. Then they start to sniff, like they have runny noses. I wish they'd just go. I start a decade of the rosary.

More giggling, more kafuffle. I can't concentrate on my prayers. Then there's a bit of soft grunting and a whole lot of panting. Oh my God, it can't be… I take a quick look.

Holy Mary Mother of God.

The sight is seared on my eyeballs. That rossie, the one in the zebra stripes, bent over the desk with her skirt up over her head. Fergus pumping away with his pants round his ankles. I shut my eyes tight again. Please God forgive me for looking. I try saying an Act of Contrition but there's nothing wrong with my ears. I can still hear the huffing and puffing, the filthy obscenities. It is all I can do to stop myself screaming out loud. But I try to concentrate on saying the Hail Marys until it is over.

After that, I definitely need a hot cup of tea.

LALA

Kirsty snogged Spike from the Wage Slaves! This was MEGA. Kirsty always said that somehow, someway, she'd make it as a Celeb. But Kirsty always exaggerated everything. When she went on about being a Celeb, I thought of it like, "what-would-you-do-if-you-won-the-Lotto?" But if she got to be Spike's girlfriend then she would be half-way there.

Spike took her number and promised to phone! She swore that whenever he brought her to cool parties she'd get me in too. Oh my god, I thought, maybe I could get to be a Celeb too! Although actually, if I was going to be a Celeb I'd prefer it to be as a writer, not just as someone's girlfriend.

NANA JO

One of the waitresses comes in and asks if I want anything, and I beg her for a cup of tea. Nice girl. Foreign of course, but very polite. That's the one thing you can't fault the foreigners for – they show respect for their elders. While she is making the tea I take the chance to powder my nose. When I get back to the den, she has already left the tea on the desk with a jug of milk and a small bowl of sugar. I turn the key in the lock. Just in case there are any more intrusions.

Silly girl, she's given me icing sugar and an old-fashioned salt spoon. She must be from one of those countries that used to be Communist Russia. Sure the creathurs, they probably never had sugar. I stir in the sugar and take the tea to my chair. It bucks me up no end.

I begin to notice things in the room that I haven't noticed before; a grand picture of a horse, a carved eagle bookstand, the banding on the edge of the desk. I get up to look. I'm feeling much better now. I notice that the last drawer of the desk has a key in it and is half open. I try to close it but something is catching. I pull it open. The problem is a plastic bag of icing sugar with one of those twist things. That silly girl! I take it out, intending to return it to the kitchen. The blotter is baw-ways. I go to straighten it. Then I notice a mirror on the desktop with white dust and more dust on the desk. I am about to wipe it all down with my hanky when everything clicks in my head and I have to sit down. The filthy scene flashes before me: the chopping, the snorting, the zebra dress, the fact that icing sugar does not come in plain plastic bags...

Small wonder they were at it like monkeys. I may be old-fashioned but I do watch television.

JAKE   •

Just when it looks like there might be a decent cat fight, Kirsty disappears to the garden with Spike. She looks ridiculously smug. Crisis averted, more's the pity. When she gets back she's the centre of attention and Martina is gone. I reckon Martina has shot her bolt and wants to go home. The wrinklies are all gone too. DJ Tak-Atak is whooping it up. There are smiley faces all round. Everyone is hap-hap-happy. I reckon that Es have been taken. I must scout around and see if I can score some.

EAMON

Monkey and the Wrenches went down like a dinner and Kirsty is thrilled with her present. The kids are set to dance until dawn. At last it is just the old gang plus Tracey and Colm's wife, Jenny. I go to my bar and take orders for cocktails. We kick back and relax. Fergus puts on Van the Man. *Tupelo Honey* is dripping all over the room. Next thing, the door explodes open and Josie appears like the Avenging Angel's Granny.

"I've phoned the police!" she announces.

That gets our attention!

"What the fuck, Josie? What did you do that for?"

"Mammy! Are you all right?"

"I found *cocaine*!"

Jesus!

"In the den!"

Oh *fuck!*

Tracey flings her head back, howling laughing. Fergus

lowers his head and chuckles into his chest. Bastards, they must have gone for a snort and left it out in the open.

"Don't be ridiculous, Mam," says Marian. "You don't even know what cocaine looks like."

"You can't pull the wool over my eyes, Marian. I watch television, you know. Besides I saw that pair snorting it – snort, snort, snort, like two little piggies. Oh, you lot make me sick." Josie flings her arms wide to take in everyone in the room. Thunderbolts flash from her eyes. "You think you're so modern. You think you're so smart with your computers and your fancy Range Rovers. But where would you be without our generation? The sacrifices we made, the back-breaking work, the doing without just so you'd have a life. And what do ye do? Ye drink and snort drugs and mock your religion. Ye've no backbone. Ye've no moral fibre. Ye've no sense of sin. And as for you two," she whirls round to point at Fergus and Tracey. "I was there. I saw what you did. But the Day of Judgement is coming. Christ will sit on His throne and He will judge you! He'll cast the pair of yiz straight into Hell!"

We are all mesmerised. Josie is old-style but upfront confrontation is not her usual method. She's more one for the snide remark and the martyred aside. Tracey has a look on her face that I don't trust.

"What did we do?" she asks, all innocent-like. "Was it something like this?"

She licks her finger and slowly pumps in and out of her mouth.

"I won't lower myself to your level," says Josie.

"Are you some kind of pervert who likes to watch people fuck?"

Josie can't cope with the "f" word. Used as a curse it's bad, but if it is used to mean what it actually means, that's worse.

"That's right," she yells back. "I saw you two fuck! Fuck, fuck, fuck, fuck, fuck, fuck! A filthy word for filthy behaviour!"

Marian takes her by the arm and leads her away. I go to the den to put the stuff into the safe. I find her tea-cup with the silver spoon in the saucer and the little bowl of coke beside it. That's when it hit me. She's coked to the eyeballs.

MARIAN

How much has she taken? Is she about to OD? The image of Mother in A and E flashes through my head, doctors in green, stomach pumps, tubes stuck in her arm. Jesus, what if she dies? I'll never forgive myself. Then I do what I'd do if one of the children were hurt. I take hold of myself and I check. No blood, no vomit, no injury. She is sitting on the chair in my dressing room, upright and alert, if distressed. Step one – calm her down.

"Tell me what happened, exactly?"

I make her start from the time she woke up and she tells me what happened. Luckily, she's not a great one for sugar. But I can't let her go home by herself, just in case.

"Come on, it's late, the guest room is ready and waiting."

"But I have to be ready to talk to the Gardaí!"

"You've had a shock, Mammy. Lie down and rest. I'll give you a call when they need you."

She takes her shoes off and lies down. I put a duvet over her and turn out the light.

EAMON

I wipe the desk clean, straighten the blotter and put the evidence in the safe behind the picture of Red Rum. Then I pick up the phone and dial Superintendent Heaney's number. Joe's a pal and he owes me. I invited him to the party but he couldn't accept – it might compromise his position and all that. He answers after three rings.

"Sorry to call you so late, Joe, but I need your advice."

"Shoot."

"My mother-in–law was on to the station."

"Oh yeah?"

"I'm afraid she's the worse for wear."

"I thought she was teetotal?"

"Oh she is, but some joker spiked her lemonade. Vodka we think. And she's lost it. She's gone all Wrath of God. You'd think we were running Sodom and Gomorrah out here. She found some spilt cornflour in the kitchen and she's convinced it's cocaine. That's why she phoned. I'm really sorry about this but I'm afraid it's a false alarm. Nobody knew she was quite so scuttered. Any chance you could call off the troops?"

"I'll phone you back."

No messin' with Joe. I sit back in my chair and think hard. What is the worst that can happen? They find traces of coke. But the door of the den isn't locked. There are at least two hundred people free to roam round the house. It could've been anyone. If the worst comes to the worst, that should do. The phone rings again. I snatch it up.

"Foley took the call. He's left the station already," the commissioner says. "Get him to call me."

As I said, no messin'.

Foley would know about the party, it was the talk of Balfathery and I bet he was itching to be here. All those teenage pockets to turn out! All those young ones to frisk! Bet he was out like a bullet.

I went to the door and cocked an ear for the siren. Foley loves the aul siren. Too much television. Makes him feel like he's in LA Central. *Gangsta suspect ahead wanted for drug violations and umpteen murders...*

Dickhead. All he does is make the cows skittish.

MARIAN

I call Fergus out of the room. "Get Tracey out. Now. Before the Gardaí get here."

"Okay."

"And Fergus, I don't like how she treated my mother."

"She just likes to shock."

"She's a mad bitch and she'll do you a damage."

"I know, I know, but..."

"And in future, don't bring her into my home. Understood?"

He understands.

JAKE

DJ Tak-Atak plays an awesome set. The Es are kicking in. It's all arms-in-the-air and float on your feet and crazy dancing. The vibe goes all melty and lovely and peace and good will. There's hot girls with boobs that are jiggling. A lot of hot girls. Lots of them want to touch me and play with my hair. That's okay by me. I'm wafting about with my camera, looking for an angle, a pose, a shot I can look at and think, yeah, I like that. Something catches my eye and I look. Sergeant Foley is standing by the door. Disaster.

I hate that bastard Foley, and he hates me.

Take last Saturday afternoon. Me, Niall, Fionnbar and Brian were werewolfing our way through the town and along River Quay as far as the statue. The statue is CJ Quinn, the only Balfathery man to play hurling for the county. It's a very bad statue but the wall around it is perfect for sitting. It's the place where we tell one another about our latest internet finds, especially music. We might be the geeks and titches but we don't follow the herd. We explore, we find stuff. Old stuff, new stuff, world music stuff. Our latest find is Bob Marley. He's our latest thing. I asked Dad about him and he said Marley was a legend back in the day. "No woman no cry," wails Bob as we nod along to the rhythm. "Noooo woman no cry."

We don't notice the car swinging round from Church Street. We only see it when it squeals to a stop with a skid and a small spit of gravel.

It's a squad car and it's askew on the street. Sergeant Foley's inside undoing his seatbelt. He's hoping for trouble. He's hoping we're posing a threat to the peace. Or dealing in crack. Or carrying weapons. But his seat-belt is tangled.

"He's been watching the cop shows again," says I. "This is going to be fun."

The lads laugh. Foley hates laughing. He untangles the belt and gets out of the car. His face wears its natural scowl.

"Get over here, ladies!" he roars. We saunter over with our hands in our pockets. He hates hands in the pockets. "Take your hands out of your fucking pockets," he barks, "and get those fucking wires out of your ears."

We obey with a smile. He hates smiles.

"Turn 'em out! And remember, I'm watching! I'll see if you try to drop something!"

"Turn what out, Sergeant?" asks Fionnbar politely. Foley hates polite.

"What the fuck do you think?"

"Sorry, Sergeant, I really don't know."

"You know bloody well, you insolent little faggot."

"Do you mean our pockets, Sergeant?" asks Niall.

"Of course I mean your pockets. Come on. Let me see what you've got there."

"Why do we have to turn out our pockets, Sergeant?"

asks Brian. "We're only sitting on a wall."

Foley swells up like a rain-forest toad.

"Shut up, nancy-boy!"

We shut up. He stands with his hands on his hips. A moment of silence.

"Can I ask you something, Sergeant?" I say politely.

"What?"

"Is there something wrong with being a nancy-boy?"

It's the first time I've tried this particular line. The puff goes right out of him. His gob opens and shuts like one of them real ugly fish that they find in the depths of the ocean. He twitches his shoulders. There's a splinter of spite in his eye. He looks like he's going to lamp me. I stand there, half-hoping he will 'cause then he's in trouble. My dad is very good friends with the Gardaí Commissioner.

But two women and a dog come along.

"Afternoon, Sergeant."

"Afternoon."

The stand-off is over. We turn out our pockets – iPods, bus tickets, coins, small notes, chewing gum, tissues. No guns, no knives, no alcohol, no dope, no coke, no heroin – not even a cigarette. Foley is fierce disappointed. We stare real hard at the ground to stop ourselves grinning but as soon as he's gone we fall about laughing our legs off. We get him every time and he never sees it!

But here's Sergeant Foley now with his sidekick at Kirsty's party. He's surveying the scene. This looks like trouble.The sidekick is that new fella, red-raw from Templemore, with his ears sticking out like a hat-stand. The rookie is gawking around and craning his neck. He's clearly impressed with the girls. Foley calls his attention to duty.

The Sergeant shoulders his way through the dancers

and up to the stage. I follow. I take several shots and then switch to video. DJ Tak-Atak is dancing. Sergeant Foley observes him, like dancing is grounds for arrest. He waves a hand but Tak-Atak has his eyes closed and he's grooving away. Foley loses his patience. He marches up to the desk and throws several switches. The speakers squeal, the high frequencies stop, the bass keeps on thumping. Tak-Atak opens his eyes and looks startled. Foley commands him to turn off the sound. The silence is like an assault.

Foley takes the mike, taps it.

"One-two-testing," he says. "One, two, three, four…" Dickhead. He clears his throat into the mike. "Listen up you lot. We have reason to believe there are Class A drugs on the premises. No one may leave the room till I tell them."

Everyone cheers. They're thrilled with themselves and their brotherly, sisterly, lover-ly love. There are drugs in the room but they're mostly in bloodstreams. Tak-Atak has recovered. It's not his first time with police at a gig. He takes another mike.

"There is certainly one Class A drug here tonight." His voice is lazy and slow. "It's called *luuuurve*. Am I right, boys and girls?"

"Yeahhh!" they roar back.

"Altogether now, Love Bomb!"

Everyone raises their arms towards Foley.

"Love!" they roar at him.

Foley goes red in the face.

"Shut up, you little arse-bandit," he snaps at Tak-Atak.

He forgets we can hear him.

"Love! Love! Love! Love!" we chant, and it changes to singing.

"*All You Need is Love!*" sings Tak-Atak.

"*Dun, the dun, the dun,*" we join in. "*All you need is love!*

82

Dun, the dun, the dun. All You Need is Love, Love. Love is All You Need."

"Shut the fuck up, the lot of yiz!" roars Foley. "No one leaves here till they have my permission. Have yiz got that?"

He leaves the stage and grabs the rookie by the arm. They head for the door. Tak-Atak is in charge once again. He pumps up the volume and throws a switch. His words seem to come from the heavens and his voice sounds like God.

"Show some *luuuurve* for the Gardaí," he commands. "They are the men who help keep us safe."

Jim Buckley flings his arms around Foley and enfolds him in his raspberry jacket. Three winsome girls snuggle up to young Pink Ears. He looks ready to bolt. Foley is batting Jim Buckley away. Dad pushes up through the crowd and shakes Foley's hand.

"Sorry Sergeant," he says, "I'm afraid you've had a wasted journey. And the Commissioner wishes to speak to you."

EAMON

I show Sergeant Foley to the den and settle him down at my desk. Then I leave, but I don't close over the door. All I hear is, "Yes sir. No sir. Yes sir." Then he slams down the phone, and I tip-toe hastily away from the door.

Foley emerges, looking bitter.

"Misunderstanding." His face brightens. "Do you want me to investigate who spiked your mother-in-law's drink?"

"God no, it was probably a mistake by one of the bar staff. She'll have a hangover in the morning but sure isn't that why God invented Disprin."

The lighter touch doesn't play well with Foley but he

has his orders. I bring him and his side-kick out to their car, apologise profusely and watch till the headlights vanish. I close the door and saunter back to the den. Time for a remedial toot.

CHAPTER 4

KIRSTY

Mum's at me to think about what I want to do when I leave school. She wants me to go to college. But *another* three years of studying? I don't think so. I'm planning to get famous. Let Balfathery see just how far a Kerrigan can go! Dad's with me all the way. I've spent hours on the internet, searching for info about reality shows, checking the dates of auditions and putting them in order. I have made out a chart with three headings: 1) Name of Show. 2) Date. 3) Place. Lala isn't being much help. Sometimes I don't think she takes it seriously. I've put all the dates in my mobile and set it for reminders.

Big Brother and Stargazer are the only auditions that will happen in Ireland but when I mention Big Brother, Mum goes ballistic. She makes me promise that I'll at least wait till I've left school. Stargazer is just a piddly-assed RTE singing thing. But it's worth a shot – especially as there's unlikely to be anything much in the line of competition. And the auditions are on during the summer holidays so Mum can't object. There will be loads more auditions during the autumn but they're mostly in Belfast and London so that might be a bit tricky. It'll take a bit of planning. We'll have to book flights and hotels. And plan what to wear. And I'll have to get Dad to give me his credit card.

LALA

We'd been talking about becoming Celebs since we were twelve. I was going to marry a footballer and Kirsty was going to be Ireland's answer to Paris Hilton. I knew it wasn't really going to happen, but talking about it was still fun. So I wrote about it in my diary:

Teenage Afternoon

The girls sat at the dressing-table meticulously scrutinising their spots in the mirror. Not too bad, nothing concealer couldn't deal with. Then they re-read a magazine article on "How to Create Smouldering Eyes". This was surely the most important article they had ever come across, because when you were famous you had to have smouldering eyes and they dreamed night and day of how life would be when they were famous. Limos sweeping them off to exciting events, assistants to fulfil every need, glamorous clothes, parties, summer cruises on film stars' private yachts.

They followed the instructions with dedicated diligence: cleanse, moisturise, base, smudge eyeliner, dark shadow, highlight, mascara. They made lots of mistakes and painstakingly wiped everything away and started again. Finally they were finished. They stared into the mirror and admired their Celebrity eyes.

Then they tried different hairstyles: up, down, hairpieces, ornaments, flowers, combs, Day-Glo pink wigs. Each time they changed hairstyle they chose a new boyfriend from the following categories: Premier League Footballer, International Rugby Player, Formula One Driver, Pop Star, Soap Star and Film Star. They passed the long afternoon in a phantasmagorical cornucopia of dreams and illusions. One girl knew it was make believe. One girl didn't.

Mrs Brady, our English teacher, was right. It was indeed very interesting to write about my own life from the outside.

KIRSTY

I've been thinking a lot about having to go back to school. Do I really want to do that? It's so boring. And who needs to do the Leaving Cert anyway? You don't need a Leaving Cert to be a success. Look at my dad.

When I say it to Lala she gets all po-faced.

"Are you *seriously* thinking of leaving school?"

"It's not like we've never discussed it before," I remind her. "These are the best years of our lives. We can't waste them with our heads in a book. There's things to do, places to see. We ought to be out there, enjoying ourselves, living the dream."

"Yeah, right, okay. Let's leave school – like your folks will go along with it, or mine for that matter."

"Don't worry about the folks, we can get round them."

"Of course we can, like your mother's a pushover, just like mine!"

"Seriously though, we could live in the apartment in Baggot Street, go to auditions during the day and at night go dancing in Lillie's Bordello. It's Celebs wall to wall in Lillie's so we're sure to meet loads of people who can help with our careers."

"Goodbye, Balfathery," says Lala. "Hello, Red Carpet! Hey Kirsty, this time next year we'll be on the Late Late Show!"

"Stuff the Late Late," I say. "This time next year I want to be on Oprah. Can you imagine, Lala, sitting on the sofa with Oprah?"

"Awesome!"

We do our *"Whoo-ooh!"* dance.

LALA

We had often talked about leaving school but it was just talk. Mum wouldn't let me and anyway I didn't want to. I

87

wanted to go to college. And I couldn't see Marian letting Kirsty drop out the year before her Leaving Cert. That would be mad. Marian had a thing about education; she told us one time that she was the best in her class but she'd had to leave and get a job after her dad died. Once she'd got wind of Kirsty's plan, it would all be over. Kirsty could pout and moan and throw herself on the bed in a sulk but really, really, *really*, she'd be relieved. And then it would be like it had never happened and she'd be on to something else.

She was great like that, Kirsty – real devil-me-care. Didn't give a damn for what anyone thought. I wished I was more like that.

MARIAN

Sixteen's the age when they turn normal, according to Minnie – seventeen at the latest. That's when their hormone-riddled brains settle down and they start to behave like civilized Christians. Not Kirsty though. She's eighteen now and still in that parallel world I call Kirsty-land, a world where her fantasies rule and reality doesn't exist.

We sit down to Sunday lunch and, while Eamon is carving the leg of lamb and I am dishing out roast potatoes, she makes her announcement.

"Oh by the way, Mum, I'm not going back to school. Me and Lala are going to live in Dublin."

"Oh really?" She argues the point, giving all the reasons why she should leave. I don't argue back. I wait until she is finished. "And where will you live?"

"What's wrong with the flat in Baggot Street?" says Eamon, switching off the electric carving knife.

I kick him under the table and give him my filthiest look.

"That's what I was thinking too." Kirsty beams at her daddy.

"Can you afford the rent?" I ask. Her jaw drops. Eamon is going to say something but I kick him again. "Your dad and I are more than happy to support you while you are in school and all the way through college but not if you're just going to sit up in Dublin doing… what, exactly?"

"Pursuing my career."

"Oh, right. Do tell me more."

I have to pry it out of her and then point out that applying for reality shows is not a career and that if she continues with this scheme of hers, believe me, she'll be paying for her own keep. And with no skills, no experience and no qualifications, she has zero chance of getting a job that will pay her enough to live on.

She grabs her dinner and flounces off to her room for a sulk.

"You're very hard on her," says Eamon.

"No, Eamon, I'm being realistic and if you go on encouraging her to do stupid things you'll be sleeping in the spare room."

That always works. Eamon likes his home comforts.

EAMON

Kirsty's an adult. If she's determined to leave school, how can we stop her? We can't drag her to class every day! And even if we did, there's no guarantee that she'll stay. Then what? Sit outside the school gates with a rifle?

Is it really such a tragedy if she doesn't do the Leaving? I didn't. Marian didn't. No one belonging to us did. The truth is, Kirsty doesn't need a job when she leaves school. I'd be more than happy to give her a decent allowance. Isn't that why I worked my butt off all these years, to be able to support my family? But when I suggest that to Marian she has a double conniption. Calls me a dinosaur. I'm not, am I? I mean I'm all for Women's Lib and all that malarkey but if she doesn't have to work why make her?

KIRSTY

Mum thinks I'm useless. Well, I'm going to prove that she's wrong. I've thought and thought about it and I have a great idea. I am going to demonstrate my business skills by raising money for charity.

I learnt how to be an entrepreneur in Transition year, the year after Junior Cert. Transition year is supposed to be a doss, only it wasn't for us because Mrs Dempsey, the brainiacs' favourite, was in charge. She entered us for the Gaisce Award – that's the President's Prize. It's supposed to be good if you want to go to college and Mrs Dempsey insisted that employers like it as well. One of the things we had to do was raise money for a community project.

"Why not just donate it?" I asked.

"It's not just about the money," she said in her teachery voice. "It's about you girls learning how the other half lives. It's about developing entrepreneurial and organisational skills. It's about taking part in your local community."

Which was ironic, as I couldn't wait to get out of my local community.

Anyway, me and Lala made these key rings. I did the design on the computer and printed them out. Dad got them laminated, Lala added the key-ring. We sold them at five euro each in school and at the country market, and Dad sold a load to his rich pals. Mum too. We made five hundred and ninety five euro for St Gobnait's special school. Nearly six hundred euro! But that's buttons, really. So I'm going to raise thousands for St Gobnait's. That'll show Mum.

MARIAN

Kate acts very nice, very polite, when she tells me what Kirsty has done. But I can tell that she's furious.

Kate's a bit older than me. I met her soon after we came back to Balfathery. She and Joe are our nearest neighbours. Joe is hideously rich. He's also gay, although that's not generally known. Kate knew this before she married him. He needed the cover, she wanted the money. They even have a son, Max, her pride and joy – courtesy of Señor turkey-baster. She and Joe appear together when socially necessary but generally they live separate lives. Joe is generous and Kate is discreet. Max is grown up now and has a job in Moscow. Kate was bereft when he left and decided she had to have a *cause* to give her life meaning. Then she found a lump in her breast that turned out to be nothing, but she took it as a sign from the universe that she had been spared to raise money for breast cancer research. So she set about organising the Ballyhoo Ball. I was just glad she'd found something to occupy her time, but Kate turned out to be a great organiser and the Ballyhoo Ball has become *the* social and charity event of the season.
But it's Kate's Ballyhoo Ball and don't you dare touch it.

Last night, Kate tells me, she was at home in her old caftan, just out of the bath and doing her cuticles. Sex in the City is on the TV, a glass of Merlot to hand, when the doorbell rang. She wasn't expecting anyone so she didn't answer but it rang and it rang and it rang. She was afraid then that something had happened to Joe – or worse, to Max – so she opened it only to find Kirsty on the doorstep, pink-cheeked and windblown after cycling over. She brought her in.

Kirsty then proceeded to outline how she could help to organise the Ballyhoo Ball, sell tickets and – get this! – share the profits. I should mention here that tickets for the Ballyhoo Ball cost one thousand euro a head and are snapped up the instant they go on sale. The problem is dealing with disappointed customers and keeping track of the waiting list. Kate always employs the same two reliable local women to answer the phones and deal with the correspondence. There is absolutely nothing that Kirsty could bring to the party. I explain this to Kirsty.

"Kate was so rude to me," she complains.

"Good," I say.

Kirsty mopes.

"If you're so anxious to raise funds for St Gobnait's," I suggest, "why don't you weed out your wardrobe and sell the clothes you don't want on eBay?"

LALA

Kirsty was in a major sulk because Kate wouldn't let her help with the Ballyhoo Ball. I was totally on Kirsty's side because why would Kate be so rude when Kirsty was only trying to help? And besides, Kirsty was doing it to show her mum that she was responsible. But, typical Kirsty, she didn't let it get her down for long.

She was still determined to leave school and to show her mum how responsible she was. She decided that we should both get summer jobs in Dublin with her dad's friend Seán. I was happy to go along with that. I didn't mind the idea of earning a few bob.

"Besides," she said, "it means we'll be in Dublin for the Stargazer auditions at the end of August."

Her mum wasn't that keen on the Dublin idea, although her dad gave off an air of silent approval.

"Please, please, please, Mum," Kirsty begged.

"Okay, fine," said Marian, with a frown at Eamon.

Kirsty threw her arms around her.

"Thank you, thank you, thank you."

"Well, Eamon, why don't you give Seán a call?"

He looked surprised, like none of this had anything to do with him.

"I think it'd be better coming from you, Marian. Sure, he thinks you're a walking wonder, he'll do anything for you."

"All right," she sighed, "but before I do *anything*, Kirsty, promise me that you won't ask Seán to share his profits with you."

"*Mum!*"

"Well, that's what you asked Kate to do."

"That was different."

Ah, now I understood! So that was why Kate chewed Kirsty's head off! But I said nothing.

MARIAN

Eamon's right, Seán thinks I'm God on a stick. It's not that I did anything for him that any decent friend wouldn't do. But maybe that's the point. There's times when you know who your friends are.

When Seán came back from London he brought Tommy with him. This was the real thing, the love of his life. They were living in a fabulous apartment close to Temple Bar, view of the Liffey, everything cool, contemporary. I used to drop in to see them any time I was in Dublin and they'd feed me cocktails and bring me up to date with all the latest city gossip. Tommy was HIV positive but doing well on medication. But then he got ill, really ill. The flu turned into pneumonia, complications developed. It wasn't looking good. Seán was in bits. None of his friends in the gay community wanted to know so whenever things got him down he'd phone me. I liked Tommy, he was very funny, even when he was in hospital, even looking like a corpse warmed-up, he could make me laugh. And when things got really bad I went up to the hospital a couple of times to sit with him and give Séan a break.

Then there was the funeral. And Tommy's bloody family turned up, including the father who, when he discovered that Tommy was gay, drove him to Dublin and threw him out on the street. Bastard. The boy was only fifteen! Then he went home and told the neighbours that Tommy had gone to Australia. The brothers and sisters weren't much better.

"Tell the family I'm dying," Tommy said near the end.

He kept hoping they might come and see him. Fat chance. Séan couldn't bring himself to speak to those bastards but I spoke to every one of them. Did they visit? Phone? Send a card? Hell, no. But they turned up for the funeral! They sat up at the front on their fat arses alongside the coffin. If you didn't know better, you'd think he had meant something to them. They ignored Seán. He had to sit behind them as though he was nothing, like he didn't exist. I've seldom felt so angry. I wanted to go up and punch them in the face. But I sat and held Seán's hand instead.

The priest ponced about on the altar spouting meaningless crap. How could he say anything relevant? He didn't know Tommy. He mentioned the grieving father, and each of the brothers and sisters by name. He did not mention Seán.

"Would anyone like to say a prayer?" he asked when it came to that part of the Mass.

And fuck me if one of the brothers didn't get up and mumble some shite about Tommy now resting in peace. Then a sister got up and prayed for the Pope. The Pope! Fuck the Pope. Why was nobody praying for Seán?

The priest was about to get started again when something came over me. I could no more have stopped myself than I could stop the wind. I don't remember how I got there, I just found myself at the mike. The priest smiled. The family shuffled. And then I heard the words coming out of my mouth.

"Tommy was a wonderful man," I said, and I was surprised to hear myself sounding quite calm. "He was funny and kind and hardworking. He brought joy to my life and the lives of his friends. He loved people and people loved him." I stopped and looked at the three rows of family. I wasn't sure what I'd say next but something about the way the father was clutching his rosary beads spurred me on. "Tommy was gay," I said. "A homosexual." The family coughed and got red. The priest examined his fingernails. Tears streamed down Seán's face. "He was gay because that was God's plan for him. He did not have a choice. It wasn't some lifestyle he chose in a moment of madness. It was deep in his genes and therefore it must have been God's plan. And because of God's plan he was rejected, despised and called ugly names. But Tommy was strong, he made a good life for himself and found love with Seán. Seán loved Tommy when he was well and cared for him all through his final illness. Seán washed him and fed him and looked after his medicine. And now Seán is grieving. So please, let's say at least one prayer for Seán." Seán covered his face in his hands and sobbed like a child. The family were getting redder and redder. Good. "May the Lord heal his hurt and help him find consolation. Lord hear us."

When I got back to the seat I was shaking. Seán put his arms around me and the two of us sobbed our hearts out.

When I ask Seán if he can give Kirsty and Lala some

95

work for the summer he says, "Certainly". Kirsty is thrilled. She thinks she'll be swanning around at celebrity parties. A dose of reality will do her no harm.

KIRSTY

Mum finally agrees to let us stay in Baggot Street. Yeeey! I know she'll be dropping round to keep an eye on us but she can't be here all the time.

Seán's office is cool. Floor-to-ceiling windows overlooking the Liffey, glass, wood, abstract pictures, Japanese flower arrangement and a bronze nude of a man aiming a bow and arrow.

"Esther will show you what to do," he says.

Esther is old, at least thirty, blunt bob, rectangular glasses, good blouse, black trousers, chunky green matching necklace and earrings, good shoes.

"Come with me, girls," she says, and leads us out of the office and round the corner to the Fiesta! Fiesta! shop in Fleet Street.

It has to be *the* best party shop ever. Pedro, Seán's partner, runs the retail side of the Fiesta! Fiesta! business. Pedro is from Columbia and he's sweet and I know he likes me and when he looks at me with those puppy-dog eyes, Oh! My!! God!!!

"*Buenos días chicitas,*" he says. "I have plenty work for you today."

"I don't think so," I say. "We'll be working in the office with Seán."

"No way. You are working with me. Now roll up your sleeve and come."

You'd think we were slaves! He brings us through the back of the shop to this horrible warehouse lined with shelves.

"We have seven big orders that must go today. Here is list of all things what they want." He hands me a clipboard with papers and a biro on a string.

"Look you see here, name of client, all what they want. You find items on shelves, you see everything have a name. Ladder over there if it high up. You find Fiesta! Fiesta! box in this section here. Pick right size box, pack with order, tape up proper so it not open. When everything okey-dokey, leave here on shelf beside door ready to deliver. Then next order and next. Okay. Call me if you need help."

And off he went. Just like that.

"This is stupid," I say. "I'm going home."

"No you are not," says Lala and she takes the lists from my hand. "You're going to help me to get these orders filled. I thought you wanted to prove to your mother that you're capable of doing a job."

LALA

Kirsty was really pissed off. She felt that she belonged at Seán's side in that beautiful office! The warehouse was a huge let down and she dragged around making everything ninety times harder than it needed to be. It was a simple job really but Kirsty could never find the items even when they were staring her in the face. So of course I did most of the work. In desperation, I reminded her that we needed to sort out our ideas for the Stargazer auditions. And then, typical Kirsty, she perked up and we discussed songs and names. Over the next couple of weeks we decided to call ourselves "Girlicious".

MARIAN

I don't think going for Stargazer is a great idea. It's a competition for singers and Kirsty can't sing. Plus, I've seen the judges on these things, they're not just nasty, they're smart-arse, sound-bite nasty. I suppose it makes for good television. But it's not fair to the youngsters, making eejits of them like that in front of the nation. I don't want Kirsty to get hurt. But she is hell-bent on it so what can you do.

LALA

I wasn't expecting much from the auditions because basically neither of us are singers. We're not even in the school choir. But I thought that it might be a laugh. We got "Girlicious" printed in sparkly pink on white t-shirts and we wore them with pink rah-rah skirts and pink sequinned ankle boots. One weekend my mum came to stay the night with us in Dublin and even she thought we looked cute and my mum is not into Pop. Now all we needed was a song. We settled on *I'm a Barbie Girl* because we knew all the words so we could concentrate on the performance.

We practised every day in the warehouse and any time we got a minute – which wasn't as often we'd have liked, as it was astonishing the number of mega parties that were going on in Ireland during the summer. Still, we worked out a dance routine. I suggested having hairbrushes like pretend microphones, so we got pink ones and stuck glitter all over them. And the more we practised the more I was looking forward to it.

KIRSTY

We have to queue for ages outside the Montrose Hotel before we get registered. We are number 93 so we aren't going to be called for ages. They bring us into this big room to wait. People are doing their make-up, though why anyone thinks peacock-blue eye-shadow does anything for them I don't know. Others are rehearsing in corners or singing along with their iPods which always sounds a bit weird. Some people are changing their clothes and you'd want to see some of the get ups! HOR-RIF-ICK! Wobbly fat covered in Spandex is not a good look. Me and Lala look great though, like real professionals.

Then these cute guys start chatting us up. Oz, Poz, Pat and Georgie. I fancy Georgie. They want to be the next Westlife and they called themselves Zipidee. They are good gas. Georgie has a brother who is a barman in this new club that's opened in Harcourt Street called Sultan and Bob. It's supposed to be dead cool. The lads are going there that night to check it out and they ask us to come as well and of course we say, yes.

Next thing there is this huge commotion. Who has come in, only Louis Walsh! THE Louis Walsh!! Everyone is jumping up and down and screaming. Louis waves to everyone. I stick out my hand as he passes, he shakes it. He goes into the room where the judges are.

"This is our chance," I tell Lala. "I know for a fact that he's looking for a new girl band. I saw it on the web. We could be it, Lala! We could really be it! Louis Walsh could be our manager!"

"Except none of his girl bands ever get anywhere."

Lala can be so negative.

LALA

People were going in for auditions but none of them were getting through. It was depressing. No one had got through since the fat girl with the glasses and that was ages ago.

"I wouldn't mind but she's ugly," said Kirsty. "How come they picked her?"

"Maybe she can actually sing. I'd heard her practising

in the toilets and she's brilliant. "

"But she's ugly!"

Just then, Oz, Poz, Pat and Georgie came out shouting and jumping and high-fiving everyone in sight. Zipidee were through.

"When you're famous," I told them, "we can tell people we know you."

"Excuse me," said Kirsty. "We'll be famous as well."

Then the man called out five more numbers, including us. We were on.

"Good luck!" cried the lads as they left. "See you tonight!"

"Sultan and Bob!" agreed Kirsty. "We'll be there."

We had to wait outside the audition room while Colm Sharkey interviewed us. He was the compere for Stargazer and you could see he was bored. But once the camera was on him he came alive. I was so nervous I couldn't answer but Kirsty took over so it was all right. Then he told us to go in.

The judges sat behind a table with Louis Walsh to one side.

"By the way girls," Louis said, "I'm not a judge. I'm just an associate producer but while I'm in Dublin I wanted to see how the auditions were going."

The judges asked about our ambitions. Kirsty ignored them and talked straight to Louis and went on about wanting to be bigger than Girls Aloud. I said nothing.

KIRSTY

I've never heard of any of the judges. One is an old woman, bottle blonde, scrawny, with too much make-up. Beside her is a fat man in a scruffy black shirt. The third is a guy in a biker jacket. These no-names keep asking questions but obviously Louis Walsh is the most important person in the room so I smile and speak directly to him. Finally they tell us to go ahead and thrill them.

Everything is going fine until Lala messes everything up. She gets the moves wrong. She kicks left instead of right and it catches me on the shin and makes me trip. I could kill her.

"Please, please let us start again," I beg.

Louis says it's down to the judges, he obviously wants us to sing again, but they won't let us. Bastards. I have to blank what the judges say out of my head because they are downright rude. But Louis Walsh isn't. He says he likes us! He says our outfits are cute and that I have potential. He advises me to finish school and try again. No wonder those other judges are no-names, they wouldn't recognise talent if it jumped up and kicked them in the goolies.

LALA

The audition was a disaster from the start. Kirsty insisted on talking only to Louis.

"I'm not a judge, Kirsty," he said at least twice. "Speak to the panel."

But she didn't and I could see the judges getting annoyed and giving one another looks.

Things went wrong from the moment we started. We were supposed to start standing back to back and then turning to the front, except Kirsty didn't turn because she was facing Louis Walsh and that completely messed up the routine. Then when we got to, *"I'm a blonde bimbo..."* Kirsty went straight into *"Come on, Barbie, let's go party!"* I tried to catch up and do the twist-kick, twist-kick that went with *"Come on Barbie"*. But, apart from being turned the wrong way, she was doing the bunny-bob, bunny-bob that went with *"I'm a blonde bimbo"*. My twist-kick caught her on the knee and she fell over, splat on the floor. I knew it was all over then. But Kirsty never gave up that easy. She went down on her knees imploring the judges to let us start again and made a complete eejit of herself.

"There's no point." said the woman. "You can't sing, you can't dance and you haven't even the manners to address us properly."

The two guys agreed. At least Louis was kind.

"I love the outfits," he said, "and the hairbrushes are a clever idea. But look, girls, you're never going to be pop divas. You're young, go home and finish school before you decide what to do with your lives."

I was thrilled that he liked the hairbrushes.

As usual, Kirsty tried to blame me. Most of the time I just let it go but not this time. I reminded her that she was the one who was turned the wrong way and she was the one that sang the wrong words. She sulked for a bit but then she started to plan what to wear to Sultan and Bob and off we went shopping like nothing had happened. I was surprised. Maybe I ought to stand up to her more.

KIRSTY

There are two big burly guys on the door wearing black puffa jackets with Topaz Security embroidered on the back. Even though there is a queue and they aren't letting some people in, we get in with no bother at all. Sultan and Bob is awesome, all done up like a palace in the Arabian Nights.

We find Oz, Poz, Pat and Georgie in the middle of a crowd in the Kashmir Bar watching two barmen making cocktails while juggling bottles and glasses. One of them is Georgie's brother and he makes us Tequila Sunrises. Then we go down to the Turkish Rondo Room where they have cool techno music and we dance. George tells us that, if we like, his brother can get us into the VIP lounge. He doesn't have to ask twice!

The VIP lounge is double awesome. The walls are covered with gold brocade and pictures of dancing girls and sultans on elephants. There are brocade divans all round the room and silk cushions with embroidery and beading and little brass tables and fretted lantern lights. In the background, Indian music is playing. Mum would love it.

A lot of people look vaguely familiar but I can't put a name on any of them. The waiters are tanned and handsome and naked from the waist up except for embroidered boleros teamed with their Aladdin trousers and curly slippers. In one corner there is an arch with gold fretwork doors. Every so often the doors open as someone comes out or goes in. Inside, I see a huge pile of silk cushions and a man with a curly moustache and a hookah. He looks vaguely Indian but it might just be a fake tan.

"Who's your man?" I ask.

"That's the Sultan," says Georgie. "He'll read your palm."

"Among other things!" adds Oz.

A party of people come in with some of the actors out of Fair City; they are the centre of attention. People are still going in and out to visit the Sultan. It's like he's hearing confessions.

"That palm reading is very popular," I say.

Georgie looks at me as though I am thick.

"That's not why they're visiting him."

"But Oz said…"

"Isn't it obvious?"

"No."

"He's the house dealer. Whatever you need he'll sort you out."

"So if I wanted to get a bit of blow?"

"Sultan's your man."

We dance around and drink cocktails and chat to all kinds of people. Next thing, who should come in only Tracey. She looks fierce. Black vintage Balmain, gold-beaded Manolos. Two of the bouncers are right behind her.

"Hi Tracey," I say. "Is that Balmain?"

She whips round and stares at me.

"Jesus fucking Christ, if it isn't little Miss Daddy's Girl."

"You know her?" Georgie asks me, looking surprised.

"She's a friend of the family."

"Jesus!"

Tracey goes straight to the gold fretwork doors and slams them open. The Sultan is sitting there scratching himself. She grabs him by the throat and hauls him to his feet.

"I hear you're ripping me off," she says. The Sultan looks very scared. She calls over the bouncers. "Clear the room. Now!"

She drops the Sultan back on the cushions and slaps him across the face. The bouncers move everyone out so we head back to the Turkish Rondo room.

Afterwards, we see the bouncers strong-arming the Sultan into a van outside, with Tracey watching.

"What's that all about?" we ask Georgie's brother.

"He was cutting the product with baby powder and pocketing the extra money he made. I said it was a dangerous game – but would he listen?"

Wow. Exciting.

CHAPTER 5

LALA

Sometimes, when he had to go and do other things, Pedro left us in charge of the Fiesta! Fiesta! shop. This was way more fun than packing deliveries. You could have a bit of craic with the customers and make suggestions for their parties that they might not have thought of, like having glitter bombs go off when everyone was singing *Happy Birthday*, or getting balloons personalised.

Some of the customers were tricky. I couldn't believe how rude they could be. Some people seemed to think that just because we were behind a counter they could treat us like their personal slaves! Kirsty lost the head with one woman and wanted to throw her out of the shop. Luckily I was able to save the day. Kirsty marched off into the warehouse and I lied. I said she was bi-polar and on a week's trial! The woman bought it but made up for it by being extra unpleasant to me.

It was during our last week that we heard what Kirsty described as "the most mega news of the century". Pedro had to go to Seán's office for a meeting. Everything in the shop went smoothly. Just after twelve, Pedro came back. He was fanning his face and looked like he was going to faint.

"*Díos mío. Díos mío!*" he exclaimed. "I have seen *la Madonna.*"

Pedro is your typical Latin male, never darkens the church door but considers himself a very devout Catholic. He wears a cross round his neck and kisses it every morning before he opens the shop. He even has a little altar with lights all round it in among all the boxes of glitter and confetti. It has a picture of Our Lady of the Rosary of Chiquinquirá – she's the patron saint of Columbia – and he puts a fresh flower in a vase for her every day. So when he said he had seen the Madonna I assumed that he thought he'd had some kind of vision.

"Where did you see her?"

"In Seán's office."

"Where in the office?"

"On the computer. On video conference."

"*You were having a video conference with Our Lady?*"

"No, no, with *the* Madonna, the singer... The Material Girl!"

"Oh, Madonna."

"She say hello to me. *Díos mío*, my heart, it is jumping out from my chest."

Kirsty's ears pricked up.

"Is Seán doing something for Madonna?"

"Yes, but it is very big secret. Trade secret, you must to tell no one."

Kirsty begged and she cajoled but he wouldn't say any more. But she wasn't about to get put off that easy. Later that afternoon, she made Pedro a cup of tea.

"About Madonna," she said.

"I say nothing," said Pedro, dramatically miming a lip zip.

"Do you think Seán would be angry if he knew you told us abut the video conference?"

"He would kill me."

"Gosh, Pedro," she said with a grin. "I hope it doesn't slip out the next time Seán's in our house."

"Oh please no, Kirsty, please no, you cannot say."

"Okay Pedro, I promise – but on one condition."

"Anything, anything."

"You have to give me all the details."

KIRSTY

Madonna is having her Christmas party in Blackwater Castle in County Cork and everyone who is anyone will be there. Me? I'll definitely be there. Apart from the fact that I've always adored Madonna, I am pretty sure that when we meet we'll become good friends. I know she's a lot older than me but we both have the same drive, the same Blonde Ambition! Her Christmas party will be the perfect place to chat with her. She might even want to include me in her entourage. Besides, it's a golden opportunity to meet A-list Celebs who can offer me all kinds of opportunities to further my career. I just have to find a way of getting there.

I ask Seán straight out if he can get me on the guest list. He gets very snotty and wants to know how I found out about the party. I don't rat Pedro out. I say I picked up a hint when I was delivering sandwiches to the office and put two and two together. Seán says to forget it because Madonna is hyper-neurotic about who gets invited. But I'll think of something.

EAMON

You see, I was right. Kirsty is fine up in Dublin apart from the Sultan and Bob episode. So she went for a night on the town! Where's the problem with that? Fergus says I have to warn her not to go back, because some of Tracey's associates are… Well, let's say they're not big into good works. I don't tell Marian, she'll only worry. But I have a quiet word with Kirsty. She always listens to me because I'm not on her case all the time and of course, as I knew she would, she understands perfectly. Underneath the mascara and lip-gloss, she's a sensible girl.

LALA

Imagine meeting Madonna! How cool would that be? Except it wasn't going to happen. Although there was no telling Kirsty that.

She insisted that we check out the Blackwater Castle's website. It was very "ye olde" – suits of armour, panelled rooms, portraits of ladies in high wigs and Cinderella dresses, four-poster beds, archery, falconry, horse-riding…

"Horse-riding, Kirsty!" I said. "I bet Madonna goes horse-riding. "

"Give us a look." She found the phone number for the Blackwater Castle stables and called. "Hi, I'll be in the area the weekend of December the twelfth. I'd like to book a couple of horses for trekking."

They were fully booked up that weekend. Private party.

Kirsty flung herself on her bed and picked up Pogo and started fingering his ears. Pogo is the cuddly monkey she's had since she was little, and stroking his ears is always a sign she's fed up. She put Pogo down, came to the computer, pushed me aside and got on to Google Earth.

"Bingo!" she said, after a few minutes. "Crannóg Lodge, blah, blah, blah, weekend pony trekking… And look, Lala! It's right beside the grounds of Blackwater Castle! We could book in there, find a back entrance and crash the party."

"There's a much simpler way," I suggested.

JAKE

Kirsty's back home and drama reigns in the house once again. She and Lala have been spending hours on the web so they must be planning their next attempt to be Z-list Celebs.

"Jaaaaake!" It's Kirsty. "Can you sort out this glitch?"

"Turn it off and re-boot!" I shout back. I'm busy working on a project I'm planning for the film club that Mr Geoghan runs. Mr Geoghan encourages us to do both still photography and video. He says that each feeds the other and everything you learn about either informs your visual language. Over the summer, I took a lot of photos of people in Balfathery and I'm morphing them. I'm trying for kind of photographic cartoons. I did a lot of the girls at Kirsty's party – mostly pretty, pretty stuff, butterflies and fairies, because that's what they want. But now I'm on to the serious ones. I finished one of Mrs Lawless in The Gem that makes her look like a comfy cardigan, and I'm working on Sergeant Foley. I'm turning him into a Nazi bullfrog. And I want to turn Dad into Napoleon commanding an army of breeze blocks. I haven't decided yet what I'll do with Kirsty but maybe a kind of freaky fashion shot with her spiky heels trampling the fairies and butterflies.

"Jaaaake," Kirsty whines. "Take a look at this pleeeeeeease!"

If I don't answer, she'll just keep on whining. I go to her room, turn off her laptop and re-boot. Everything's fine. I notice that she's been looking at horsey sites. Why is it that girls like horses and riding but boys want to be in a band? It's something we've talked about over a toke in Niall's den. Niall thinks it's a sex thing. The bouncing up and down turns the girls on but they can pretend it's nothing to do with sex, because nice girls have to pretend that they don't like sex. While the boys think that once they're on stage with a guitar, they'll have no problem pulling the girls.

MARIAN

I thought working at a very ordinary job might give Kirsty the shot of reality she needs. I am wrong. She's still pestering me about leaving school and living in Dublin pursuing her "career". I have downright refused to consider it.

Minnie and Jimmy are here this weekend, in full "I'm right! No, I'm right!" mode about the name of some house, and I am a bit short on what Minnie calls "stardust". I certainly don't need Kirsty harassing me about leaving school.

"It's not going to happen, Kirsty!"

"You should try to find the common ground with your daughter," says Minnie suddenly deciding that she's Dr Phil. "A win-win result is what you need. There is no need to be confrontational about everything." Then, without batting an eyelid, she turns right round to Jimmy and snaps, "The house is not called *Mountain Lee*, that's plain stupid, it's called *Monalee*."

"Okay, Kirsty," I say. "What can I do to persuade you to go back to school and finish your Leaving Cert?"

"Well, there is one thing you could do," she says. "Persuade Seán to take me on as staff for Madonna's Christmas party. If you do that I'll go back to school."

"There you are Marian," says Minnie, smugly. "Compromise. It always works."

Why I don't bite a lump out of her leg…

GRANDMA MINNIE

Young people nowadays are so independent and full of confidence. I think it's great. You should have seen how Kirsty was able to negotiate with her mother. When I think of myself at her age... I was convinced I was as ugly as sin.

No-one in them days ever said you were pretty, or praised you or paid you a compliment. Afraid you'd get a swelled head and commit the Sin of Pride, which of course was one of the Seven Deadlies. I wouldn't mind but we wouldn't have known pride from a hole in the wall. We were proud of nothing, not ourselves, not our family, not even our country.

When I look back now at photos of me and my sisters I realise we were gorgeous. Every one of us. Even sitting on a stone wall in our home-made dresses. There was no such thing as cheap finery then, no Dunne's Stores, no Penney's. We used to swap Simplicity patterns and on Saturdays we'd hitch a lift to Athlone and head for Fay's Fabrics. Fay's had a bin full of remnants and all of our finery came from that bin.

We didn't have a sewing machine either but Mrs Duggan, next door, gave us the lend of her sewing machine. She was the best dressmaker around in her heyday but she was crippled with arthritis and couldn't sew any more. In return for us getting her shopping and tidying up, she'd give us dressmaking tips. The machine was a big, old-fashioned Singer, a beast of a yoke, with a treadle you worked with both feet.

Many's the evening we spent in Mrs Duggan's house chalking and cutting and pinning and tacking and her, cocked up in her wicker armchair, supervising. I think she enjoyed the company but she'd never allow us take short-cuts. We'd gossip and giggle about fellas we fancied and she'd egg us on. And on special occasions, when a band came from Dublin to play in Parish Hall… Boy, but that sewing machine could fly.

Of course we had to be careful. Canon Casey always stood at the back of the hall keeping an eye on proceedings. If he thought your dress was immodest he'd make a show of you.

"Occasion of Sin!" he'd shout in your face and he'd march you out of the door.

The mere fact of being female in them days made you an Occasion of Sin. Mrs Keogh, the primary school principal, explained it to us the day we were leaving. Mrs Keogh, by the way, was a very big wig in Balfathery – President of the Ladies Sodality, Chairwoman of the Altar Society, Vice-President of the Pioneers – well got with the clergy and general pain in the ah-do-stand-back.

"Remember girls," she said. "Eve was the cause of Original Sin. Eve tempted Adam to eat the Forbidden Fruit. And, because of her, Original Sin stains the soul of every human born since and it can only be removed by the Sacrament of Baptism. Always remember that you are the Daughters of Eve and as such you are walking Occasions of Sin. Boys have powerful urges and, when you flaunt yourselves in tight skirts and low necklines, they cannot control themselves. Keep that in mind when you're dressing yourself for a dance or a party because, if things get out of hand, you'll have only yourselves to blame." She held up two fingers, rested them under her collarbone and made us all do the same. "Necklines should be no lower than this."

Mary Colgan, who was very well developed for her age, put her fingers half-way down her chest.

"What do you think you are doing?" roared Mrs Keogh.

"Is that not my collar bone, Miss?" asked Mary, all big eyes and innocence.

"You are destined for Hell, Mary Colgan," spat Mrs Keogh and she hit Mary's hand with the edge of a ruler.

Bad-minded bitch. If she was alive today I'd take great pleasure in rubbing her nose in it because Mary brought up four wonderful boys and since they left home she's been raising thousands for the Chernobyl children. Thanks be to God, those days are well gone.

Look at young Kirsty, pretty as a picture and knows it. And why wouldn't she? Wears the latest in fashions, shows off her legs and isn't she right? She's young, that's the time you can do it. And as for confidence! She has buckets of it.

MARIAN

I nearly fall out of my standing when Kirsty mentions the Madonna party because that's the kind of thing that Seán is extremely careful about. He insists on total confidentiality for his clients, especially celebrities who are paranoid about the press. So I take her aside and warn her to keep quiet about it or she won't have a chance of getting within an ass's roar of Madonna and her party. I warn Minnie and Jimmy as well but they'll never do anything they think might harm their darling grand-daughter.

The problem for me is that this is probably Seán's most important and financially rewarding gig of the year. I've no doubt at all that he will not want to employ amateurs like Kirsty who might mess things up. Seán only uses professional staff and I can't see what kind of job Kirsty could do, unless it's skivvying in the kitchen – and I suspect that's not what she has in mind!

My only hope is that he'll be sympathetic when I explain about trying to keep her in school and, who knows,

WICKLOW COUNTY COUNCIL
LIBRARY SERVICE

he might be able to come up with something. I'll take him out to dinner before I spring this on him. Somewhere really nice.

KIRSTY

Seán would do anything for Mum, I think he's in love with her although Jake insists that he's gay but maybe he's only gay because Dad got her and he didn't. Jake thinks that's a stupid idea too, but who knows? Maybe he's bi.

So – deep breath – *are you ready for this?!?* I'm going to Madonna's Christmas party! Eeek!! Oh my God I can't wait!!! I only wish I could tell people but I can't because if Mum found out she'd ground me for the rest of my life, and Mum always finds everything out – Every. Single. Thing. But in school, when Mrs Melia is being especially annoying, I just think, I don't care, I'm going to Madonna's Christmas party and I'll get to meet Lourdes and Rocco and all her celebrity friends!

For some reason Seán insists that Lala has to come as well which is all right although I'd really prefer if it was only me. But I won't say that to Lala. And I can't decide what to wear. I'm thinking Lacroix, McQueen, maybe Dolce and Gabbana. Madonna likes way-out clothes and those guys can do way out. Or maybe Jean Paul Gaultier. But I don't want to look like I'm slavishly copying her style. I could always do Stella, in fact that might be good because she's quite likely to be at the party. I read somewhere that they are friends. Mum will probably want me to wear my birthday dress because it cost so much but that's more summer wear. I'll need something seasonal and anyway Dad will cough up.

LALA

Maybe we were going to get to see Madonna after all! It

was killing Kirsty not to be able to boast about it, especially to Martina Curran. She came home from school every day and threw herself on her bed in frustration. I had to keep reminding her that she could boast all she wanted after Christmas. She was pissed off with Martina because she'd had the gall to get a good haircut. And the difference it made! Now she looked pretty, especially as her spots had cleared up. To hear Kirsty go on about it, though, you'd think Martina had gouged a baby's eyes out in Market Street.

Actually I quite liked Martina, she was clever and ambitious and she was applying to Trinity like me. It would be nice to have someone I knew when I started college. All the Dublin ones would already know one another and would think I was a culchie so, yeah, I thought, I wouldn't mind being friends with Martina. But when I smiled and said hello to her in The Dozy Donkey, Kirsty accused me of stabbing her in the back. She wasn't a bit pleased when I told her to grow up and remember that we lived in a very small town and needed to be able to get on with people.

"You're as bad as my mother," she said.

Kirsty didn't know that Seán had asked specially for me to come and work with her at the party. He wanted me to keep an eye on her, Marian told me in confidence. It seemed that Pedro had reported that I was the only one who could handle her. I didn't know about that. When Kirsty wanted something...

Kirsty knew perfectly well that Seán was only letting us come to the party to work, but in the part of her mind that was wired to the moon, she saw herself as a guest. She kept thinking up clever lines to say and trawling through websites to look at designer dresses. I kept reminding her that we would have to wear some kind of uniform. I might as well have been talking to the wall.

115

KIRSTY

The sky is blue, the birds are tweet-tweeting – well, not exactly, because it is winter, all I mean is that everything is perfect and at last we are on our way. We leave early because Seán wants us there by three at the latest. Lech, Dad's driver, brings us down in the Merc. His wife Beata is with us because they're going to visit Cork city and pick us up when it's all over.

We come to the top of a hill and there is the sea doing its glinty thing down below. Then I notice the roofs with turrety bits sticking up from the trees.

"Blackwater Castle, Lala!"

"Yeah, I can see."

"The adventure starts here!"

LALA

So there was the Castle of the Stars – film stars, rock stars, even the President of France; they have all come here. Next thing, we heard a helicopter. It flew over us and began its descent over Blackwater Castle. I thought Kirsty was going to have a stroke with the excitement.

"Lech!" she screamed. "Hurry up, we've got to get there to see who it is! It might be Madonna herself!"

But Lech just drove on at a steady fifty, because the road was narrow and winding.

"If you don't hurry, we'll miss them," Kirsty groaned.

The helicopter rose up again out of the trees. She collapsed into a sulk but brightened when another one clattered into view.

We passed a high wall and came to a huge semi-circular entrance flanked by granite pillars topped by gilded eagles, wings spread wide. The gates were huge, high and modern, made of wrought iron done like interwoven branches and leaves. A security man was standing outside. Lech turned in and stopped. The security man came to the car window and asked for identification. We showed him our passes.

"Staff entrance," he said. "Keep on going, it's on the right."

Lech backed up and drove on. The staff entrance was not so impressive and we all had to show our passes again.

None of this was going down well with Kirsty, especially when we ended up at the back of the castle in a concrete yard which was, frankly, a bit ugly and gloomy. Lech left us and we knocked at the back door. A man opened it.

"Yes?" We showed our passes and he stepped aside to let us in. "Down the corridor to the right, Anna will issue you with a uniform. Change into it, then come and see me in the kitchen."

"And you are?" said Kirsty.

"Jerry Stanley, your boss for the evening and if I say jump, you jump. Got it?"

"I'm afraid you're mistaken," says Kirsty. "We're friends of Seán's."

"I know. He told me to remind you to expect no favours and that you will have to work just as hard as everyone else."

"Well *duh!*" said Kirsty.

"Off you go then."

The uniforms were pretty standard, black trousers and white shirts, but the shirts were rather nice – collarless with pin tucks down the front. I was a bit surprised that Kirsty made no objection. She was always getting into trouble in school for trying to "customise" her school uniform.

We spent the entire afternoon polishing glasses. There were ten huge crates of them. Wine glasses, water glasses, sherry glasses whatever-you're-having-yourself glasses.

All of them were clean but Jerry insisted that we had to inspect every single one and shine it up just in case it had got dusty on the journey. And when that was done we had to fold linen napkins into a lotus shape. Anna, who seemed to be in charge of everything cloth-related, showed us how and left us to it.

Every so often we'd hear a helicopter arrive. I judged there must have been three or four of them ferrying people in from Cork airport, or maybe from Dublin. There was a window in the scullery where we were working but we only got a quick glimpse of the helicopters as they flew over the trees on the way in. Then Kirsty said that she wanted to go to the toilet.

KIRSTY

It's George Michael! I swear, I would recognise him anywhere! I'm standing at the side-gate and I can see him getting out of the helicopter with his boyfriend – at least, I assume it's his boyfriend! Madonna and Lourdes are out on the drive to meet them! I am half thinking of going over and asking if they want a drink or something when one of the stupid security men finds me and marches me straight back to Jerry. Jerry is really snotty about it.

"The cat can look at the queen," I say.

"Not this cat," says he.

Oh yes, very smart!

LALA

Kirsty was away for ages and ages and next thing she came back with Jerry.

"Any more of that lark and you're on your way home, missy," he said. "I've enough on my plate without baby-sitting Seán's little girlfriends."

Late in the afternoon Seán came around to see how things were going. He spent a lot of time talking to Jerry then he gathered all the staff together for a pep talk and to let us know what the programme was.

First the guests were going to gather for a reception in the baronial hall. That was the room we'd seen on the website with the suits of armour and the big portraits. Apparently there was a huge log fire in the fireplace and two chefs, dressed like characters from Dickens, would be roasting chestnuts on it and two of the waiters would hand them around. The rest of us waiters were divided into two groups. The very experienced ones would circulate with pink champagne. The rest of us would circulate with silver salvers of canapés.

"Remember, your job is to smile and offer food and drink," Seán warned. "*On no account* speak to a guest, unless the guest speaks to you first. If a guest asks for something the answer is "Certainly, sir" or "Certainly, madam". If it's not something you can easily provide, speak to me or to Jerry. On no account, ask for an autograph."

Part two of the event would be the arrival of Santa with his elves and the appearance of Madonna. Brian Blessed was going to dress up as Santa and Lourdes and Rocco were going to be elves.

"We need a few extra elves to hand out the gifts," Seán announced. "Anyone up for it?"

Kirsty's hand shot up immediately. Nobody else seemed that keen and Jerry had to pick a few "volunteers".

Part three was the Christmas feast itself, when the guests would move into the dining hall and sit down to a traditional Christmas dinner. Except it was being prepared by Heston Blumenthal, so I wondered if there would be lots of dry ice and smoke and surprises and nothing would look like it was supposed to look. But we wouldn't get to see that part. Only the professional waiters would be allowed to serve. Our jobs would be to shift the dirty plates when they came out and pile them into the dishwashers and do general skivvying. I was curious to see how Kirsty would cope.

KIRSTY

The canapés look like mini plum-puddings and turkeys and crackers and hams and they are decorated with gold leaf. Just before we go in, Lala leans over.

"Please, Kirsty," she whispers, "don't try to talk to Madonna. Just do like Seán says."

Well, duh! Not while I'm dressed as a waitress!

The room is amazing. The walls are hung with trailing ivy and swags of holly, gold bows and lights. There is a vast Christmas tree to one side of the fireplace, decorated with starry lights and gold ornaments. At the far end of the room, a "window" looks out over chimneys and rooftops and Santa and his reindeers are galloping in silhouette across a huge golden moon. And I *mean* galloping – the reindeer are moving and every so often they land on one of the roofs. Santa jumps out of the sleigh with his sack of presents and disappears down a chimney then reappears, gets back in the sleigh and gallops again across the sky. Brilliant. Underneath the "window", there is a big fake fireplace. Up in the minstrel's gallery there is a chamber orchestra playing Christmas music and the whole place smells divine, like the best Christmas you have ever had.

I take a good look at the guests – the room is wall-to-wall A-listers. Wow. And obviously there is a colour theme, because everyone is wearing red, green or gold.

LALA

The guests, one hundred and sixty-eight in all according to Jerry, were gathered waiting for Madonna's arrival. I listened in to their conversations because Mrs Brady says that a good writer knows how to listen and I knew that this was a scene I could definitely use in the future. I circulated with my silver salver, smiling and offering canapés. Everything was going with a swing. Glug, glug, glug. George Michael was chatting to some woman with red feather eyelashes.

George M: "How's Bettina?"

Red FEs: "Worried about the dogs."

George M: "Schnauzers?"

Red FEs: "Yeah."

Riveting!

Nibble, nibble, nibble. Stella McCartney seemed to be explaining something very serious to Bob Geldof.

Stella McC: "How was the holiday?"

Bob G: "Sun, sea, sand, sex. What can I tell you?"

My God, how original!

Yack, yack, yack. Guy Ritchie was in a huddle with Seán Connery and Alexander McQueen.

Guy R: "Yeah right."

Seán C: "What did I tell you?"

Alexander McQ: "Same ol', same ol'."

Enlightening!

Ha-ha-ha-ha. Elton John was doubled up laughing in a green velvet suit, and so was David Furnish, in a red velvet suit.

Hilarious!

Note to self. The conversation of A-list Celebs – *Yawn-o-Rama.* All of them acted like we were invisible, which is probably a compliment and the way Seán would want it, but my mum always said you should always be pleasant to anyone providing a service, even if you were paying for it, because they were not your personal servants, they were people doing their job.

I was dying to try some of the canapés but I was afraid I'd get caught and land in trouble. Kirsty behaved impeccably. After about half an hour, I saw Jerry beckon the volunteer elves to the door. It was time for Santa and Madonna's big entrance.

KIRSTY

As if I'd ever dress up as one of Santa's little helpers! I have a much better idea. I've brought a dress and shoes with me. New ones. Thank God, I didn't rely on the birthday dress because it would have been totally the wrong colour. I knew Mum would have a fit if she thought I was getting a dress for Madonna's party and go on about how I wasn't a guest *blah, blah, blah*, so I told dad that I wanted a new dress for Christmas. It's Vera Wang, halter neck, simple full-length shift, scarlet with crystals all over, and it looks spectacular.

I say I'm going to the loo, grab my bag from the cloakroom and sneak up to the first floor, to the guest toilets. I slip into one of the cubicles and change. I'm just ready to emerge when I hear someone come in. At first I assume it is one of the guests, but whoever it is seems to be doing an awful lot of faffing about. I peep out and see that it is a cleaner, wiping the hand basins and tidying the hand towels. I just have to brazen it out. I march out and hand her my bag which now contained the waiter's uniform and my flat shoes.

"I found this uniform in the toilet," I say. "It looks like one of the staff changed in here by mistake. Please return this to the kitchen quarters."

"Certainly, madam. I'm very sorry, madam." She hurries out and leaves me to put the finishing touches to my make-up and hair.

I can't return down the back stairs because I might run into Seán or Jerry and the elves, and I can't make my entrance to the party through the staff door. I carry on down the corridor and find the main stairs down to the front hall. I open a door that I assume must lead into the party room. It doesn't. It leads into the dining room where Séan is supervising the final arrangements. I close the door quickly before he can see me. All I can tell you is that there are huge silver candelabras and the tablecloths are white. A waiter passes me, pushing a trolley with a wine rack full of bottles. I am terrified that he'll recognise me but he doesn't.

"I've got a bit lost," I tell him. "How do I get back to the hall?"

He gives me directions and pushes the wine rack into a room across from the dining room. I make my way to the hall and slip in.

LALA

The orchestra struck up *Jingle Bells* and then quietened down to just the sound of sleigh bells. Brian Blessed's voice boomed out of nowhere:

"*Ho, ho, ho.*"

Santa's boots and legs appeared dangling from the fake chimney and then a very convincing Santa dropped into the fireplace. He pulled down his sack of presents and stood with his hands on his hips *ho-ho-ho-ing* like crazy. Then Lourdes and Rocco dressed as his elves jumped down from the chimney and bowed and everyone clapped and cheered. The other elves followed and they all sat beside

Santa. The guests gathered round and the staff stood back. I saw no sign of Kirsty but then I couldn't see all the elves. Even still, not seeing her made me feel nervous.

"And now," boomed Santa, "I have a very special gift for you all."

The elves ran back to the fireplace and helped to lower a giant parcel from the chimney. It was wrapped in gold foil and was tied with a red ribbon in a bow. The elves pulled the bow open, the sides of the parcel fell down and there was Madonna in a white halter-neck dress, floor-length shift, covered with crystals, a tiara of stars made of diamonds, a long rope of sparkling rubies and a jangle of ruby and diamond bracelets on each of her well-toned arms. The orchestra started playing *Material Girl*. The guests went berserk with cheers and applause. Were those real rubies and diamonds? I reckoned they probably were.

Santa did his *"ho-ho-ho"* riff again. The musicians played *Santa Claus is Coming to Town*. The elves started delving into Santa's sack and bringing out small parcels. Some were wrapped in green foil and tied with red ribbon; some wrapped in red foil and tied with green. The elves handed them round. People began opening them and I could hear the squeals of delight.

Next thing, I saw a familiar figure accepting a box from one of the elves. It was Kirsty, dressed to the nines in a dress that was uncomfortably like a red version of Madonna's. She was chatting to a man who looked like Jean Paul Gaultier. I had to get her out of there before she did something daft. But how could I do that without making a fuss? I wouldn't put it past her to pretend not to know me and ask security to have me removed. I moved towards her with a plate of canapés.

"Would you like some?" I asked, with a charming smile.

"Go away or I'll kill you," she said through her teeth.

"O eet ees so beeyuteeful!" said Jean Paul showing her a mother-of-pearl box with a pair of emerald and ruby holly-leaf cuff links. Someone called his attention.

Kirsty was opening her box. Inside there was an emerald and ruby holly-leaf brooch.

"Oh my God, it's divine," squealed Kirsty. "I must go and thank Madge!"

And before I could do anything to stop her, she swept off down the room.

Madonna wasn't difficult to find, she stood out as the only person not wearing red, green or gold. She was turning from one group to greet another when Kirsty rushed up to her.

"Madge, Madge," exclaimed Kirsty. "I adore it, it's divine, thank you so much."

Madonna stopped in her tracks and she seemed to grow taller.

"And you are?" she asked icily.

"Kirsty, Kirsty Kerrigan,"

"I repeat – and you are?"

"Ireland's answer to Paris Hilton!"

By this time everybody was watching. Then a voice from behind called,

"Paris who?" and everyone laughed.

Madonna's icy expression did not change.

"How did you get in?"

"Funny story actually," said Kirsty, preening herself at the sound of laughter. "I pretended to be a waitress."

Madonna raised one arm in the air.

"Security!" she snapped, and turned on her heel.

"But Madge, Madge, we have so much in common!" pleaded Kirsty. "The least you can do is talk to me!"

Madonna kept her back firmly turned. Kirsty grabbed a

handful of canapés from the plate I was holding.

"How dare you ignore me!" she screamed and flung them at Madonna's bare back. Two of them stuck.

Madonna didn't even twitch. Two security men were already marching Kirsty out. A woman appeared with a cloth and wiped Madonna's back. The orchestra struck up *Last Christmas, I Gave you my Heart*. George Michael took Madonna's hand, kissed it and sang the song to her. The elves continued giving out the presents and people continued to squeal with delight. It was like the appalling debacle had never even happened.

EAMON

Marian is all of a do-dah. I mean, crashing a party, big deal! We've all done that in our day. I am looking forward to a feed of fried bread and rashers and a couple of hours with the Sunday papers, but Marian just won't let it rest.

"You have to talk to her, Eamon, she'll listen to you."

"Like you haven't crashed a few parties in your day!"

"It wasn't just a party. This is Seán's business, his *livelihood*. How would you like it if someone messed with your business? Say if you found some of Jake's pals rearranging your files?"

God forbid. Not that there's anything dodgy but... Well, some information is best kept to yourself. Marian insists that both of us phone Seán to apologise. Oil on troubled waters and all that.

It's a sticky conversation. Ever since Seán turned gay he's gone very sensitive, can't take a joke, always accusing you of being homophobic. The thing that gets me is that he used to be a fierce man for the women. I know, I saw him in action. Marian says it was only a cover, but I don't agree. She says you're born queer but I've known him longer than

126

she has. I'm convinced that he was converted.

When we first went to England, Seán fell in with a theatrical crowd and, as everyone knows, they're all benders. This was before the AIDS thing got big. There were some very wild scenes – mind you, this was before my sister and Marian came over. They don't know the half. Orgy rooms, blow-job rooms, women in black leather corsets and whips, fantasy rooms, men dressed in leather chained to each other, gimp masks, dildos and all kinds of drugs. For a country lad like myself it was quite an eye-opener or, as Fergus said, wanking material for the rest of your life! But it wasn't really my scene and once Marian came along I never went back. But Seán did. I think he fell in with queers and just got addicted. Which is why I worry about Jake going into the film business because, no matter what anyone says, that sort of thing isn't natural or normal.

I promise Seán that I'll get Kirsty to write a letter of apology both to him and to Madonna. Anything for a quiet life.

MARIAN

That's Kirsty grounded until she's finished her Leaving Cert. I hoped Lala would be a steadying influence but clearly she is too innocent for Kirsty. Lala knew nothing about her plans. And Kirsty really and truly imagines that she can hold on to the emerald and ruby brooch! I have handed it back to Seán myself.

KIRSTY

I'm grounded for the rest of my life. But I don't care. It was worth it. Everyone wants all the details. And Martina Curran, looking like a Pekinese sucking a lemon, pretends she's not listening but I know she is.

But I've gone off Madonna.

CHAPTER 6

KIRSTY

Freedom at last! No more homework, no more school uniforms, no more jewellery bans, no more getting grounded. I can do what I like. Eat pizza in front of the telly, get drunk, get stoned, have sex, stay out all night. I open the window and stick out my head. What's this I smell? It's FREEDOM!!!

Mum has been on my back day and night all year – forcing me to study, study, study! – but Madonna-gate was sooooo worth it. Who else do you know who has had a one-on-one with Madonna? Boogied with Jean Paul Gaultier? Made jokes with Stella McCartney and George Michael? Mum must be the only person on earth who wasn't impressed. She even sent me to a psychologist. Well, okay, a careers psychologist. He gave me all these tests and he said I had artistic talent. Well, *duh*. We all knew that! He told Mum I should apply for some kind of art course. Mum kept hounding me to decide which one, so I thought, where do you find the A-listers? Givenchy, Dior, McQueen, all sitting in the front row? I'm going to do fashion design!

Unfortunately, the course takes *three years*. But the good thing is, I will be in Dublin and I have my own credit card. That means I can apply for all the reality shows I like and fly to London for auditions if need be. Top of my list is Big Brother!

MARIAN

The night before Kirsty heads for Dublin, I have the Book Club girls over. The book is *Eat, Pray, Love* by Elizabeth Gilbert – not really my cup of tea. Some of them agree with me but most of them think it is marvellous. It's always great craic when the girls disagree about a book and this time we get so fired up that we go on till all hours. And the more we go on, the more wine we drink. It's way after midnight when we finish and no-one is fit to drive so husbands and taxis have to be called. I invite Kate to stay the night and when the others have gone we have another glass and smoke a joint and turn on a bit of Dolly Parton.

I go to the kitchen to get sparkling water and get distracted by a packet of honey-roast almonds. You know how it is when you're stoned. As I wander back to the sitting room, I hear Kirsty's voice.

"I can't really ask Mum. I mean she's fine for the basics but… Well, you're cool."

"Thank you." says Kate.

I hang back and earwig. I know, I know – I'm not proud of it but she's my daughter and she is about to leave home.

"You had boyfriends before you were married, right?"

"I've had my moments."

"So, you know, oral sex… Is that something that all boyfriends expect?"

"I've never met a man who objected," laughs Kate. "But Kirsty, you do know it works both ways?"

"Yeah, of course."

It sounds like bluster to me.

"So… What's it like?"

"That depends on who's doing it."

"Yeah… Right… And what about, you know, kinky stuff?"

It's time for me to re-appear.

"Kinky stuff?" I say, as I put down the tray. "You want my opinion? Men might like it but let me tell you from my own experience, it's way over-rated."

"Mum!" squeals Kirsty, sticking her fingers in her ears. "La-la-la-la… I don't want to know."

"So if you're not sure just say no."

She disappears back up to her room.

I am all up in a heap but, as Kate points out, everyone's curious about sex. With all the stuff on the internet, kids know about things that we'd never heard of at their age. And isn't it much better that Kirsty feels she can talk to us? That's when I begin to have palpitations about young fellas who have learned all they know about sex from looking at porn… Oh, sweet Jesus…

I know, I know, I have to let her go, but… Every mother worries, especially with girls, because no matter how well you prepare them they'll make their own mistakes. I know I made my fair share. I suppose that's how you learn. But I don't want to know about Kirsty's mistakes. As long as they don't include getting pregnant. Mind you, if she did get pregnant, I'd have her on the next plane to London. Not that I approve of abortion, I don't, but I wouldn't want her ruining her life. I just hope and pray she'll be all right in Dublin. At least Lala is sensible. I'm glad she and Kirsty are sharing the flat.

LALA

The apartment in Baggot Street belonged to the Kerrigans, so it was way better than the usual student digs. And it cost me nothing, except food and electricity, which Kirsty and I shared. Mum wanted to pay rent but the Kerrigans wouldn't hear of it. I think despite the Madonna debacle, Marian was still hoping that I would act as a restraining influence on Kirsty. I wasn't sure I liked being cast as Goody Two-Shoes.

Kirsty was going to the Stella Institute of Fashion Design, just off Grafton Street, and I was in Trinity reading English and European Studies. When I was finished my basic degree, I hoped to do the MPhil in Creative Writing. The flat was very handy for college but even handier for when we were out on the town, as we could easily walk home.

The first night we were in Dublin, Kirsty made me sit down and draw up a plan of action.

"Because, Lala, you must have a plan if you want your dreams to come true." Kirsty was always a great one for plans. The problem was, her plans were never that practical. "So," she said. "What are your ambitions?"

"Have a nice time in college. Pass my exams. Write."

"And then?"

"It depends."

"This is the Rest of Your Life, Lala!" she urged. "Didn't you always want to marry a famous footballer?"

"When I was *twelve*. Seriously, it's not going to happen."

"Not if you don't *plan*!"

"I'm not sure that me and the striker for Chelsea would have much in common," I said.

"It doesn't have to be Chelsea."

Clearly she wasn't hearing me. She had a notebook at the ready and her pen poised to start one of her lists.

"Number one." she announced. "We have to lose our virginity between now and Christmas."

132

"Why Christmas?"

"Because at our age it's ridiculous."

"Yeah but, it has to be someone you really, really like and what if you don't meet him between now and Christmas."

"No, Lala, no. It has to be someone who's really, really fit and older! Kate told me that older men make better lovers because they know what they're doing."

"Oh gross."

"I don't mean ancient, I mean older than us, around twenty-two, twenty-three. The only reason I haven't done it already is because Balfathery boys know nothing about erogenous zones or foreplay or any of that and I want the first time to be amazing."

"I'd like it to be the first time for both of us."

"Oh God, Lala, you're such a romantic, you'll never learn anything that way!"

EAMON

Marian keeps saying I'm a Doting Daddy but the point is, Marian does not understand about men. She thinks she does but she doesn't, not really. No woman does. Women think it's all about flowers and feelings and love and will-you-still-respect-me-in-the-morning but it's not. That stuff's fine when you're older and tired of the chase and want all the home comforts. But for guys of Kirsty's age, forget it. All they're after is sex. Nothing else. They'll say anything, anything at all, even the dreaded "L" word to get a girl into bed. For them it's a game and you know us fellas and games, we just have to win. And there's Kirsty, young, good-looking, innocent as the day is long, all by herself up in Dublin surrounded by randy young guys. That's why I'm worried.

Marian assures me she has had "the chat" – but then

she blithely informs me that she has given Kirsty a supply of rubber johnnies! I'm fit to be tied.

"You're encouraging her!"

"So you won't mind if she gets pregnant or picks up an STD from a one night stand?"

"Kirsty would never have a one-night stand."

"Oh yeah?"

"*Never.*"

"I'd love to think you were right, Eamon, but we've all done stupid things in our day and I'm sure Kirsty will too."

I know it happens. Of course I know it happens. Go down Temple Bar any Saturday night and you'll see half-naked young ones out of their skulls. No prizes for guessing where they'll end up. But Kirsty's not like that. She has too much respect for herself. She knows she only deserves the best, I've made sure of that.

And no, I'm not stupid, I know she's going to have sex. And I know it'll probably happen before she gets married. But Kirsty will wait till she finds the right one, I know she will. Marian can raise her eyebrows, but I know my Princess.

LALA

I thought Kirsty would have gone off the whole Celeb thing after Madonna-gate, but no, her new plan was to apply for Big Brother. The Dublin auditions were coming up. She was at me to do it as well, but I wasn't really interested. I wouldn't have minded going along for a look, maybe writing about it, but there was no way I was going to appear on that freak show. When I said that to Kirsty she told me to show some ambition. But I had plenty of ambition. I wanted to make something of my life, I just didn't know yet what all the possibilities were. My degree was going to take three years. Maybe then I would take a gap year and travel the world. I had plenty of time to decide. Meanwhile I intended to enjoy myself.

Of course, Mum was delighted that I was going to Trinity. I suspected she thought it was the perfect place to snag a brain surgeon or a barrister or some other professional husband who would earn lots of money. She was going to be disappointed. I had no intention of even starting to look for a husband until I was at least twenty-five.

It was handy that me and Kirsty went to different colleges. I would get to meet all her fashion lot and she would get to meet my Trinity crowd. Hopefully that would mean being asked to lots of parties. One thing though – and I was going to have to break this gently to Kirsty – I had met up with Martina Curran a couple of times and I thought we were going to be friends. She was doing biology.

KIRSTY

College is boring. It's mostly lectures about the importance of a good pinking shears and how to make patterns. There's twenty in my class, seven guys, the rest girls. The guys are nice and all but I'm not interested in any of them...

Until *HE* arrives.

Mrs Williams is giving a lecture about natural fabrics when the door opens and in walks this guy. Unruly black curls, blue eyes, long lashes to die for. He is wearing a mint-green cashmere sweater and a scarf knotted just so, the exactly right shade of mauve. Every girl in the class is drooling. Mrs Williams nods at him and smiles, which astonishes us all because she's always very sarcastic when somebody's late and this guy is *late* – not just for class, but for the term. Maybe she fancies him, even though she's much too old. I catch his eye on his way to his desk and he gives me a wink. *Swoonerama!*

The next day I sit beside him in the canteen. His name is Ross Fahy. He's a mature student and he knows all about fashion because he works in it. So I've made a decision. He's going to be my first lover.

JAKE

Dad is right. I don't exactly wake up with my feet hanging out of the bed but I put on a sudden spurt. I'm five foot ten now and I'm hoping for six foot because I don't think I'm finished. Now Kirsty's gone to college, Dad is getting interested in my photography. I think he's quite surprised by my stuff. When I finished the photo cartoons I made a video about what local teenagers do to amuse themselves. And no, it's not all video games and drinking cider! Dad makes me show it to Seán, because Seán knows Liam Fitzsimon. Yes, THE Liam Fitzsimon.

"Would you like to meet him?" Seán asks.

"Would I give my right arm!"

"Bring some of your work. Maybe he'll give you some pointers."

I can't sleep with the excitement.

The plan is to go to Dublin on Thursday after school and meet Liam Fitzsimon early the next morning. It has to be then because he is flying to Bolivia to shoot a documentary on the most dangerous road in the world, then off to New York for some award. Mum writes a note to Fr Cronin saying I have to see a specialist. Which is true – in a manner of speaking!

I ring Kirsty to say I'll be staying in the flat. She is not very happy because she and Lala are having a Big Brother party.

"I can handle a Big Brother party," I say.

"You're not invited."

"I'll take photos for you."

"You always make me look horrible."

"I'll do some nice ones, I promise."

"No."

"Okay. But Mum will want to know why I'm staying in a hotel."

"All right. All right. But you have to make up your own bed."

"Deal!"

LALA

The Big Brother party was all set. All my Trinity friends were invited including Martina. I was expecting Kirsty to have a canary when I told her but she was cool. I imagined it was because all the fashion students in their bizarro get-ups would be there and because the "fabulous" Ross was coming and she was convinced that this was the night they would finally do it.

I'd met Ross a couple of times. He was very handsome and all but I suspected he was a bit of a chancer. He was definitely an Olympic class flirter. I'd watched him in action. He batted those baby-blues at every female who came within fifty metres, including me. Kirsty was convinced that they had "chemistry" but I suspected he had "chemistry" with anything in a skirt.

JAKE

If you think boys are untidy you should see the mess girls live in!

The spare room is a dump. I shove everything that's on the floor into a corner, shoes, shoe boxes, clothes, books, papers. Then I wrap the clothes, hangers, more shoes, make-up, dirty towels et cetera that are on the bed in the bedspread and dump that in the corner as well. I perform an archaeological dig in the hot-press to unearth pillowcases and sheets. Kirsty's not used to looking after herself because Maria, the Polish girl who does the house-keeping at home, clears up after her.

At least Lala is tidy.

Friday morning I wake at six and jump out of bed. The girls are still in zzzzz-land. The sink is full of dirty dishes. There are no clean cups in the cupboard. I wash a cup and make tea. I shave – yes, I shave, have to do it every day now – wash my teeth, comb my hair, put on my black shirt, best jeans and trainers, grab my jacket and my portfolio. I check myself out in the hall mirror still half expecting to see the titch that I was. But no… I'm still tall.

I meet Seán in Sally's Cafe for breakfast at seven. Sally's Café is in the Financial Services Centre. I'm so nervous and excited I can hardly eat. The thought of Liam Fitzsimon seeing my work makes me feel sick. What if he thinks that it's rubbish? At the same time I can't wait.

We take the elevator up to his office. It's six stories up. Liam Fitzsimon sits behind a huge table examining video on a computer. He looks like he's just tumbled out of his bed. He doesn't look up.

"This is Jake," says Seán.

Liam Fitzsimon grunts and waves his hand at a chair. I stand there feeling the sweat breaking out on my palms.

"Sit down, Jake," says Seán.

I sit on the edge of the chair.

"Right," says Seán. "I'll leave you to it."

He leaves.

The room is white and bare. A large window looks out

at the Custom House dome. Liam Fitzsimon continues to work. The table he's at is old, gouged, hacked and stained all over. I look around. On the wall behind me there is a poster-sized black and white photo of hands. The hands are old and they're folded over the crook of a stick. A hand-rolled cigarette is stuck between two of the fingers. One of the fingers is only a stump. It gives me a kind of a shiver. I can read a whole life from these hands. It must be a shot from one of his films. I don't know which one but it's brilliant.

I turn back. Liam Fitzsimon looks up and holds out his hand. I give him my memory stick. He puts it into his computer and watches the video about teenage pastimes.

"Any stills?" he asks. I hand him my portfolio. He opens it and flips through my photos. His face is without expression. He gestures at the screen where my video is on pause. "If you had five minutes to sell this to a TV company which shot would you use?"

This is a test but I've thought about it already and I know.

"The one of Paddy White drawing Fall-About Girl."

"Why?"

"It's funny, it's sexy and he's bloody good."

He nods briefly and grunts. It feels like some kind of approval.

"Do you have a holiday job?"

"No." My heart is pounding.

"When do your holidays start?"

"December fifteenth."

He scrabbles through a big desk diary.

"Sixteenth. Be here. Seven-thirty. Okay?"

"Okay."

"That's seven-thirty in the morning."

"Of course."

His phone rings. He takes the call and waves me away.

I'm too excited to take the lift. Instead, I skip down the six flights of stairs.

KIRSTY

Tomorrow could be THE most important day of my life. It's the Big Brother auditions. I've done a list of the questions they'll ask and the answers I'll give. The important thing is to get as far as the interview. But I have something in mind that will definitely help. Once I've got as far as the one-on-one interview, it'll be a cinch.

I ask in college if anyone is up for the BB auditions and tell them about the party. Nearly everyone in my class is up for it – Ross too, which surprises me a bit. Ross is quite old for a student – twenty-four – but that's because his dad died and he had to go to work to help his mum. He works in his uncle's clothing factory so he's been to all the trade shows and he knows about fashion. He hasn't asked me out yet but I know he's attracted because every time I talk to him I can feel the spark. Also he's a brilliant designer and the teachers all rate him.

Lala invites her Trinity crowd, including, ho-hum, Martina Curran. They'll come along to the auditions as well but really, they are not Big Brother material, not the ones I've met so far and definitely not Martina. They've no sense of adventure, no style. Still, it takes all sorts and BB often has a brainiac-anorak type – so who knows?

LALA

Even if they picked me, there's I'd be no way I'd go on Big Brother. I'd hate the thought of millions of people watching me! Apparently, there were even people who watched Big Brother live, during the night, when the housemates were asleep. How crazy was that! Plus, I wasn't about to sign up to live with fifteen people I didn't know and probably wouldn't like. It was bad enough living with Kirsty –and I'd known her since we'd made our First Communion. But I did have a brainwave.

The college magazine was called *Daedalus* and was published by the Lit.Soc. On the previous week's back page there had been a request for contributions, especially for articles which, "reflect and comment on the times in which we live." So I was planning go along to the BB auditions, take notes and then write something for *Daedalus* and hope that they accepted it.

JAKE

Before the party everyone meets in Fiddlesticks which, to quote Kirsty, is *"trendissimo"*. Red sofas, low black tables, glowing lamps, murals in hot colours, cool Cuban tunes, cocktails, lattes and good-looking waiters in black t-shirts and floor-length aprons.

Three girls drift in.

Girl A: Hair streaked with luminous pink highlights, gelled to stand up like flames on her head.

Girl B: Midnight blue angular bob.

Girl C: Blonde hair wrapped round pink foam rollers and the occasional escaped curl hanging down. Apparently they're statement hairstyles. All three wear "edgy" make up, red eye-shadow, blue stripes on their cheeks, diamante lashes. Their clothes have been customised ie with lumps hacked out and bits stitched on at odd angles. Kirsty greets them with squeals and kisses. So this is the future of fashion in Ireland!

A flock of woolly pullovers arrive. They have strange facial hair – I spot an Abe Lincoln beard, a waxed moustache and a soul patch, fluffy sideburns. They greet

Lala with witty quips. Several well-brought up girls with long straight hair follow them in. More fashionistas and still more woolly jumpers arrive. None of them talk to me. But why would I care? I'm going to work for Liam Fitzsimon!

Seán was impressed when I phoned to tell him. Mum and Dad too. Then I told Kirsty.

"So what's he paying you?"

"I don't know."

"Why didn't you ask?

"'Cause I don't care. I'd work for him for nothing. Remember Kirsty, we're talking about *the* Liam Fitzsimon."

"So what?"

"He's internationally famous, Sundance, Cannes, featured in Vogue, Rolling Stone. Even professional film makers would pay thousands just to spend a day with him."

"I still think you're an eejit." She doesn't get it.

One of the Trinity girls sits beside me.

"You're Jake," she says. "You probably don't remember me, I'm Martina Curran. I was in school with Kirsty."

I didn't recognise her for a second but now I remember. She wears a cream lace top, a brown velvet skirt and looks gorgeous. I like her. She's doing biology in Trinity.

"You've changed," I say.

"So have you," she says.

She's the only one who bothers to talk to me. She asks what I do and I tell her about Liam Fitzsimon. She knows who he is. And she's impressed.

As I said, I like her.

KIRSTY

The living room looks fab with fairy lights all round. We've got a big plastic baby-bath filled with sangría, *muy serioso* sangría with plenty of fruit and loads of vodka. As well as that, lots of people have brought bottles. Jake is looking after the music – it's the least he can do considering he's crashing our party. Soon everyone is dancing and the party is buzzing. But Ross still hasn't arrived. I've told him about meeting in Fiddlesticks. Maybe he has something to do for his mum and he'll be along later. The party is going to go on all night and then we'll all head for the auditions. Ross knows that too. I know that he definitely wants to be on Big Brother.

He does arrive eventually, well after midnight, with a girl.

"This is Emma," he says.

"Hi," I say, even though I want to kill her.

"Hi."

"There's sangría if you'd like to go get some," I say to her.

"Sangría! Great!" he says.

"Get one for me, Ross," she calls, as he pushes through the dancers.

Me and Emma are left eye-balling one another. She is quite old, at least twenty-five. Cheap High Street top and not even customised.

"So you're Ross's girlfriend," I say.

"I'm not 'his'; anything. We're more, you know, 'buddies'."

She sketches quotation marks in the air and smirks. And I instantly know what she means. I am taken aback. I mean I know about "fuck buddies" but I've never met anyone who'd say it out straight. Also, I am very pissed off. If she is his "buddy" that means I'll still stay a virgin tonight. My God, there's twelve year olds who've done it. Why can't I?

She is smirking away and I can see what she's thinking: *Poor little culchie, hot from the sticks and she's shocked.* I may be from the country but I've travelled, probably more than her, and I'm not easily shocked. I've seen things on

YouTube. But I don't say any of that. Instead, I leave her there smirking, and go to find Lala.

JAKE

I move round the party taking shots, nothing especially interesting. Kirsty and Lala looking sweet; Kirsty's classmates making rabbit-ears over one another's heads. Hilarious – *not!*

Three guys come out of the loo, rubbing their noses and talking a mile a minute. So they've cracked open the drugs. I find Martina in a corner by herself. She is smoking a joint.

"Wanna hit?"

I sit on the floor beside her and have a toke.

"Siege of Ennis," she says.

"What do you mean?"

"Look at them." She nods at the dancers. "Advance retreat, advance retreat."

"What are you talking about?"

"Did you never do Irish dancing?"

"No."

"Siege of Ennis. Part one, advance retreat, advance retreat."

We smoke together in silence and I watch the dancers. They're all flirting and throwing shapes. Advance, retreat; advance, retreat. Now I get it! I must use it sometime in a movie.

"Tell me, Jake," she says. "Do you ever look up at the stars and suddenly get the shivers?"

"Not really."

"I do. They make me think of the blackness out there, the distances, the black holes, the cold and all the alternative worlds where there might be intelligent creatures, entirely unlike us, living their lives."

"That's why you're doing science and I'm taking photos."
She laughs and gets to her feet.

"Wanna dance?"

We jiggle about to Aleisha's new album and then on comes Anthony and the Johnsons. Martina moves into my arms and we dance cheek to cheek. I get an erection. I try to keep some space between us and hope she won't notice. She comes in close. Should I say something? Or should I pretend it's not happening?

"Don't worry," she says. "Nobody knows except me. And I like it."

That makes it worse. I feel like I'm going to burst. I wish I had the nerve to take her down to my room but I haven't. The music changes to something loud and bouncy but we're still dancing cheek to cheek. She bites my earlobe.

"Is there anywhere that isn't so noisy?" she asks. Her breath is warm on my neck.

"We could go to my room."

She goes out in front of me so I won't be embarrassed. I've butterflies in my stomach. I think maybe she fancies me. I want to grab her and kiss her but maybe I'm wrong. She is older than me and she probably just wants to get away from the noise.

I lock the bedroom door and turn on the bedside lamp. Martina sits on the bed and pats the duvet. I sit beside her. She falls back on the bed. I fall back too. We look up at the ceiling.

"Pity there isn't a hole in the roof," I say.

She laughs.

"Mightn't that be a bit cold?"

"We could see the stars though. And I could find out if they make me shiver."

She laughs again and takes my hand.

"Have you ever done it?" she asks.

I used to think that if a girl asked me that question I'd say, yes.

"No," I say.

Maybe it is because we are both looking up at the ceiling, that it feels easy to tell her the truth.

"Me neither."

"Do you want to do it?"

There! I've said it. She doesn't reply. The universe stops for what seems like an age. I am certain I've blown it. My erection starts to go down.

"I don't know," she says at last. "Kiss me first and we'll see how it goes."

She doesn't have to ask twice. After a while she breaks away and looks me in the eye. "Have you got a condom?"

"No."

I want to kick myself. How can I be so stupid? Why don't I keep one in my wallet like other guys do? And I used to think it was just for effect!

"Lucky for you," Martina says, "I was in the Girl Guides."

She dives into her bag, pulls out a packet of three and wiggles it.

"*Bí ulamh,*" she grins. "It's the Girl Guides motto."

She is definitely the most wonderful girl I have ever met. She unbuttons my shirt and starts stroking my chest. Then we're flinging our clothes on the floor and we're at it like Adam and Eve in the Garden.

It is awesome.

I think I might die.

When I've recovered, we lie there laughing and talking and I put my hand on her breast and get another hard-on and we do it again! It's even better this time, longer and slower and I'm not so tense. Afterwards, I look at the ceiling and imagine all the stars out there and I can't keep the grin off my face. The party is still going strong outside. We hear a lot of shrieking. We decide to get dressed and go out and see what's happening.

They are playing a Big Brother game. Putting one another in order of snogability. The girl in fourth place thinks she should be in second. Several guys decide that the only way to find out is to snog her. She is perfectly willing. More people decide they need to try someone out. There's a lot of fake groaning and writhing and smacky sounds. I look round for Martina. For a horrible moment I think that she's gone. Then I see her in the corner chatting with Lala. She gives me a wink. I wink back and look round for something to drink.

Am I her boyfriend now? I like her a lot and I'd definitely do it with her again, but she's at college and I'm still at school. And I can't keep coming to Dublin every weekend because my Leaving Cert is next summer. Should I ask for her number? But would that make her think… No, better not. I'll wait and see what happens.

LALA

Oh! My!! God!!! Martina did it with Jake! I was really surprised. I had never even looked at him like that. But then after she told me, I did take a good look at him, and he *was* kinda cute. Tall and funny and smart. But I could never have done it with him. I'd known him too long; it would have been like doing it with my own brother.

"Did you do it to piss Kirsty off?" I asked her.

"No! For crying out loud, Lala, we're not in school anymore."

"Jake is."

147

"Only till June! Anyway, if it does piss her off, I won't be stricken."

KIRSTY

After the Big Brother game we play Spin the Bottle. During the game I discover that Ross first had sex when he was sixteen, that Emma likes S&M, and that Martina had sex for the first time tonight. At *my party!* With *my little brother!* I can't believe it. How dare she? How dare he? When Martina announces it everyone cheers and claps and the two of them stand up and take a bow. That's so typical of Jake, he always has to be the centre of attention. Bastard. It's not fair. I'm going to tell Mum.

I've been watching Ross and Emma all night. I don't think they're together. She's been dancing with one of the Trinity guys and chewing his face off. Several times during the night I feel certain that something is going to happen between me and Ross. But so far, *nada.* I don't understand it. I'm pretty sure he finds me attractive. Maybe when I get into the outfit...

JAKE

I pull open a curtain. The sky's getting light. Some people have fallen asleep on the floor. Couples are half-heartedly feeling one another up on the sofa. A group in the corner are singing a raggedy, out-of-tune version of *You'll Never Walk Alone.* The place is a mess. Kirsty is looking at her watch. She rattles a spoon in a glass.

"It's time to get ready!" she says.

People start rubbing their eyes and yawning. Some people leave. Kirsty ushers several girls into Lala's room to change their clothes and repair their make-up. She follows them in, saying over her shoulder,

148

"Jake, could you go to my room and get my outfit?"

"How am I supposed to know what you want to wear?"

"It's on the bed."

Kirsty's room is a predictable mess. The curtains are closed so it is dark except for the bedside lamp which lets me pick a path through discarded clothes, tissues, cups, glasses and make-up. Tracey Emin could take lessons. Kirsty's outfit is thrown on the bed. It's a red, PVC catsuit. It glistens like a skin freshly cut off a body. I take a couple of shots that I hope will look gruesome when I blow them up. Then I bring it to Kirsty.

Back in the living room everyone's wasted. People scrabble around for the makings of a joint or shake cans and drain them. I take some more shots. If they turn out right it will look like an orgy in a low-rent brothel. One guy shakes a can and swigs from it. Then he starts coughing. He goes red in the face and his eyes start to pop. Someone slaps him on the back. It doesn't help. His face gets darker and darker. He's not coughing any more – he's silently choking.

"Help him," I shout. "He's choking to death!"

Everyone panics. People crowd round shouting instructions at everyone else. But Martina puts her arms around the guy and does the Heimlich manoeuvre. Two soggy fag ends shoot out. He takes a deep breath and sits down on the floor. Then he starts gagging again. Another fag end. He is like a magician. I get him some water. Just then Kirsty flings open the door and poses in the doorway. She is wearing her shiny red Cat Woman outfit, complete with tail, hood and cat ears.

She looks obscene.

LALA

Kirsty had all the guys drooling. Including Ross. And for extra kudos, the smug girl Ross had brought with him

149

to the party now looked like she wanted to slit Kirsty's throat.

Kirsty had the outfit specially made. Fair dues to her – I wouldn't have had the nerve. She saw the original in black in Fiesta! Fiesta! Pedro knew the guy who made them and Kirsty ordered it in high-gloss scarlet. It had a hood with little cat ears that completely covered her hair. She had Amy Winehouse style cat eyes and false lashes teamed with scarlet gloss lipstick the same colour as the suit. She looked like one of those sexy avatars that guys love.

"Jesus fucking Christ!" said Ross. "That is some outfit."

The whole party then decamped to Hoofers where we ordered gallons of coffee and full Irish breakfasts. We were all a bit faded but, once the protein kicked in, we were back at full steam. The plan was to be in the Big Brother queue by eight. As I sat there sipping my coffee, I decided it was time for me to start taking notes.

We weren't the first in the queue. There were at least fifty people before us, all huddled up in their coats. It was bitterly cold, with a thin wind sneaking in through our clothes. They finally opened the doors and we trooped into a white exhibition hall empty except for a few taped-off areas. Guys in black t-shirts with STAFF on their backs corralled us into a queue. More black t-shirts arrived with video cameras and clipboards. People in the queue began to get giddy. The chatter and laughter grew louder. People took off their coats. Some were in ordinary clothes, others had dressed up and many were wearing outlandish costumes.

There were students from Galway and Cork and Sligo and Waterford and Donegal. Some were only there for a laugh but most were deadly serious. Several people told me that if they were picked, they'd give up their studies.

There were girls with blonde hair and tans that came from the Costa del Chemist. Boys with mad hairstyles. Girls dressed in sexy basques, micro-minis, Bunny Girl outfits and French maids. There were at least four panache-free transvestites, with bad wigs and huge Adam's apples. There was an old guy in a grubby white suit and scarecrow hair attempting to break-dance. There was a man with a brown paper bag on his head with a badly-drawn face on it. Behind us there were overweight twins wearing pink tutus and wings. A teenager with a face full of roaring-red pimples arrived in a chalk-stripe, three-piece suit, starched shirt, club tie and trousers with creases so sharp you could slit your wrists on them. Three belly dancers tinkled. A scrawny Superman failed to look cool. The excitement was catching. I was almost sorry I hadn't dressed up myself.

JAKE

I have my camera on video. This stuff is too good to miss.

They pull this guy from the queue. He is tall, blonde, handsome and wearing a kilt. It's the full regalia: socks, jacket, tam o'shanter and hairy *sporrán*. One of the BB staff films him while another asks questions. They are too far away for me to hear what they're saying. Pity. They ask him something. He nods, takes a deep breath and does cartwheels all down the hall. That makes every head swivel. He's not a real Scotsman. He has cycling shorts underneath. They are luminous green!

Kirsty still has her coat on. She watches intently. They pull out two people in Bunny Girl outfits! One of them is a guy. He walks like a builder carrying a hod up a ladder. He's possibly not a real tranny, just one of those guys who always dresses up as a woman for fancy dress parties. The other is a girl. She is wobbly-fat. After some chat, the tranny steps back and the fat one steps out. She puts her hands straight by her side, points her right toe and starts to do something that might be related to Riverdance. Everything jiggles. Her bunny ears flop to the floor and her furry white tail hangs on by a thread.

KIRSTY

The instant I take off my coat the Big Brother staff are all over me. They pull me out of the queue for a screen test. They asked me loads of questions about myself and then asked me to do some Cat Woman poses. I've been expecting that and I've practiced at home in front of the mirror. They tell me the camera loves me. Then they send me back to wait my turn.

While I am waiting I watch carefully. They are taking groups of ten or so and getting them to do things like wheelbarrow races and cheer-leader chants. Also there is a woman with a clipboard making notes. Obviously she is looking for the people who stand out.

When my group is called, I throw myself into the games, heart and soul. I also make sure to encourage the others. Every time I catch the eye of the woman with the clipboard she smiles at me. She must think I stand out. We are sent to a cordoned-off section at the other end of the room. The woman in charge makes us interview each other and then tell the group about the other person. I am paired with a drab little primary school teacher who has somehow been included in our group, and I make her sound like Mother Theresa. There are more games and more questions and then she asks us to line up behind a rope and hold out our right hands, palms down. With a rubber stamp, she marks the hands of all those who are going on to the next stage.

I am the first to be stamped!

Lala doesn't get stamped and neither does Jake, which doesn't surprise me. But I am very surprised when Ross doesn't either. I think he'd be perfect. He says he doesn't care but I can see he is disappointed. Next thing, the stamp woman's phone rings and she has to leave. She gives the stamp and the clipboard to one of the other BB guys. Someone calls him to help with something or other, and he leaves the clipboard and stamp on the floor. I pick up the stamp and mark Ross's hand.

LALA

Jake did not put his hand out and neither did I. At least there's someone with some common sense, I thought – but a few minutes later, it struck me how stupid I was being.

"I'm an eejit," I said to Jake, "I want to write about this."

Jake had seen Kirsty taking the stamp so he took it too and stamped both our hands. The BB woman returned just as he was putting it back.

"Did you nick my stamp?" she asked.

Jake gave her one of his angel-boy smiles.

"Go on," she said. "I was going to put you through anyway."

JAKE

I video Kirsty being Cat Woman. She cannot stay still. She's up and down, prowling the corridor, clawing the air and going, "*Rharrrrgh*". The only one that seems impressed is Ross. Dad would burst into flame if he saw her.

A guy dressed as a schoolgirl sashays in and sits next to me.

"What's *your* name, sweet-cheeks?" he asks, stroking my face. I grin uncomfortably.

"Jake."

"Fancy some chick with dick?"

"No, but thanks all the same."

Lala is watching and chortling her head off. Kirsty doesn't notice.

"You should try it some time," he says.

This time yesterday a comment like that would have made me wonder. Does he fancy me because he can see that I'm gay? Not that I really thought I was gay, but everyone wonders don't they? Today however, after Martina, everything's different.

"It's not really my kind of thing," I say.

"You don't know what you're missing."

When we were leaving Hoofers this morning, Martina squeezed my hand and slipped away. I expect she was going to lectures. I wonder if I'll ever see her again.

"Jake Kerrigan?"

Another woman with a clipboard is calling me into a room for my interview. I find the whole thing ridiculous and at the end they tell me I haven't got through. Which is fine by me.

KIRSTY

The interviewers are nice. They asks lots of questions, and I have the answers all ready.

Q. Why do you want to be on Big Brother?
A. Fun, laughter, sunshine.
Q. How would you describe yourself?
A. I'm a Daddy's Girl, a Princess, and my mum calls me Little Miss Sunshine.
Q. Why did you choose this costume?
A. Because I think it's sexy and because I can! There aren't many girls who could get away with it.
Q. What work do you do?
A. I'm a student. I'm studying fashion. I'm going to have

my own line and branch out into jewellery and accessories as well. I'm going to be the Stella McCartney of Ireland.

Q. What would you do if somebody in the house got on your nerves?

A. I'd have it out with them.

Q. So you're not afraid of confrontation.

A. No way. Actually, I enjoy it.

They mutter together for a couple of seconds, then say, "We'd like you to come back tomorrow."

I scream and jump up and down with excitement. I feel like I am going to explode. Then they give me a form to fill in before I leave.

The form is bright green. They want the usual CV stuff but then they ask questions like:

Q. Are you happy?

A. Yes.

Q. What are you passionate about?

A. Fashion. Life. Travel.

Q. What are you afraid of?

A. Nothing.

Q. Are you a virgin?

I don't know what to say to that. If I say "Yes" they'll make a thing of it and I don't want that. So I write "No".

Q. When did you last have sex?

I write "today". It isn't even a lie because Ross got to the next stage too and I have asked him back to the flat so it definitely won't be my fault if nothing happens.

JAKE

Me, Lala, Kirsty and Ross go back to Baggot Street. The flat looks like a mortar attack and smells like you'd stuck your head in a bin. It looks even worse empty than it did when the people were here. Every surface is covered in cans, bottles, bits of clothing, ashtrays with butts spilling over, cushions, paper plates, hairclips, cups, Rizlas, torn bits of cigarette packets and two pairs of sunglasses.

Kirsty and Ross are still on a high because both of them are on to the next stage of the Big Brother auditions. Kirsty shifts a couple of glasses round, lifts an ashtray from the arm of a chair and puts it on the table. Ross sits on the sofa and discovers a bit of tinfoil down the side with a small lump of dope still wrapped in it. He finds a discarded packet of Rizlas and skins up. Kirsty sits beside him.

The doorbell goes. It's Martina. She is wearing jeans and a simple red jumper. She looks great, like an ad for a high-fibre breakfast. She offers to help with the clearing up.

"You weren't at the audition," says Kirsty.

"I know," replies Martina. "I've got a life."

I laugh and so does Lala. Kirsty looks daggers.

Kirsty and Ross start a deep discussion about what to wear for Big Brother tomorrow. Kirsty asks him to come to her room and help her choose. They lock the door. Me, Lala and Martina clear up. All I can think of is – will Martina do it with me again? I decide that I'll ask her but I don't want to sound like a yobbo. I try out several lines in my head but none of them seem right. We are filling sacks with the rubbish and we both go for the same paper plate.

"Ladies first," I say, with a mock bow.

"Thank you, kind sir," she replies. "And by the way, would you like to stay over in my place to night?"

She really is one amazing girl.

"Anything else to be washed?" Lala calls from the kitchen.

I bring out the last of the glasses and she fits them into

the dishwasher. "I'm going over to Martina's," I say. "Tell Kirsty that I'll go straight home from there."

"Good for you, Jake," says Lala and she reaches up and tousles my hair.

Martina has a studio flat in Ranelagh. We make spaghetti with sauce from a jar and drink lemonade. When we get to bed I realise that I'm really quite tired, so we only do it once. Next day however it's different. We stay in bed till it's time for me to leave for the bus.

"Give me your number," I say as I leave.

"Sure," Martina says. "But really, you don't have to ring. You've things to do and so have I. But it was fabulous fun!"

"I'll be in Dublin over the Christmas holidays, working for Liam Fitzsimon."

"Text me and we'll see. Who knows, I might have to stay in Dublin myself, to study!"

How cool is that.

EAMON

There's something about Jake. The minute he stepped off the bus I can see it. He has a swagger about him. Jakers, I say to myself, you've had sex up in Dublin.

"Congratulations on the holiday job," says I, playing the long game. "Liam Fitzsimon eh? Seán tells me he's the bollocks."

"Yeah, he really is."

"So, apart from that, did you have a good time?"

"Yeah." He can't keep the grin off his face.

"Good party?"

"Great."

"Meet anyone interesting?"

"Yeah loads."

157

"Anyone in particular?"

"Not really."

"Do you know something? You're a terrible liar."

He blushes to the roots of his hair. He opens the door of the car and gets in. I get in as well and before I put on my seat belt I pat his knee.

"Well done, son," I say. "Well done."

MARIAN

Eamon could be right. There's definitely something about Jake. He suddenly seems more grown up. Of course, he's thrilled about working with Liam Fitzsimon but I feel there's more to it, especially after he hugs me. It isn't the usual 'do-I-have-to-do-this' kind of hug; it's a proper hug! I try, subtly, to find out about the girl but he isn't telling. In fact, he just does to me what I always did to my mother – he chatters away about everything except girls. Fair enough. I hope he remembered to use a condom. I've warned them both often enough. I'm not ready to be a granny and I'm not raising their babies.

This Big Brother thing is a worry. Kirsty doesn't realise what could happen. People might hate her. The press could write all kinds of hideous lies and there's always jealous people out there willing to sell made-up stories. Big Brother can seriously damage your health.

I can't think what I could say that might change her mind. There's still a way to go before they make the final choice so I'm still hoping. I even thought that if she did get chosen I'd leak her name to the press. That'd put the kybosh on it. But I won't. My mother did something like that to me. And I still haven't forgiven her.

I'd wanted to do nursing, but in Ireland you needed the Leaving Cert and I'd left school early. It was easier in

England, so I applied to a whole rake of hospitals. Every morning I came down hoping to find a letter in the hall. And every morning I was disappointed. After a month or two I knew that was that. I mustn't be good enough. I had a bit of a weep, a bit of a sulk, kicked a few walls then I went into Market Street and told Mr Carnew that I'd take the job he had offered.

Mr Carnew had sausage fingers and smelled of cigarettes and sweat. He owned a bar with a bit partitioned off near the door that was a hardware shop. The bar was dark and old-fashioned with a low counter shined by eighty-two years of drinking men's elbows and there were always a couple of ne'er-do-wells hunched over the dregs of a pint. But, when the local fleadh ceol started up, the very fact that Carnew's was old-fashioned made it popular with the tourists. Mr Carnew was so thrilled with himself that he introduced beer mats! The style of that! The permanent residents drew up their stools, adjusted their caps and got set to engage the tourists with makey-up stories in the hopes of free drink.

Mr Carnew wanted me for the hardware side and when things got busy, to help in the bar. Besides spades, forks, fertilisers and cures for liver fluke, he sold rubber boots and tweed caps. I decided to hang a display of them outside the door. We sold out in no time. No wonder Mr Carnew developed a crush on me. Mrs Carnew, however, was not pleased at all and kept coming in and being critical. That's why I went off to England.

Fast forward to my hen night. Me and my sisters Bernie and Jazz, and several girlfriends, are whooping it up a pub in Camden. I have a rose in my teeth, a white feather boa and several Pink Ladies on board. My sisters are ginned to the eyeballs. Bernie starts reminiscing. She flops a very drunk arm around my very drunk shoulders.

"Jesus, Marian," she says. "You could have married a doctor."

"Stop talking shite."

"But you could of! If only Mammy had let you go for the nursing."

Drunk as I was, I caught the whiff of betrayal. I sat up in my chair.

"What do you mean?"

"She burnt all the letters."

"What letters?"

"The hospital letters. They all said they'd take you and she burnt every one."

That's not what you need on your hen night.

"She's a bitch!" I declared. "And I'm going to ring her this minute."

But Mother was back in Balfathery. We had no mobiles then. I'd have to find a public phone that was working, get the right change, ring Burke's across the road, ask them go to my mother's house and bring her to the phone and I knew I was too drunk for that.

But I got the chance to have it out with her the day before the wedding. And a fat lot of good it did me. It was like flinging lemonade at a pebble-dash wall. She only did it to save my immortal soul! Some priest told her that English hospitals are hotbeds of immorality. The nurses are well-known for their low morals and the doctors perform operations expressly forbidden by the Catholic Church.

When it comes to "saving your immortal soul" there's no place to go with my mother. She has the hot line to God. In her book any action, no matter how cruel, is perfectly justified if it saves you from the maw of the devil. On the morning of my wedding, as I knelt beside Eamon up at the altar, I made a promise to myself. I will never, ever interfere with what my children want to do with their lives. But now that I'm at that point myself, I'm beginning to know how she felt.

I still think she was wrong.

KIRSTY

The second audition was great and I'm through to the next stage in London! How lush is that? And even better, Ross is through too!

Last night when we went to my room we didn't waste time choosing clothes.

"Jesus, you're sexy," he says.

At last, I think.

"Come here," he says. "Let me help you with that zip."

He turns me around and then slowly, very slowly, he pulls down the zip and kissed me all down my spine. Oh! My!! God!!! Next thing we're on the bed and doing it like crazy. Afterwards I feel all giggly and floaty. We sleep for a bit and wake up and do it again. We do it so many times that now it feels burny. But I like that feeling. It reminds me of Ross and makes me think about wanting to do it again. And it definitely helped in the second Big Brother interview because it made me feel ready for anything. Ross said he felt the same.

LALA

So, Kirsty and Ross did it. Great. Big deal. Afterwards, she acted like she was first girl in the world ever to have had sex. She declared she was now a "real woman" and much more mature than me. But I was worried for her. I knew Ross was a poser the first time I laid eyes on him, and nothing I had seen since had changed my mind. He was always telling everyone what a design genius he was and how he couldn't wait to take London and Paris by storm. At the same time, he would do this whole Alpha Male/Love God thing. Maybe that was just to prove that he was straight – fashion was not coming down with butch men. But he never gave it a rest. Once, when Kirsty had just popped out to the shop, he suggested that he and I get together sometime. I told him to go and get stuffed. I decided I had to tell Kirsty but when I did, she said I was over-reacting. That Ross was naturally flirty and the reason was because he had been brought up by women.

Then he pissed me off even more by making endless "jokes'" about me being an "ice maiden". He would sit there on the sofa with Kirsty wrapped around him and tell me that lots of hot sex might cure my "condition". And Kirsty would agree and between the two of them I began to feel like a virginal freak. Maybe they were right?

But I didn't trust him.

He was sexy, though.

CHAPTER 7

EAMON

I miss Kirsty something desperate. I miss finding her high heels under my chair. I miss her lipstick rolling round on the floor of my car. I even miss the arguments between her and her mother. But then I love a woman with a bit of spark, a bit of don't-mess-with-me fire in her eye; it's what first attracted me to Marian, and Kirsty has it in spades. And when the two of them clash –*wey-hey!* – seconds out of the ring! Surprising really, the things you miss.

So, the first day Kirsty is home for Christmas, I take her to Galway. A day out in Galway, it's been our "thing" since she was little. She mentions needing a new saddle, so we drop in to see Pat Ward. I like to do business with people I know and I've known Pat for a long time; he's one of Ireland's top saddlers. He promises to have it ready for Christmas.

I let on to Kirsty that I have business with Tom Joyce, the jeweller. But it's a game, she knows it's a game, Tom knows it's a game. I know they know but hey, what's wrong with a game? Kirsty likes a bit of sparkle and Tom's my first choice for that kind of thing. I knew him in his wild days in London.

I chat to Tom while Kirsty looks round the goods. I

make a call on my mobile, pretend that the signal is bad and go out on the street. Kirsty tells Tom what she fancies. When Kirsty is busy admiring a display of crystal animals Tom points to a pair of diamond studs, and I give Tom the nod. Christmas gift solved. I'll come back some time before Christmas and Tom will have it gift-wrapped to the max.

"Has Kate been in yet?" I ask Tom.

When I'm stuck for a present for Marian, I ask Kate to pick something. Another game. Marian knows but she pretends that she doesn't and I pretend that I don't know that she knows and collect the brownie points for getting exactly what she always wanted!

"Not yet."

"Okay, let me know."

After lunch, I give Kirsty my credit card and send her off to the shops. I don't do shops, Jesus no, only when I absolutely have to. Besides, I have to go and stick a rocket up Joe Duggan's ass. He was supposed to send out solar-energy boffins to survey Carpathi Castle. Some cock-up with passports, okay, fine, so now get a move on, time is money, my friend, time is money. They get plenty of sunshine out there and the more of our own energy we can supply the better – these cowboy countries are flaky when it comes to basic services. Besides, we can market the castle as environmentally friendly. It adds kudos, ups what you can charge the punters.

I want Carpathi Castle up and running and earning its keep ASAP and I'm thinking ahead. It'll need publicity. A celebrity wedding would be ideal. I'll offer the castle for free if I can find the right face – a face that sells magazines. You can't buy publicity like that. Exotic location, all the facilities – including bear hunting! – what macho man with a few bob to spare could resist? And I've just found out

164

something great. Every New Year, the locals dress up in bearskins and parade through the streets. Handled right, that could be a major attraction! Meantime, the bloody castle is full of unexpected niggles. Modernising old places like that, you need time and ingenuity. But that's what my lads are good at. These old places also take money but that's the least of my problems. Oliver Cooney in the bank is always happy to see me right. I reckon it should take about forty, forty-five million. Make that fifty to be sure.

NANA JO

God be with the days when you never heard a word about Christmas till December the eighth, the Feast of the Immaculate Conception. The children had a day off school so that's when you took them to town to see Santy. Nowadays Christmas lights are flashing straight after Halloween. And it's "*Jingle Bells*" all the way. They don't even play Christmas carols, just that tin-pan-alley rubbish written by atheists to make money out of Our Saviour's birth. If a Martian landed on earth in December they'd never know Christmas was intended to celebrate Jesus's birth in a stable in Bethlehem.

But then everything's money these days, especially in Ireland. It's all anyone thinks about. Money and the foolish ways you can spend it. But make no mistake, God is watching and a reckoning is coming.

My daughters see me as a burden – they *say* they don't, but they do, especially at Christmas. I expect it's all the bother and fuss, building up inside them, like pus in a boil. You make the simplest remark and *whoosh!* they explode. Marian has invited me over this Christmas. Her turn I presume.

She doesn't make her own Christmas cake or pudding

these days, she's too high and mighty for that. She says she gave it up because she doesn't "enjoy" it – as if work was supposed to be enjoyed! But that's the other side of money: self-indulgence. "Me, me, me!" "I deserve it!" "Because I'm worth it!" Did you ever hear such nonsense? She buys her Christmas provisions from one of those free-range, organic, everything-comes-in-wicker-baskets type shops that cost ten times what you'd pay in a normal shop.

"We're hardly on our uppers, Mum," she says. "We can easily afford it."

It's Sinful Extravagance. And it's also Sinful Extravagance to throw out last year's decorations and buy a whole new set. This year's decorations are purple! What has purple to do with Christmas? Even the tree is purple; artificial of course. God be with the days when you stuck a bit of holly over the picture of the Sacred Heart and lit a red candle in the window to welcome the Holy Family.

They have friends in for drinks and fiddly food on Christmas Eve. It's all very nice, I suppose, but I'm not a great one for small talk and I find it an effort. Minnie and Jimmy of course can chatter for Ireland. Minnie sits in the middle of that white leather sofa holding forth as only Minnie can. She has reindeer horns on her head and a blouse made entirely of sequins and if you ask me she's had too much Bailey's. Jimmy has a ridiculous flashing tie that plays *Mistletoe and Wine*.

I used to love Midnight Mass with the Crib and all the candles and the smell of frankincense and Father Mullery in his white and gold vestments. It was a beautiful way to welcome the Baby Jesus but Father Mullery had to put a stop to it. Too many bowsies were coming in drunk. It's a terrible shame but that's what Ireland has come to.

I do like Father Mullery's Mass, he says it with such

devotion. Not rushing through it like some. And I like his sermons as well, he always says something that makes you think about your religion. Some people think he's old-fashioned but I think he sticks to his guns. I like that in a priest. I don't hold with priests who try to be "with it".

Before I slip off to bed, I mention to Marian that I want to go to eight o'clock Mass in the morning.

"But Mammy, no-one will be up. Why can't you wait till we're all going?"

"If I walked down to the gate maybe one of the neighbours might give me a lift."

"I'll take you, Nan," says Jake.

"Thank you, Jake," I say.

Jake's a good boy.

Jake takes the roads nice and easy. He's a good, safe driver, not like Eamon. I always feel nervous when Eamon is driving.

There is only a scattering of people in the church, mostly women and older folk. Everyone else is having a lie-in. Marian says it's because people work so hard nowadays, but that's nonsense. People always had to work hard. When the girls were small I was up at half-five every morning to help milk the cows. Rain, shine, Sundays, holidays, it made no difference, the cows had to be milked. But people don't have that kind of grit any more.

Jake has some grit though. That lad knows what he's at. Not Kirsty. She's full of this Big Brother nonsense. If she was mine, I'd have taken the wooden spoon to her long ago.

GRANDMA MINNIE

We have a lovely Christmas. We start with Bucks Fizz and scrambled eggs *oh-feen-erb*, which means with chopped herbs. Josie sits there with that lemony puss on her and just has toast. She'd dragged Jake out of bed because she wanted to get early Mass. Why, I don't know. Surely one Mass is as good as another? But she does like to act the martyr.

Eamon and Marian do everything just right, like they do things in movies. They have Christmas stockings hanging from the mantelpiece, with our names embroidered on them and crammed with lovely little presents. I get hand-made soap with real flowers in it, Belgian chocolates shaped like Baby Jesus – which, incidentally, Josie puts aside, I suppose she thinks eating them would be some kind of a sin – pretty gold earrings, a gardener's diary, my favourite perfume. Then we have more champagne before we open the proper presents. They are piled under the tree and wrapped in silver. And, the tree! Huge, up to the ceiling and shimmering purple, with decorations and lights in silver and lilac and mauve. Fabulous. My present is a voucher for Brown Thomas and the dotey silver jug that Marian and I had seen in a Galway antique shop. She remembered! That's Marian for you!

Needless to say the excitement is fierce with everyone opening their presents. Josie spends most of the time picking up wrapping paper, smoothing it out and folding it. I wouldn't be surprised if she brings it home to use again.

The Christmas dinner is perfect: candles, silver, turkey, champagne. Even Josie, eventually, cracks a smile. She goes so far as to read out a joke from the crackers and she puts a silver paper crown on her head!

Now that, for Josie, is going totally wild.

MARIAN
I hadn't been looking forward to handling Minnie and

Jimmy as well as my mother for Christmas, but then Fergus gave me a call. He had a new consignment of Jamaican Mary J, very laid back, very smiley, very peace on earth, goodwill to all men and joy to the world. I put enough into Minnie and Jimmy's scrambled eggs *"aux fines (Jamaican) herbes"* to keep them from starting a row. And another good dose into the extra portion of stuffing which I was keeping aside for my mother! Mother does love her stuffing! Ding-dong merrily on high!

KIRSTY

Dad is so funny. He really thinks I don't know what he's up to when we go into Tom Joyce's shop. But I've known since I was ten. And Mum knows about Kate because the two of them go to buy whatever Mum fancies. Kate wraps it and gives it to Dad. Dad hands it over on Christmas morning. Mum gasps with delight and Tom Joyce says nothing to no-one.

Christmas at home is nice and everything but I can't wait to get back to Dublin and Ross. I'm definitely going back for New Year's Eve. I told Gran about Ross.

"I hope he knows what a treasure he's got," she says.

I hope so too.

Among all the cards a letter arrives for me from England. I thought my heart would burst out of my chest. I was afraid to open it but I did. I'm into the next round of Big Brother in London! Awesome! I want to phone Ross and tell him but I've decided to wait and see if he phones me first. He hasn't. Does that mean he hasn't got through? Now I don't know what to do.

I haven't figured Ross out yet. We have lots of sex and that's good and we're both interested in fashion and he comes round to the flat all the time but I still keep wondering. Are we an item or are we not? Most people assume that we are. But when one of the girls in our class asked him out straight he just looked deep in her eyes and smiled. Well that's not on, so I asked him out straight myself. He looked deep in my eyes and smiled:

"Are you jealous?"

"No!"

Even if I was I wouldn't let on. Anyway, I'm not so much jealous as not sure. While I'm home here in Balfathery, is he seeing that girl from the party? I don't know. I keep telling myself that the reason he hasn't phoned is because he didn't get the call to London. Well if he hasn't, he hasn't. I won't let it hold me back.

Mum ruins Stephen's Day by taking me for a walk and a "serious talk". According to her, Big Brother will ruin my life, people will hate me, the papers will write vile stories. It's happened to others so it could happen to me. *Duh!* I know all that. But I also know that it only happens to housemates who are thick! I'm not thick, plus I'm popular and on top of that I've studied Big Brother. I know what it's all about. That's what Mum doesn't get. If I get in the Big Brother House I *will* be famous! I'll be a Celeb and I might even invite Madonna to my next Christmas party – *NOT!*

CHAPTER 8

JAKE

Kirsty asks what I do for Liam Fitzsimon. I tell her. She doesn't get it.

"So basically," she says, tossing her hair, "you're his bitch."

"It's Liam Fitzsimon!"

"You're still his bitch."

What's the point? She thinks what I do is boring and boring is only for Losers. She still hasn't copped that every job has boring bits, even the glamorous ones. And, if you don't do the boring bits, nothing happens. *Duh!*

Tidying the studio, making tea, phoning the crew, checking supplies and so on may not be glamorous but I get to see Liam at work. He's amazing. I've learned more watching him find the right angle than I learned in the Camera Club in a year. And don't get me going on what he can do at the editing stage. Pure genius. We're very different characters, me and Liam, but we're both hooked on visuals. So we get along on fine. He even asked me to work for his company full-time but that would mean leaving school and Mum would go ballistic.

"I'll finish my Leaving Cert first."

"Hnhuhh." That means he approves.

"If you like," I say, chancing my arm, "I could work weekends till Easter."

"What about school work?"

"It's under control."

"Good."

So now I'm up in Dublin every weekend and staying with Kirsty, although most Saturdays nights I stay with Martina in her tiny flat – yes, Martina Curran! We're still seeing each other but it's still, you know, casual.

Now it's the last week of January, and the weather is vile. We're in Trinity College. National Geographic have asked Liam Fitzsimon to do a documentary on Dr Phelim McConville, aka The Water Doc. The guy who developed "Uisce", the low-tech water treatment system. He's a major star in development circles.

We're in the car in the car park. It's chucking it down. Liam pokes his laptop with one finger. I pull up the hood of my rain jacket and lug the gear out of the boot, across the car park, round the rugby pitch, along the side of a building and across the slippery cobbles to Doc's office. The east wind takes slivers off my face. Rain needles my eyes. I have to go over and back three times. Remind me: Why am I doing this?

Doc sits at his desk. He is white-haired and handsome. He seems slightly bemused at the invasion. Liam arrives and starts looking around for angles and light. He's in one of his grumps.

"Be gentle with me," smiles Doc Water. "I hate being photographed."

"Don't interrupt," snaps Liam.

At the best of times, he's not good at the chit-chat. I set up the camera and lights. I smile at the Doc. He smiles back. Liam prowls round, like a hyena surveying a carcass.

He wants to get some establishing shots.

"Stand by the window," he growls.

"Not at my desk then, looking solemn?" jokes the Doc.

"No," snaps Liam.

Doc stands obediently by the window.

"Take off your jacket."

Doc takes off his jacket. He hangs it on the back of his chair. He stands by the window again with his hands in his pockets rattling his change. He looks very uptight.

"Try smiling," says Liam.

The Doc gives it his best passport smile.

"Jesus!" complains Liam.

It's not going well.

"What's Africa like?" I ask, even though I'm supposed to say nothing.

"Extraordinary place," says the Doc.

And that's all it takes. The man is a natural. He tells stories. He laughs. He gestures. He ruffles his hair. He forgets about Liam and the camera. Meanwhile Liam shoots it all.

You should see the footage. You could use every bit. But one sequence is special. It looks like it was shot in black and white. Doc's face is alight. He flings his hands in the air. His hair looks like a spiky white halo. Raindrops shimmer on the window beside him, like water that's just been invented. It says everything. Genius.

So now I'm the official chatter-upper! I talk to Martina about it. She says I'm like her, a good chatter-upper because – and this is her theory – we were brought up in the country. City kids avoid adults, she says, because they mostly hang round with each other. Country kids have to talk to everyone.

She could be right.

KIRSTY

When I get back to Dublin, the flat is a tip. Lala had stayed on in Dublin to finish an essay – she's such a swot – and I was sure she'd do one of her big tidy ups. But she didn't. On top of that Jake stayed till the end of the holidays. Now he's announced he's going to stay here every weekend until Easter! Who does he think he is? The way he goes on about Liam Fitzsimon, you'd swear it was brain surgery. It's taking photos. *Duh!* Point the camera, press the button. How hard can it be?

I still haven't heard from Ross. We've been texting of course: *Happy Christmas! U2! Miss you! Me2!* that kind of stuff. I clear a space on the sofa, phone a cleaning agency, order a Chinese and turn on the telly. But suddenly I can't bear not knowing. I ring Ross.

"Hi, it's me!"

"…?"

"Kirsty."

"Hi, Kirst."

"Good Christmas?"

"Family, the usual,"

"So. Any news?"

"Well, I got through to London if that's what you mean."

"Me too! Me too!"

That's why he didn't ring. He didn't want to spoil my Christmas in case I hadn't got through! You see? Underneath all the cool stuff, he's a dote. Later that night he comes over.

We sit on the sofa drinking a couple of beers and discussing Big Brother. Next thing Ross takes my hands and stares deep into my eyes. I love when he does that. It's very romantic and a little bit scary as well.

"When we go to London," he says. "How would you

feel about telling Big Brother that we're a couple?"

"Really?"

"Of course."

"Will BB like it?"

"Trendy young Irish couple? It would make headlines. And BB wants to make headlines."

"It'll be like living together! Except… I'm not having sex on TV."

"God, no."

LALA

Kirsty was like a three year old high on Smarties. What with Big Brother and London and her and Ross being an item… Oh! My!! God!!! she just couldn't keep up with her life! So she started skipping classes to "research" her Big Brother outfits. Also, she was late with her project, which was important because it counted towards her final mark. But there was no talking to her.

And going on BB as a couple? Toe-curling kafuffles under the duvet, recorded by infra-red camera? It would kinda put a blot on her CV.

"It did Paris Hilton no harm," Kirsty snapped when I raised it.

Also, about them being a couple… I just didn't know. It suited Ross, that much was clear. But Ross only did what was good for Ross – he was quite upfront about that.

"Now that it's official," I asked, "does that mean he'll stop flirting?"

"Don't be stupid Lala, that's just how he is. It means nothing."

I was pretty sure that when he came on to me – which he did at least once a week – that if I gave him an inch it would definitely mean something. But I didn't say that out loud.

I had to be careful or Kirsty would say I was jealous. She knew I wasn't mad about Ross but she'd convinced herself that it was because he was unconventional, creative, blah-de-blah and I'm a country virgin.

Wrong!

I didn't like Ross because he was totally selfish. He was only interested in two things: fashion and sex. Fashion was fair enough – it was his future career. He was already selling stuff on line and going to clubs to show off his creations. And that included gay clubs, by the way. I mention the gay thing, because Ross was also into all kinds of sex. It was his second obsession. He made no secret of the fact that he'd taken "a walk on the wild side".

"The body's an organ of pleasure," was one of his mantras. "We should explore it."

The day I got back to college I found an email from the editor of *Daedalus*. He had accepted my article! Yes, yes, yes, yes, *yes, yes, yes, yes,* YES! It was due out in March but I decided not to tell anyone… except maybe my mum. I planned to wait till it was in print and then I would show it to everyone in the world. In the note, the editor asked me to meet him.

The minute I saw Mark Brennan I realised I'd seen him before at Lit.Soc. meetings. He was the chairman. I'd always thought he looked interesting. Final year student, quite good-looking, glasses, curly brown hair, black polo-neck shirts. I'd never spoken to him. Final year students didn't mix much with first years. He was a poet and – get this – he told me I had talent!

After that, I kept running into him all the time. Then he asked me out. We went to a Mexican movie. I didn't tell Kirsty. She'd want to know all the details, and there weren't any to tell. He didn't even hold my hand and I wondered, is he asking me out as a friend or what? I asked Martina about him. She went to Lit.Soc. as well and her cousin was on the committee. Story was, Mark was okay. So when he asked, I went on a second date and a third. It finally happened on the fourth. *Hallelujah!* No longer a virgin.

Mark was very intelligent, sometimes a bit serious, but I made him laugh. He thought I was hilarious. He gave me his poems to read which I took as a compliment, although poetry wasn't my thing and I didn't really understand them. He used a lot of words I'd never heard of. I looked them all up but even then I still didn't understand. Well sort of… but not properly. I tried to think what I'd say if he asked what I thought.

"So what did you think?" he asked the next day.

"I'm not finished yet," I improvised and, to make myself sound more intelligent, I added, "I want to let them resonate."

The instant the words were out of my mouth I thought, Jesus that sounds pretentious. But Mark smiled. Not his usual ironic grin but a little-boy smile. He looked so cute. Of course, I had to give back the poems in the end. I decided to say they were "deep". And there was that little-boy smile once again.

At least now Kirsty and Ross can stop with the ice maiden jokes.

KIRSTY

I've so much to do before going to London, what with all the research! I'm checking out all the Big Brother websites – there's squillions of them! – because, like Mum always says, information is power. Then there's tactics to discuss with Ross. And I have to plan my wardrobe.

I've decided to go urban casual: killer jeans, great shirts and chunky jewellery to add some pizzazz. I have to make so many shopping trips, you've no idea, I'm totally stressed. One day I find myself in a shop wanting to buy every blouse on the rack because I *can't decide*. That's when I give in and ask Ross for help. He saves my life.

He makes me calm down and start applying the principles. Choose things that flatter your figure. Then, whenever I can't decide or he thinks I'm making a mistake, he does the choosing. I ask him to pick the accessories as well. He has such a great eye. My favourites are the mirror-glass swallows he teams with a midnight-blue jacket.

For himself, Ross scours the charity shops. I go with him once and frankly once is enough. All those smelly clothes that strangers have sweated in! *Yeeeeuch!* Ross washes everything, of course, and then cuts, re-jigs, starches, appliqués, embroiders, whatever, and comes out with his hyper-cool, punk-dandy look. That's why he's going on Big Brother, to show off his talent and hopefully find his own Isabella.

The first time he told me that, I threw a wobbler. I was furious. How dare he? He only laughed and that made me madder. Then, he showed me a picture. I couldn't believe it.

"She's ugly!"

"And dead."

Then he explained about Isabella Blow. Apparently she made Philip Tracey. Wore his hats to all the best parties. Instant fame. Also Alexander McQueen. Okay, now I get it. And that makes me think – I wouldn't mind someone like that as my agent.

I tell Mum what a great help Ross has been and she says I should buy him a thank-you gift. Mum's hot on doing the right thing. But I don't know what to get him. Boys are hard to buy for. Then the very next Saturday, me and Ross are passing through Brown Thomas menswear when I spot this *fabulous* jacket. I stop to feel it. Buttery leather, great cut, sharp design, totally fierce. Ross takes it from me and holds it at arm's length, giving it the laser treatment (that's the look he gets in his eye when he's styling). He picks up a couple of scarves and tries them against it, then a couple of shirts.

"Go on," I say. "Try it on, you know you want to."

He does and it looks cool. He loops a forest-green wool scarf round his neck and it looks *killer* cool. An assistant appears.

"There's twenty percent off in the sale."

"Would you take ten euro a week?" jokes Ross.

"Sorry, sir?"

He helps Ross out of the jacket and hangs it back on the rail. Ross shrugs on his old biker number. And I have a brain wave.

"Try it on one more time."

"No, I like it too much. I might make a dash for the door and end up in the nick."

"But I'm going to buy it for you. As a thank-you present for all your help."

"I couldn't take that, it's too much." He so wants me to buy it.

"Then it's your birthday present as well."

"My birthday is not till July." *He so wants me to buy it.*

"Then you definitely have to have it now."

"Why?"

The assistant is hovering around earwigging so I can't say it out straight. Once you get picked for BB you can't tell anyone, not friends, not family, not anyone because, if it leaks to the press, you're a goner.

"Hopefully, the only shopping we'll be doing in July is ordering the groceries."

Ross gets my drift.

"Yeah right, fingers crossed."

"At least try it on!"

He tries it on. Perfect. It was for nothing really, considering the quality.

After that we decide to have a send-off party. It was Ross's idea.

"After London," he says, "it's heads down until the exams."

"Also," I remind him, "it's our last chance to celebrate getting so far in Big Brother."

LALA

I had never seen Kirsty behave the way she was doing around Ross – she was totally dazzled by him. I decided it was because Ross just didn't care what she thought. Kirsty's a Daddy's Girl. She's used to twisting men round her little finger. But this one wouldn't twist. Plus, he was good-looking and had undeniable talent. He was also a dick. But she didn't see that.

The party was his idea but needless to say he left all the arrangements to us. He promised to do one thing but even with that Kirsty had to help him out. The night before the party, I had got the fairy lights out and was checking to see were they working. Ross was sprawled in an armchair with his mobile, texting and making calls. Kirsty was trying on another new outfit.

"Kirsty!" he called, "He's not answering!"

"Try him again later," Kirsty called back.

"I've been trying all day. Word is he's 'under pressure' and he's 'on holiday'."

Kirsty came into the room in killer jeans and a simple white shirt with deep cuffs.

"What do you think?"

"Fierce babe, fierce. Don't you know someone?"

"Yeah but… He's a friend of my dad."

"Give him a call."

"He might tell the folks."

"Is there no way you could twist his arm? I mean, did he never make a pass or anything?"

"No way."

"Pity."

"I think that's called blackmail," I said.

KIRSTY

Fergus sounds surprised.

"To what do I owe this honour?" he asks.

"I'm having a party."

"Good for you."

"I thought perhaps you could help me."

"How do you mean?"

"I need some, you know, 'fun stuff'."

"Fiesta! Fiesta!'s your best bet."

"Not that kind of stuff."

"Sorry Kirsty, you've lost me."

"Nothing heavy, just, you know… The fifth letter of the alphabet."

He hangs up on me.

I text: *'Maybe ur grlfrnd can help.'*

He phones back instantly.

"Don't do that," he says. "Don't ever do that. I'll drop by at lunchtime to morrow. Do you have a boyfriend?"

"Yes."

"Make sure that he's there."

"Okay."

He hangs up. I've never known Fergus so jumpy.

When he comes round, he makes me and Ross sit on the sofa while he paces the floor.

"This is really important," he says, "so listen and don't interrupt."

It was like being back at school!

"First, and I cannot emphasise this enough, Never contact Tracey. Not for any reason. Not ever. "

"But she was at my party…"

"And your mother was very pissed off. Do you want to know why? Tracey has certain connections."

"Who's Tracey?" asks Ross.

"My girlfriend. Tracey O'Hagan."

"Not *the* O'Hagan's?"

"The very same."

"Heavy."

"Very heavy. Now, secondly, I'm not selling drugs to you, Kirsty. Your father would kill me."

"I won't tell if you don't."

"No. That's not going to happen. However, this once, and this once only, I'll do a deal with your boyfriend. Okay?"

"Okay."

"And last but not least, contact me like this again and I'm telling your dad. Are we clear?"

"Sure."

Ross and Fergus go into the kitchen.

FERGUS

If Eamon ever finds out, I'm for the high jump. But the silly tart would have gone straight to Tracey and I can't let her do that. Especially not now while she's having one of her "episodes".

The first time that Tracey went off the rails I thought it was me, that I'd done something wrong, but I didn't know what and she wouldn't say. She screamed that I was useless, called me a shit, then disappeared for ten days. Two months later, it happened again. And it still happens, but now I know it's not me, it's her. She has psychological problems – which isn't surprising, all things considered.

So why am I still with her? I keep asking myself that question. Séan says I'm addicted to danger and maybe I am. But, unlike most women, Tracey is never boring. And she makes up for her "episodes" – boy, does she make up for them! We don't need to go into the details. But let me say this much. It's worth it. *Well* worth it. Still, it's better for Kirsty to stay away.

JAKE

Kirsty doesn't want me at the party and I think I know why. She's afraid of the camera. She says she loves it but she only loves it when it shows her at her best. But I'm not into flattering portraits, I'm into human behaviour, and that's why parties are interesting. With the barriers down people do things, you see stuff, you store it away and maybe sometime it'll be in a film. Also, she's afraid that Mum and Dad might see my work and have a fit.

"Why don't you stay with your girlfriend?" she asks.

"Because she'll be at the party. Lala asked her."

Kirsty's convinced that me and Martina are only together to spite her. We're not. So she acts like Martina doesn't exist. Martina couldn't care less but she stays away from the flat, unless there's a party.

LALA

Ross arrived looking like he'd come off a Gaultier catwalk.

He wore the thank-you present that Kirsty had bought him. Hello? It must have cost squillions. He also wore one of his customised shirts with starched quills of material sticking down the front instead of ruffles. His signature punk-dandy look.

JAKE

I'm working late. Liam's off to Venice tomorrow to collaborate with a theatre director on a set for a ballet. There's a lot of things to clear up before he goes and I don't get out of the office till after eleven.

I get back to Kirsty's flat. The party has begun, music is pumping and, from the look of the dancers, their bloodstreams are coursing with E. I find Martina and we go to the kitchen to cook some spaghetti and heat up some bolognese sauce.

Lala comes in and drags Martina away to help settle an argument about the Large Hadron Collider. I'm starving. I put the spaghetti into a bowl and larrup it up. Ross comes in and takes out a beer from the fridge.

"Jake." He claps me on the back. "Have you taken your medicine yet?"

He hands me a tab of E which I'm happy to scoff. He leaves his hand on my back and starts caressing my spine. I finish my meal and move away to put my dish into the machine. I go to the sink to rinse my hands. Ross comes up behind and puts his arms around me.

"You are beautiful," he says.

"I know," I say, keeping it light. "Now please let me go."

He rests his head on my back.

"Ever done it with a man?"

"No." I try to disentangle myself.

He holds on tight.

"Why don't you try it?"

"With my sister's boyfriend! A bit too Jerry Springer for me."

"You're funny." He laughs. "Have you any idea how sexy that is?" Martina comes back looking for me. Ross lets me go. "Try a walk on the wild side sometime," he says. "You might like it."

I bring Martina back to my room and tell her about it.

"He just wants to shock you," she says, " he's that kind of guy."

The E starts to kick in. Me and Martina start getting it on. Afterwards, I'm lying on the bed looking up at the ceiling wondering, if I was on a desert island, with no women, only men... Would I?

LALA

As the party went on, the starch in Ross's shirt wilted but not his libido. About one in the morning things got a bit messy. Ross and Kirsty and several others tumbled into her room and they left the door open. I saw lots of sucking and writhing. Mark saw it too. He was shocked but pretended he wasn't. I got up and pulled the door closed.

KIRSTY

Lala says it was an orgy, but it wasn't. Like Ross says, it was humans being totally loving. Love given freely and taken with joy. Except for the bit where he was sucking the tits off that blonde one, abandoning me to the ear-licker guy.

"You're not jealous are you?" he asks.

"I thought we were an item."

"We are." He comes up close and nuzzles my neck. "But we don't have to be exclusive. Unless of course you're one of those uptight Catholics, riddled with guilt. Are you?"

"No way."

"I didn't think so. Sex is for pleasure. Any chance that you get you should grab it. The thought of you with someone else is so hot. I want to watch you and help make you come. How about I broaden your horizons?"

I guess I'm all on for broad horizons.

CHAPTER 9

MARIAN

Kirsty has dashed off to London in a flurry of last-minute panics and phone calls. Glad I wasn't in Dublin for all the drama. Poor Lala got the brunt.

The further it goes on the more I worry about this Big Brother thing. Even if the press and the public adore her, what then? A rash of Red Carpet dos. A couple of modelling jobs for the lad mags, and they'll want her to get her tits out. God forbid she goes topless. Eamon would punch someone out.

And a year later, where will she be? Invites drying up. Agent busy every time she calls. What then? I can't see her going back to college. So I'm concentrating on getting her through her first year and keeping my fingers crossed that she doesn't get chosen. Because she has talent. She could become a good designer. Mrs Williams has said so several times, she just needs to focus.

Kirsty complains that fashion college is just glorified dress-making. Well probably, yeah, but it's important to know the basics. I've explained this to her several times but she's not convinced, she thinks she'll have lackeys to do the basics. If I can just get her through this first year then I think she might settle. A year makes all the difference at her age.

I've started dropping in to the church and saying prayers to Our Lady begging her to make sure that Kirsty is not picked for Big Brother. Me, that's never darkened the door of a church since I was sixteen! I even asked Mammy to say one.

EAMON
Kirsty would be terrific on telly. She'd make an ace presenter, I know she would. This Big Brother thing could be the start of something. I must ask around. I've been very generous to the Party over the years, it's time that they gave something back. Some of them must know someone with the right contacts.

Marian's convinced that even if Kirsty does get on Big Brother it will all come to nothing and she'll have ruined her chances in college. But so what? It's not the end of the world. I can take care of her. Why do you think I fly to Romania, spend nights in crappy hotels, get stranded in airports? To take care of my family, that's why.

Carpathi Castle is taking its time. Colm warned me it was par for the course in Eastern Europe where nothing is ever straightforward. I sent over two of my Romanian lads to supervise. They keep me up with the gossip. But I need to be out there myself. I believe in dealing with problems before they grow horns.

The forest is essential to our plans, it's one of the main attractions. But the locals smell money, so they're manufacturing problems: ownership, traditional hunting rights, blah-blah-blah... all that stuff. It'll work out in the end, them ex-commies love the old capitalist buck.

We'll employ an eco expert and put him in charge of the hunting, that'll keep the tree-huggers happy. It's the only way to go. The more doom and gloom people read in the papers, the more eco bling they demand. Give the people what they want, I say, and let them pay through the nose.

NANA JO
Marian knows that I'm off to Athlone next Thursday to start the Novena to Our Lady of Perpetual Succour, that's why she's asked me to say one for Kirsty. But I can't waste Our Lady's good time on all this Big Brother malarkey. She has far better things to be doing. It's like praying to win the Lotto. Our Lady has no time for that kind of nonsense. Of course I will pray for Kirsty, same as I pray for all my grandchildren.

KIRSTY
There are mad people at the London auditions! One guy wants to do everything naked but a lot of the girls object so they make him wear pants but if he gets into the House, he *insists* he'll go naked! I'm not sure he'll make it because apart from going nude he is *Dullsville*. Me and Ross though wow everyone and the Big Brother crew adores the idea of us as a couple.

We have to play all kinds of games and have debates and discussions and stuff. Sometimes they put me and Ross together and sometimes they separate us. Of all the men there, Ross stands out the most and I know I am *smokin'*… one of the staff told me so. Lots of the people there are, you know, a bit odd, a bit kooky, but all in all, I'd say me and Ross are by far the most interesting. They'd be mad not to pick us.

I'm dying to tell Lala all about it but, when I get back, her mother is there. It seems Lala has an article in some little student rag. Mrs Bergin is so chuffed that she has come up to Dublin specially to celebrate. It's not like it's such a big deal but then people with small minds are easily impressed.

We go to The Water Palace to celebrate. It's a Thai restaurant and Mrs Bergin is all of a doo-dah because she's never had Thai food before! She is excited with all the gold Buddhas and the water feature and the silk outfits the waitresses are wearing. And when she isn't wittering on about the décor she is banging away about Lala's "achievement".

We are well into our main course before Lala remembers to ask.

"What was London like?"

"Brilliant."

"So tell all!"

I give them the official version. Later, when her mother is gone I fill Lala in on the details.

LALA

Kirsty was still faffing around and not doing anything for college. She spent all her time shopping and drinking coffee with friends.

"How are your designs coming on?" I asked.

"Fine."

"Have you sorted the patterns?"

"I'm still doing the sketches."

That was the problem, right there. She'd do sketches all day but she never got down to the real nitty-gritty.

"You'd want to get a move on."

"Jesus, Lala," she snapped, "stop nagging, you're worse than my mother."

She was like a briar. According to her, Ross was being unreasonable. She thought they needed time together to prepare for the Big Brother House – she was convinced she was going. I hoped it kept fine for her. He thought he needed time to prepare for exams. They had several rows over it but, for once, I was on his side.

MARIAN

Why can't it be Eamon who picks up the phone for once? But no, every time Mrs Williams calls to complain about Kirsty, he's off in Romania. This castle has taken over his life. I know he works hard but he doesn't have to work nearly as hard as he likes to pretend. Truth is, he loves it. For him, it's like stepping into the ring where he's the Big Dog, the Champ. Except I'm left alone with the house and the children and all the responsibility.

It happened before when the kids were small.

"It's all for the family!" he said, when I faced him.

"A family you never see."

He didn't listen that time so I had to take steps. I took myself and the kids off to Spain and didn't tell him. That got his attention. When I rang a week later he was frantic, grovelling and ready to promise me anything.

Now he's at it again. I expect he thinks it's okay because Kirsty and Jake are grown up. But they're not independent. They still need their parents. And I'm fielding the phone calls from Mrs Williams.

"I'm very concerned about Kirsty," she says. "We haven't seen much of her lately."

"She says she's enjoying the course."

"She's certainly enjoying something. I've given her a final warning. I thought you should know."

I want to drive up to Dublin, take Kirsty by the shoulders and shake her. But I don't. I go out to the pool and swim fifty lengths. Even that doesn't calm me. I ring Eamon and tell him but, as usual, he is all loosey-goosey about it.

"Stop worrying, Marian," he says.

Jesus, Eamon!

LALA

The more I got to know Mark the less impressed I was. All he wanted was an audience for his literary theories – and regular sex. The regular sex was nice. But the other stuff, not so much.

For example, there was the way he used big words. He knew lots of them because he actually did read the dictionary – not just a normal school dictionary, but the Shorter Oxford Dictionary, which isn't short at all. There's nothing wrong with expanding your vocabulary but Mark uses jaw-breakers like "adynamia", "inchoate", "ancillary" and "palimpsest" to impress you with his intellect.

At first I thought his poems were brilliant, mainly because I didn't understand them. He was, after all, a final year student and I was just a first year who wasn't great on poetry. I read them several times but I still didn't know what they meant. I asked him to explain one particularly obscure verse. You'd think I'd committed a crime.

"Art," he said, looking down his nose at me, "speaks directly to the soul."

So maybe my soul was deaf. Or maybe his poems weren't Art.

KIRSTY

Mom is so mean. She landed in Dublin out of the blue. When she asked Lala to leave us alone I knew I was in for the riot act. What can I say? College is BORING. They're not teaching design, they're training dressmakers. Which is all very well if you want to end up as some little Mrs McFerrity, making debs dresses for spotty school-leavers.

But that's not what I want. I want to be Stella McCartney. Does she make her own patterns? I doubt it. She has people for that. Or Posh Spice? She *definitely* doesn't.

Mum says if I don't finish college, she'll charge me rent. I don't care. I'll get a job.

MARIAN

I decide to stay the night in the flat – just to see for myself how the land lies. While I'm giving Kirsty her options, Lala is in her room writing an essay. I've noticed that Lala is standing up to Kirsty more than she used to. Good girl, Lala.

We order an Indian takeaway and, while we're waiting for it to arrive, this creature appears at the door. Child-of-nature hairstyle, three shaved bars in one eyebrow, tiny white tusks sticking out of each side of his nose.

"That cyclamen bra of yours?" he says to Kirsty. "Can I borrow it?"

"Sure."

Familiar with her bras *and* wants to borrow one!

"Cyclamen your colour then?" I ask, by way of a joke.

"I'm not sure," he answers quite seriously. "I hope so. It could be just the colour I need for a trim."

"I'm Kirsty's mum. Call me Marian."

"Hi Marian, I'm Ross."

So this was Ross! All-round fashion genius and current boyfriend. I'd pictured a baby-faced youth. This was a full-grown man. Six years older than Kirsty at least – maybe seven. It's too much at her age, she's still a child. You do all your growing up in those first years of freedom. Wait till Eamon sees this.

"We've ordered Indian," says Kirsty and from the way that she flutters, I can see she has it bad. "Want to join us?"

"I've eaten," he says, "but I wouldn't mind a quick coffee."

He glances at his watch. He's one of those swaggery men who knows he's attractive. He is wearing a beautiful jacket.

"Nice jacket," I say, by way of being pleasant.

"Thanks."

"It's a present from me," says Kirsty.

"Really?"

I do my best to sound neutral, but Kirsty immediately goes on the defensive.

"It's a thank-you present for helping me out."

I'd be thanking him with a bottle of wine. This jacket must have cost at least five hundred euro. I don't blink.

"It's very nice."

She knows what I'm thinking.

"*And* it's a birthday present as well."

What's wrong with a book? Aftershave? A good pinking shears? But I hold my tongue. Ross doesn't stay long. He has to get back to the cutting room. I hope Kirsty takes note.

Over beer and a Tikka Masala, she opens up – well, a bit. I don't know if I'm sorry or glad. It seems that Ross is also up for Big Brother. He wants to let the world see his genius, fair enough. And they plan to go into the House as a couple. His idea, of course – I can see how it would increase his chances. Maybe this will wake Eamon up.

While Kirsty goes to the loo I ask Lala what she thinks of Ross. She tries her best to be neutral.

So it's not just me.

EAMON

I get back from Romania wrecked. The changeover in Budapest was a nightmare. Five-hour wait. I need a hot

194

bath, a good steak and onions, and bed.

I am barely in the door when Marian starts on about Kirsty and this fellow Ross. I'm starving. I open a packet of chocolate Kimberley and start eating them.

"Leave it, Marian, it's going to be fine."

"Oh really?" Marian persists. "Will it be fine when she's there on the television having sex in front of the world? Is that what you want?"

"Are you blaming me?"

"You're the one that encourages her, that tells her how great she'd be on TV." She slams out of the room.

How come I'm to blame? All I've ever done is love and protect Kirsty and if Marian doesn't get that then that's her problem. All her life I've done it, since the day she was born…. I'll never forget that day. All those hours waiting. I've never been so nervous in my life. Then the nurse puts her into my arms. The tiny fingers clutching my thumb, that shock of black baby hair. I was hooked. Like a lamp had lit up in my heart.

If anyone's to blame it's this Ross guy. He said they should go as a couple. I'd drive up to Dublin and give him a piece of my mind only I'm knackered. Anyway, she not going to go on television and have sex! Marian always exaggerates.

Just as I'm thinking that, Marian bangs open the door of the kitchen again.

"Your little Princess, having sex at peak viewing time! How does that suit you?"

"Kirsty would never do that."

"Oh really?"

"Leave it Marian, I'm knackered."

She snatches up the packet of Kimberly and throws it at my head. I duck. It falls to the floor and bursts open.

195

"This is not over!" She slams out again.

I leave the biscuits scattered all over the floor, get into the car and drive to the Sheraton in Athlone. I might get some peace there.

KIRSTY

I hate all the waiting. Sometimes I'm sure we'll be picked and I get all excited just thinking about what I'll wear going into the House. I can picture it now, me and Ross, hand in hand, getting out of the limo, talking to Davina McCall, standing on top of the steps, everyone cheering. Other times though, I start having doubts. I hate that, it makes me depressed. I happen to think that when you're feeling down and depressed, the least your boyfriend can do is be there for you. But no. Ross is too busy sewing. He's more concerned about a few yards of cloth than he is about me! It really pisses me off. When he does eventually come round he asks about Mum. Says he liked her. I tell him that the only reason she was in Dublin was to get on my case and how I'm pissed off with her.

"I don't blame her," he says. "She's dead right. You're a spoiled little brat."

That's a joke. He only says that because he knows that we're rich. His mum's a single parent so they're poor. He seems to thinks being poor is somehow better. I don't see why.

"I'm not joking," he says. "You can't keep missing classes, it's stupid. You'll fail your exams. And what are you going to do then?"

"Jesus, you're as bad as my mother," I say.

"If you can't see that your mother is right then you're stupider than I thought."

"You're jealous."

196

"Of what?"

"My dad is rich. You have no dad at all."

That shuts him up. He goes out to the kitchen for water. He comes back, drinks the water in one go, puts the glass down, looks at me.

"Jesus Kirsty," he says, "you really are a *very* stupid cunt."

Nobody calls me that. Nobody.

"*Get out!*"

"Gone already."

"And don't come back."

"I won't."

It is only after he'd left that I remember about Big Brother. This could be awkward. What will we do – assuming we're chosen? But anyway we won't know for sure for weeks yet. He'll come crawling long before then.

EAMON

The presidential suite is nice. Comfortable. Great service plus peace and quiet. I have a lovely long bath with bubbles up to my ears. Just what the doctor ordered. I ring down to room service for a steak and switch on the telly. RTE is showing one of those the-way-we-were programmes. Black and white stuff, some time in the seventies. Holy Christ, it looks grim. And I was alive then! Council workers digging a ditch. My dad was one of them. Jesus.

At ten years of age I was working. Collecting pig slop for Tommy Joe McIntyre's piggery. Girls in school went "oink, oink" and held their noses when I came near them. Silly cows. But Tommy Joe was my inspiration. He lived in a Dallas-style house out the Derrybawn road and I swore that one day I'd live in a house just like that. No Leaving Cert, no college, no nothing. And look at me now! That's why I'm not bothered if Kirsty flunks out of college.

KIRSTY

Mum picks me up at the station. I haven't been looking forward to spending the Easter holidays at home. Why can't Mum just let me live my life the way I want to live it? The traffic is gnarly which suits me fine because Mum doesn't like talking in traffic and I'm in no mood for a chat. But, come the last roundabout, she goes all Miss Marple.

"So, how are you?"

"Fine."

"That doesn't sound fine to me."

"I'm fine."

"Okay."

We drive on in silence. I count the lambs in the fields. There are loads of them.

"So how's Ross?"

"Why don't you ask him?"

"Funnily enough, I don't have him on speed dial."

"Ha, ha, ha, Mum, very funny."

More lambs, a horse with a foal... Ah, that's dotey...

"Have you two had a row?"

I shrug, and tears come into my eyes.

"Oh, I'm sorry."

"No you're not. You hate Ross."

"I don't hate him."

"But you don't like him."

"I never said that."

"You don't have to. So, you'll be happy to know that you were the cause of our row. Why do you always have to keep on at me? You're ruining my life."

Tears burst from my eyes. Mum begins to say something and stops herself and starts her yoga breathing. The tears are hot on my face. She keeps on with her breathing. After a bit, I dry my tears and watch out of the window for horses and foals.

"Last chance, Kirsty," she says, in a nice calm voice. "That's what Mrs Williams said. I'm concerned."

"Well stop being so fucking concerned!"

For a moment I thought she might hit me. Then it passed and she started doing her yoga breathing again.

I look out of the window. Cows. Three little black lambs wagging their tails. So cute. An abandoned car stuffed with rubbish outside a house. Why do people do that? It's so ugly! You'd think that, at least, they could leave it somewhere round the back.

"Your father and I had a row."

So what? More sheep and lambs. Five Charolais cows. Quite pretty for cows...

"Your Daddy's left home."

"What do you mean he's left home?"

"I mean he's left home. He's living in a hotel."

"Did you throw him out?"

"No..."

"I bet you did, you're so mean!"

"I did not throw him out. He just walked."

"Because you were being horrible to him!"

She shrugs. I examine her face. It looks kind of drawn and sad. Oh. My. God. This is serious.

"Are you getting divorced?"

"No we're not, he's just taking a break."

They are. They are getting divorced. My parents are getting divorced. I refuse to believe it and at the same time I know it is true. I don't know what to do. My head is in a whirl. I look out the window and started counting the lambs in the fields again. I count fifteen in one field.

LALA

At the end of term, I still had an essay to finish. Kirsty had gone home. She was clearly in the dumps about her split with Ross, although she was putting a brave face on it. Then Jake arrived, perky as ever, thrilled to be up in Dublin for a whole week before Easter and another one after.

"Martina's coming over for something to eat," he said, before leaving for work. "Is that okay?"

"Kirsty's not here, so of course it's okay. Is she staying the night?"

"We'll probably go back to her place."

"Make love on the rug in front of the fire?"

He grinned and blushed and looked about twelve – so sweet, no wonder girls love him. I was sure they were made for each other, but Martina insisted it was nothing like that. She said they were just friends and that anyway they were too young for commitment, especially Jake. I didn't agree. I thought when you found the right one you ought to hold on tight. Of course they'd got things to do but they could do them together.

I sat down to tackle my essay: "Fear, Loathing and Lear." That was the title. God how I hated it. I had to read Hunter S. Thompson. Vomitorious, as Jake would say, but the Prof. said it was a seminal text. The guys in class loved it. I thought it was vile; just self-indulgent head-wankery. And King Lear was a rough ride as well. They were both about people acting like eejits.

I sat at my laptop and stared up at the bright scuddy sky. I stared down at the cherry tree out in the courtyard. The blossom was taking its time. I felt suspended. My mind was a blank. I stared at the cherry tree some more. Then I had a sharp word with myself.

"They're both about people acting like eejits" – that was

an opening line.

I stayed at it all day until it was finished. It wasn't world-shattering but, with a scattering of the requisite number of Lit.Crit. buzzwords, I reckoned a modest C plus. Maybe even B minus.

"Come and get it," called Jake. The table was laid with daffodils and candles, courtesy of Martina. Jake had made a lasagne. All I had to do was sit and enjoy.

"We're going to Fiddlesticks, later, want to come along?"

I was definitely ready to go out and party.

Tuesday in Fiddlesticks was New Talent night. It was where students went to show off. All the Dram.Soc. crowd went there, all the would-be comedians, the bands, the dance crews. Most of the acts were quite rough-and-ready, but the atmosphere was great. And some day, some of those acts would be famous.

We found a table and ordered drinks. The third act up was a fashion show. The amateur models strutted their stuff. Lady Gaga territory, corsetry, holes in strange places, skirts supported with wire, hairstyles that could do you a damage. Some just looked silly but a couple stood out. We argued about whether fashion could ever be Art. The designers came out to take their bow. Ross was among them. He was wearing the famous jacket and looked sexy as hell.

I thought he'd avoid us but no, he came over.

"So what did you think?"

"Which ones were yours?" I asked, just to annoy him. I knew perfectly well: the two best.

"The black and white polka dot and the chilli red with the forties style peplum."

"Oh yeah. Not bad."

He went back to his fashion college friends. Later, he

201

came over again.

"We're going clubbing," he said. "Want to join us?"

He was looking at me as he said it. It was one of his smouldering looks. Jesus, he was sexy. Something pinged in my stomach. I may have blushed.

"Sure, but I'll have to go home and get changed."

"Don't bother, I'll customise you. You'll look fabulous."

"Okay."

Jake and Martina left soon after that, and Ross brought me back-stage to the "changing room". It was more like a cellar. There were cigarette butts on the floor. Boxes of crisps stacked against a bare wall were the only furniture. There was a broken mirror leaning against them and make-up and accessories strewn on top. The only light was a forty-watt bulb and it was bloody freezing. Ross took a scissors out of his pocket, made a couple of snips in the air. He stood back and looked at me hard, not smouldering this time, assessing. It made me feel shy but excited. I knew he'd do something way out.

"What colour bra are you wearing?'

"An ordinary white one."

"Pity."

"I wasn't planning to show it in public."

He cut off my sleeves and stood back. He cut a slash over my chest and another. He tried out a couple of belts and chose a red one, a waist nipper, boned and shaped like a mini leather corset. He jagged the hem of my t-shirt to show glimpses of skin. How did he do that? I'd lost several tops trying to customise them like that. He back-combed my hair, swirled it into a clip, pulled bits out, primped and sprayed. Then he started the make up. When I finally looked in the mirror I could have easily passed for a member of the Pussycat Dolls.

There's something about knowing you look great that gives you a swagger. I was Queen of the Ball. Got loads of attention. Danced my ass off. And, when they threw us out of the club at three in the morning, Ross offered to walk me back home. It was cold. He put an arm round my shoulder. I had a feeling that something might happen. I wanted to bury my face in his chest. I willed him to make the first move. We stopped in a doorway and kissed. He put his hand on my crotch – I let him. Work the rest out yourself.

I felt a bit bad the next day. I kept having to remind myself that Kirsty and Ross were finished, but there was still no way I could tell Kirsty about it. Or Martina either, as she'd be sure to tell Jake. Not that I wanted to tell anyone. It wasn't like I was after Ross as a boyfriend, Christ no. It was just one of those things.

Then there was Mark. He didn't need to know either. I'd have to end it with him though. It was the right thing to do. I would have done it right then, but he had already gone home to Wexford and the least I could do was finish it face to face. I packed some things and caught the twelve o'clock bus to Athlone. I had the whole of the holidays to work out how I was going to break it off.

CHAPTER 10

KIRSTY

I've been checking my calls, texts, e-mail, Facebook... Nothing. I was sure he'd have made contact by now. He's probably doing this to annoy me. I think about texting a million times but I can't think of anything sarcastic enough. Let him stew. He's the one who should apologise. He never takes my side. Even when my mother sticks in her oar, he sides with her! I'm really pissed off.

EAMON

My dad, God help his wit, thinks five-star hotels are the business. The time I sent him and Ma off to Dubai on a trip, you should've seen the grin on his face.

"It's like being James Bond!" he said.

I'm glad I can do it. Six kids in a labourer's cottage on a labourer's wage! That was no joke. I'm glad he's enjoying the five-star. Me, I hate hotels. Avoid them as much as I can. Whenever I'm working too far away to drive home, I hire the whirlybird. Well worth it in my book. I'm a home boy at heart.

It's the curtains that get me down the most. I don't know why. They are perfectly fine curtains but each day when I wake up, I detest them more. Funny how little things like that get to you.

"I don't like either of you," I say as I jerk them apart.

Broken cloud, dry, not much of a breeze. Good day for building. I do as I do every day, I check my phone diary. Not too bad, a couple of hours in the office then out to the golf course. I'm not much of a hand at the golf but it gives you a walk and fresh air and a chance for some business.

The phone in my hand rings. Marian. I let it ring a couple of times. I've decided to play it cool, as though nothing has happened.

"Hi babe," I say.

"I'm sorry, love." It all comes tumbling out of her. "It's my fault. I shouldn't have hit you with all that stuff about Kirsty. At least not until you'd had a night's sleep. I was worried, that's all."

"That's okay, love."

"Come home, babe, please. I miss you, we all miss you."

"Me too."

Result! I go back to the window and smile at the curtains. Easter coming up. Big church day today. Big church week, washing the feet, purple drapes on the statues, long gospels, renouncing the world, the flesh and the devil. Hocus-pocus I call it. Still, I used to love going to church. Great place to meet girls! Winking at them from the back of the church. Making them laugh. Hanging round after in groups. I often saw Marian then with her sisters, a tight little group, pretending not to notice us. Even back then I fancied her.

The minute I get into work I phone Nunu, that flower shop she likes, and ask them to send her a bouquet. I call Kate. She says, sapphire earrings. I phone Tom Joyce to bike them over. Then, on my way out to lunch, I call into "Shannon Chocolates" and pick out their biggest and fanciest Easter egg.

My old dad's right: I am a lucky son-of-a-gun.

JAKE

A woman comes into the office. Not good-looking exactly, but oodles of oomph. Long legs, high hooked nose, dark eyes, blunt black fringe. Liam goes all goofy and grinny.

"Maya!"

"Hi."

"That's Jake."

"Hi Jake."

"Hi Maya."

She looks straight at me and smiles and I feel ridiculously pleased. Liam shows her some recent takes; he's all of a doo-dah. I've never seen him like this. But I do understand, there is something electric about her.

"We're closing up for the weekend," he says. "Take some time off, relax. Go now if you like."

I can take a hint. I tidy a few things away and head into town. I have time for a coffee before the six o'clock bus.

As the bus rumbles through Leixlip, Maynooth and Kilcock, I think about Maya. There's a divan on the set. She stretches out on it and beckons me with a finger. I try sitting beside her but I keep slipping off so I change scenes and think about Martina instead.

Lech picks me up at the station. Lech's not a talker. We get home in no time. Mum's in the kitchen arranging flowers in a vase. Kirsty's listening to Jenny Elixir on her iPod. I find Dad in the den reading the paper.

"How's she cuttin'?" he asks, like he was never away.

"Grand," I say.

EAMON

I don't like the sound of this Ross chap. Sounds to me like a freak and a weirdo. I want to go straight up to Dublin and tell him to stay away from my family. But Marian says no.

"Use the head, Eamon," she says. "If Kirsty thinks we disapprove, she'll stay with him to spite us. Besides, I don't think it'll last. They're not suited."

Marian is usually right on these things. So I promise to take Kirsty aside and have a serious talk 'cause I know Kirsty listens to me.

With that in mind, I take her to Galway on Saturday. She needs a new riding hat for the Easter Gymkhana. The Easter Gymkhana is a Balfathery tradition. The whole town turns out. People come here from three counties. Rich people on horses, I used to think when I was a kid. Now I know that they're not rich at all. I could buy and sell the lot of them.

We go to Orsini's for lunch. I wait till we've ordered our meal and are sipping a glass of prosecco. I want "the talk" to be over and done with so we can settle down and enjoy our lunch.

"Kirsty," I say, "your Mammy is worried."

"Yes, Daddy," she says.

"Just get through the first year. Okay?"

"I think I might want to do something else."

"You can think about that over the summer. In the meantime, just do your best, love. Will you promise me that?"

"Yes, Daddy."

The lunch was delicious.

LALA

It was storybook perfect, the chestnuts beginning to spread their green hands, swans landing feet first on the river. The whole town was heading to Hannigan's Field for the Easter Gymkhana. I'd always loved the Easter Gymkhana. Before I looked for Kirsty, I did a tour of the show. It was not just horses. There were displays of rare breeds of cattle and sheep, a Fluffiest Rabbit competition, a Cutest Dog competition, a Guess the Weight of the Pig competition, the ICA ladies' cake stall, and countless hippy types selling chunky hand-made jewellery and dangerous-looking soaps.

I spotted a pair of Shire horses. Magnificent beasts, groomed to perfection, so gorgeous I just had to stroke them. They had fetlocks like fluffed feather dusters. I could have stayed there all day, but the tannoy interrupted.

"One two, one two... Would competitors for the Junior Ladies please report to the chief steward?"

I wished I owned a horse. I'd have loved to enter for this competition but all the good horses were booked when I asked at the Paddocks. Kirsty was so lucky to have her own horse. Whispa was everyone's favourite. I found Kirsty in the waiting area, making a last-minute check of her saddle.

"Nervous?" I asked.

"Not really. I know I'm not going to win."

I was surprised to hear Kirsty sound so downbeat.

"You never know."

"I haven't had enough practice. I'll be happy to get to the second round."

The Junior Ladies was two rounds. Only the top ten would get into the second, which was against the clock. A gang of us stood at the rail and cheered when our friends were riding. Kirsty got into the second round with only four faults. The second round killed her though, ten faults – she rushed the fences, trying to make up the time. Still, she got a rosette. I helped her unsaddle.

"I've still heard nothing from Ross," she complained.

I felt a sharp stab of guilt.

MARIAN

Because the Gymkhana is on Easter Sunday, we have the folks over on the Monday – Minnie, Jimmy and my mother as well. Eamon serves drinks and keeps the peace with his parents while I get the dinner together. Kirsty sets the table and Jake helps me out in the kitchen. I have roasted a goose, with my own "special" stuffing, of course, and my own chocolate brownies for afters. Jake looks after the veg. It's the first chance I've had to talk to him. I try to find out what he thinks about Ross – without being too obvious.

Jake doesn't like him.

The goose is perfect, juicy and golden, and the roast spuds are crispy. Everyone eats up and goes for seconds. The stuffing and brownies have everyone smiling. Minnie, as always, wants the recipe.

"So Kirsty," she says. "Tell us about this boyfriend of yours up in Dublin? I hope he's not a smart-aleck Jackeen?"

"No, he's not."

"So when are we going to meet him?"

"Don't mention the war, Gran," says Jake. "Don't mention the war."

"What are you talking about?"

"The boyfriend – they've had a row and it's over."

"Oh, I'm sorry, love."

"It is not!" said Kirsty. "Jake doesn't know what he's talking about, Gran. We had a bit of a row that's all."

"Well, if it isn't, it ought to be," says Jake.

"And what would you know about it?"

"I know that Ross fancies men."

"He does not."

"So why did he try to get me into bed?"

Eamon suddenly comes to attention.

"What's this? Did some dirty shirt-lifter attack you?"

210

"He's not some dirty shirt-lifter, he's Kirsty's ex-boyfriend."

"God, Jake," says Kirsty. "You're soooooo naïve. Don't you get it? Ross was messing with your head and it seems he succeeded."

"Where does this bastard live?" Eamon looks like he is going to explode.

"Chill out, Dad, nothing happened."

"It's a lovely afternoon," I say, getting up out of my seat. "Why don't we go for a walk by the river?"

NANA JO

There was no such thing as homosexuals in Ireland till they brought in the cable television. That's when filth started flooding into this country. I wouldn't have bothered with cable myself, I'm happy enough with just RTE One and Two, but the girls said it would give me a bit more variety. It certainly does that. Sometimes of an evening, after I've said the rosary, I flick through the channels looking for a nice quiz programme or a detective series and I see things that would scorch the eyeballs out of your head.

But then that's the English for you. They're never content. They take our land, rob us blind, treat us like slaves, starve us, exploit us and, when we finally throw them out, they send in the BBC to destroy our religion and give people notions. Of course, they've always held our religion against us.

I lived most of my life not knowing what a homosexual was till Marian explained. I didn't believe it at first but she said that I definitely knew at least one. I asked who he was, but she wouldn't tell me. I wonder does she mean poor Frankie Cregan who, God help us, is not the full shilling. Mind you, when it comes to sex, I'd expect anything off men. They have no control of themselves. Nothing they do would surprise me. Marian also said that there are women like that as well. I said flat out that I didn't believe her. But now I've got the cable, I see them on the telly all the time, bold as brass. I don't think the woman thing happens in Ireland, not yet anyway – though the way things are going, who knows?

MARIAN

I feel my stomach turn over. Not because of Jake, he's a sensible lad – because of Kirsty. When she came back from Galway she'd said she was not feeling great, a bit of a burning sensation. It sounded to me like cystitis. I'd told her to drink lots of water. But if Ross has been playing both sides of the field…

"You did use a condom?" I ask, as we stacked the dishwasher after dinner.

"Of course."

"Every time?"

"Yeah yeah yeah." There is something about the way she turns away from me as she says it.

"I'm taking you to a clinic tomorrow, first thing."

"*Muuuum!*"

I not telling Eamon. Not unless I have to. Meanwhile I try not to show how worried I am.

JAKE

Poor Dad, he is totally freaked! Kirsty has to assure him several times that she definitely doesn't have AIDS. Later, when they've all gone home, he comes to my room for a "serious" talk.

"He didn't try – you know – to convert you?"

"Afraid I'll be doomed to a life of musicals and sparkly

high heels?"

"It's no joking matter."

"They're not the Moonies, Dad."

"Don't be so sure, son. That Ross guy, he didn't do anything – you know – *bad?*"

"No, Dad, he didn't."

"You can tell me, you know. I won't blame you."

"There's nothing to tell."

"They say it's addictive, once you start…"

"Who told you that?"

"Believe me, I know…"

"Is that what you think happened Seán?" He doesn't answer that. I decide to put him out of his misery. "I've a girlfriend, Dad. I see her every time I'm in Dublin."

"Good lad, good lad," he says.

LALA

I told Kirsty, casually, about meeting Ross in Fiddlesticks, in case Jake had said something.

"Did he ask about me?"

"No, he was busy with the show. "

"Was he with someone else?"

"He was with a gang from your college."

I felt terrible saying it. It wasn't exactly a lie but it felt like a lie and I'm not good at lying. I swore to myself there and then, on the spot, that what had happened with Ross would never happen again.

The next day I got a text from Mark. *'We have 2 stop cing each other. I have to study. Xams coming up.'* I felt three parts relief because I didn't have to do the breaking off and seven parts anger because he got to do it instead of me. He must have seen it coming and decided to strike first – *by text!* Because he hadn't had the guts to face me! Stupid bastard.

I finished the article I was writing for *Daedalus*. It was about college hierarchies and was called *"Pecking Order"*. What made you a star or a wallflower, a klingon or merely one of the herd? The types I described were based on real people, but I'd changed it enough to keep people guessing. It was great fun to do and I thought it was funny. I decided to go up to Dublin and put it into Mark's hand. I wanted to see his face. Also I knew he'd be back, studying for his finals. He was hell-bent on getting a first.

I saw him in the library but he didn't see me. I went round the long way so that he wouldn't see me till I sat down in front of him. He didn't look up. I waited. Then he saw me. I pushed the envelope across the table.

"The article you asked me to write."

He nodded and coughed and shuffled his notes.

"So why didn't you tell me face to face?"

He turned bright red and squirmed. I let him.

"Just don't have the guts?" He squirmed a lot more. Then I leaned over the table and said loud enough for people to hear, "And by the way, that so-called poetry you write. It's not deep, it's shite."

I didn't wait to find out what he might say to that.

I went to the Student Union, but there was nobody there that I knew. I went up Grafton Street and into Bewley's. No one there either, they must all have been still at home. I got a coffee and found an Irish Times that someone had left on a seat. I phoned Martina but her mobile was off. I'd done what I'd come up to Dublin to do and now I felt a bit flat. The next couple of days stretched before me with nothing to do but sit in the empty flat. I decided I might as well go back to Balfathery. Half way across Stephen's Green, I ran into Ross.

"What are you doing at the moment?" he asked.

"Nothing much."

"Come down to Murphy Sheedy's with me to look at some fabric?"

Where was the harm?

After that we went back to the flat. What can I say? I wouldn't trust him as far as I'd throw him, but he was kind of addictive.

I once overheard a girl in the ladies' toilet saying that men with small dicks try that much harder. I hadn't seen that many dicks but Ross's was smaller than Mark's. And he did try a lot harder. Which was nice.

KIRSTY

The doctor in the clinic quizzes me up down and sideways and okay, there were a couple of times when we didn't use condoms. She immediately insists on all kinds of tests, including an AIDS test. Oh! My!! *God!!!* Too scary. My brain starts to whirl and, when she whips out the needle for taking blood, I faint. When I come round, she gives me a glass of water.

"There's three rules for sex, Kirsty," she says. "Condoms, condoms and condoms."

She returns to her desk and writes a prescription.

Five days. That's how long I have to wait. That's five whole days with me in a state. What takes them so long? All they have to do is stick it under a microscope. How can that take five days? I swing from thinking everything's fine to "oh God, I'm dead". Every itch, every slight mark on my skin, throws me into a panic. I open the tabloids and headlines jump out at me: "HIV Heroes!" "Condoms are a Girl's Best Friend!" The same when I turn on the telly...

Lala is pissed off with me, I know she is, so I tell her why I'm so upset. She goes mental – but then, Lala is easily shocked. When she calms down, she starts trawling the internet for STD sites. That doesn't help.

LALA

When she told me... Holy shit! I went on the internet. From what I could see I had no symptoms yet but then it often lies dormant, maybe even for years. I went straight to the Well Woman clinic for tests. Fucking Ross! Why the hell did I do it? Okay, I knew why I'd done it.

An A4 envelope arrived in the post. It was from Mark, rejecting *"Pecking Order"* with a scrawl on the cover page, "Not substantive enough." I thought the piece was rather good. But I knew what he was up to. He was punishing me. I thought, *"Okay Mark. It's done. I'm not playing that game."* Besides, I had other things on my mind.

KIRSTY

They phone at last, to say they have the results. *But they won't tell me over the phone.* Oh Jesus, I realise, it's bad news. I'm too scared to find out by myself. I ask Mum to come and she does. We sit in the waiting room, waiting. I stare at the big purple dinosaur on the TV. I go on staring at it until the doctor sticks her head around the door.

"Kirsty?"

I grab Mum by the hand and she gives my fingers a squeeze. We follow the doctor into her office and sit. She fusses for a bit with my file and lifts a number of papers.

"Now, your results." She smiles. Is that good or bad? Mum squeezes my hand. "You're a very lucky girl." Oh thank God, oh thank God, *oh thank God*.

"Hang on, I'm not finished. You're clear for all the biggies – HIV, syphilis – but you do have chlamydia, which is serious as it can cause infertility. However, I think we have caught it early enough so hopefully there'll be no ill effects. Finish those antibiotics I gave you and if you don't see an improvement, come straight back here."

Mum takes me for lunch in the Shelbourne. I am expecting a lecture. She says nothing. And you know something? In a way that's worse.

I'm totally finished with Ross. There's no way now, not even if he comes crawling. But when Big Brother says yes, I will have to deal with him. I'll have to think about that. First though, I need a boost. I decide to have my hair cut. I phone Gregor in Galway to make an appointment.

LALA

Kirsty's results were some relief but still, I couldn't rest easy till I saw my own. Same as Kirsty – chlamydia, which they think they caught early. They gave me the same antibiotics. Anyway I'd learned my lesson. That was me and Ross finished. Never to be mentioned again. I hid my antibiotics in my underwear drawer in case Kirsty saw them.

KIRSTY

Gregor is a genius.

"Why you want cut it?" He fluffs up my hair and tosses it about.

"I broke up with a boyfriend."

"So, you want 'fuck-off' hairstyle. I understand perfect. I been there."

He makes me look totally fierce, Manga heroine style. He changes me from blonde to black and cuts it to look wind-tossed and spiky. I love it. I look in the mirror.

"Don't mess with me babe," says my reflection.

"'Cause you know it will hurt!" I say back.

LALA

Every time I went into the library I saw Mark, but I kept well away. He'd handed *Daedalus* over to his side-kick, that was how serious he was about his exams. His side-kick was a lanky second-year called Paddy. I printed a new cover page for *"Pecking Order"* and left it with him. He loved it! He thought it would get everyone talking.

I told Kirsty about it but I'm not even sure if she heard me. She has a new haircut and she was all business. She'd even started going to class to keep her mum off her back, but in reality there were only two things on her mind. How to style her Big Brother wardrobe, because, as far as she was concerned, Big Brother was a foregone conclusion. And secondly, how to get back at Ross.

She had a plan to sneak into college when no-one was around, and slash Ross's designs. But there were always people around. She even thought about getting me to lower her on a steel cable through the skylight in the dead of night. I declined.

KIRSTY

This haircut has given me confidence, changed how I think. At first I planned to cut up Ross's designs but then I thought, No, that's the old Kirsty. The new Kirsty would do something better. Give him a fright. Make him suffer like I did.

LALA

We were waiting for Ross. He was ten minutes late and Kirsty was pacing the floor.

"Are you sure you don't want me to leave you two together?" I asked, wishing she'd let me go.

"Please stay."

Ross arrived. Kirsty answered the door wearing her mauve off-the-shoulder angora with cerise bra strap showing, great jeans, hair all spiky. His eyes popped.

"You look great!" he said.

For the very first time in her life, Kirsty ignored a compliment.

"I have something to tell you," she said.

She made him sit on the low sofa. She sat opposite on a wooden chair, towering over him. I hunched in the corner on the leather beanbag, trying to blend into the background. Kirsty took a drink from a glass of water. Put the glass down carefully on the table beside her.

"I have a disease," she said. She let that one sink in for a bit. Ross sank into the cushions. "I've been to the doctor and I've had all the tests. " She let that one sink in as well. The silence grew gnarly.

Finally, Ross asked shakily,

"And?"

"I got the disease from you."

"*Me?*" He tried to act indignant.

"I haven't had sex with anyone else. "

"You think I believe that?" Yes he did.

"I don't care Ross. I'm doing you a favour. I'm letting you know I've been tested for AIDS."

"*AIDS?*" Suddenly, Ross looked really concerned. "Did you get the results?"

"Not yet."

"Jesus!" Then he turned to me. "Did you get tested as well?"

Oh *fuck*.

"Why would Lala get tested?"

He was still looking at me,

"You didn't tell her?"

"Tell me what?" asked Kirsty

I opened my mouth but nothing came out. Ross leaned back on the sofa. Then Kirsty got it.

"When did this happen?"

"When you went home for Easter," my voice sounded like an asthmatic crow. "after you and Ross split up…"

Instead of exploding, Kirsty tossed her spiky head in the air like it was nothing.

"Oh, yeah. You're right, it was over by then."

"That's the only reason I…"

Was she okay about it or not? I shut up then and curled up on the beanbag. Kirsty turned back to Ross.

"We need to discuss Big Brother," she said. "I assume you'll still go if you're asked?"

"Sure."

"Here's how it'll be. We'll act as a couple beforehand but, first week in the house, we'll have a big row and break up. Okay?"

"Okay."

"I'll let you know about my results. But you should go get your own tests done."

Ross got up and left, visibly shaken. When Kirsty came back from the door there was a bit of a silence.

"I hope it turns green and falls off," I said, I didn't know what else to say.

"I'm not speaking to you anymore," she said.

"But Kirsty, you said it was over between you and him…"

She didn't reply.

I thought she'd give up on not speaking to me eventually, but she didn't. For the rest of the term I spent most of my waking hours in college revising.

CHAPTER 11

LALA

I decided to wear my new top because I wanted to look my best. *Daedalus* was due out, and my article was in it, so I was all excited. Once I had the magazine in my hands, I planned to go into the library to show it to my friends but really to run into Mark and chant: *Nah-nah-nee-nah-nah!* in his face. Not out loud, just in my head while smiling enigmatically and looking devastatingly gorgeous. Let him see what he was missing.

Kirsty was sitting at the table in the living room, spooning cornflakes into her mouth and reading a copy of Grazia.

"Good morning, Kirsty!" I said.

She ignored me. Was this going to go on for the rest of our lives? I'd already apologised umpteen times. I'd told her I hadn't been trying to steal him, it was just one of those stupid things you did when you'd had drink and a couple of tokes. I'd explained that I'd genuinely thought it was over between them. Was that not enough grovelling? Did she enjoy watching me squirm? I went to the kitchen to make coffee for both of us.

I'd often thought that being around Kirsty twenty-four seven was too much like hard work but since she'd stopped talking to me I couldn't believe how much I missed her. Although she didn't speak to me, I kept on speaking to her. I remarked on the weather. I kept her up to date with my news. I did everything I could think of to get her to talk.

Returning to the living room, I put her coffee on the table beside her and sat down with my own.

"*Daedalus* will be out to day," I said, to start another one-sided conversation. She turned a page of Grazia and started reading an article about the beautiful home of an EastEnders actress. I sipped my coffee. "My article will be in it."

She turned another page and seemed totally absorbed in the photos of the actress and her three labradoodles. Her mobile rang. She picked it up, looked at the screen and leaped to her feet splashing coffee on the floor. She pressed the button to answer.

"Hello?" she said in a small and squeaky voice. As she listened her eyes popped and her jaw dropped. Then she started to scream. And I instantly knew, and jumped up as well.

"Congratulations!" I said when she'd finished the call, "You're going to be a star!"

She gave me a look.

"Are you being sarcastic?"

"God no, Kirsty, I really do think you'll be a star, you have the look, the pizzazz..."

"I have pizzazz?"

"By the cartload."

We stood there feeling awkward for a bit.

"So," I said. "Are we talking again?"

"I suppose."

"You know I'm sorry..."

"I know. And anyway, he's not worth it."

"You're right."

She sat down and took up her bowl of cornflakes again, but she was too excited to eat it.

"What am I going to wear for my entrance into the House? And what clothes will I bring in with me? It's been driving me crazy, I can't make up my mind."

"Can I help?"

"Would you?"

She dashed into her room and came back with an armful of clothes. Most of them were new and still had the labels. I had been looking forward to my victory lap around the library, but I stayed. I owed her that much. She tried on several dresses including a silver one that I thought looked great.

"That's the dress for your big entrance," I said. "Are you still going in as a couple with…?"

"Bastard," she said. "He got away far too lightly."

"I bet he had a few sleepless nights though."

"It's not enough. Once we're in the House I want to do something that makes him look really stupid. Any ideas?"

"Go easy on that, Kirsty. You never know what the papers will make of it, especially if you guys have just staged a break-up on screen."

I stayed while she tried on a million different outfits and I gave my candid opinion. It was just like the old days. We made carbonara for lunch and I reminded her about *Daedalus – and she asked me to get her a copy!*

I got in to college too late in the afternoon and searched the library. No sign of Mark. Pity. But I found Paddy. He instantly closed his notes and said he was ready for a break.

"You've caused a bit of a stir," he said, taking a copy of the magazine out of his rucksack and handing it over. "Page seventeen."

And there it was: *"Pecking Order"* by Alanna Bergin. It looked great, ten times better than I remembered. Print made it seem more important, like my words were words to be reckoned with. On our way to the Buttery, Paddy said,

"We're almost sold out. That's a first. And it's all because of your article. It's the talk of the college. Well done. Great social satire."

I'd thought my article was just a bit of a laugh, but he thought it was social satire! I was thrilled.

"Mark's not pleased though," he laughed. "He was furious with me for publishing it and he's jealous as hell that we've sold so many copies. Apparently I'm 'pandering to populist sentiment'. What an eejit! He should try taking his head out of his arse."

For a week I was famous in college. People came up to congratulate me – people who wouldn't have looked my direction before! And everyone wanted to know who was being lampooned. Several were certain they knew and mentioned some names but I refused to confirm or deny. It was fun.

I sent a copy home to my mother even though I knew what she'd do with it. She'd put it on the coffee table in the sitting room to show off to relations and friends. Embarrassing. But hey, I wasn't there and it if it gave her a kick... When she was sure that everyone had seen it, she would stash it away in her old boarding-school trunk, the museum of all my achievements.

MARIAN

Kate and I are in Gregor's in Galway having our roots done. Gregor is blow-drying my hair and telling me about his holiday in the Canaries when my mobile rings. It is Kirsty.

"Mum. Brilliant news but I can't tell you over the phone!

224

I'll be on the first bus to morrow. Can you pick me up?"

Damn, blast and bugger. She's been called for Big Brother. May the curse of the crows be upon them.

I lie in bed that night making fantasy plans to kidnap her and lock her up somewhere to keep her from harm. I've seen Big Brother, I know what happens. After the first couple of days, people forget about the cameras. They forget about being on their best behaviour and start acting normal. And I know my Kirsty, if somebody gets on her wick she'll throw a wobbler. The viewers will love it, Big Brother will love it – but can you imagine the headlines? Then there's the photos they'll dig up from her friends. The kiss-and-tell stories... I fear for my daughter. I really, really do.

KIRSTY

Mum and Dad are great. They bring me out for a meal to celebrate. I keep waiting for Mum to give me a lecture, but she doesn't.

"We're so proud of you, Kirsty," she says. "I remember the day you were born. When they handed you to me I thought my heart would burst out of my chest with the love, you were so perfect. And look at you now, all grown up, intelligent, talented, beautiful… You've no idea how proud you make us."

Dad nods and pats my shoulder. He has tears in his eyes. So have I. Mum gives me a box. Inside there's a silver bracelet, plain but classy. Engraved in beautiful writing are the words: "Intelligent. Talented. Beautiful." The tears spill down my face.

"I love it!" I sniffle, dabbing them away.

Dad raises his glass.

"To success in the Big Brother House."

The three of us drink to that.

EAMON

Marian is terrific. I know how she feels but she hasn't said a cross word. She is lovely to Kirsty. My steak is perfect, the wine is top class and everything is sweet as Lamb's Jam till the coffee arrives. That's when I discover that Kirsty is going to the Big Brother House with that fucking shirt-lifter. And there is Marian, acting like nothing is wrong. Jesus.

I've met freaks like him before, perverts that swing both ways – well, I won't have him swinging his thing near my daughter. I don't know how I do it but I keep my trap shut till Kirsty goes out to the ladies.

"I thought you said it was over," I say to Marian.

"It is."

"Obviously not."

"How many times do I have to remind you, they were picked because they're a couple so they have to go in as a couple."

"Will they be sharing a room?"

"Oh Eamon, everyone shares the same room in Big Brother."

"And you're okay with that?"

"Don't worry love, I trust her on this one."

"It's not her I don't trust."

KIRSTY

I'm glad I've made it up with Lala. It was so hard not to talk to her. I kept wanting to tell her things and having to stop my self and that takes a lot of energy. Now I'm free to concentrate on how I'm going to get back at Ross because I'm not finished with him, not by a long chalk. I want to spit in his big Don Juan eyes. I want to smash his face with my fist. I want to tear up his dresses and set his collection on fire. But Mum made me promise I'd do nothing stupid.

"Revenge," Dad always says, "is a dish best served cold."

I take pen and paper and write: *"Cold Revenge"* in the middle and draw a circle around the words. I sit back and think, then I write:

Post a photo of Ross on Facebook with the caption: This man has the pox. Destroy stuff/his customised clothes/his collection. Tell his mum something he wouldn't want her to know…. Do something when we get to Big Brother… what? Beat him to a pulp/kill him but I'd end up in prison….

Then I have an idea. I search through all my handbags and find the receipt. I pour Parazone into a Ballygowan water bottle and put it into my bag. I put on my new, silk, Pucci-print top over skinny black jeans and go straight into college. My plan is to find him, then, while chatting to him, casually take out the bottle like I want a drink. Then I'll pour the Parazone over the jacket. Yes, that jacket, the one I bought him. The one that makes him look "film-star cool" as one of the girls in my class told him. And if he kicks up I have the receipt. Technically, the jacket is mine. I paid for it with my credit card.

But when I get to college I can't find him. Instead, I find Mrs Williams who brings me into her office and reads me the riot act for missing classes. As if I haven't enough on my mind.

When I get home, Dad phones to see how I am and before I know it I am telling him what happened.

"There's only one thing you can do," he says. "Draw a line and get on with your life."

He's right. I have to think of the future. I refuse to look back. But I'm not quite ready yet to draw that line. I get out my computer and I type: *"Ross Fahy is spreading disease.*

He has sex with men, women and trannies and he won't use a condom. He has infected several people already." I print it out, stuff it in an envelope, address it to Ross's mother and set it aside to post. But then I have an even better idea. Once that's done, I can draw the line.

LALA

Big surprise! Kirsty took her exams! And she thought she did well enough on the theory. She knew she'd failed the practical, but she didn't care. She was going to be on Big Brother! I was the only one who knew except for her Mum and Dad and Jake. She made me swear on my life I'd tell no one. I wouldn't, of course. If a contestant's name came out before the show started, BB would dump them.

Marian and Eamon came up to Dublin to see her off. They brought us both out to dinner the night before. Next morning, there were the usual Kirsty dramas and last minute panics before the taxi arrived and we all trooped down to the lobby. Ross was standing by the back door of the taxi and for once he failed to look cool. He nodded at Kirsty. She nodded back. The taxi-man put her suitcase in the boot. Marian was sniffling and dabbing her eyes but Eamon was smiling. Ross held the door while Kirsty got in the back. The door closed and we waved them away.

KIRSTY

It's all very hush-hush. When we get to the airport we have to wait at the end of aisle ten for a contact, who turns out to be a woman in a dark business suit with a clipboard. She makes us hand over our phones, and anything else you could contact the world with.

"From now on," she says, "you're in the Big Brother Bubble."

The Big Brother Bubble! *Eeeeeeeeek!*

She hustles us through security and down to the Ryanair flights. We're flying budget! I've never flown budget before. Is it even safe?

"Of course it is safe," snaps Ross. "I've done it loads of times."

The flight goes to Charleroi. That's in Belgium. I assume we'll be changing planes there, to go some place you can't fly direct to from Ireland. Maybe Morocco. But when we arrive in Charleroi we are ushered into a car.

Belgium is boring, like being in a dentist's waiting room. We aren't even staying in Brussels! They stick us in some god-forsaken seaside resort in a third-rate hotel. The kind you'd expect a minor eurocrat to pick for a dirty weekend.

Ross is civil enough. I don't ask whether he's gone to a clinic and he doesn't tell. We explore the town; it doesn't take long. We eat frites with mayonnaise and waffles with aerosol cream. Ross has brought playing cards and Scrabble and we play them for hours. This is an awesome opportunity for both of us so neither of us want to wreck it. We talk about how we will act going in. We practice our walk up the steps, how we'll turn at the door of the House and wave to the crowd. We remind each other that we might be booed by the crowd. Everyone gets booed, especially the really cool people like us.

They bring us our Big Brother suitcases and give us a list of all the things that are forbidden: books, paper, notebooks, anything electronic, games, paint... you're not even allowed bring your knitting! All you have in the House is yourself and your housemates. I am excited and nervous. Both of us are.

The hotel breakfast is crap: cheese, cold meats, tepid coffee. But our next breakfast will be in the House!

JAKE

Dad is hilarious. He needs so much reassurance. He comes to my room and leans on the doorpost making small talk... blah, blah, blah. What does he want?

"That Ross guy..."

"*Daaaaaaad!* How many times do I have to tell you I don't want to walk on the wild side?"

"Yeah, yeah, I know. I just wondered if you had any photos of him."

"What for?"

"Nothing. I just want to remember his face."

"What *for?*"

"I just want to, okay?"

"Okay, Dad, chill."

I show him a couple of shots on my laptop. He stares at them for a bit and grunts like a silverback male, protecting his troop. He forwards a couple of pictures to himself. Any moment now he'll thump his chest and roar.

EAMON

I make sure the envelope is properly sealed. I don't want anything essential lost on the way. I have copies of course, but still. Then I phone Terry Foley. Terry edits Ireland's premier gutter press.

"Eamon Kerrigan here. I've a little something here that might be of interest to you."

"Can you give me a hint?"

"No hints, no clues. I'll have it biked over."

"Dad?" Jake is standing at the door of the den. How long has he been there?

"Yes, son?"

"You know she'll never speak to you again."

"I don't know what you're talking about."

"Are you thinking of leaking Ross's name to the papers?"

How did he know?

"I'm protecting my daughter."

"You think he'll take that lying down? If he gets kicked out he's sure to blame Kirsty and how do you think he'll retaliate?"

That lad's so sharp that one day he'll cut himself. Measure twice and cut once. That's what Marian says when she thinks I'm going off half-cocked. She's right. Sometimes I don't think things through, especially when it comes to protecting my family. The more I think about what Jake has said, the more I realise I could ruin Kirsty's chances. I wouldn't do that for the world.

CHAPTER 12

KIRSTY

They fly us to London, EasyJet this time, and bring us to a hotel. I am so excited I can hardly stay still. I decide I need a long hot bath with plenty of suds and a final exfoliation. I leave Ross watching Spongebob Squarepants on the telly. The hair and make up people arrive at six and the limo will pick us up at eight.

I wear my Hervé Leger silver-sequinned, off the shoulder, bandage dress, lots of fake tan, silver torc, silver bracelet, silver Manolos. Hair and make up, fierce. Now I am ready to rumble. I spend the next twenty minutes pacing the floor.

Knock, knock, knock on the door.

Deep breath.

Showtime!

MARIAN

My heart is in my mouth as we sit down to watch. I am sure something awful is going to happen. I don't quite know what. Kirsty and that bastard Ross are the eighth to enter the House. Kirsty looks great and, if I didn't know better, I'd be saying how they made a beautiful couple. They answer Davina McCall's questions with pleasantries

233

and run up the stairs to the House hand in hand.

Eamon starts to splutter.

"Relax love," I soothe him. "I know they're holding hands but it's only for show."

Once they get inside and Ross lets her hand go and they start talking to the other contestants, Eamon relaxes.

"Does she knows that we're watching?" he asks.

"Of course."

"Good."

LALA

I was curious to see what was going to happen. I knew they'd planned to have a row and split up on screen once the first vote was over but Kirsty was going to do something else. She'd hinted at it but all she'd say was that she'd play it by ear.

The first person to go was the health freak girl who kept going on about mung beans. She got nominated because the housemates were afraid she'd hijack the weekly shopping and the viewers voted her off because she was boring.

It was getting time for Kirsty and Ross to have their fake row. I watched Ross flirting with everyone. I watched the other girls batting their eyelids and making up to him. That was part of the plan. Kirsty was supposed to discover him flirting, and start a row. But that didn't happen. And it wasn't because Ross didn't try. He was outrageous – so bad that everyone gossiped about it and some of the girls reported it back to Kirsty. She shrugged it off.

Nomination Day arrived, the day when the housemates go to the Diary Room to nominate who would be next to face the public vote. Everyone in the house was awake and up. Kirsty was in the kitchen making tea for herself. Ross sat on the sofa eating toast. One of the girls brought her cornflakes over to join him. She leaned over to brush something off his cheek.

"Bit of fluff," she said.

"I left it there specially," grinned Ross.

"I'll be your de-fluffer any time!" she smirked.

"How about my fluffer?" The two of them laughed.

"Oh you are awful!" She gave him a mock slap on the wrist.

"But you like it!"

"Depends… What kind of a lover are you?"

That was the thing with Big Brother, all they ever talked about was sex. Maybe they were all so sex-deprived that talking was the nearest they could get to it. Anyway, Ross batted his baby blues.

"I'm a generous lover," he said. "I like to take my time, give my lady what she wants."

"Most guys just want what they want and then it's all over."

"Not me, babe."

At that point, Kirsty joined them with her cup of tea.

"Is that true Kirsty?" asked the girl. "Is he a generous lover?"

"Oh yeah, he's generous all right." replied Kirsty. "He likes to share his dick around. Men… women… He doesn't mind and he'll give you all the STDs you like."

The girl stared.

"STD… *What?*"

Ross was speechless. Just like the time Kirsty told him he might have AIDS.

"Sexually Transmitted Diseases," said Kirsty, articulating the words loud and clear. The other housemates drifted over, all ears. "He has them, and he's happy to share them. He shared them with me AND my best friend."

Ross by this time had recovered himself enough to jump to his feet and face her.

"What the fuck are you saying?"

Kirsty turned to the rest of the group.

"Ross doesn't use condoms. Not because he's selfish, it's all to heighten your pleasure. Except then you find yourself in a clinic getting tested for AIDS. But I still don't know if he ever got himself tested."

She turned on her heel and went out to the garden. Ross ran after her and dragged her round by the arm. The force knocked the cup out of her hand. He raised his hand to hit her but one of the other guys held him back. He screamed all kinds of abuse and called her all the vilest names you could think of.

Later that day, he was called to the Diary Room and sent home.

Later they called Kirsty to the Diary Room to see if she was all right. She was more than all right. She was glowing.

JAKE

Even though you know Big Brother is stupid and you think the housemates are awful, you still get pulled in. I think it's because you're wondering how you'd deal with all the stuff that goes on. Would you lose the head? Would you be the voice of reason? Would you put up with the crap? Would you stand up to bullies? You always hope you'd be the sensible one. But the rest of the time I think you'd be bored.

Now that Ross has been evicted, I can see Kirsty getting bored. I'm sure Big Brother is disappointed. The row has made headlines in all the papers. I bet they are hoping for even more drama. But mostly she lies around and yawns. Not very long into the series, she goes to the Diary Room and announces she wants to leave. It doesn't surprise me. Kirsty has a low boredom threshold.

LALA

She left, because she was bored. So no agents came running, no Red Carpet invites plopped through the letterbox. That was it for Big Brother. Kirsty insisted that the only reason she went into the house was to get back at Ross. Mission accomplished. She was drawing a line under that and getting on with her life.

Marian, clearly relieved, suggested that she, Kate, Kirsty and me take a "girly" trip to Marbella.

I always loved it when we went to Marbella. The Kerrigans have an amazing house there. Me and Kirsty could do our own thing or hang out with Kate and her mum. Mostly me and Kirsty spent the morning on the beach, getting a tan. When we were younger we used to flirt with the local boys. It was the dark eyes that did it and the accents and the fact that Spanish boys said what every girl wanted to hear: "You are soooo beautiful." "You are soooo sexy." "You have captured my heart with your eyes." Irish fellas are no good at that stuff.

But then you discover your dark-eyed Spanish boy is going out with three other girls besides you! These days, we stick to the tourists.

A couple of London lads chatted us up. They recognised Kirsty from Big Brother. They were fairly good craic until they got maggoty drunk.

"Get your tits out for the lads," they chanted.

We refused. They moved on. We were not devastated.

Then we met the Dutch guys but God, they were dull. It was more fun going to El Molino Azul with Marian and Kate.

El Molino is very trendy. Marian and Kate would get tiddly on cava and flirt with the waiters in Spanglish. Kirsty was mortified, I thought it was gas. Flamenco dancers come out with their castanets and their heel-stomping and chose guests to join in. They picked Kirsty and put her in a costume. She hammed it up at a fierce rate. The audience cheered. Kirsty took several bows.

"God, I love being on stage," she announced afterwards.

"Sure you're never off it!" said Marian.

"It's because I'm a natural actor." says Kirsty. "How do you think I got through Big Brother? Right up to the row with Ross, that was acting. Afterwards it got me thinking. I should be an actor. So I've decided. I'm leaving Stella College and applying for the Gaiety School of Acting."

"Sure, off you go," laughed Marian, quaffing more cava.

"I'm serious, Mum."

"What about your fashion design?"

"Dullesville."

"Well let me tell you, madam…"

Kate gave me a nudge.

"Bathroom," she murmured, "come on."

I followed her out, a little surprised.

"Mothers and daughters, Lala," she said. "Never take sides."

She took her time combing her hair and applying fresh lipstick and, by the time we got back, Kirsty was starting in drama school in September.

JAKE

The last time Kirsty was on stage, she was an angel in the nativity play in High Babies. Her wings fell off and she cried. I was too small to remember but Dad has it on video.

"Why acting?" I ask.

"It's useful."

"So you're aiming for Hollywood then?"

"Get real Jake. Open your eyes. Every presenter on television has been to drama school, and every Celeb. You learn loads there. How to pose. Which is your best side. How to present yourself on camera. How to do interviews. That's why it's useful."

Dream on Kirsty. Dream on.

I'm starting college and I can't wait. I'm going to the Ballyfermot Film School. Liam lectures there sometimes and he said it's the best. I'll be living in Dublin and sharing the apartment with Kirsty and Lala.

My project over the summer has been to train my gut instinct. I'm trying to learn how to identify faces that light up the screen. It's something Liam can see instantly. Some people look great on camera, others don't. At first I thought it was to do with good looks but it isn't. Then I thought it was camera technique but it isn't that either. Liam said there's no rule, you just have to go with your gut. So that's why I'm training my gut. When I see a face that strikes me I ask can I take a couple of photos and then I can check if I'm right. So far I'm right about half the time.

So what better place to go looking for faces than Open Day in the Merry Andrew Academy of Acting? It's Kirsty's new school. She didn't get in to the Gaiety.

I'm in the living room ready to leave but Kirsty decides she doesn't like the top that she's wearing and just has to change.

"Hurry up or we'll miss the whole thing," I call.

Twenty minutes later she's ready.

Mrs Cunningham is the principal of the school but she's not into drama herself. She runs the business end and, from the look of the place, it's a very good business. The Leeson Street basement is a cool, tasteful reception area in neutral colours and natural wood. An arrangement of lilies and roses sits at the end of the counter and the walls are hung with black-and-white blow-ups of famous Irish actors. I don't think they're past pupils, or if they are, their names are not in the brochures and Mrs Cunningham is not the type to miss a trick like that.

The school proper is in the converted mews at the back. It's a light airy space with a proper stage. Parents and pupils mill around the teachers who sit under signs that say 'drama', 'speech', 'presentation', 'television', 'stagecraft'. I leave Kirsty to do her own thing and start taking photos. There's no shortage of people willing to pose. They all want the photos for their "books". I promise to e-mail them to the school.

"Who are the most famous past pupils?" I ask each aspiring actor as I snap them.

They name two. One got a part in Fair City, the other won Stargazers two years ago.

Mrs Cunningham gets up on the stage to introduce the final year students. They do *All That Jazz* from *Chicago*. I don't think Broadway will be beating their doors down.

On the way back to the flat, Kirsty is all excited.

"They do two shows a year," she says. "And they invite all the agents and the TV casting directors."

"Yeah, but do they come?"

"Ha ha, very funny. "

"Did you ask?"

She ignores the question.

"They're not just looking for actors you know, they're looking to spot presenters, game show hosts, all kinds of things."

"And if nobody spots you?"

"I have a plan B."

She won't say what it is.

EAMON

I was beginning to think we'd have to bomb the Town Hall to get a decision. It's the same everywhere – the locals object at first and kick up a fuss then a few bob in the right pockets does wonders. But this lot is getting greedy, so I've just been over there threatening to pull out of Carpathi Castle. That will have them leppin' on board pretty smartish.

We should have it ready for autumn. We've poached the sales manager from the Prince Rudolf in Heidelberg. Turned the old Prince from failing grandeur to a top-notch seven-star, sales up eighty percent. Plus, he's Romanian. He already has the gun clubs of Germany, Italy and Spain excited.

Now we're looking at Ohrid. Little town in Macedonia – lake, mountains, lots of outdoor stuff. Ohrid pearls for the ladies – don't ask me, it's something they make out of fish-scales – and for the culture vultures, they're up the yazoo with icons and Orthodox churches. Colm is over there now doing a recce. Me, I'll have a word about finance with the bank, then I'm off to Old Trafford.

Me and the lads have leased a small private jet we call The Monkey Wrench – what else? It's a legitimate business expense but it's handy as well for going to Old Trafford. We're lifelong fans of Man U. My dad too, he comes as well. When I gave him life membership for his sixtieth birthday he actually cried. That's how much he loves the Red Devils. He adores being in the executive box – another legitimate business expense – and the first time he met Alex Ferguson he was tongue-tied. Probably for the first time in his life! Jake used to love coming to matches but he spends his weekends nowadays working for that photographer fellow.

Kirsty has never been a fan so imagine my surprise

when she asks if she and Lala can join us! I'll make sure she meets the TV people. I've said it before and I'll say it again – Kirsty would be great on TV. I'm glad she's changed college courses. But it's not what you know in the old TV game, it's who you know. And I've got hold of a few names who can help her.

LALA

Kirsty took to going to football matches with her dad, claiming a new-found passion for Manchester United's sporting achievements. He was thrilled, of course. I was too, to be honest, because I got taken along for the ride – in the luxury private jet!

When I was a kid I used to think that being a WAG would be cool. Then I got sense. Kirsty, it seemed, still thought it would be cool. We always stayed over on Saturday night and went out clubbing to the places where footballers go. The clubs weren't really my scene, too much hair gel for me, too many tattoos and I liked my conversations to cover more than your favourite Xbox characters, your wicked motor, the "toons" you've downloaded, your super-cool iPod and your monumental ego! But everything's grist to the mill for a writer.

We met a lot of guys from the first and second divisions. But these, according to Kirsty, were a Lower Form of Life. She had her eye on the Premiership. She was looking for a player from one of the top four teams – a true star. Someone, I supposed, whose super-cool iPod was studded with diamonds.

FERGUS

Half of Ireland is in the hotel, all of them wearing red shirts and all of them celebrating the extra-time goal. 2-1 against

Chelsea. *Come on you Reds!* By midnight the bar is rocking. Even that little scut Pedro for once isn't whining at Seán to leave. Eamon's dad is standing on a table leading a rowdy chorus:

"U-ni-ted, U-ni-ted,
United are the team for me.
With a knick-knack-paddy-whack-give-a-dog-a-bone,
Why don't Chelsea fuck off home?"

"Once more boys," he roars. "Why don't Chelsea fuck off home?"

He loves acting as general MC, cracking jokes, flirting with women and generally behaving the way only a man whose wife is at home can behave.

"There's the girls," declares Eamon, pointing to the door and waving. Kirsty and Lala come into the bar, dressed in their finery. Eamon is mildly etiolated, nothing he can't handle, but he is getting effusive. We all budge up on the sofas to let them sit down.

"I thought ye were off gallivanting," says Eamon.

"Someone started a fight so, we decided to leave," says Kirsty.

"What did I tell you?" Eamon declares, every inch the proud daddy. "My Kirsty is sound as a pound!"

Yeah, right.

He beckons to Cristos and orders more drinks. Cristos brings them in seconds. Market forces. We look after him, he looks after us. The Columbian scut is slumped in his seat with a pout on his gob, because Seán is chatting to the girls. Christ almighty, grow up! When he's is out on the town, Pedro likes his company exclusively male. The gas thing is, in Fiesta! Fiesta! he's all Latin charm and baby seal eyes. And I hear that for a consideration, some lady customers get a much better service than others! Seán on the other hand is Mr Faithful and True so I don't know what Pedro's complaining about.

I happen to glance towards the door and there, striking a pose at the top of the steps that lead down to the bar, stands Tracey. Men are openly staring, one guy gawking so hard that he falls off his barstool. She looks awesome. Hair stylishly tossed, carnivorous eyes, fetish heels, and her fabulous, fabulous, tiger- skin coat. And yes, it is real tiger skin. She had it made in Bangkok. Very eco-unfriendly. She wears it on special occasions and, when she does, the future of tigers is the least of your worries.

KIRSTY

Tracey's coat! Oh! My!! God!!! Pure Russian Princess and totally fierce. Yes Lala, I know, not "politically correct", but Tracey's coat is completely bodacious. She looks like at star at the top of those steps. That's the way I want to look.

"Is it real?" asks Lala.

"Definitely." I can spot a faux-fur a mile off.

"But they're endangered!"

What can you do? This tiger is long dead by now.

FERGUS

She spots us and waves. I wave back. Then she punches the air with her fist.

"U-ni-ted, U-ni-ted," she chants and every man in the room chants back:

"United are the team for me.

With a knick-knack-paddy-whack-give-a-dog-a-bone,

Why don't Chelsea fuck off home?"

Then she stalks through the cheering crowd like she's on a catwalk. I don't understand, I thought she had business in Dublin. She flings off the coat, takes my head in her hands and plants a big, soft kiss on my lips. She runs a nail down the front of my shirt.

"You look fabulous darling," I choke.

"Thanks, sweetie."

I catch Cristos's eye and order a gimlet for her. The room is vibrating with envy. She sits on the sofa beside me. I stroke the back of her neck – it's one of her hot spots.

"What a lovely surprise."

"Bit of business."

"Went well?"

"So well I got you a present."

"Oh honey, you shouldn't." I mean it.

She dives into her huge leather handbag and brings out a box which she tosses in my lap. It might be chocolates but I know that it isn't.

"Aren't you going to open it?" asks Kirsty.

"No, Kirsty, I'm not."

"Why not, darling?" grins Tracey.

"I suspect that it's something quite naughty."

Tracey giggles and runs her hand up the inside of my thigh.

Kirsty backs off.

Even before she has finished her drink, Tracey is yawning and wriggling her shoulders. She can even make yawning look sexy.

"Tired, love?"

"It's been a long day." She stands up and stretches. A long, slow, luxurious stretch.

"I suppose there's no chance of a ride?" some bozo shouts.

Tracey put her hands on her hips and stares.

"Wanna try?"

He buries his face in his pint.

"Come on, big boy," she says, taking my hand. "Time for beddy-byes."

It's going to be wild.

KIRSTY

I stretch out my hand and stroke the coat. It is thick and gorgeously soft. First chance I get I'm going to ask Tracey if I can try it on. I'm sure it would suit me.

Lala strokes it as well.

"That's not any old tiger," she whispers. "I think it's Siberian."

"So?"

"There's only a few of them left."

"Can you raise it from the dead?"

"No..."

"Well then."

Before I get the chance to ask, Tracey is gone off with Fergus.

An hour or so later I'm beginning to feel that there's only so many times I can cheer for United. When we finish our drinks, me and Lala go up to bed. I brush my teeth and am about to strip off when I remember my coat. I've been so busy thinking of Tracy's, I've left my own in the bar. It's Stella McCartney, so I have to go down and collect it. The lift takes ages to arrive. I'm thinking of taking the stairs and then it comes. The doors swish open and there, with her tiger coat over her arm, stands Tracey. This is my chance.

"Hi, babycakes," she says.

"I'm loving your coat."

"I saw you stroking it before. Want to try it on?"

It is bliss. I look at myself in the lift mirror. Oh! My!! God!!! Stunning! Totally fierce! We reach the ground floor.

The lift doors open and sadly, I have to give back the coat. Tracey slings it over her shoulders and takes out her mobile.

"Thanks for letting me try it," I say, but I don't think she hears me.

I collect my Stella McCartney, which is very nice.

But it's not tiger skin.

LALA

Two things I've always hated about hotels. The curtains let in no chink of light, so when you wake up you never know if it is morning or not. And secondly, if you forget to turn down the heat before you go to bed, you wake up in a lather of sweat.

We'd forgotten to turn down the heat. I wiped the sweat from my neck with the sheet and tried to judge the time by closing my eyes and seeing if I felt that my body needed more sleep. I wasn't sure. I got up and peeped through the curtains. It was cloudy and grey but the sky was light and, this being November, it had to be time to get up. I pulled back the net curtains and opened the window a crack.

Our room had a view of the forecourt. I could see a silver Range Rover that was parked baw-ways beside a sign that said "Parking at Rear". Several policemen were standing around it and, just like you see on the telly, a man in a white plastic jump-suit and mask was examining the inside. I watched but nothing much happened. The policemen looked bored.

"What's up?" mumbled Kirsty, stretching.

"The police are outside."

The one thing I *adore* about hotels is the buffet breakfasts, especially in five-star hotels. They have things you never get anywhere else, like fresh mango, kedgeree, eggs Benedict, mini doughnuts. I *love* mini doughnuts. We piled up our plates and sat down. There was no sign of the men. The hotel manager came to ask if everything was all right. We asked for more toast. He sent a boy for it.

"A car was abandoned last night in our forecourt," he said. "The police believe that it may have been used in a crime so they wish to speak to all our guests. I hope this won't inconvenience you, ladies."

"Hey Kirsty," I said when he'd left, "this could be your chance to be famous. You could be witness in a high profile case with your photo all over the papers."

"Ha ha, very funny," she said.

FERGUS

I wake suddenly. It is one of those "where-the-fuck-am-I?" moments. The light is still on. Then I remember.

Tiger-coat sex is the best, better than make-up sex. Images race through my head. If I know Tracey, she'll be ready for more. But when I stretch out my hand the bed beside me is empty.

"Tracey?" I call.

No answer. I glance round the room. The tiger-skin coat is gone. That's Tracey for you. Oh well. You take what you get and you're grateful. I turn off the light and lie down to sleep but something scratches at the back of my mind. The present. I turn the light on again.

When Tracey threw it into my lap in the bar my first thought was, it's a gun! But Tracey's not stupid. If she had a gun to get rid of, she'd make sure I knew nothing about it. On the other hand, Tracey gets her kicks out of walking the edge. That's the difference between me and her. I have a line beyond which… But she seems to have none.

It is a shiny-red gift-box, tied with a fancy gold ribbon. I tear off the ribbon and lift the lid. It isn't a gun. Whew.

I'd scared myself shitless for nothing. It is... Well, it is a present, just like she said. And a very nice present indeed. Let's just say it isn't pan pipes and it isn't a poncho. I put the lid back and slip it into the special compartment I have in my bag. I lie down and conjure up Tracey again and, eventually, sleep like a log.

When I go down to breakfast, a couple of policemen are waiting in the foyer.

"Something up?" I ask.

"We're investigating a stolen vehicle, sir. Do you mind if we ask you a few questions?"

The police take me into a room and quiz me up, down and sideways. Fortunately, I am able to account for every second since I left Dublin yesterday morning and I assure them I have witnesses. Then they ask about Tracey's movements. It's at times like this that I'm glad I know nothing. She's had brushes with the law before but she's never been charged. Oh Tracey, I think, what have you done now?

LALA

It was one of those rooms with a large oval table that they hire out for meetings. The two detectives sat facing the door.

"Good Morning, Ms...?" He had one of those bland English faces that's hard to remember.

"Alanna Bergin."

"Ms Bergin. I'm Detective Weames. This is Detective Whittle."

Detective Whittle had a broken nose and his head was shaved. He would have looked tough if he hadn't spent most of the time blowing his nose into a hanky.

"Head cold," he said, by way of apology.

I was surprised at how nervous I was. I didn't know why, I had nothing to hide.

"We're investigating a crime, Ms Bergin so we have to be thorough. I hope you'll bear with us."

I did my best to look relaxed, but scenes from the cop shows teemed through my head: crooked cops, evil perps, witnesses framed, innocent people sent down. At the same time, it was kind of exciting and a useful experience for a writer. *Why had I travelled to Manchester? What had I done since I arrived? Who was in the group? Who joined the group?* And on and on. It stopped being exciting quite soon.

Kirsty's interview was apparently much the same.

EAMON

My head is thumping so I go for the cure. Several gallons of OJ, rashers, eggs, sausages, beans, tomatoes, toast, strong black coffee and a couple of aspirins. It works every time. At least by the time I face the police, I am able to think.

"Tracey's mad as a box of babies," I tell them. "Crazy, bonkers, apt to go off at half-cock."

There's not much else to say. If they pin something on her and put her away I won't lose sleep. Fergus will be far better off without her.

It's after midday before we get the all clear, so we miss our time slot at the airport. We finally get off the ground around four. Once we are up we crack open the champagne and toast the Reds once again. A fine weekend, all things considered.

That night, me and Marian are watching the news on the Beeb. A multiple murder in Croydon, the police think it may be drug-related. Was that what the police were investigating? I won't be stunned if Tracey turns out to be mixed up in it in some way.

CHAPTER 13

LALA

Over the football season we must have been in every one of the footballers' hang-outs, but we still never got to meet any Premiership players. Then one Saturday, after a mind-numbing match against Birmingham, Kirsty's dad was invited to drinks in the Board Room, so naturally we tagged along. Talk about a yawn-fest. It was wall-to-wall middle-aged suits, pouring drink into themselves and tearing strips off the referee. Kirsty and me were going to leave but next thing the players were herded in. That perked Kirsty up no end.

The suits took out their phones and snapped themselves with their favourite players. Kirsty geared up for advanced eyelash-batting. She chatted to Rio Ferdinand. He smiled politely and moved on. She rushed back to me all excited.

"Look what I got!" She pushed a card into my hand. *You are invited to join us in Smokin'*, it said.

Be still my heart! The Premiership's favourite night-spot, located in a boutique hotel in Alderley Edge, entry by invitation only.

It took Kirsty two and a half hours to get ready. When she was finally satisfied with her look we took a taxi and made our entrance into Smokin'. It was loud, lots of purple and gold. All the girls seemed to be blonde and fake-tanned, with laser-white teeth, smoky eyes, cleavage and jewel-decked navels. The guys were designer-suited, necking champagne and fingering the huge diamond studs in their ears. The girls mobbed the guys like sparkly starlings. The guys lapped it up. Some of the faces were famous and others were vaguely familiar. I was blinded with bling.

While we were getting the feel of the place, this guy swaggers over with a couple of pals in his wake. He was middling tall, his face sort of lop-sided and pock-marked but his teeth were too perfect and his clothes were pure Mickey Dazzler. He takes Kirsty's hand, lifts it to his lips and kisses it.

"Belissima," says he.

Kirsty went all squirmy.

"Io sono Filippo, Filippo Lippi. I am Italiano."

"I guessed," simpered Kirsty. "I'm Kirsty, this is my friend Lala."

"Lala," he said, making my name sound faintly obscene.

"Any relation of the artist?" I asked.

He looked blank. He was Italian. Surely somebody, somewhere, had told him his name was the same as that of a famous Italian artist?

"All Italian people, we artist," he smiled.

Good save!

Filippo was Europe's best midfielder. He scored the crucial goal in some final or other. Manchester United paid fifteen million for him. How did I know this? He told us... several times. Kirsty had her flirt mode turned up to max. Filippo looked deep into her eyes.

"Belissima," he said and topped up her glass.

I noticed that he was topping up her glass quite a lot.

252

The way she was knocking it back, she'd need me to get her home safe.

"There is party," he said. "Private party, very… How you say… Very exclusive. I invite you."

Kirsty went weak at the knees.

We took the private lift, which Filippo unlocked with a key. It brought us straight to the penthouse suite – knee-deep white carpet, chandeliers, mirrors, champagne bottles, orchids, platters of food and a bowl full of coke. One guy was chopping lines on a mirror and snorting it with a silver straw. Another snorted it through a crisp rolled-up fifty pound note. Several others were lounging around drinking champagne. The vibe in the room was unpleasantly jaggy. There were no other women. Kirsty took a bottle of champagne from one of the coolers and necked it.

"Hey Kirsty," I said, "take it easy."

But she only had eyes for Filippo. He took the silver straw and gave it to Kirsty. She did a line. I slipped my hand into my bag and took out my phone. While Filippo was taking his snort, I snapped him and forwarded it to my e-mail address.

"Come," said Filippo. "Now we make jiggy-jiggy."

He pulled Kirsty towards the bedroom beyond. The other guys followed them. I snapped all the faces I could and sent those to my e-mail as well. I slipped my phone back in my bag, as one guy came over and stuck his hand up my skirt.

"What about this one?" he asked.

I dragged my high-heel down his shin. He screamed like a girl.

"Hey, you lot!"

I called over his head to the guys crowding into the

bedroom. They ignored me. I grabbed a bottle of champagne and flung it at one of the mirrors. It made a satisfying crash and shattered all over the carpet. That got their attention.

"What the fuck?" shouted Filippo, appearing at the bedroom door. "Why you do that?"

"To stop you raping my friend!"

He started towards me, bunching his fists. I brandished my phone at him, showing the photo of him snorting cocaine. He snatched it off me and threw it out of the window. Kirsty burst into tears.

"That's okay," I shouted. "I've sent the pictures to my laptop at home and there's plenty more. I snapped every one of you. So go ahead, rape us both if you like. We'll be reporting you to the police."

It worked.

NANA JO

Marian has been making a ridiculous fuss about Kirsty's "traumatic" experience but if you go round half-naked, what do you expect? Marian doesn't want to hear that, but the truth is the truth. It's time that young one learned a lesson. And I'm not even talking about morals, I'm talking about nature. When it comes to S.E.X., you can't trust any man. As long as they can put one leg in a trouser, no woman is safe, for they're all supplied with the devil's equipment. The Almighty should have known better. Did He realise the harm He was doing to women when he gave men that thing? When it comes to morals, it's up to us women to put a halt to their gallop and Kirsty should know that.

Marian, as usual, doesn't agree. Instead of giving Kirsty a good telling off for exposing herself to the world, she's sent her to Spain with her pal, to recover.

I hope for everyone's sake that Kirsty didn't get pregnant.

KIRSTY

Azafrán looks over the sea and because I know Alfonso, the owner, he gets me and Lala a terrace table. Marbella in April is heaven. He brings the menu with our *tinto del verano* and a dish of olives. We order *tortilla de patatas* and a salad and watch the boats. There must have been a regatta on because Marbella is heaving with yachting types. My phone goes. It's Dad. I have an audition in Galway for a commercial, even though I'm still only a student!

Lala is thrilled for me.

"It just goes to show I was right to change to acting!" I say.

A waiter arrives with our food and shortly afterwards Alfonso seats two guys at the next table. One is on crutches and has his leg in a cast. As Alfonso leaves them, he gives us a tiny wink. He's always trying to fix us up. He's mostly way off the mark but this time he's right. They are wearing Ralph Lauren and they are a bit of all right. I fancy the one in the cast.

The guys read their menus and then look over to see what we're eating.

"How's the tortilla?" one of them asks.

"Delicious," I say.

It turns out they are Irish and brothers as well and they ask us to join them. Michael is a student in Limerick and Brendan has a job in Swansea. He's fallen at work and fractured his leg so they've sent him here to recuperate. Afraid he'll sue them for millions, I expect. We arrange to meet for drinks that evening.

I wear my favourite floaty Vera Wang dress that makes me look taller and with my tan, my diamond studs and my Manolo sandals, I look pretty hot. But Brendan sits beside Lala! Next thing, they're rabbiting on about some book they've both read and I can't get a word in edgeways.

LALA

Brendan turned out to be the loveliest guy and we had so much in common. We'd read all the same books and we even liked the same music, except for U2. He thought they were The Greatest Rock Band Since Time Began and that The Edge was God on a Guitar. But they just gave me a headache.

Kirsty was not happy even though Michael was obviously interested. That's because she fancied Brendan and he fancied me. Well tough! She thinks that she's the good-looking one and I'm the plain friend and therefore she should have first dibs on everything. I used to think she was right but not anymore. She practically did double-somersaults to try and get Brendan's attention but he thought she was an airhead. I told him she wasn't really.

We met every day after that and the more time we spent together the more we discovered in common. But I never found out what he did exactly. I knew he was working in Swansea but was about to move to London. I kept thinking that something would happen but it didn't. I don't really know why. I fancied him and I'm pretty sure he fancied me. He said it was the wrong time for him to get involved.

"Does that mean you've a girlfriend?" I asked.

"No… Just… It's hard to explain."

I reckoned he'd been recently dumped so I didn't push it. I appreciated that he didn't pretend he wanted a relationship just in order to get some holiday sex. In the end, he gave me his number.

"Text me," he said, "and next time you're in London give me a shout."

"As it happens I might be working in London for the summer."

"Great!" He seemed genuinely pleased.

I decided I would text him if I got an internship in London. I'd sent CVs to about twenty publishers. I thought it might be the way to go when I'd finished in college. But I'd heard nothing back so far.

KIRSTY

God but I hate flying commercial, especially when the plane gets delayed. Hanging round airports is not my idea of fun. When we *finally* arrive in Dublin, I've missed the bus and there isn't another till seven that evening and my audition is in Galway the next day. I try getting a taxi but none of them will take me, not even as far as Athlone, not even when I show them my platinum card. Bastards.

Lala heads off back to the flat because she's staying in Dublin to study, so I'm left waiting all by myself for the late bus.

I ring Seán. He uses helicopters for clients all the time, maybe he can get me a lift. He can't. Or rather, won't. I have another idea. I try Fergus.

FERGUS

She is wearing her tiger-skin coat over a peacock-blue teddy and she has a hold of my goolies.

"Morning sweetie," I say. "You're taking advantage."

She snarls and twists. It hurts like hell.

"Where's that packet I gave you to mind?"

Ah. I should have known. Tracey's presents are not always presents, especially when she's in one of her moods.

"It's all gone, love, I told you – a lot of parties."

The present was a tiny proportion of the windfall she'd acquired during that business in England. Mind you, it was still worth a lot. (Although not as much as the Gardaí would claim it was worth, if they got hold of it. They like to big up their seizures, give the impression they're winning the war against drugs. Everyone knows they don't get within an ass's roar of winning – never have, never will. Legal or not, people will always want drugs.)

"Where the fuck is it?" Tracey twists again.

I scream. She jumps from the bed and starts pulling out drawers. At least she's let go of my goolies. I put on my jockeys and jeans for protection. She is throwing my stuff all over the room.

"Like I said, Tracey, it's long gone."

"So why the fuck don't you show some appreciation?"

"I have something in mind, sweetie," I lie. "But it's not ready yet."

She lifts the Lalique bowl I keep keys in and flings it at my head. I duck. It hits the metal frame of the bed. Bits of glass spray all over the place. Some hit the side of my face, some get stuck in my shoulders.

"Get the fuck out of my house!" she yells.

"No!" I yell back. "'Cause it's my fucking house!"

She whirls out of the room, down the stairs and slams the front door. And, presumably, walks down the street in her tiger-skin coat and peacock-blue teddy.

I pick out the glass with a tweezers and dab on antiseptic. Then I phone Brown Thomas. They have a new line in handbags, just in, from Judith Leiber. I ask them to deliver the most expensive one to Tracey at Topaz Security in Molesworth Street. Three thousand eight hundred smackeroos! But when Tracey gets over her fit, it'll be well worth it.

As the day goes on, I get more and more paranoid. I've lied to her. I still have the stuff in my safe. I like to save for the lean times because, when Interpol gets lucky, times can get very lean indeed. But my customers do not believe in lean times, so I like to have a reserve. The problem is, Tracey knows professionals, guys who can easily break into my safe. And even more easily break my neck.

Jenny Elixir, the singer, phones. She's been on tour and she's tired and emotional and badly in need of some "me" time. I ask Shay to pick her up from Limerick. Then Kirsty phones. Now there's an idea. Two birds, one stone.

KIRSTY

Fergus arrives half an hour later and while we are waiting to hear from the pilot, he orders black coffee. He looks nervous and keeps glancing around, like he is expecting something to happen. His phone rings. He sets it on the table and stares at it till it stops. I can see Tracey's name on the screen. It rings again. Tracey again.

"Why don't you answer?"

"She's in one of her moods..."

She rings five more times. The next time it rings, it is the pilot.

Out on the tarmac, Fergus gives me a red gift-box, sealed with gaffer tape.

"Give that to your dad," he says. "Ask him to keep it safe till Tracey gets over her mood."

I put the box in my suitcase.

I love flying by helicopter, there's so much to see. Shay, the pilot, has flown Dad loads of times so I've met him before. He points out towns as we pass but when he lands, it isn't at our house.

"This isn't Balfathery!" I say.

"No love, Fergus said to take you straight to your dad and he's in Bannagher."

Dad's building a shopping complex in Bannagher so he can drive me home but it means more hanging around and

I can't wait to run a hot bath and relax.

"You know we've a landing pad near our house," I remind him. "You could drop me there."

"I know. But I'm on a schedule and I'm doing you a favour. You can get out here or I can drop you in Limerick, so make up your mind."

So bloody rude.

The shopping complex is still a building site, all muck and foundations. I pick my way over to the pre-fab which is the office. Dad is inside talking to Miroslav.

"Princess!" he exclaims. "What brings you here?"

I tell him what has happened and give him the box.

"Fergus wants you to mind this."

"Jesus!" he says.

"What?"

"Never mind."

FERGUS

I'm on my way back to town when my phone beeps. A text from Tracey. '*Why r u in airport with Princess?*'

How does she know that? Jesus she's having me followed.

'*Arranging copter for Jenny E,*' I reply, sweating. '*P. called, needs a lift.*'

I phone Brown Thomas again. They assure me the handbag has already been delivered. Good. I call Nunu and order a ludicrously expensive bouquet for Tracey. Then Eamon rings.

KIRSTY

"Fergus," Dad says into his mobile. "Is this what I think?"

He listens a bit then he snaps his phone closed.

"I'm going to kill Fergus."

He walks up and down and punches the wall a few times.

"What? What? What is it?"

"Let me think, Kirsty. Let me think."

He walks up and down some more then turns to Miroslav.

"Take my car," he says, "and drive Kirsty to her Aunt Phyllis."

He writes down the address.

"I don't want to go to Aunty Phyllis's house."

"I'm sorry love, but you're going."

"I've an audition tomorrow."

"I know, I arranged it and I'll sort it out."

"What's going on, Dad?"

He throws his car keys to Miroslav.

"Fill her up."

Miroslav leaves. Dad sits down.

"Remember the police in Manchester? They're looking for Tracey to 'help with inquiries'. It's about a multiple murder."

"Wow. Did she do it?"

"I don't know. But I do know she's wanted in England and I know she's refusing to go."

"What's that got to do with me?"

"Tracey's a very loose canon. And this box... It's the present she gave to Fergus, remember?"

"He said it was something naughty…"

"Yes. Fergus wants to keep it but Tracey wants it back."

"That's not very nice."

"It gets worse. Somehow Tracey knows he met you in the airport which means she'll put two and two together and come after you."

"Why don't you phone the police?"

"Sure… Yeah… But first I want to make sure that you're safe."

He makes me get into the back of the car and lie under a blanket. Tracey must be completely insane. All that fuss about a sex toy!

EAMON

Once Kirsty is safely away I want to drive up to Dublin and beat the shite out of Fergus. Kill him. Have his balls on a griddle. But Miroslav has the car and I have to find a taxi to get me home. I sit at my desk and stare at the box. I know well what is in it but I have to make sure. I find a Stanley knife and slit the tape. Inside is a sealed plastic bag the size of a fairly thick paperback. I make a small slit. White powder spills out, I pick it up on my fingers and rub it on my gums. It is the good stuff all right, pure and uncut. I'll have to bring it home and stash it in the safe. Before I stash it away, I decide I deserve a small snort. It is bloody amazing. Then I stick it into my briefcase.

I go outside to talk to the men. Yesterday's rain has caused a bit of flooding. While we're discussing the options I hear the sound of a chopper. It comes closer and closer and starts to descend. Holy shit! Tracey! Somehow she must have tailed Kirsty! I dash back to the office and take the stuff out of my briefcase. She'll definitely look there. I stare wildly around looking for a hiding place. There is nowhere. I am about to be toast.

By now the 'copter has landed in the field and the pilot is helping Tracey out. Oh fuck, fuck, fuck, fuck, fuck. Then I see the answer. It is standing a few yards away. I grab the box and take it outside. Two of my Russians are mixing cement. I told them to vamoose. Russians don't question orders.

The mixer is churning away. I open the box, take out

the plastic bag and empty the good stuff into the cement. It near breaks my heart to see that white streak get absorbed. I keep a bit in the end of the bag, put it back in the box and kick it under the prefab. Then I go inside and sit down at my desk. I grab some architectural drawings and spread them out. My hands are shaking.

The door opens, I pretend to be absorbed while frantically wondering what Tracey might do.

"Bloody pop stars!"

I look up. It's Shay. I know Shay well. He's brought me home umpteen times.

"How's she cuttin'?" I ask.

"I've Jenny Elixir out there," he moans. "She's throwing up everywhere. These young ones, they want the rock and roll lifestyle but they don't have the balls. Not like us Eamon, eh? Any chance of a cup of tea? It might settle her for the rest of the journey."

KIRSTY

Aunty Phyllis is so fat, she wobbles when she laughs. Plus, she has no sense of style. You should see the house, she collects china dogs. They're everywhere. Then there's my cousins. Molly and Mabel. The twins. Big balls of fat dressed in pink. Uncle Frank's fat too and when he decides to fart he gets one of the twins to pull his finger while he lets rip. Hilarious! I have to sleep in the box room in a bed surrounded by junk.

I have a terrible dream. I am being chased by a tiger and it's tearing my clothes. I wake up with my heart in my mouth. After that I can't sleep again. I keep thinking of Manchester and the police. I try to remember what I've told them. What if Tracey finds out? Will I have to go into witness protection?

First thing next morning, I phone Dad.

"Don't worry Princess," he says. "There's CCTV in the hotel, they'll have her arriving and leaving on tape. What you said doesn't matter."

The other problem is my drama classes. I have a part in the end of year play but if I don't get to class I'll be dropped and that will mean I'll miss my chance to be spotted. Uncle Frank says he'll drive me door to door on his way to work and pick me up in the evening. It means getting up at an ungodly hour. I hope he doesn't expect me to pull his finger when he wants to fart!

NANA JO

As soon as I hear she is staying with Phyllis it sets off alarm bells. Phyllis and that lump of a husband of hers don't have the luxury lifestyle that Kirsty is used to. I can't see her staying there willingly, unless there's a very good reason.

"Someone was stalking her," Marian says when I ask.

Now there's a cock and bull story if ever I heard one. I try to probe a bit more but Marian clams up and that confirms my suspicions. Kirsty must be pregnant.

At least she has enough modesty not to display herself in front of the whole of Balfathery. Not like the shameless young ones you see in skin-tight clothes, tummies exposed to the world, parading their babies in buggies and no sign of a wedding ring.

I always said Kirsty would get into trouble. I expect she'll have it adopted. That's the most sensible thing.

MARIAN

I arrange to meet Fergus in Dublin. Some things can't be said on the phone.

"What were you thinking," I ask, "putting Kirsty in

danger like that?"

"I'm so sorry Marian, I panicked… If it's any consolation, Tracey didn't suspect her. She suspected Shay the pilot, but she's over it now."

I tell him what Eamon did with the stuff.

"Ill-gotten goods," he shrugged. "Serves me right."

"She's no good for you, Fergus."

"I know."

"Why don't you dump her?"

"She's not the type you can easily dump. Besides, I'm crazy about her."

After lunch he gives me a bag of the finest Jamaican.

"Peace offering," he says.

JAKE

I'm in Nana Jo's house with my camera at the ready. Nana Jo wants a portrait of her cat. The cat is called Dino. Dino is old and sick and might die at any minute. He's Nana Jo's favourite cat of all time.

Dino doesn't like me. Every time I approach, he humps his back and stares at me with malevolent yellow eyes. I take loads of shots but I know that they won't be what Nana Joe wants. Dino is not a cat that lights up a screen.

"Have a cup of tea," Nana Jo says. "Give him a chance to get used to you."

She makes tea and gives me a slice of rhubarb tart with a dribble of cream. There's not enough rhubarb.

"So," says Nana Jo. "Is it true that Kirsty has a stalker?"

"That's what Mum says," I reply. "But I suspect that it's Kirsty being over-dramatic because, as you know, every Celeb has to have their own stalker!"

"She hasn't been sick or anything?"

"I don't think so."

"No tummy upsets?"

"Not that I know of."

When we've finished the tea she lets the cat into the garden and I get a couple of very nice shots with the telephoto lens.

LALA

Houndstooth Press were taking me on! Wow! I'd be spending the summer in London. I'd be paid buttons of course but I had an aunty in London. She worked for Médecins Sans Frontières and she was going to the Congo so I was going to be able stay in her flat in Swiss Cottage. All I had to do was feed myself. I couldn't wait.

Kirsty was back in Dublin again. She told me all about Tracey and the murders. I wondered if she was making it up, it sounded like a movie. Now she was up in a heap about this play that she was in. It was an end of term thing. She was convinced that her future depended on it and that if she did well, agents would beat the door down to sign her up. But it was a very small part and, between you and me and the wall, I wasn't sure she was that much of an actress.

I asked if she'd like to come to London with me for the summer. She said she'd think about it.

GRANDMA MINNIE

We all go to Dublin to see Kirsty's play. It's "Lady Windermere's Fan" by Oscar Wilde. To be honest, I don't think it is very good but Kirsty does look lovely. She is playing Mrs Cowper-Cowper which is a small part but, in my opinion, she should have been playing the lead.

Josie is there as well, looking like she is suffering from piles. When Kirsty comes on she leans over to me.

"Has she put on some weight do you think?" she whispers.

"No," I hiss. "It's the dress."

Even if it were true that Kirsty had put on weight, which it clearly isn't, I wouldn't give Josie the satisfaction of agreeing with her.

LALA

We were in London at last. In the end, Kirsty came with me. My aunt's place is a two-bedroom flat in a nineteen-thirties apartment block. It's full of things she'd brought back from her travels. Kirsty thought it was old-fashioned and fusty and maybe it was – but it was free, so who cared?

I started work in Houndstooth mostly helping Jeremy Winters, the commissioning editor. He was Eton and Oxford, very languid, very grand and a bit la-di-da-condescending at first, but he knew everything there was to be known about publishing. My job was getting coffee, answering the phone, photocopying stuff, but once he saw I was willing to work, and that despite being "a wild Irish lass" my knuckles didn't drag on the floor, he gave me a load of manuscripts from the slush-pile to read and told me to find him a jewel. Sadly, I found no jewels. I couldn't believe how bad most of them were.

I'd texted Brendan but he was away in a clinic in Switzerland. It seemed his fracture was complex and because he'd injured himself on the company premises, they'd sent him off for the very best treatment.

Kirsty didn't last long in London. I thought she might go for auditions but she mostly went shopping or hung round the flat. Then her dad phoned to say he'd set up the audition in Galway again and she was off.

I quite liked being on my own. I could eat what I liked

when I liked, watch what I liked on the telly and keep the place clean and tidy. Then there was Brendan. He phoned the minute he got back from Switzerland and we got it together at last. It was nice to have the place to ourselves without Kirsty getting annoyed or demanding to know all the details. And now at last he told me what he did. He was a footballer! Arsenal were about to buy him from Swansea – they'd just been waiting till he got the all clear on his leg. He hadn't liked to tell me before because he feared his career was over, and he didn't want me getting all interested in him because he might be going to be famous, then dumping him if he didn't make it.

"But Brendan," I said, "I don't care if you're famous or not."

"I know that now, but I had to be sure."

I knew someone who would care! Kirsty was going to have a seizure when she found out. But for the moment we were not going to tell her.

NANA JO
Kirsty is back home from London and her tummy is flat as a pancake. Marian's story is that she went over for auditions. But we all know why girls go to London. How can I stand idly by when my first great-grandchild has been murdered by foreign doctors? I should do something about it but I don't know what. I keep praying to Our Lady to guide me. The answer comes when I am saying my rosary. I need a long chat with Fr Mullery. He's a good man and a good priest and we're on the same wave-length.

JAKE
We gather round the TV in the den waiting for the ads. This is Kirsty's big moment. The ad that Dad set up for

her was with one of his buddies. It's due its first screening to-night. Steven Spielberg, take note! We're watching the end of the news and weather forecast in Irish because the ad only features on TG4, the all-Irish station. The news ends and on come the ads: washing-up liquids, mobile phones, car insurance. Then Kirsty appears on the screen. She is wearing a blue dress with a plunge neckline. The background is yellow.

"Do you need the volume turned up?" she asks us. "Have you problems hearing what people are saying at parties? A hearing-aid will help." She turns her head and points to her ear. "Especially an invisible one like mine."

Cut to Dad's pal, Barry Lavelle, standing outside his hearing-aid shop in Eyre Square.

"Come on in to us, we'll look after you." Says he with a big cheesey grin.

That's it.

Everyone claps and tells Kirsty how great she was. Well, Nana Jo doesn't say much but Gran and Granda and Mum and Dad make a huge fuss.

NANA JO

I have a long chat with Father Mullery and he advises caution.

"Time was," he says, "when the Church could speak out but these days the media is waiting to do us down at every hand's turn. We're effectively gagged. The last time I preached about immodest dress I had fifty complaints and a scurrilous piece in the Western People. The press are so anti-Catholic these days."

He's right. We've known for a long time that the likes of RTE and the Irish Times are riddled with left-wing atheists and liberals, hell-bent on destroying the Catholic Church.

But now it's the local newspapers as well, even the Midland Express. When Ireland was poor we had standards but nowadays money's destroyed us.

"But what should I do about Kirsty, Father?" I ask.

"I don't know, Mrs Murray," replies Father Mullery. "I honestly don't know. Abortion's a terrible evil. Sure the guilt alone must be crippling."

"Perhaps you could speak to her, Father?"

"I'm not sure about that Mrs Murray. Young people today resent priests interfering. But you're her grandmother. I'm sure you could take her aside and have a word. Persuade her at least to go for counselling. I can recommend a very good Catholic lady."

JAKE

Finally, we get a sunny weekend. Dad slides open the roof and the walls of the pool to take advantage of the sun. We're all in our togs, playing ball and splashing about. All that is, except Nana Jo. She sits on the patio in her pink cardigan, her tights, her white lace-up shoes and, for all I know, her thermal vest. Dad wears a Hawaiian-print shirt open over his swimming trunks. He puts on his barbeque gear, a full-length white apron and a tall white chef's hat. He fires up the stainless steel, top-of-the-range Hitachi. He has a beer in one hand and barbeque fork in the other.

Granda comes out of the kitchen with a plastic container of steaks. He wears a luminous green Speedo and his skin is the colour of leather. He too puts on a chef's apron and hat. He joins Dad at the Hitachi. He spears a huge steak from the plastic container and lets it fall on the griddle. It spits in every direction. The two of them jump away from the steak spit. They josh one another and cackle and laugh their lads'-night-out laugh. They're in their element and on their third beer.

Gran gets out of the pool and wraps a sarong round her waist. She flicks through the Sunday Times Style magazine. Kirsty swans out of the pool like she's Manga Girl: bikini, ankle bracelet and film star shades. She sprawls in a deckchair and spikes up her hair. Nana Jo stares at Kirsty's bare midriff and the shiny gold star in her navel. Gran looks up from her magazine and sees Granda opening his fourth can of beer.

"Go easy on the beer, Jim," she calls. "We don't want you falling down drunk."

"I've never been falling down drunk in my life."

"Well I beg to differ."

"The food will soak it all up."

"We can only hope that it does."

Mum arrives out from the kitchen with a bowl of potato salad. She puts it on the table.

"Minnie," she says with a smile, "can you give me a hand?"

Gran loves feeling useful. She jumps up and goes to the kitchen.

Crisis averted.

Gran carries a tureen of gazpacho to the table and ladles it out into bowls. Gran and Granda have developed a taste for gazpacho in Spain. Mum comes out with a dish of chopped peppers and stuff for the soup. She sprinkles them in Gran and Granda's gazpacho. I notice little brown flecks that are not in the rest of our bowls. Nana Jo doesn't believe in gazpacho. She thinks cold soup is unnatural. She has pineapple juice instead. Dad and Granda take their soup standing up while they watch the steaks. Everyone goes for second helpings and the mood of the party gets mellow. Nana Jo drinks her pineapple juice in small, disapproving sips.

Granda marches over with a platter of steaks held high on the flat of his palm.

"All hands to yer knees," he shouts. "The ship's going up a hill!" He lays the platter in the centre of the table. "Olé!"

Dad takes charge of dishing the meat out. I hand out the plates. Kirsty sits beside Nana Jo in her bikini. Nana Jo looks at her long and hard and shakes her head.

"Don't you want to put something on?" she asks.

"No," says Kirsty.

Nana Jo breathes in and out through her nose. You can see she's restraining herself.

I help Mum bring out the desert. Strawberries, hazelnut meringue, cream, ice-cream and cava. Nana Jo doesn't drink, but she lashes into the meringues, ice-cream and strawberries. Needless to say, all that sugar is catnip to wasps. One arrives. It buzzes round me a bit, I stay quiet. There's no point in flapping, it only pisses them off. It zooms off to Gran.

"Wasp, wasp!" she squeals.

She flaps at it with her serviette. The wasp zooms about. All the women are squealing and trying to flick it away. Understandably, the wasp gets really pissed off and starts buzzing real loud around Kirsty. Kirsty flaps at it and succeeds in hitting it into her bosom. The wasp stings. Kirsty screams, jumps up and pulls off her bikini top. The wasp wisely escapes. Mum runs inside for the first aid box. Granda turns away and whistles at the sky. Dad looks away too. I cover my face with my hands but this is too good to miss so I watch through my fingers. Kirsty holds her stung boob in one hand and looks down at the red mark. She tries to lick it. Gran laughs. Nana Jo glares.

"Kirsty! Cover yourself up at once!"

Kirsty ignores her. Mum arrives back with sting cream and a t-shirt for Kirsty. It's safe for us men to look once again.

"You're just too sweet, Kirsty," says Granda. "You've a fatal attraction for wasps!"

"Just as well it's not sharks," says Gran.

"Ah Minnie, come on," says Granda. "We're too far inland for sharks."

"Not when *you're* in the pool!"

That starts the laughs. That and the beer and the cava. Everyone laughs except Nana Jo.

"Ah Josie," says Granda, "why don't you loosen your stays?"

That makes us laugh even more.

"It's the silly half hour," says Dad and that cracks us all up again.

Granda holds up one little finger and waggles it and that makes us laugh even more. After a while we're all laughing so much we no longer know what we're laughing at.

Nana Jo is not laughing. She's sitting there looking like the Wrath of the Gods. She lifts her hands over her head and slams them down on the table.

"That's quite enough!" she yells.

We're all shocked into silence.

"Mammy!" says Mum. "What's your problem?"

"My problem? Your daughter strips off her clothes in front of the men and you ask me what's wrong?"

"Ah Josie, relax," giggles Gran.

"You Kerrigans were always the same," says Nana Jo. "Lax in your morals." Gran bursts out laughing. Dad and Granda go into convulsions. Mum tries her best to keep a straight face. "And as for you, young lady..." She turns on Kirsty who is peering down the neck of her t-shirt and blowing on the sting. "You're a right little trollop. "

"Oh Nan, take a chill pill."

"More's the pity you didn't take yours."

"What?"

"At least if you'd been on the Pill you needn't have had that abortion."

We all sit up in our chairs and gawp.

"Woah there," says Dad. "Rewind. What abortion?"

"The one your daughter had when she was in London."

Dad turns to Mum.

"Is this true?"

"No it is not." Mum stands and takes Nana Jo by the elbow. "You have a very bad mind," she says. "Come inside. We need to talk."

They disappear into the house. The rest of sit there in silence. After what seems like an age Gran takes the bottle of cava out of the cooler and fills her own glass to the brim.

"Why don't we all have a drink?" she says.

CHAPTER 14

MARIAN

Kirsty doesn't deal well with rejection but even the very best actors get turned down for parts and Kirsty's not that good an actor. After a one-year course in stage school she can't believe that she hasn't been spotted, that producers haven't see her potential.

I suggest that she volunteer to work in a theatre company. Help out with props or costumes or something because, if she's on the spot, she might get offered some small parts. You'd think I'd suggested street-walking! Kirsty believes that God has it down in His book that she, above everyone else in the world, deserves to start at the top!

Meanwhile, she needs some kind of a job. Just hanging round doing nothing in Dublin is bad for morale, especially when Lala and Jake and all her friends are back in college working for their exams. But Kirsty won't take any old job. It has to be something she thinks is cool. I phone Fergus.

LALA

Working for Houndstooth in London was fascinating. They specialised in avant-garde authors and I got to meet a whole lot of them. One writer I was dying to meet was

Gert Vrille. He wrote outrageous short stories. I expected to meet someone flamboyant, like, for example, Will Self. Instead, he turned out to be white-haired and shabby and painfully shy. It just goes to show, you never know what's going on inside people's heads.

When I was leaving to come back to college, Jeremy said that when I'd finished my degree I should contact him and he'd give me a job. Wow. That was of course if Houndstooth hadn't folded by then because apparently all the money-men want is chick-lit, celebrity autobiographies and gory who-dunnits, even though lots of that stuff doesn't sell. But whether I worked for Houndstooth or not, the minute I finished my degree I was moving to London to be with Brendan.

The more I got to know Brendan, the more I was impressed. I began to think he might even be The One. He was so easy to be with – not like the guys in college who were so far up their own arses that even talking to them gave me constipation. Brendan made me laugh. When we were together we laughed all the time. I knew being funny was a sign of intelligence; that was why women always put "sense of humour" at the top of the list.

His leg was better although the physio checked it all the time. He was back in training and in the gym. He was seriously fit. I couldn't get over his six-pack. I hoped he would get to play a match before too long.

Mum met him. She came to London one weekend and I was dreading it because she could be a bit snobbish. She had always told me to look for a man with a good profession ie a doctor/dentist/lawyer. I didn't know what she would think of a footballer with no university degree. But Brendan did all the right things: opened doors for her, held chairs, helped her on with her coat, brought us to see "Les Miserables" on the Saturday and to lunch the next day in a snazzy place on the river, then off to the Tate Modern. And of course he was her type, tall and athletic. Plus she knew damn well that footballers earned way more than doctors or dentists or lawyers. So he got the Mammy Seal of Approval!

I missed him desperately after I went back to college. He phoned every day and we e-mailed and texted but it wasn't the same. He sent me tickets to come to London for his birthday, which was the day of his first game for Arsenal. He was having his family over for a big celebration and because he didn't want me to feel overwhelmed by Hickeys, he sent a second ticket so that Kirsty could come with me.

I told Kirsty that Brendan had been signed for Arsenal, but she only laughed and reminded me that she had met him in Marbella, and she knew he had some bog-standard job in Swansea. I explained his job was playing football for Swansea, and suggested she check him out on the Arsenal website. She rolled her eyes and asked was I ever going to grow up. It was pointless trying to convince her. I would just let her find out, in her own good time.

What birthday present do you buy for the man who has everything? I thought of a book but, after hours in Hodges and Figgis and more hours on Amazon, I couldn't find anything that was just right. Then I had a brainwave.

Brendan and I had taken a trip to Hampton Court in the summer. There was a dragon outside the front entrance. He stopped in front of it:

"Look Alanna, Falkor!"

That's the dragon from The Neverending Story, which was his favourite book when he was small. I loved it too. It wasn't a bit like the dragon in my mind but clearly we all had our own versions.

As it happened, I had a dragon at home which I called Falkor. I found it at a Christmas bring-and-buy sale in aid of the Vincent De Paul which my mother took me to when I was ten. I was in serious Neverending Story mode at the time and I loved the little dragon so much that I spent a whole week's pocket money on it. It was a dotey little carving of a dragon curled up on itself and playing with a ball. Since then I had discovered that it was a bargain because it's a Japanese netsuke, made of genuine ivory and quite old. I was sure Brendan would like it.

KIRSTY

Quayside Studios is where all the big names in music come to record. They love coming to Dublin because they don't get hassled on the street and the Irish journalists don't stalk them like they do in England. And I've got a job there, which is fab because, as well as meeting the stars, I get to talk to their agents and managers.

My job is to meet and greet and see to the artists' needs. Guess who walks in on my very first day? Only Bono! I know some people don't like him but that's because they haven't met him, I think he's lovely. No bullshit, not like some I could mention! And guess who arrives later, to pick him up? Only Bruce Springsteen! I nearly faint on the spot. But you can't do that stupid fan stuff, you have to be professional. He turns out to be really nice too.

Lala wants me to come to London for Brendan's birthday party which might be fun but when I take a look in the studio diary I see that The Wage Slaves are due in for the weekend. That meant that Sparks will be here. After our "thing" at my eighteenth birthday party he never phoned, never even texted, so I need to give him a piece of my mind. After that he will probably ask me out to make up for not calling. So I have to keep my options open.

"What time are the Wage Slaves due in?" I ask Nikita – she's the manager of Quayside. "It's not in the book."

"It depends," she says, "on whether Sparks has been on a bender. And by the way, don't get left alone with that bastard or he'll have you against a wall with his cock at the ready."

"I can handle him," I say. "I've met him before."

I tell Lala I have to work. She's pissed off because she'll be meeting Brendan's parents and she's nervous and wants my support. But she has to learn to do without me some time.

Sparks arrives about midday on Friday, which apparently is early for him. He has the band with him and several hangers-on. I bring them to Studio Four. He doesn't recognise me but then he isn't really looking, he is too busy horsing around with the lads. Besides, my hair is totally changed.

"Run out love," says he, "and get us a dozen tubs of Ben and Jerry, any flavour. And a couple of bottles of vodka."

I stand right in front of him and look him in the eye.

"Any particular brand of vodka?"

"Wet, alcoholic, and the bigger the bottle the better." Not a flicker.

His manager follows me out of the studio.

"Forget the vodka," he says. "I want this thing finished today. And don't worry, I'll take the rap."

Later, I'm heading for Studio Five where a fiddle player is cutting one of those crappy "Best Of Irish" CDs. I have to check if they needed water or anything. There is nobody else in the corridor. The door of the men's toilets opens and out comes Sparks.

"Hi, Sugar-tits," he says.

"Good afternoon, Sparks."

I act totally professional but *Sugar-tits*… really! Then, just like Nikita warned me he would, he jams me up against the wall and tries sticking his tongue down my throat. I remember all the time I wasted hoping he'd call and I bite down hard on his tongue and give him the old knee-up.

"Bitch!" he screams, doubling up and clutching his privates. "Fucking bitch!"

He makes a swipe at me with his fist. I duck. He misses. I scream for help although that's a bit pointless because the studios are sound-proofed. Fortunately his manager comes out of Studio Four and sees him bent over and groaning.

"Jesus, Sparks," he says. "Kneed in the nuts again! How many times do I have to tell you? One more harassment suit and you're screwed!"

I text Lala that things have freed up at work and I can go to London after all.

LALA

Kirsty was surprised that Brendan didn't meet us in the airport. (I knew he wouldn't be able to, because of the paparazzi.) But even she was impressed when we were met by a chauffeur and whisked away in a limo through the city to a truly awesome hotel.

"Jesus, Lala, this must have cost your man a year's wages!"

Kirsty had a fabulous room, and she was delighted until she found that I was booked into a suite. Chandeliers like big balls of twinkling stars; silk curtains ceiling to floor; balcony with a view of the London Eye; suede-covered sofa and chairs; flowers, fruit, plasma TV… And an emperor-sized bed in the bedroom with loads of silk pillows! On the nightstand was bouquet of gorgeous cream roses, and a sexy note from Brendan which I hastily hid in my pocket. I could tell Kirsty was deeply confused. Things were the wrong way round. Wasn't she the Princess?

My room phone rang. It was a woman.

"May I speak to Alanna?"

"I'm Alanna."

"I'm Brendan's Mammy. We're having lunch in the Orchid Room. Why don't you join us?"

"That would be lovely," I squeaked. I put down the phone, shaking. Jesus, Mary and the Holy Saint Joseph... I hadn't thought I'd be meeting his folks quite so soon.

Down in the Orchid Room the whole of the Hickey family was sitting around a big table, grinning at us like a basket of chips. Michael, the brother we'd met in Spain, did the introductions to Mr Hickey – "call me Frank", Mrs Hickey – "call me Pat", Angela the sister, three uncles, two aunts and both sets of grandparents.

Mrs Hickey sat me beside her. I expect she wanted to check if I was good enough for her son. Kirsty sat beside Michael because she knew him from Spain.

"Where's Brendan?" she asked.

"At work," Michael replied and gave me a wink.

Brendan had told him that Kirsty thought he was an office worker or something.

"Oh, has his job moved him to London?"

"That's right."

The Hickeys turned out to be lovely, ordinary people and easy to talk to. When we had finished our coffee, Mr Hickey tapped on a glass with a spoon for attention.

"Now ladies," he announced. "Don't spend too much time titivating. The limo is due in ten minutes. And remember we'll be outdoors, so wrap up well."

There was a fridge in the limo stocked with champagne and a cabinet with glasses. Mr Hickey opened a couple of bottles and poured.

"To Brendan," he said, raising his glass. "May his touch never fail him!" The Hickeys and I clinked glasses and giggled and laughed, and Kirsty joined in though she looked a bit confused.

The Emirates stadium was gigantic. It dominated all the streets around. The chauffeur left us outside the main entrance. Crowds of people in red and white scarves, hats, jerseys and rosettes where pouring in. Some had red and white flags and several were waving giant-sized, foam-rubber hands. The Hickeys all wore red and white scarves and produced one for me and another for Kirsty.

"Dad will kill me if he ever finds out," giggled Kirsty, wrapping the scarf around her neck and linking arms with Michael. "He's Man U through and through."

"Don't say that out loud here," laughed Michael.

"Isn't Brendan going to join us?"

"Maybe after the game," said Michael, laughing even more. "He's got his job to do first."

"Poor Brendan, he'll miss the game."

"Oh, I hope not!"

She cast him a puzzled glance.

It was a league match, Arsenal versus Newcastle, and we had the best seats in the house, right on the half-way line, two rows from the front. I actually preferred them to the executive box in Manchester. Here you were part of the crowd, part of the excitement. The atmosphere made me tingle all over. The noise! Wow, the noise... It was so loud, you could feel every bone in your body vibrating. And the singing.

"And it's Ar-sen-al,
Ar-sen-al FC!
We're by far the greatest team
The world has ever seen!"

It didn't scan all that well but what the heck! The crowd chanted it over and over again and me and the Hickeys joined in. We'd definitely caught the fever. I hoped Brendan was playing for sure and I hoped he'd play well and I hoped his leg would hold up and I hoped he wouldn't get injured.

Mr Hickey gave me a programme. I had a quick flick through and saw he was playing centre field. Kirsty glanced at her programme as well but she still didn't cop. The players came out on the field to warm up and the crowd let out a roar that would deafen a stone. The Hickeys leaped to their feet and started punching the air and shouting:

"Brendan, Brendan, Brendan, Brendan, Brendan, Brendan, Brendan, Brendan!"

I joined them.

"What's going on?" asked Kirsty, standing up.

"See anyone you know?" I asked, pointing him out on the field.

"No. Who?"

"Brendan!"

"Brendan *who?*"

"Brendan Hickey! My Brendan!"

"But.. But…"

I opened the programme and showed her his picture.

"You never told me!"

"Yes, I did."

"I thought you were just saying it for a laugh. Like when we were kids. "

KIRSTY

Arsenal wins 2-0. Big deal. Newcastle are obviously useless. Brendan doesn't score either of the goals, but the Hickeys won't shut up about their stupid son: his brilliant assist, his brilliant defence, his brilliant runs, his brilliant tackles. Mr Hickey has tears in his eyes.

"He's going to be one of the greats! Roy Keane better look to his laurels!"

The one thing that was keeping me going was the idea of the hospitality suite after the match. Instead, we go straight back to the hotel. And the Hickeys rabbit on and on about Brendan all the way to the restaurant, all through the dinner, all through dessert. Lala is as bad; she pays me no attention at all.

And the *fuss* they make when he eventually joins us. You'd think he was God on a stick. And the birthday cake is in the shape of a football! So not cool.

LALA

We didn't get a chance to speak properly till after the party. The Hickeys were ready to boogie all night but Brendan had to go easy on the drink and make sure that he got enough rest, so we went up to the suite.

"Happy?" I asked.

"Happy," he grinned. "But I better warn you, you're in the grip of the Hickeys now."

"What does that mean?"

"My dad described you as 'a very intelligent young wan'. It's his highest praise for a girlfriend and Mam and Gran drew me aside to whisper 'hang on to her she's lovely'." I was thrilled. "Before I left home to join Swansea," he added, "Dad gave me two bits of advice: take care of your money and don't get engaged to some orange-faced,

284

wannabe WAG."

"So if I want to escape from the Hickeys, I've got to wear lots of fake tan?"

"Even with fake tan I'd still want you."

I gave him his birthday present then, my own personal dragon, and he loved it.

CHAPTER 15

KIRSTY

Lala wants me to be chief bridesmaid, which is what I'd expect because Lala has no sisters. Then I find out that the other bridesmaids are Brendan's sister Angela, okay fair enough... and bloody Martina Curran! I'm *furious*.

"What do you want *her* for?"

"Because she's my friend and she's from Balfathery."

"I thought *I* was your friend."

"You are. You're my best friend, that's why you're chief bridesmaid."

"Well, I don't want her there."

"Well, I do."

This wedding has turned Lala into Bridezilla, totally unreasonable. She's just lucky that I can rise above petty jealousies. Jake is still friends with Martina even though she has a new Swedish boyfriend. I don't get it... But then, Jake is weird.

I've decided that after Lala's wedding, I'm leaving Quayside. It's boring and the "stars" or, as Nikita and I like to call them, "the shit-heads", treat us like glorified slaves. I thought it would be a good place to make contacts but a year or more later, *nada*, zilch. Irish people don't recognise talent.

Sure, Fergus has managed to swing me a couple of gigs. My left hand has featured in a music video for an already-forgotten boy band called Hot Fat. You can see it holding a cocktail glass (full of coloured water). I also appear in a low-budget, made-for-video (actually, made-for-bin) horror movie. I am a sexy nurse with a huge scary syringe who has to inject her patient with a mad doctor's experimental virus. The patient explodes and flesh-eating zombies form out of the splatter. I scream my head off. The zombies eat me alive.

So I have to move on. I need something bigger and better, something fabulous, something to show off my talent. I'm thinking of Hollywood. There's so much more I could do there. Hollywood recognises talent.

Jenny Elixir came in today to record her new album. Her real name is Maura Brogan but that's not very rock'n'roll. She's out of rehab. Again! And according to Fergus who does her PR, this time she's fully de-toxed and rarin' to go.

She arrives late, all bra straps and red lipstick, flops into a chair in the foyer and lights up a fag.

"Sorry," I say. "I'm afraid there's no smoking in here."

She stands up and blows smoke in my face.

"Do you know who I am?" she asks.

"You're Maura Brogan."

She gives me a poisonous look.

"I'm Jenny Elixir, I have three platinum discs. Two Brits and a Grammy."

"Wow, I'm impressed."

I was being sarcastic. In Pop terms that's peanuts.

"Where's my band?"

They'd been waiting in Studio One for an hour and a half.

"First put out that cigarette."

"Who the fuck do you think you are?"

She takes a drag, stares me in the eye, taps cigarette ash on the floor, crosses her arms, takes another drag and blows more smoke in my face. I take out my mobile and call Mario. That's Mario Benini, her manager stroke agent whom I've been trying for ages to meet. He is in Studio One with the band.

"She's here," I say.

Mario is small and fat, with highlighted hair and lots of black leather. He comes bustling out. He waddles straight up to Jenny Elixir and snatches the cigarette out of her mouth.

"Jesus, Jenny," he says. "You are one stupid bitch. You know what that does to your voice."

Jenny give him a look that would pole-axe a bullock and sashays off towards the studio. Then she bends over, pulls up her skirts and wiggles her arse. She has no knickers on. Mario shrugs.

"As long as she gets this album finished," he shouts after her, "I don't give a shit what she does with her rancid old arse."

I've heard about Mario. Everyone has. He's a rottweiler agent and everyone wants to be on his books, me included. I've asked Fergus to swing it for me but so far he's come up with nothing but now is my chance. He goes to the door and throws the cigarette out in the street. I stand where he can't help but notice me.

"*Ciao, Bella,*" he says. "What your name?"

Why is he bothering to fake an Italian accent? Sure, I'd heard him a only minute before! He's one of the chip-shop Beninis, brought up in Ringsend.

"Kirsty Kerrigan," I say. "And I'm looking for a good agent."

"What you do?"

"I'm an actress and model."

"*Si, si, si...*" He looks me up and down and obviously likes what he sees. "I could get you some modelling work. You have CV? Photo?"

"Sure."

I am so excited. I tell Nikita.

"Let me guess," she says. "He can get you some modelling work?"

"Yes!"

"That's what he tells all the wannabes."

"So? I'm not a wannabe."

"Whatever... But if he sends you to Sackville Studios, don't go. That's his brother's place. His brother specialises in topless modelling and internet porn."

I don't believe her, not really. But when Mario phones me two days later and tells me to go to Sackville Studios, I don't go. Nor do I mention it to Nikita.

It's not fair. It really isn't. Lala does nothing at all and she gets the job she wants in London and gets engaged to a Premiership player. And not just any old Premiership player – since he started with Arsenal, Brendan's gone mega! You should see her engagement ring. Baguette-cut diamond from Asprey's, at least a carat and a half.

Why am I always the bridesmaid?

EAMON

Lala brings Brendan to meet us. Nice enough lad, considering he plays for The Enemy. I tell him he ought to play for a real team and he laughs. He can take a bit of slagging. Of course, he's sure to be playing for Ireland as well because he is good. Not as good as Roy Keane – he'll never be that good – but still, they'll have to select him. So

I can forget about The Enemy and think of him as an Irish international!

While the girls are squealing over Lala's engagement ring, I have a thought. Brendan's a fine-looking lad and the press love him, magazines too. His face alone on the cover sells. How about his face beaming beside his blushing bride?

So here's my thought. Carpathi Castle is perfect for a footballer's wedding. It can be our wedding gift. I'll throw in the reception, accommodation, whatever extras are needed. It'll be money well spent. Every editor west of the Great Wall of China will want to publish it.

LALA

We were so grateful when Mr and Mrs Kerrigan offered us Carpathi Castle – for free! We'd been desperate to find a secret location, somewhere we could have a wonderful day far away from the press. Just in case, we didn't even tell the guests where the wedding was going to be held – just that they had to turn up for a flight to "a mystery destination"! It was the only way to stop leaks to the press. Already our friends and Brendan's team mates were being offered big money to spill the beans.

Brendan was a big disappointment to the tabloids. He never got drunk, he didn't have punch-ups in nightclubs, he didn't do three-in-a-bed romps with surgically-enhanced models. He trained. He came home. He went to bed early. He took me out now and again. And, shock horror, he read books!

Since the paparazzi first snapped me with an engagement ring, I'd had to change my number three times and my parents had had to go ex-directory. Every time I went out I had to make sure that I was properly dressed and made-up because there was always someone lurking behind a hedge with a camera, hoping to catch me looking like a troll. I had decided to go the friendly route. I would smile, wave, say "Hi guys" and move on.

Meanwhile, the tabloids kept running wedding "exclusives".

The Sun revealed that we were getting married in a castle, which gave us a bit of a fright. But they thought it was Luttrelstown Castle, like Posh and Becks. The News of the World went for a tropical wedding in the Maldives. The Mirror knew for a fact that it would be in the Elvis Chapel, Las Vegas. Reporters were checking out all the most famous locations. But the press had never even heard of Carpathi Castle, so the place was an absolute godsend.

Mum found this great woman who made bridal wear for all the best shops in Spain. She was making the dress and bridesmaids dresses as well. When Kirsty heard that she did a fandango.

"You're not going designer?" she squawked.

"Pilar Morena is a designer."

"But she's not famous."

"She's famous in Malaga."

"Lala, it's the greatest day of your life!"

"I'm not asking Mum and Dad to pay mega money for a dress that I'll only wear once."

"Get Brendan to pay."

"No way."

"Why not?"

You have to spell some things out for Kirsty, because she lives in a different world.

"Your Dad is giving us the Castle and the reception. Mum and Dad want to pay for the dresses at least, okay?"

"But I saw a Dolce and Gabbana that would be perfect

for the bridesmaids…"

"Sorry Kirsty, that's not going to happen."

She went into a sulk.

When I told Brendan he laughed. He understood money. His family wasn't well off. He was earning squillions but he knew how to budget. He was investing his money and, when the football was over, he was planning to go to college and study sports psychology.

JAKE

It's my first film premier. It's not Hollywood. It's a weekend of student shorts in the film centre that me and the guys in my class organised. They're showing *"Gymkhana"* this evening. It's no big deal, just a fifteen-minute documentary I made about the Balfathery Easter Gymkhana. It's not going to rock the world or anything but I'm reasonably happy. At least I was until today. Now I feel like a cat on a raft. We've invited everyone who's anyone in film in Ireland.

Liam Fitzsimon turns up, which chuffs me no end, and some people from RTE. Mum and Dad are here of course and Gran and Granda and Nana Jo. I was hoping Martina would make it but she's in Stockholm on an Erasmus. Kirsty is working.

The lights go down and the titles come up. I am squirming. I find it hard to look at the screen. I can see every tiny flaw. The credits come up. I brace myself. The audience claps. They even seem enthusiastic. Wow.

There's a cheese and wine thing that Dad has paid for. Liam Fitzsimon can't stay very long but he gives me a nod and thumbs up. That means that he liked it. Whew. He'd tell me if he thought it was shit. Now I can face the others. People congratulate me and I feel a bit of a fraud because I know some things could have been better. Dad struts about with his hands in his pockets and a grin on his face. He puffs out his chest.

"How's she cuttin'?" he says to anyone who stands still long enough. "What did you think of "*Gymkhana*"? Wasn't it brilliant? My lad made that."

They all agree. What else would they say? Afterwards he takes me aside.

"You're not half bad," he says. "How would you like to make some money?"

I'm all on for making some money.

"You'll have the camera at Brendan and Lala's wedding?"

"Yeah."

"There's plenty would pay for those photos."

"No way, Dad."

"A bit of exposure would do the Castle no harm."

"It's their wedding, Dad, and they want it private."

"It's my hotel and I'm paying for the reception."

"If you gave them a toaster, would you go to their house every morning and ask them to make you some toast?"

"Now you're being stupid."

"I'm not doing it."

EAMON

It's like trying to talk sense to a rick of wet turf. I know he thinks that all that I ever think of is money. But if I don't, who will? How does he think he got his education? His holidays abroad? Who paid for his cameras? Who keeps him in college? Who dresses him? Feeds him? Puts the roof over his head? And what about the fine lifestyle he has? That all comes from money. My money. The money I make from hard graft. He should remember that the next time he gets all high and mighty.

MARIAN

Eamon has gone and invited Seán and Fergus to Lala's wedding without checking with her! He wants them to recommend the Castle to their clients! Lala and Brendan are being more than gracious about it. Lala even suggests that Monkey and the Wrenches might do a turn at the wedding. She doesn't have to ask twice. Now Eamon's going round like a dog with two tails.

My biggest worry is Tracey because who knows what that mad bitch might do? But she's not coming. Fergus assures me she can't leave the country. She's too busy avoiding extradition. Good.

JAKE

I will take photos at the wedding. But only for Lala and Brendan. The professionals will do the formal stuff and I'll do the candid shots. I'll put them on a CD and print up the best ones for their album. It'll be my wedding present.

I have Martina to thank for that idea.

Martina has arrived back from Sweden with Sven in tow. He's the new boyfriend. (We had agreed that both of us had things to do and that we should see other people.) Sven is tall and blonde and a Class A eejit. He asks if I suffer much from existential angst. Seriously! I say no. Apparently he has the existentials real bad. He seems to think it's a good thing. That it makes him tortured and deep and by implication, I must be shallow. I don't think he'll last long with Martina.

Carpathi Castle is very impressive. It looks like Mr White's villa in that scene at the end of Casino Royale. Except everything's grander and bigger, including the scenery. I'm mooching around in the grounds admiring the orange-gold light of the sunset on the lake when a herd of cows wanders up the avenue. Their udders are swollen and swaying. A local teenager in jeans and wellies lopes behind. He whistles and swings his switch. He gives me a wave and says something. I wave back.

There's a fountain in the gardens in front of the castle. The water tinkles and casts the odd rainbow. The cows amble past. A few cows stop for a drink. The boy chivvies them on towards a gate on the far side. The gate leads into a lane. He holds the gate open. I watch till they disappear round a corner. A few minutes later two of the staff from the hotel come out with a bucket and brush. They inspect the gravel for cow shit. There isn't any this evening.

Later I ask Dad if he knows about this. He does. It's a traditional right of way and it has to be honoured.

MARIAN

Carpathi Castle is amazing. It was built as a hunting lodge for a Prince. Some lodge. When the Commies took over, Ceausescu used it for holidays. Can't say I blame him. Eamon has put in an infinity pool overlooking the lake, a luxury spa, tennis courts, golf course, a marina, decent heating and air conditioning, every mod con the wealthy traveller needs. The staff are up to standard as well: good-looking, charming, efficient and they speak pretty good English and several speak German and French.

Lala and Brendan will get married in the local chapel which is in the castle grounds. It is totally cute and the walls are decorated with brightly coloured paintings that Eamon has had properly cleaned and restored. According to the brochure, which Eamon commissioned from a local professor of history, the paintings were done by a shepherd. The Prince found him one day drawing with chalk on a rock. He took him under his wing, bought him paints and brushes and brought him to live with him in his castle. Hmm! I wonder what that was about! But it's the kind of story guests love. Let's see how the staff handles the wedding reception.

FERGUS
Tracey would love this place. Especially the bear hunting. She was dying to come but we could only fly via Heathrow and she's wanted in England. Though I wouldn't put it past her to take the risk anyway as a sort of "up yours" to the police. I never ask her about why she's wanted because I definitely don't want to know. I keep telling myself that she'd never be stupid enough to get involved in a murder. On the other hand, when she loses it, she really does lose it and if somebody pissed her off enough...

Why do I fall for whack jobs like Tracey? And who am I kidding when I ask myself that question? It's the sex, I know it's the sex. Marian says it must go deeper and maybe it does. She thinks if I got some decent counselling I might find out what makes me fall for the lunatic fringe. But what kind of a life would it be without the excitement?

EAMON
A scruffy pap in a filthy anorak! Jesus, I told Terry to send someone who'll blend in. It's a footballer's wedding for Christ's sake, there's no anoraks. I have to buy him a suit. He's supposed to mingle, pretend he's one of the guests and e-mail the photos in time for the Saturday deadline. For Christ's sake, that's not much to ask. I'm doing him a favour. He's getting a major scoop. I'll be billing him for the suit.

GRANDMA MINNIE

I'm so thrilled that Lala has invited us to the wedding! Of course we've known her since she was a child and it is Eamon's hotel, but still, it's nice to be asked. Jimmy is up in a heap about meeting the footballers. You'd think he was meeting the Pope. And he a dyed-in-the-wool Man U supporter! According to him, once you join Arsenal FC you sprout horns and a tail and take pleasure in poking poor little Man U with pitchforks! But give him the chance to down a few pints with an Arsenal player and he's up in his hat with delight!

The invitation says "formal dress" but Jimmy says he's not going to spend the day looking like a penguin. He wants to wear that magenta jacket he bought in Spain years ago. I tell him he looks like an ad for Ribena. Why do men hate wearing dress suits? They look great in them, handsome and manly. Even Jimmy.

"Fine," I say, "wear your aul jacket. Make a fool of yourself. I don't care. I just wonder what the footballers will think? Because you can bet your last cent they'll be turned out in style."

That softens his cough for him.

KIRSTY

I hate the bridesmaid's dresses. Lala thinks they are lovely. But who wants to be dressed the same as two other women? Especially when one of them is Martina Curran and there's loads of fit men around.

Being chief bridesmaid is no fun at all. It's like being the bride's personal slave!

"Kirsty, get me some hairspray."

"Kirsty, where's my blue garter?"

"Kirsty, fix my veil."

"Kirsty, straighten my train,"
"Kirsty, help me into these shoes."
"Kirsty, do I look okay?"
"Kirsty, where's my mascara?"

On top of that I have to look after Amy, the flower girl. Nobody warned me about that until the last minute. Amy is Brendan's little cousin and she's only five. She's taken a great shine to me which was cute at first but enough is enough.

Lala is lucky she has me, otherwise she wouldn't be able to cope.

MARIAN

It's a fabulous day! Sunshine, blue skies and just enough breeze from the lake so the heat doesn't melt your make-up. I'm so thrilled for Lala and Brendan.

When we arrive at the church, we find all the locals have turned out to see them. Brendan is recognised the world over, even here in the middle of nowhere. Lala arrives at the church in an old-fashioned open Chrysler. The car is swagged with flowers, which is a local tradition. She looks stunning and when she walks up the aisle on her dad's arm, Brendan wells up. So sweet.

NANA JO

This church has very peculiar pictures all over the walls. Our Lady has plaits and she's wearing some kind of folk costume. Jesus is wearing a sheepskin jacket!

The priest is a "friend of the family", one of those so-called "trendy" priests. I don't like the way that he does it at all. I'm sure Fr Mullery would agree with me.

"Marriage is a sacrament," says he, "which Brendan and Alanna confer on themselves."

299

And then he stands aside and lets them say their own makey-up promises! And instead of a sermon, he asks Brendan's and Lala's parents to come to the altar to speak! Everyone thinks it is great but of course most of them aren't even Catholic. God be with the days when the priest would remind the newly-wed couple of their Christian duties.

Why they have invited me to this so-called wedding, I have absolutely no idea.

JAKE

I take shots of Brendan's aunties getting tiddly on champagne. They're getting mock flirtatious and want me to stay but the camera gives me an out. I take more shots of WAGs in cackling bunches with their heads exploding in feathers. They also want me to stay. I snap Granda standing five-foot-five in a group of six-foot-plus footballers. He's telling stories and they're laughing their heads off. He's clearly the belle of the ball.

Martina looks great in the bridesmaid's dress. She circulates among aunties and grannies and mammies, doing her bridesmaidly duties. Sven's by himself in a corner being existential and angsty. He sees me and approaches. He seems to think I'm his friend. I'm not. I tell him my battery's low and that I have to replace it.

I escape out the front door and breathe the fresh air. I walk down to the lake. It is silvery blue. The sun is low and the mountain peaks are pink. It's deliciously balmy and warm.

KIRSTY

The WAGs stand around sipping champagne, watching their husbands and boyfriends like hawks. Just for the craic I decide to flirt. Each time I speak to a couple of guys, the girlfriends gather and push me aside and drag the fellas away. Not that I'd touch any of them with a forty-foot pole. Footballers are just so dim.

This guy starts chatting me up and he strikes me as vaguely familiar.

"Have I met you before?" I ask.

"Don't think so, love."

He goes on about some match that he played, and then I remember. He was one of the guys at that horrible party. I'm trying to think of some way of letting him know when his girlfriend arrives and almost knocks me down.

"That's my fiancé," she hisses.

"Lucky you," I say. "Do you know he's a rapist?"

She goes bright red.

"Shut your stupid mouth!"

"Fine." I take two steps away. Then I turn back again. "And I have the pictures to prove it."

Just then Amy, the flower girl, tugs at my skirt.

"Lala wants you," she says, taking my hand and pulling me away.

I leave the footballer and his WAG having an almighty row.

"Can you get my make-up bag please, Kirsty," demands Princess Lala. "I've left it outside in the car."

JAKE

I hear a melancholy moo. Milking time and the cows are heading for home. I turn back to look at the castle. Kirsty is coming down the front steps. The bridesmaid, alone in the gloaming. I take a couple of long-distance telephoto shots. Kirsty gets into the open-top bridal car and starts rummaging.

Romanian cows are just like Irish ones, curious. I switch

301

to video. They crowd round the car. One scratches her arse against the door handle. A child's voice is calling,

"Kirsty! Kirsty!"

"Hang on, I'm coming!" Kirsty calls. She tries to open the door of the car but the cow's arse is right up against it. "Get away! Shoo!" The cow doesn't pay her a blind bit of notice.

"*Kirsteee!*" wails the child.

Holy shit, it's little Amy the flower girl. She must have followed Kirsty out and now she's trapped in the middle of the big, jostling cows; she looks tiny and she's clearly terrified. Kirsty comes to the rescue; she climbs over the door of the car and whacks the cow with a bag on its bony behind. The cow lifts its tail and sprays a huge jet of shite all over Kirsty, in her hair, on her face, all down her organza dress. Kirsty freezes for a moment in shock, but Amy has fallen down among the cow's hooves and she is hysterical.

"I'm coming!" screams Kirsty and she pushes her way through the herd like a mad thing until she reaches Amy and lifts her up. The two of them are destroyed with cow-shit. The cow-herd comes running and drives the cattle away. The staff come out with their buckets and brushes and help Kirsty and Amy into the hotel.

Kirsty has to ditch the bridesmaid's dress and wear one of her own. I think she's pleased about that and when she joins us again she's the hero of the hour. I show people the video of the rescue. Amy's parents are grovellingly grateful. Dad is puffed up with pride. Mum is beaming. Even I'm impressed – I didn't think she had it in her. And who knows what might have happened to Amy, if Kirsty hadn't been so brave?

Later that night, I post the clip on YouTube.

CHAPTER 16

KIRSTY

When I get back to Quayside after the wedding, Nikita hands me bunch of messages. Twenty-three are from Mario Benini, the rest from journalists. It's like something you dream of but I have no idea what it is all about.

"Please call Mario," says Nikita. "He's been on the phone non-stop."

"I'm not doing topless for his sleazy brother."

"It's not that," she says. "You're a celebrity now."

"No, I'm not."

"Of course you are. You're Cow Girl."

"What are you talking about?"

"You're on YouTube. Didn't you know? It's gone viral. Five million hits and climbing."

Oh my God! Oh my God!! Oh my God!!! *Oh my God!!!!* This is it! I never expected it to happen like this, but... I realise that Nikita is saying something.

"What?"

"You're going to need a manager , Mario may be a shit but he cuts the best deals for his clients. But before you sign anything for him, get someone who knows what they're doing to check it. He's known for his lethal small print."

Mario takes me for a very nice lunch and orders

champagne. He tells me why I should choose him as my manager. Then he outlines his plans. I like what I hear but I keep my cool and tell him I'll think about it.

"*Ciao, Bella,*" he says, as I leave.

I am walking on air.

Dad checks Mario out with Fergus and insists on putting him through his paces. Then he gets his lawyer to go over the contract. They find a couple of booby traps. Mario grins when they point them out.

"God loves a trier," he says.

The lawyer deletes the traps and I sign.

"Glad to have someone who knows what they're doing," Mario lies, as we shake hands on the deal. He has dropped the fake accent. "Let's get down to business. I checked before I came out, Cow Girl is all set to have the highest number of hits ever on YouTube! So let's do America first."

Mario goes to work. I resign from Quayside and go shopping – no patterns, no tartans or checks, because they go all funny on screen. By the end of the week he's lined up spots on Jay Leno, Conan, Rickey, Oprah and several others I've never heard of. He gives Leno first dibs because they've paid the most. Then he moves on to England and Ireland and gets Graham Norton, The One Show, Lorraine Kelly, Richard and Judy, Pat Kenny and Ryan Tubridy.

On Monday, we fly to Los Angeles. I still can't believe that it's happening. I really am a Mega Celeb at last. It feels great. I must buy something lovely for Jake.

MARIAN

Kirsty's got all the fame she wants now. It's so unexpected! I think it's hilarious how Jake made her famous. She's a heroine now on both sides of the Atlantic and everyone wants her. I hope she enjoys it, I really do, it's what she has wanted forever.

NANA JO

Remember that song, *Thank God We're Surrounded by Water?* I like it because being an island is a blessing. It helped preserve our faith and our culture. Sadly, those days are over. I blame Joe Walsh and his Travel Agency.

It was fine when he organised pilgrimages to Lourdes but then there were the holidays to Spain. The Irish started drinking wine and wearing bikinis.

Now it's the computers. Marian tells me I could order my groceries in winter and have them delivered but I won't have a computer in my house. Fr Mullery tells me there's all kinds of depravity on them.

Still and all, computers have made Kirsty famous. Well, she did save that little girl's life and I'm very proud of her for that. I didn't think she'd have the guts but she did. She gets that from our side.

I can understand why she might get in the papers but I can't quite understand how she got famous all over the world. Marian says it's the heady cocktail of cow dung and heroism. It makes no sense to me.

EAMON

The Sunday Gazette gave Carpathi Castle a fabulous spread and of course it was picked up by the British papers. Now there's magazines from all over the world wanting to do features. Job done.

Lala and Brendan suspect nothing. They think that either one of the guests or one of the staff was trying to earn a few bob. I have promised to investigate the staff and if it was one of them, I'll make sure they're fired. I think Marian suspects what really happened but she doesn't know for sure and I'm saying nothing to no-one.

But the best thing about the wedding is what's

happened to Kirsty. She's done the Kerrigans proud. Put that in yer pipe, Balfathery – my daughter's a heroine. You should see her with the paparazzi! Boy, can she turn it on. I'm delighted for her.

KIRSTY

America is fierce, fab, wicked and totally cool! My photo is in all the papers! I have screaming fans and autograph hunters! I've been staying in top hotels and the studios send limos for me! I've been invited to lots of Hollywood parties! Loads of directors have promised to call me! I've even been properly stalked, by a genuine stalker! In Chicago!

I've met Harvey Kietel on the Jay Leno show – he is cool and he's promised to look me up when he comes to Ireland. I've met Hilary Swank on Montel. She is just the nicest person and she's given me great tips for handling the paparazzi – accept them as part of your life, always smile, always be pleasant, be especially nice when they're being obnoxious and never leave home without make-up. Conan can't wait to have me back – of course, he's Irish, so we have a connection. I'm sure Ellen de Generes hit on me, I swear to God… Mario says she was just being charming but I don't know. And the audiences! When I walk out from the wings, they go super wild. I'm a hit in America! A major hit!

Of course, there are downsides as well. After every show Mario makes me watch the recording. (It's horrible but it's useful. You see why crossing your feet at the ankle looks better that crossing your knees and why waving your hands can make you look manic.) Plus, the press are a pain. They act like they own you, like you owe them something, like you don't have a life of your own and your own things to do.

Then the Oprah show goes horribly wrong. I am in the green room waiting for my call. Mario is off schmoozing as usual. In comes an assistant producer. She's one of those scary, efficient types, all skinny black jeans and rectangular glasses.

"Bad news, Kirsty," she says. "I'm afraid we're gonna have to bump you."

"Bump me?"

"Yeah. Bette Midler called and asked could she come on the show, so sorry, but no contest. Sorry."

"Who the hell is Bette Midler?"

She raises one of her angular eyebrows and looks at me like I've crawled from the slime.

"Watch the show," she says and she clatters away on her cheap platform heels.

I find Mario in the wings laughing his arse off with some of the crew. He is no help at all.

"It's just one of those things," he says. "If you want to stay in this business, you better get used to it."

I go back to the dressing room. An assistant brings me coffee and a danish, like that makes up for being dumped! She turns on the TV.

"Enjoy the show."

As if.

Oprah does the big build up:

"*Blah, blah, blah… blah, blah.* Please give a huge welcome to…" dramatic pause: "The Divine Miss Midler!"

You'd think it was the Second Coming. The audience stands and goes wild. Bette Midler waddles on and air-kisses Oprah. I can't believe it. Showbiz fake if ever I saw it. She's ugly, she's dumpy, she's old and she's wearing a dress that looks like it came from a rag bag. She has a tour coming up and a CD to flog.

"I'm the people's diva," she smirks.

People's diva my arse.

Afterwards, Oprah comes to the green room and apologises to me. She looks much older in real life.

MARIAN

Kirsty is off to England next week to do shows there. If she thinks the American press are bad, wait till she meets the British. Animals. Already they're calling her "Sh*t Girl". They've sent reporters here to Balfathery. Three of them this morning were hanging round our front gates, and I had to get Eamon to give them the bum's rush. Mrs Lawless in "The Gem" tells me they're asking everyone questions. They're looking for old boyfriends, old school friends, neighbours. One of them even tracked down my mother – like an eejit, Mam invited her in for tea! I dread to think what she's told them.

JAKE

A guy from the Observer phones. He writes a regular column about YouTube. Because "Kirsty and the Cows" has gone viral, he's checked out my other YouTube clips. He interviews me then and there on the phone. It'll be in the paper next Sunday, in his Talent To Watch section! The only one I've told is Liam Fitzsimon. He didn't say much but he did crack a smile and he nodded as well.

The guys in college are going to be super-sick. Especially Jeff Warren. I often wonder why he's doing this course at all. To hear him talk, you'd swear Kurosawa, Antonioni, Billy Wilder and Tarantino could learn at his feet!

This week we have to construct a three-minute narrative, which the class then has to critique. I keep mine simple:

It is dark. A mother waits at a bus stop with a child in a stroller. A tattooed skinhead joins the queue. He makes her nervous. Others join the queue. All avoid the skinhead. The bus arrives. The mother has difficulty lifting the child and folding the stroller. All the passengers except the skinhead crowd on to the bus. He grins menacingly at the mother. His teeth are metal. He lifts the baby out of the mother's arms and rubs noses with it. The mother folds the stroller. They get on the bus. He hands back the child. Through the bus window we see him play peek-a-boo with the child.

I think it's fairly okay. It needs better editing and the acting is definitely hokey. The class make their criticisms, and most are positive.

"I thought it was puerile, derivative, ingenuous and faux naïve," says Jeff and off he goes on one of his "nature of cinema" rants. I let him rant. His piece is up next:

Two guys in anoraks stand hunched against a graffitied wall. They smoke cigarettes and mumble. A plastic bag blows about. They smoke and mumble some more. The plastic bag blows about a bit more.

That's it. No narrative. Just moody blue filters and lots of weird angles. And the plastic bag is hijacked straight from American Beauty. I decide to say nothing. Everyone slates it. Jeff throws a hissy fit.

"You're missing the inner meaning," he whines.

"But Jeff," says Helen. "how come all of us missed it?" Helen is a mature student and she knows what she's up to. Jeff doesn't like her. "It can only mean one of two things," she continues. "Either there's no inner meaning or you failed to bring it out."

"I don't do *simplistic* Hollywood narrative," sniffs Jeff. "I follow the European tradition."

"O-kaaay," says Helen, and she gives me a dirty big wink.

KIRSTY

I've been shopping all day, looking for something to wear for the Graham Norton show. It is taking forever, because people keep stopping me and asking for autographs, which is nice and all but it really does get to be a pain. Even when I am having my lunch, this guy comes over and insists on yacking on and on about how I must have been inspired by angels to save the child. Total crap.

Eventually I find a dress and shoes and accessories but by the time I am finished I am completely wrecked. Typical Dublin, I can't find a taxi. I decide to walk towards the apartment and hope that I'll pick one up on the way. I'm on my way down Molesworth Street when I hear the shout:

"Shit Girl! Hey you! Shit Girl!"

I walk on, wondering what that's all about.

"Shit Girl! Shit Girl!"

A group of people run past me, and the next minute they're standing in front of me, blocking my way.

"Hey, Shit Girl!"

There are reporters sticking their microphones into my face and a photographer snapping away. Me, Shit Girl? *Bastards.* I back away up the steps of a house.

"My name is not Shit Girl."

"Is it true you had an affair with Chris de Burgh?"

"No!"

"Did he get you pregnant?"

"What are you talking about?"

"Did you have it adopted?"

"Did you have an abortion?"

"Did you have it in London?"

"Is your dad a millionaire?"

"Are you a Princess?"

By now, I'm right up against the door with these guys

310

firing questions so fast that I'm totally confused and I'm frightened as well. I don't know what to do and I panic. So I scream and press the bell. The door opens behind me and a hand pulls me in. The door closes again and there's Tracey. The reporters are banging on the door, ringing the bell and hammering on the knocker.

"They're shitehawks," says Tracey. "Come on, we can you get out the back."

The reporters had caught up with me directly outside the Topaz Security office! How lucky is that? I don't know what I'd have done if it hadn't been for Tracey.

I'm starting to get fed up with reporters. And I really miss Lala.

MARIAN

Kirsty is very excited about going on the Graham Norton show. She's a big fan. We all are. I travel with her to England because Mario is busy and Lala is no longer easily available now she is married and living in England. I think Kirsty misses Lala more than she'll ever admit. So do I.

"Graham may act the eejit," I warn Kirsty. "But don't be fooled. He's very bright, he's very professional and he can think on his feet. You do realise that he'll make jokes at your expense?"

"I know that, Mum, I'm not stupid."

The first thing we see when we land in Heathrow is a newspaper stand with a photo of Kirsty, hair tossed, eyes wild, splayed against the door of Topaz Security under the headline 'SHIT GIRL DEFENDS HER HOME'. I try to divert her attention but of course Kirsty sees it and bursts into tears.

"Why are they doing this to me, Mum?" she sobs.

What can I do? I just hug her and tell her she doesn't deserve it. Poor kid.

KIRSTY

I phone Lala the minute we get to our hotel. She's seen the headline as well. She understands because she's had the press after her.

"Whatever you do, don't let them see you cry," she advises. "Don't lose your cool and don't say anything nasty, that'll only make it worse. Grit your teeth, smile and act like you're having a wonderful time."

It's so good talking to Lala.

MARIAN

It's a strange thing, meeting someone you've been watching on the telly for years. You feel he's your friend except he wouldn't know you from a may-bush. When Graham comes in to meet us he is wearing jeans and a t-shirt like any ordinary fella. He's really friendly and warm but all the time he's chatting to us I'm thinking, this guy went to Liza Minnelli's wedding! He's best friends with Hollywood stars!

Later, in the green room, we meet the other two guests: Catherine Deneuve and Bette Midler! It's all I can do to stop myself gushing and begging for autographs. Then the show starts. We watch it on the screen. Graham does his introduction, telling his jokes about the guests and showing the pictures.

"She's the Face of France and a goddess of stage and screen," he announces. "It's Catherine Deneuve!"

Out she goes, and appears on the screen, and Graham kisses her. She sits on the sofa in her silver-grey, silk dress, simple, expensive and totally perfect. God, she looks elegant.

"Now let's meet our next guest," says Graham, "the Divine Miss Midler."

Bette is not the most beautiful woman God ever created but she has oomph by the cartload. When she walks out on set, she makes you feel happy. She sits on the sofa oozing charisma. I pray that Kirsty will be okay.

"And finally," he announces, "you've seen her on YouTube, all together now, give a big welcoming Moo for the One, the Only, Shit Girl Heroine!"

"Moooooooo," moos the audience.

"For fuck's sake!" says Kirsty.

"That's you," says the assistant, who is standing beside us. "Go on, go, go."

"My name is not Shit Girl," says Kirsty, through gritted teeth.

"He's only joking. Now GO!"

She refuses to move. The assistant turns away and says something into her microphone to Graham. I assume they'll stop the recording but no, he turns to the camera, puts his finger to his earpiece and cocks his head.

"Ladies and Gentlemen!" he says. "I'm told that her name is not Shit Girl. It's *Kirsty*. And this is her very first professional strop! *Awwwwwwwwwww!*"

The audience howls laughing. "Catherine Deneuve, you might learn something here. Bette Midler, you'll have to keep up! Neither of you have sulked once." Everyone howls once again. "Please welcome our final guest, Kirsty Kerrigan!"

I give Kirsty a push and she walks out on set looking like thunder. Graham kisses her on both cheeks and, as she sits on the sofa, he turns to the camera: "Known to us all as Shit Girl!"

I panic that Kirsty will clock him but she doesn't. She takes a deep breath and smiles. Good girl, Kirsty.

Graham goes on with the interviews. Catherine

Deneuve looks bemused. She doesn't get any of the double meanings. Bette Midler does – she's enjoying herself. And Kirsty is managing fine. Graham makes it clear that cows are big and scary and that Kirsty was very brave to save little Amy even while a cow was shitting in her face.

In the last part of the show, Graham always gets someone to act out some nonsense while the audience and guests watch on screen. In this show, Kirsty has agreed to act out the YouTube video. They get her into a "bridesmaid" dress and sit her in a big plastic car. They push a black and white cut-out of a cow, tail first, up to the car. Graham asked the audience to provide the sound track.

"Moooooo!" they roar. "Moooooo, moooooo!"

Kirsty hits the fake cow with a handbag. The tail goes up, brown goo sprays all over her. She climbs out of the plastic car and saves a doll.

Next morning, the papers are full of "Shit Girl" stories again. Most of them lies.

FERGUS

Tracey's been on the rampage since this extradition business began. Old Man O'Hagan has got the best lawyer that money can buy but it's not looking good. Four days in Mountjoy hasn't sweetened her any. She's convinced that a business associate has grassed on her and when she finds out who it is… Well, the Lord only knows. She's wearing her tiger-skin coat all the time now.

And I'm left with a problem. Tracey has disappeared and the police are convinced that I know where she is. They've taken me in for questioning and grilled me for hours on end. Fortunately I know nothing because, after the first ten minutes, I'd have spilled every bean in the can.

KIRSTY

Why did nobody tell me? Fame sucks. After Graham Norton, the British press make my life hell. I can't scratch myself, literally, but they get the photo. I try doing what Lala and Hilary Swank have advised me to do – be nice, don't show you care – but they still write the vilest of lies and publish photos that make me look deranged. What have they got against me? I saved a child's life!

Finally I tell Mario that enough is enough and I don't want to do any more but he said I have to because I've signed contracts. I'm definitely not signing anything else. I just want my life back.

The One Show goes fine. But afterwards I have to appear in a club called Oblivion. Mostly in the clubs, I just appear on stage, everyone cheers, I smile, I wave, I say a few words, and that's that. But apparently that won't do for Oblivion.

First of all everyone is out of their skulls. A gang of fellas start a fight with bottles, and the security men who manhandle them into the street get badly cut by broken glass. And the management must have been watching Graham Norton because while I'm on stage a member of staff rushes up and sprays me with sticky brown goo! It ruins a beautiful Gaultier dress! The drunks love it, they fall around laughing and chanting "Shit Girl". Hilarious! Ha, ha, ha! And right there I know that there'll be a lot more of this in my future.

In the taxi back to the hotel, I bawl my head off. I'm so glad that Mum has come with me.

"You don't have to do this, you know," she says.

"But Mario says I have contracts to honour," I sob.

"Your dad and his lawyer can easily sort that."

It is after two in the morning when we get back. The

lobby is deserted except for the night porter and a couple of men in dark suits who eye us suspiciously. We take the lift up to our floor and walk down the empty corridor to our suite and when we opened the door, who is standing in front of us – Tracey.

"Okay, Shit Girl," she says. "Payback time."

MARIAN

What is Tracey doing here? What payback? How did she get in? Yeah, how did she get in?

"How did you get in?"

"I told the maid I'd locked my key inside by mistake and gave her a fifty pound note."

"But... But... How did you know we were here?"

"Shit Girl told me, the day I saved her from the reporters."

"Don't call me Shit Girl."

"Okay, whatever. And another fifty got me your room number. Now cut the crapola, I need to get out of here, pronto. So, Shit Girl, now it's your turn to help me."

"Don't call me Shit Girl."

"The police are downstairs, glued to the CCTV. So, Shit Girl, here's what you're going to do."

It's one "Shit Girl" too far. Kirsty snatches off her shoe and throws it at Tracey.

"*I said don't call me Shit Girl!*"

Tracey ducks. The shoe hits the wall with a clatter.

"Woah there, Shit Girl. Calm down."

"*Then don't call me Shit Girl!*"

The people in the next room have woken up and are thumping on the wall.

Kirsty ignores them.

"If anyone's Shit Girl, it's *you* Tracey O'Hagan!" she

yells, hands on hips like a fishwife. "You're the one that buys shit and sells it!"

Tracey throws back her head and laughs.

"And how do you think your Mammy and Daddy set themselves up?"

Oh damn and blast.

"They worked hard and saved up their money!"

"Oh they saved up their money all right. The money they earned from the drugs that they smuggled." I *never* wanted the kids to know about that. Tracey is laughing like a manic Goldfinger about to feed Bond to piranhas. Kirsty is looking stunned. "And they act so superior!" Tracey continues. "So Goody Two-Shoes, so fucking tight-arsed and conservative when their own fortune is based on drug-dealing!"

I start to move towards the phone.

"Get away from that phone," she snaps.

I lift it up.

"Says who?"

She sticks her hand in her handbag.

"Says Mr Glock."

I let the phone fall. I can hear my heart pounding. The gun is gold-plated with a tiger-skin grip. Oh Jesus, oh Jesus, oh Jesus.

"Now. Shit Girl, here's what you do. Put on my tiger-skin coat and my hat. Take the lift down to the car park. Make sure the security cameras can see you but don't show your face. Get into my car. Then drive like the hammers until they catch you."

"And then?"

"I don't give a shit. I'll be long gone, so tell them whatever you like. But don't mess it up, I have your mother here and a gun." She lifts her tiger-skin coat from the back of a chair and tosses it to Kirsty. "Car keys in the pocket. Silver Range Rover, close to the lift. Press the key-ring and the lights will flash."

Kirsty catches the heavy coat, opens it out and swings it around her shoulders – but instead of putting it on, she swings it around all the way and throws it over Tracey's head. Tracey staggers backwards blindly, the gun goes off and a bullet lodges in the ceiling. The people in the next room stop thumping on the wall. I kick Tracey hard in the elbow, and the gun flies out of her hand, another bullet splinters the wardrobe door. Now Tracey is on the floor, wrestling with her own tiger coat, and together me and my daughter kneel on top of her and pin her down. Then we phone the police.

That's twice in six months that Kirsty has saved someone's life!

KIRSTY

"Is it true?" I ask, after the police have taken Tracey away. "About smuggling the drugs?"

"Yes," Mum says. "We bought dope in Holland, some went to Tracey. Fergus sold some at gigs. We were very naïve, we believed it could bring peace to the world."

"Is that how you got money to set up the business?"

"We saved what we earned in the pub as well."

"What about heroin?"

"No way."

"Okay."

"Don't tell people."

"As if!"

MARIAN

Kirsty's been very quiet since she gave up on being a Celeb.

She's spent a lot of time in the stables grooming Whispa or out riding.

Tracey's been charged with two murders and bail has been refused. But Old Man O'Hagan's lawyers might still find a loophole. I hope not. Kirsty and me will probably be called as witnesses when she comes to trial. I'm not looking forward to that.

Poor Fergus. He's in bits.

"You're as well out of it." I tell him when we meet for lunch.

"I suppose."

But I know Fergus. This time next year he'll have another mad bat for a girlfriend.

JAKE

I'm at home in Balfathery editing some film. My mobile rings. It's Jenny Elixir.

"Will you direct my next video?" she says.

"Love to," I say.

She gives me her manager's number.

"Call him and firm up the details," she says and hangs up. Wow!

I go back to my editing but I'm finding it hard to concentrate. Kirsty knocks on my door.

"Can I come in?"

"Sure." I tell her about Jenny Elixir.

"Cool!"

"Would you like to be in it?"

"No, I'm done with all that."

I nearly fall off the chair.

"And by the way, watch out. Jenny's a man-eater and you're just her type."

"I can think of worse fates."

"You'd be far better off with Martina. You should ask her over some time."

Am I hearing her right?

"Coffee?" she asks.

"Please." Kirsty is making me coffee! Seems like saving lives suits her! She comes back with two mugs. She gives me one and sits down in the armchair. I go back to my editing. Kirsty watches me for a bit.

"Can I ask you something?" she says.

"Shoot."

"Do you think it's too late for me to go back to college?"

"There's a woman in my class who's well over thirty."

"Yeah? I'd like to go back to do fashion design properly in the College of Art. I'm getting a portfolio together."

"Good for you."

"Any chance you might... You know... Give me some tips?"

"Sure."

"Thanks."

She gathers the mugs and goes out.

THE END

WICKLOW COUNTY COUNCIL LIBRARY SERVICE

Author: Brophy, C .   Acc.No.:

Please return this book by the last date shown. Overdue items will be charged at a rate of 25c per item per week or part of a week. Readers will be charged for lost and damaged books.